The Coat

Alan Reynolds

Fisher King Publishing

The Coat

ISBN 978-1-910406-31-1

Fisher King Publishing Ltd
The Studio, Arthington Lane
Pool-in-Wharfedale
LS21 1JZ
England

www.fisherkingpublishing.co.uk

With gratitude to Rick Armstrong for his
unstinting support, guidance and friendship;
also to Samantha Richardson and
Rachel Topping at Fisher King Publishing.

Dedicated to my family and friends, and to all those
who have supported me in my writing –
your encouragement is greatly appreciated.

Much love

Also by Alan Reynolds:

Flying with Kites

Taskers End

Breaking The Bank

The Sixth Pillar

The Tinker

*"The worst decisions are sometimes made
with the best of intentions"
Alan Reynolds - The Coat*

CHAPTER ONE

The Topaz Night Club, Tirana, Albania. Thursday 2nd August 2012, heavy bass lines reverberated in the night air.

Inside, eighteen-year-old twins Edita and Delvina Enja were at their favourite haunt with some of their college friends. With seminars the following day, Thursday was not a regular night but a birthday celebration prompted this visit. Despite the club's rather drab appearance there was a party atmosphere and the evening was in full swing. Pulsating rhythms and flashing lights created just the right ambience; the dance floor was crowded.

The two girls were inseparable, and identical; even their best friends had difficulty telling them apart. Both were pretty with long black hair, pale complexions and green eyes. As for many local teenage girls, Albanian fashion icon Emina Cunmulaj was their role model. They were dressed in party gear, short skirts and spangle tops; Edita was in black, Delvina, blue.

The girls were from a comparatively wealthy family. Their mother was a teacher and their father, a civil servant, worked for the ministry. The family had eschewed the traditional Muslim culture for a more secular upbringing and schooling. They would be considered liberal in their views.

As the girls danced together they attracted a lot of attention from male admirers. Two of them dressed in black leather bomber jackets were taking more than a passing interest. One of them was speaking animatedly into his mobile phone.

Around nine o'clock, the girls left the dance floor and headed for the toilets.

They walked down the dimly lit corridor at the back of the club, chatting continuously. Edita was rummaging in her handbag for her mobile phone. It wasn't a long passageway, and was adorned with posters of bands and pop stars pasted to the wall. Some were peeling off, giving the club a shabby look. To the right were the male toilets, identifiable by the smell emanating from them; to the left, the ladies' and directly in front, at the end of the corridor, was an emergency exit. They would have taken little notice of the rough-looking man who was stood in front of it, distracted as they were by conversation and the need to send text messages to their friends. Against the noise of the music they would not have heard or sensed the two bomber jackets following them. The men took one each, grabbing them from behind, hands across the girls' mouths and noses. The girls kicked and flayed their arms but the door was opened and they were bundled out into the yard at the rear of the club and into the back of an awaiting van. Pinned down on the floor of the van, one of the men produced hypodermic needles and within seconds, the girls were asleep.

The men were jubilant, like a military exercise, a job well done. They would be well rewarded for their night's work.

Within an hour the van had arrived in the port town of Durrës. It's a town with over a quarter of a million inhabitants and a popular destination for tourists dating back to Roman times. It boasts the largest Roman amphitheatre in the Balkans. The occupants of the van, however, were not interested in ancient artefacts.

At this time of night, the area around the docks was deserted, and the van attracted little attention as it made its way to the quayside where a small fishing boat was waiting. The van parked alongside and the two bomber jackets got out and checked the coast was clear. The boat's skipper was waiting on deck next to the wheelhouse and, in a shouting whisper, urged the men to hurry up. The girls, still fast asleep, were dragged unceremoniously from the back of the van. The two men lifted them onto their shoulders and carried the girls on board up a narrow gangplank. The skipper beckoned them to follow him down a short flight of steps. He was cussing under his breath at the time it was taking. There was a door immediately in front of them. The captain opened it and the men went in. It was cramped, with just two small beds and a bucket as furnishings. Two other girls were asleep on the far bed just below a small porthole. Edita and Delvina were placed on the other, nearest the door.

The ferry crossing to Bari in Italy takes over nine hours; the fishing boat would take twelve, a lot longer than the speedboats that were used regularly until the recent clampdown by Italian naval forces. With bribery rife, transporting girls into the Italian port was not in itself a dangerous occupation; moving them to other destinations would be more problematic due to border checks.

The kidnappers left the boat and watched from their van as the gangplank was pulled in and the trawler chugged its way gently out of the harbour.

The four girls were sleeping in their cabin below deck. One of the men checked on them periodically; they would be starting to wake up in a couple of hours. For this voyage, there was a crew of three: the captain, a mate and an engineer, who was also on cooking duties. There were four gang-member passengers plus the 'cargo'. Weather was good, with just a moderate swell.

'Should dock mid-morning,' said the captain on enquiry from Georgiou, the Romanian leader of the kidnappers. The boat owner would be making considerably more money for this run than a normal fishing trip, and without the physical effort.

It was not a large vessel; the room where the girls were being kept would normally be the sleeping quarters for the crew when the boat was being used for its intended purpose. There was a galley which also acted as a communal room and the gang spent much of the journey playing cards there.

It was a warm night. All four were dressed in jeans and tee shirts, swarthy looking with dark, trimmed beards; a trademark appearance, it seemed, in their line of business. The three other members, another Romanian and two Albanians, took it in turns to check on the girls.

Below deck, it was Edita who woke first, disorientated, woozy and quickly very, very scared. She shook her sister. 'Delvina, Delvina wake up.' She saw the other girls both sleeping in the next bed.

'Mmm,' moaned Delvina. 'What is it? What's happening?'

'Wake up, wake up... I think we've been kidnapped,' said Edita.

Edita was the elder sibling, but only by a few minutes. Nevertheless, she had a dominant personality and was a much stronger character than Delvina. Edita would do all she could to protect her sister.

Both girls were disorientated, and still feeling the effect of the drug that would take several hours to wear off.

They listened to the rhythmic chug-chug of the engine and felt the sway as the boat rocked from the impact of a passing wave.

Edita tried to sit up, the room swirled. 'I feel sick,' she exclaimed, and just managed to reach the bucket before disgorging her evening meal.

'Urgh,' she moaned.

Delvina slowly sat up. 'You ok, Ed?'

'No, not really, my head hurts,' she replied.

'Where are we...? And who are they?' said Delvina looking at the two girls who were on the next bed, still sleeping.

'Don't know,' said Edita, holding her head in her hands.

'Wait, one of them's waking up,' said Delvina.

There was a moan coming from one of the other girls. She tried to sit up but dropped back on the bed. Gradually she opened her eyes and tried to focus. The single light in the ceiling flickered as another wave hit the boat. A swell had got up.

The girl looked at Edita and Delvina. 'Who are you?' she said feebly. 'Where are we?'

'We're on a boat somewhere. We've been drugged. I think we've been kidnapped,' said Edita. 'I'm Edita, this is my sister, Delvina...Who are you?'

'I'm Sadia, Sadia Vata,' she groaned, and held her head.

'Where are you from?' asked Edita.

'From Kavajë.'

'Who's your friend?' asked Edita.

'Don't know, I was at a disco, I think, but... that's all I can remember.'

'How old are you?' asked Edita.

'Fifteen... You?'

'Eighteen,' said Edita.

'What's going to happen to us?' said Sadia.

'I don't know,' said Edita. Delvina started to cry.

Edita looked around the cabin. 'They've taken our stuff.'

There wasn't much room: the regular crew's sleeping quarters was designed to hold six, but in bunks. The cabin had been converted to hold two beds, three-quarter size.

'I need to pee,' said Sadia.

'It's the bucket,' said Edita. 'It's not pleasant, sorry.'

'It's ok,' said Sadia, and she climbed over Edita and Delvina's bed, removed her pants and stood over the bucket.

She too was dressed to party but the much-loved outfit that her mother had saved for weeks to buy for her was crumpled and soiled.

Edita and Delvina gradually got off the bed. Delvina too needed to use the bucket. Edita looked at the bed, a bare mattress with several dark stains, unmistakably blood, and others that looked like water. She put her hand to her mouth and gasped in horror as she started to comprehend their plight.

A few minutes later, they heard footsteps, then the door unlocking. The three girls moved to the corner; Edita standing in front of the other two protecting them.

The door opened. The girls stared at the man in a state of terror. He was young, mid-twenties, and in different circumstances the girls would have found him attractive; but not now.

He spoke in Albanian.

'Ah, you are awake. That is good... Keep quiet and do not cause trouble and you will not be hurt. Wait, I will get you water.'

Before the girls could say anything, he left the cabin and went to inform the rest of the gang.

'Georgiou, the girls, they are awake.' He went to the fridge and removed a litre bottle of water.

'Good, Etrit, yes give them some water, we must look after them. They must be in good condition when we hand them over,' said Georgiou.

Etrit returned to the cabin and unlocked the door. The girls were still huddled in the corner with Edita in front.

'Here, I bring water for you,' said Etrit, and handed Edita the plastic bottle.

'Where are you taking us?' said Edita, her voice trembling with fright.

'Do not worry. You will be well looked after if you do not cause trouble,' he said, and passed her the water. Edita handed it to Delvina, who started to drink.

Etrit watched.

'Your friend is not awake yet?' he said looking at the still sleeping girl on the second bed.

'Stay there,' he said, and went to look at her. She was on her side facing away from the others towards the far wall of the cabin.

Etrit turned her over. There was vomit all around her mouth, her eyes were wide open.

He cursed and rushed out of the cabin, locking it behind him.

Edita looked at Delvina then Sadia.

'Oh my god, she's dead,' said Delvina, putting her hand to her head in horror.

'It looks like it,' said Edita, and hugged her sister.

A few moments later, the door opened again. Georgiou entered, went to the girl and felt for a pulse. The three others were still in the corner.

'Here, give me a hand,' he barked to Etrit. He spoke in English, the common language.

Georgiou sat the girl up and put her over his shoulder in a fireman's lift.

'Shut the door,' he said to Etrit, and left the cabin. The girls were trying to console themselves.

Georgiou carried the girl into the galley, where the others gathered around.

'Is she dead?' asked Constantin, the other Romanian.

'Yes,' said Georgiou. 'Here help me. We must remove her clothes.'

They stripped the unfortunate teenager and put her clothes in a plastic bag.

'Give me a hand,' said Georgiou, and the men carried the girl on deck and threw her over the side. It was two a.m. and pitch black. The boat was in the middle of the Adriatic; her body would never be found and her grieving parents would never learn what had happened to their beloved daughter. She would be just another of 'the missing'. Beer bottles and other bits of rubbish were added to the carrier bag containing her clothes. Enough weight to send it dropping gently to the seabed.

'Here, Etrit, get rid of this,' said Georgiou. As the youngest member of the group he was used to getting the dogsbody jobs.

He took the plastic bag up the stairs to the deck and dropped it over the side; an ignominious fate for a once-prized possession.

Back in the cabin, Edita was trying to console the other two. Meanwhile, Georgiou was beginning to count the cost of the girl's demise.

'Five thousand Euros, that is how much we lose now,' he said. 'Who gave her the drug?'

'It was me,' said Constantin. 'I gave her the same as the others... She must have been drinking.'

'But they were at a party. It is what they do,' said Georgiou.

'But how was I to know?' said Constantin.

'Next time we must get them without drugs. It is too dangerous. We lose too much money,' said Georgiou.

Constantin had been admonished. In other gangs he might well have been shot for his error.

'What do we do?' said Etrit. 'We are supposed to deliver four.'

'They will be one short this trip. We will have to make extra next time,' said Georgiou.

'Here, see to the girls,' and Georgiou produced a holdall. 'You know what to do.'

Etrit went back to the cabin with the holdall and unlocked the door.

The girls were back in the corner of the room against the wall.

'What have you done with her?' said Edita.

'Your friend is with the fishes,' said Etrit.

The girls gasped.

'What do you want from us?' asked Edita.

'You are going on a special journey... You are to wear these.'

He pulled out four tracksuits from the holdall and four pairs of slip-on sandals.

'We are not doing it,' said Edita defiantly.

'You will do it, or we will put you to sleep again and you see how dangerous that can be.'

Edita looked at Delvina, who was starting to cry again. Sadia just seemed oblivious to what was going on and started undressing; reluctantly, the sisters did the same. Etrit watched as the girls took off their clothes.

'Put them in here,' he ordered, 'quickly.'

The three bundled their party dresses and shoes into the holdall, then put on the tracksuits.

'Now you sleep. We have a long way to go.'

Etrit left them and locked the cabin.

'What are we going to do?' said Delvina. Sadia was starting to shake uncontrollably.

'Sadia,' said Edita, 'Sadia.'

Sadia looked at Edita but her eyes were not registering.

Edita hugged her and Delvina. 'I don't know what is going to happen, but if we stay strong we will get through this,' she said.

'Here, drink some more,' said Edita, and passed the bottle to Sadia. She took the bottle; her hands were shaking so much she had difficulty in controlling it. She passed it to Delvina. There was little left now.

Edita, in desperation, tried the cabin door handle; she knew it would be futile.

'We are locked in,' said Edita. 'There's nothing we can do. We should rest; we will need all our strength.'

All three were still suffering hangovers; it would take a day at least for the relaxant to completely leave their system, and in a few minutes they were asleep again. It was not a comfortable sleep; anxiety mixed with narcotics produced frightening nightmares, and the girls woke frequently. The ship lurched occasionally as larger waves collided with it. The bucket had been in regular use and was now almost half full; the smell in the cabin was nauseating.

There had been regular checks but no more than a cursory glance by one of the gang and the door relocked. Edita was fully awake again by eight o'clock.

'Delvina, are you awake?' she said to her sister, who was facing the other way.

To Edita's relief her sister started to stir and gingerly raised her head to acknowledge her.

'Yes... Oh, my head, I feel terrible.'

'What about Sadia?' said Edita.

Delvina shook her gently. 'Sadia, wake up.'

Sadia too opened her eyes.

'How do you feel?' said Edita.

'Not good,' said Sadia, and groaned. 'My head aches... and I'm so thirsty.'

'The water's all gone,' said Edita.

'What are we going to do?' said Sadia anxiously. 'I'm so scared.'

'I know. Me too... We're all scared,' replied Edita.

The three lay there for a while before they heard footsteps coming down the stairs outside the cabin. Quickly, they got out of bed and cowered in the corner. The door was unlocked; it was Etrit again.

'Ah, good, you are awake. I have brought more water. You must drink. It will be good for you,' he said, and handed over another bottle to Edita.

'I will empty this,' he said, and took away the bucket.

He returned a few minutes later; the bucket had been emptied and cleaned. He was carrying some bread.

The girls were still in the corner; Delvina was gulping down the bottled water. Sadia was just stood behind the sisters, her eyes wide with fright.

'Here, you must eat,' said Etrit, and passed the bread to Edita.

'Why have you kidnapped us? What will you do to us?' said Edita, handing the bread to the other two.

'If you do not cause trouble, nothing will happen to you.'

'But you have taken us. What about our family? Our parents will be worried,' said Edita. Delvina was starting to cry; Sadia was dumb with terror.

'I am sorry,' said Etrit. 'Try to rest; we will be in port soon.'

'Which port? Where are you taking us?' said Edita.

Etrit left the cabin without answering.

The pitching and rolling to which they had become accustomed was gentler as the boat headed into the port of Bari.

It was Georgiou who opened the door. The three girls were back in the corner. In the daylight he looked more sinister. There was a scar on his right cheek

'What is happening?' said Edita. 'Where are you taking us?'

'Soon you will leave the boat. You will be put on a lorry to continue your journey. If you do not cause trouble you can walk. If you do, then you will be put to sleep again.'

He produced a syringe from the pocket of his leather jacket.

'No, no we will not cause trouble,' said Edita.

'That is good. I will come for you soon,' he said, and left the cabin.

The girls sat on the beds not saying anything, locked in their own thoughts and wondering what lay ahead.

Bari is a busy port with regular ferries to Croatia, Albania and even Corfu. As they approached the outer reaches, the captain could see the ancient Castello Normano and the Basilica di St Nicolas in front of him, familiar landmarks to anyone arriving by sea. The boat entered the harbour, passing the passenger terminal on the left where the ferry from Dubrovnik was berthed. To the right there was a long causeway which led to the marina. This part of the port was derelict and deserted, an ideal place to dock and deliver the cargo.

It was ten-thirty when the boat jolted as it bumped against the jetty, and then steadied as the engines were turned off.

The three girls were back in the corner as the cabin door was once again opened. Georgiou was accompanied by Etrit and Constantin.

'This is what we will do,' said Georgiou in English. 'Do you understand English?'

Edita nodded.

'We will walk off the boat; the lorry will be close by. You will be our girlfriends... yes?'

The girls looked at each other,

'I said, yes?' said Georgiou. 'Do you understand...? Or we can carry you. It is your choice.'

'No, we will not cause any problem,' said Edita.

'Right, you come with me,' said Georgiou.

The girls left the cabin and followed the men up the stairs. There was an opening on the side of the boat next to the wheelhouse; a gangplank had been placed leading down the short distance to the jetty.

The three men walked across, followed by the girls. The fourth crew member remained on board to help with the refuelling for the return journey.

'We won't be long,' shouted Georgiou to the captain as he led the party off the boat.

He put his arm around Edita's shoulder like a courting couple might do. Constantin did the same to Delvina; Etrit was with Sadia.

There was a road in front of them, the Molo Pizzoli, which ran the length of the quay; beyond that was just waste ground. The area looked derelict. The group turned left and walked down the road about a hundred yards or so. They could see the transport parked in front of an old, deserted shipwright's, a soft- top container lorry. There were three men in the cab, and one of them got out to wait for the party to approach. It was a cloudless sky, the earth dry and dusty. The odd weed was trying to make its presence felt, a hardy genus of thistle, but otherwise nothing seemed to be surviving in the arid ground. As they walked by, a lizard, disturbed from its hidey-hole, skittered across the broken paving slabs in front of them and took cover under a jagged piece of concrete, safe from predators.

The girls were still disorientated from the drug and were compliant but reluctant, and very scared, as they reached the truck.

The man approached Georgiou and spoke in Albanian. Edita was trying to listen but could only catch the odd word. There appeared to be a problem; the man from the lorry was remonstrating with Georgiou and it was clear he was not happy that there was one less girl than expected. Georgiou explained the circumstances and there was then a renegotiation of the price. This time it was Georgiou who appeared agitated but eventually money was exchanged and the three left the girls and returned to the boat.

'What are you doing with us? Where are you taking us?' said Edita, again in Albanian.

'You... be quiet!' said the man in fractured English. 'You come, do not cause trouble or you will be hurt.'

Edita had a basic understanding of English from school and took Delvina's hand and complied. It was Delvina who was shaking now, Sadia was just terrified.

He was an ugly man with three days' growth of beard and greasy curly black hair which was thinning on top. He would be in his late forties, maybe older, and with his pot belly seemed to waddle rather than walk. He was wearing an old dark tee shirt with white sweat stains under the arm pits. The three were led to the back of the lorry. The man opened the container; there was a set of folding ladders which he pulled and they extended to the tarmac.

'You... go,' he said, and the girls slowly ascended the ladder into the back of the container. The man followed.

There were boxes and wooden crates stacked against the sides of the container with a pathway down the middle. The man walked past the girls and down towards what appeared to be the back of the container. There were two levers at the side, which the man turned then pulled. It was a false wall and the back of the container slid open on runners. Behind it was a small room with four sleeping bags and a bucket. It was stifling hot and claustrophobic with next to no natural light. Holes had been drilled in the wall behind the metal joists on each side, which would not be conspicuous to the casual observer or to a harassed customs official. They let in little light and even less fresh air.

'You stay here,' said the man, 'and no talking or you will be hurt.'

'But we will die here. We need water and food,' said Edita in English.

'You will get water... we stop soon and you will get food.'

He left them and slid the door shut. The girls could hear the levers turning.

'We are going to die,' said Sadia.

'No, we must not. We must stay strong,' said Edita.

'But where are they taking us, Edi?' said Delvina.

'I don't know but I think we're in Italy. Did you see the signs? They were in Italian.'

'I didn't notice,' said Delvina. Sadia sat down, put her head in her hands and started to cry again.

There was a roar and a shudder as the truck started up. The air brakes hissed angrily as the truck was crashed into gear. There was a sickening smell of diesel. Edita was thrown sideways and managed to hold onto the wall to stop her falling. Then she sat down next to her sister.

'God it's so hot,' she said, unzipping her tracksuit top and taking it off. The others did the same.

The truck headed down the Molo Pizzoli and turned right onto the dock road parallel with the Corso Vittorio Veneto, the coast freeway. They came to the outer gates which controlled the port and two custom officers carrying clipboards flagged down the truck. One approached the cab and handed a clipboard to the driver. There was activity in the cab, and the clipboard returned. No-one would see the one hundred Euro note attached to it as it was passed back.

The officer waved the truck through.

It would be a long journey as the driver eased the truck onto the coast road and out of the city on the Via Napoli, then on towards the autostrada. The route would take the truck over the southern Apennines to Naples, and then north.

In the container, the conditions were dire. Diesel fumes filled the air, attacking the throat and causing the girls to cough violently. They tried to sleep but it was impossible as the truck lurched along the highway; every gear change, every slight acceleration was exaggerated within the confines of their makeshift prison. Sadia appeared to be in a trance-like state whilst Edita and Delvina held onto each other for comfort. They were desperately thirsty. Despite promises, no water had been provided and it was two hours before the girls felt the wagon turn sharply before slowing to a stop. They were quickly alert as their survival mechanisms kicked in. They put on their tracksuit tops and, as they had on the boat, huddled together into a corner. The door was opened and a welcome blast of fresh air entered the chamber.

'You, girls... out,' said the same man who had incarcerated them, and the girls followed him down the ladder and out of the container.

They blinked in the blazing sunshine as they tried to get their bearings. Edita breathed in gulps of fresh air in an effort to expunge the irritants attacking her lungs. Delvina and Sadia did the same. As their heads gradually recovered, the girls could see they were at a truck-stop somewhere in the mountains behind a whitewashed building. The lorry park was large and potholed from wear and tear. It was not tarmac but compacted dirt and gravel. The light was blinding, and the girls shielded their eyes from the glare. There was one other truck about twenty metres away, and a couple of rather ancient-looking cars; otherwise, the place was deserted. A couple of forlorn-looking olive trees were at the far end as the ground fell away into a deep valley.

'We need water,' said Edita to the pot-bellied man who looked to be in charge.

He put on a pair of sunglasses and was joined by two other rough-looking men. They were of similar appearance but younger – father and sons, realised Edita.

'You will get water and food if you do not cause trouble,' said Potbelly.

There was some discussion between the men. Edita could not make out the language clearly, but it was possibly Italian, she thought.

'You stay here,' said the man in his broken English. They were behind the truck and not in direct view from the cafe. One of the other men went back to cab and produced a litre bottle of water. He handed it to Edita, who immediately passed it to Delvina; she took the top off and drank. It was tepid and not thirst quenching, but she drank in gulps before passing the bottle to Sadia.

The two younger men walked towards the front entrance of the cafe, out of sight of the lorry, and went inside. Ten minutes later they came back with more bottles of water and six focaccia filled with ham and cheese. They shared them out and handed the girls one each. Sadia took a bite but she had to force it down. After three mouthfuls she gagged and brought it up. She was bent over coughing as the watery bile stung her throat.

'Do not try to eat too much now, just small pieces. We must save some for later,' said Edita in Albanian. She passed Sadia the water and she drank. There were tears in her eyes induced by the vomiting.

Delvina had withdrawn and was nibbling the side of her bread in a world of her own. Edita could sense what was happening; she needed to do something.

'I need toilet,' she said to Potbelly in English.

'You go bucket.'

'No, I am... bleeding,' she said.

The man thought for a moment and said something to one of his 'sons'.

'You go with him. He will stay with you. You cause problem you will be hurt,' he said. 'Understand?'

'Yes,' said Edita.

Edita walked towards the cafe with the younger of the two men. He would be in his early twenties but had the same menace as his 'father'.

Inside the cafe it was refreshingly cool from the air conditioning. There were around twenty tables but only three were occupied. All the time Edita was thinking; she needed to get away and try to get help. The younger son was close to her, within touching distance, so running would not be an option. She saw the 'toilet' sign and walked towards it. He nodded and she went inside. It was a single cubicle with a pan that looked as though it hadn't been cleaned for some time. Above it was a small window which was open. Edita made a quick decision, stood on the toilet seat and climbed through.

CHAPTER TWO

There was a four-foot drop down to the ground; scrub and thistles clung to the wall below the window where leaking pipes had provided moisture.

Edita jumped and fell forward, but managed to stagger to her feet, her balance still not properly restored. She felt a sharp pain in her left ankle and winced. She could see the truck about fifty metres away to the left, the legs of the captives and captors visible. She wanted to call to her sister and try to make a run for it but her footwear would make that impossible; they would never be able to outrun the men. Her only option would be to hide and find someone who could alert the authorities.

The other truck was closer and Edita slowly backed along the wall of the cafe towards it. Her ankle hurt but she managed to climb up to the cab. She tried the door; it was locked. Just then she heard shouting and the other son ran towards the cafe. She couldn't see what was happening behind the lorry. She saw Potbelly opening the back of the container and pushing the two girls up the ladder and inside. He disappeared for a moment, then returned and descended the ladder before heading towards the cafe.

Edita limped to the back of the second truck and looked to see if there was any way of getting on board and stowing away, but the load was securely fastened; no chance of a hideaway.

There was more commotion as the three men reappeared at the back of the truck-stop and started searching. With the only realistic hiding place being the second truck, Edita broke cover and hobbled to the end of the building and back around to the cafe entrance.

She went in. There were just three tables in use; two men who looked like truckers were sat closest to the door, an elderly couple against the far wall and a man that looked like a farmer next to the serving counter. All were engaged in a late lunch.

Edita stood there for a moment; the pain in her ankle was getting worse. 'Help me,' she shouted in Albanian. 'We have been kidnapped.'

The customers stopped eating and looked at her. The proprietor was stood behind the counter wiping down the coffee machine. He turned around and saw Edita.

She shouted again, this time in English. 'Please help us, we are taken away,' she said, trying to translate as best she could. The proprietor shrugged his shoulders.

Suddenly, Potbelly and the two sons rushed into the cafe and quickly grabbed Edita. He said something to the proprietor in Italian and he laughed. The other customers chuckled, Edita had no idea what had been said but she was bundled outside and around the back of the cafe. Out of sight, Potbelly produced a syringe. The elder son had her pinned against the wall, the other son pulled up the sleeve of her tracksuit. Before Edita could do anything she felt a sharp prick in her upper arm and slumped to the ground.

The two sons lifted her up and with Edita in the middle, walked back to the back of the container as if dragging a drunken buddy. They managed to manoeuvre the sleeping Edita onto the back of the truck and carried her back to the chamber. Delvina gasped when she saw her sister. 'Edi, Edita,' she cried.

'This is what will happen if you are big problem,' said Potbelly in his broken English.

The sons dropped Edita onto one of the sleeping bags and left. Delvina bent over her and stroked her head. 'Edi, Edi,' she said. Sadia was sat on her sleeping bag just staring at the sisters, totally traumatised. The truck started again, gears crashing, air brakes hissing as it pitched forward, bouncing over the undulating surface and back onto the main road.

It was another two hours before the lorry stopped again just outside Naples; they had travelled less than two hundred miles and there was a long way to go.

Edita was starting to come round but was in a bad way, disorientated and hallucinating. She stared at Delvina. 'Mammy,' she said before closing her eyes again. Delvina put her hand to her mouth in shock. Edita was the strong one and she needed her protection.

There was still some water in one of the plastic bottles, and Delvina cradled her sister's head. 'Here, Edi, you must drink.' Edita opened her eyes again; they flickered like a waning light bulb. She made a feeble attempt to take on some water, much of it dribbled down her chin. Sadia was laid on her sleeping bag and appeared oblivious to everything.

Delvina heard the back of the container opening, then footsteps. The levers were turned and the door slid open. Potbelly appeared with the elder son. The smell that greeted them can only be imagined.

'We stop for some time, we eat. We will bring food if you do not cause more problem.' He handed Delvina another bottle of water and noticed the bucket.

'You... bring that,' he said to Delvina, pointing at the half-full makeshift toilet. Delvina left Edita, who had gone back to sleep. Sadia was not moving.

Delvina followed the two men through the container and waited while the men went down the ladder. 'Wait,' said Potbelly, and he checked to make sure the coast was clear. Delvina descended the ladder and the son passed down the bucket.

Delvina looked around. It was mid-afternoon and the sun was scorching. Light reflecting from the white gravel of the lorry park made vision difficult, and she squinted till her eyes became used to the brilliance. To the left she could see more mountains; one in the far distance looked as if smoke was coming from the top.

It was another truck-stop, but was much busier than the one in the mountains. They had crossed the Apennines and were now off the A1 autostrada just north of Naples. It was a regular stopping-off point on the journey. There were at least twenty trucks parked at the back of the main service area.

'There,' said Potbelly, pointing to an outside toilet at the back of the building.

Delvina and the son walked to the facility and he waited outside while she emptied the bucket. There was a tap on the wall outside the toilet and she washed out the pail before being escorted back to the container.

Once again, the door was locked behind her. She went immediately to her sister, who was trying to sit up.

'Edi,' she said. 'Are you ok?'

Edita moaned. 'My leg... it is very sore.'

Delvina gave her more water, then examined her sister's ankle. It was now a purple colour.

'Can you move it?' said Delvina, and Edita slowly rotated her ankle joint.

'It looks ok; it is bruised I think,' said Delvina. 'What happened?' and Edita was able to give her sister an account of her abortive bid for freedom.

'Here, you must drink,' said Delvina, and she gave Edita the bottle which she was able to administer herself.

Edita was starting to focus more fully and could see Sadia lay on her sleeping bag in just her tracksuit bottoms.

'Sadia, Sadia,' said Edita as she moved gingerly over to her. She winced as pressure was put on her injured ankle. Delvina helped her.

'Sadia, wake up. Open your eyes. You must stay strong,' said Edita as she gently shook her.

Gradually, Sadia opened her eyes but they were glazed and lacked any comprehension.

'Sit up,' Edita said firmly. 'You must not give up. We must be alert all the time, whatever happens. Sit up. Come on, drink some water. It will help.'

The assertiveness of Edita's words seemed to have an effect and gradually the life seemed to return to her eyes.

'What's going to happen to us?' she said, and started crying.

'Here drink this,' said Edita, and Sadia took the bottle and took large gulps of water.

'Steady, just sip slowly,' said Edita, and Sadia put down the bottle next to her.

Edita looked at her sister and Sadia, she talked slowly. 'I know it seems bad but we must keep together and help each other stay strong. Delvina, what did you see when you went outside?'

'Nothing; it was a truck-stop, many trucks... It was very bright. I could see the mountains.'

'Where are they taking us?' said Sadia weakly.

'It could be anywhere,' said Edita, but deep down she knew they were in trouble. There had been significant media coverage in the newspapers about gangs trafficking girls to work in sweatshops or, worse still, as prostitutes. She shivered at the thought.

The container opened and footsteps approached. The girls huddled together as the levers were turned.

It was Potbelly.

'Here, some food and things, but you make more problem, no food... understand?' he said, and handed Delvina some bread, cheese, a toilet roll and a packet of tampons. 'And you,' he said to Edita. 'If you try to escape again you will die. Do you understand?' Edita nodded.

'Yes,' she said, and looked down.

This was no act of benevolence, the girls were a valuable cargo and despite their threats the captors knew they had to keep them in reasonable condition. They would be no use damaged, or dead; they would not get paid.

He left the girls and locked the container. A few minutes later, the truck started and headed north.

Edita was still heady from the drugs and the latest dose made her feel sick again. Delvina handed her some bread and cheese. 'Here, you have some. You must eat.'

'Later,' she said, and pushed it away.

Sadia took some food and slowly started to nibble.

The journey seemed relentless. There were other stops every two hours or so, and each time the container was opened and checked. The girls were given water and some bread.

Inside the container, it was boring and uncomfortable; the atmosphere was stifling. The temperature gradually fell as the light from the air holes started to fade; it was almost ten hours since they had left the truck-stop near Naples and before the lorry hissed to the last stop of the day. They had reached some services on the autostrada near Genoa, the capital of Liguria province, Northern Italy. Potbelly made one more check on the girls. He had a torch which he shined into the chamber.

'We stop here for sleep... You make noise, you will die.'

He gave them another bottle of water and locked the door again.

It was seven a.m. before the girls heard the container being opened and the footsteps. The levers were turned and the door to the chamber slid back. The three huddled together in the corner.

It was Potbelly.

'You, come,' he said to Sadia. 'Do not worry; you can use the wash-room here. Benito will go with you. You will not be hurt if you are no problem.'

'No, no,' said Sadia.

'It's ok,' said Edita. 'You can get some fresh air. It will be good for you.'

Reluctantly, Sadia was escorted out of the compartment by the younger of the two sons, who was carrying the bucket.

Benito looked around to check again. Despite the number of vehicles, the car park was deserted, their owners tucking into trucker breakfasts or making the most of the wash-rooms. The two others were stood in the back of the container as Benito descended the ladder, followed by Sadia. Potbelly had lit a cigarette.

'Here, you take this... Clean,' he said, and handed the bucket down to Sadia.

She walked with Benito to the rear of the cafe, where there was an entrance door. There was a corridor with wash-rooms to the right and left. Sadia opened the door to the female rest-room and went inside with the bucket.

She managed to wash herself down and returned to the truck ten minutes later with Benito. Delvina was given the same opportunity. When she returned, Edita got up.

'Not you,' said Potbelly. 'You stay.'

The door was locked again and after a few minutes the truck was on its way.

From Genoa the truck headed north, through Turin, and crossed the border into France via the Frejus road tunnel and on towards Lyon, a journey just short of three hundred miles. Again there were stops where the girls were fed and watered, but only Sadia and Delvina were allowed out, under close supervision. Edita was starting to feel unwell, a mix of drug hangover and lack of clean air; her left ankle had swollen considerably.

It was eight o'clock when the truck made its final stop just outside Lyon on the main Paris auto route. Although expensive, the motorways were by far the quickest way to their destination and the rewards would more than compensate for the cost of diesel and tolls.

When the door opened, Delvina expressed her concern at Edita's health.

'She is not well; you must let her get some air. She will die.'

Potbelly went over to her. She was laid on her sleeping bag, sweating profusely.

'You bring her,' he said to Delvina. He spoke to his elder son in Italian and he helped take Edita to the front of the container. The sun had set and the temperature was a lot cooler. The truck was parked in a more secluded park of the truck-stop, well away from any prying eyes. Edita gasped as the fresh air hit her; the effect almost like smelling salts. She quickly regained her senses.

'You, go to wash-room with Federico. You try to escape, we will kill you. Understand?' said Potbelly.

'Yes,' said Edita weakly.

The elder son helped Edita down the ladder. At the bottom she collapsed as she put the weight on her damaged ankle. Federico held onto her and led her to the front of the main service area. It was bustling at this time of night but no-one took any notice as Federico helped Edita towards the wash-room. The facilities at the French service stations are far more comprehensive than the Italian version with a Routier section provided specifically for truck drivers. It included shower facilities and Federico escorted Edita to a vacant cubicle.

'You... bathe,' said Federico, and watched as Edita took off her clothes and showered. When she had finished he handed her a towel; he did not take his eyes off her for a moment. Edita was past caring.

He helped her back to the truck and the two girls were stood at the bottom of the ladder with Potbelly and Benito. As Federico approached them he said something to Potbelly who laughed loudly and replied. Edita managed to slowly climb up the ladder to the container and Federico helped her inside. The girls were about to follow when Potbelly suddenly said, 'No, no, you wait,' and started to chuckle. Benito lit a cigarette whilst they waited. They had heard the levers turn and the door pulled back. Then there were muffled screams. Then quiet.

'What is happening?' said Delvina in English.

'Don't worry, Federico will not hurt her; he will give her great pleasure,' said Potbelly, and started to laugh again. He coughed a smoker's hack, which he had trouble controlling, and his face turned red with the effort. Benito smiled and tugged on his cigarette as they waited for Federico to finish.

Delvina spoke to Sadia in Albanian. 'Do not worry,' she said, but deep down she feared the worst.

After a few minutes the door to the back of the container opened, and Federico appeared, fastening the belt to his trousers. The girls gasped. Potbelly said something to Federico, who laughed. 'Yes, very good,' he said in English so the girls could hear.

'You go, up now,' said Potbelly to the girls, pointing to the ladder, and they went back to the compartment.

The door was closed behind them.

Edita was laid on one of the sleeping bags staring at the ceiling. Her tracksuit bottoms were in a heap next to her and her top was up under her chin. Blood was smeared around her upper thighs. She had made no attempt to dress.

'Edi, Edi,' cried Delvina. 'What have they done to you?'

Edita looked blankly at her sister.

'Come on, let's get you dressed,' said Delvina gently, and helped her put on her clothes. She would need to take control now. Delvina cradled her sister, rocking her like a baby. Sadia looked on; the trauma had returned.

The truck started again, left the service area and got back on the auto route. It was another three hours before the truck stopped for the night.

Delvina was trying to look after her sister; Sadia was uncommunicative and appeared to be in a trance most of the time. Delvina had used some of the water to bathe her sister to try to make her more comfortable, but Edita was unresponsive. Eventually, the three girls slept until the door was opened again at six-thirty.

It was Federico. Delvina immediately recoiled. 'No, no,' she said, and backed away, fearing a repeat of Edita's treatment. Sadia and Edita were drowsy but awake.

'You... bring bucket,' he said to Delvina.

'No... No.'

'Do as I say or you will get like her,' he said, nodding towards Edita.

Slowly, Delvina complied, picking up the bucket and following Federico out of the container. It was another truck-stop, and about fifty wagons from many different countries were lined up in bays, their drivers making the most of the facilities or sleeping in their cabs. The sun was just making its presence felt and there was white haze rising from the fields that bordered the car park.

In the wash-room, Delvina washed her face and took the worn bar of soap from the sink and some paper towels from the dispenser. She cleaned the bucket and returned to the lorry. Potbelly and Benito were waiting by the ladder, smoking. They spoke to Federico in turn and he laughed. He helped Delvina up the ladder and she returned to the chamber. A few minutes later, Potbelly opened the door and gave them some more water and bread. By six forty-five the truck was back on the auto-route heading for Paris and Calais. It would take another twelve hours.

The ferry was booked for ten o'clock that evening.

The mental cruelty and physical abuse the girls had endured was having a damaging effect. They were now psychologically broken and totally compliant. The two-hourly stops were rewarded with water and some food. The girls received the sustenance sat on their sleeping bags with no more than a passing interest. Edita's ankle was a blue/brown colour, but less swollen, and Delvina had managed to wash her down again with some water and the soap from the truck-stop. It was now a question of survival. At least Delvina and Edita had each other, and that provided some emotional comfort, but Sadia was on her own and for the moment had virtually shut down, lost in her own world. The coughing, though, was less frequent now as the speed of the truck along the motorway dispersed the worst of the fumes. There was little conversation in the container as they continued the journey north.

After another long day, the truck eventually arrived in Calais just before eight o'clock. Federico was driving and headed the wagon off the auto-route to an industrial area about three quarters of a mile from the docks. Along the road, lines of immigrants watched the truck with interest, ironically waiting for any opportunity of getting across the Channel. After a few minutes, the wagon pulled into a deserted car park behind another lorry displaying UK number plates. The Italians flashed their headlights and the driver got out of his cab.

He approached the Italians and there were warm greetings.

'Marco. How are you?' said the Englishman.

'Bene, multo bene,' said Potbelly.

'Federico, Benito, good to see you again,' said the Englishman. The greetings were warm.

'You have the cargo?'

'Si, si,' said Potbelly, 'but three only.' He raised three fingers in confirmation to ensure comprehension. 'One, she is, how you say...? Morte, on boat.' He looked at the floor.

The Englishman's face reflected his anger, and he snarled his response.

'For fuck's sake... You tell them to be more fucking careful. We lose much money, dinare... comprende?'

Potbelly shrugged. 'Si, si... I tell them. You pay for three,' he said.

'Yeah, too fucking right. I ain't paying you for dead girls.'

The Englishman went back to his cab and pulled a fold-over leather bag from behind the seat. He opened it and counted out some money, then returned to the Italians.

'I want to see them.'

'Get the girls,' Potbelly said to Benito, and he opened the back of the container and pulled down the ladder. He walked to the back and opened the door. The three girls were laid on the sleeping bags.

'Up... now. You go,' said Benito, and the girls lethargically got up and followed him.

The Englishman watched as they descended the ladder. They were marched forward for inspection. Edita was limping badly, which the Englishman noticed straight away.

'What's wrong with that one?' he said to Potbelly, pointing at Edita.

'Nothing, she fell. That is all.'

The Englishman walked towards them for a closer inspection.

'How old?' asked the Englishman.

Potbelly shrugged.

'Do you speak English?' said the Englishman to Edita.

'A little,' she said.

'How old are you?' he asked again.

'Eighteen,' said Edita.

'What about her?' he said, nodding at Delvina.

'She too,' said Edita.

The Englishman approached Sadia. She was looking to the floor and would not make eye contact.

'This one?' he said to Edita.

'Fifteen.'

'Hmm,' said the Englishman.

'They're a bit fucking skinny,' he said to Potbelly. 'You been feeding them?'

'Si, si, they have much food.'

'Yeah, well, ok. Suppose they'll have to do,' he said. 'Here,' and he handed a wad of money to Potbelly, who proceeded to count it.

Seemingly satisfied with the transaction, Potbelly shouted at Benito and he returned to their truck and closed the container. Moments later it started up, and the Englishman watched as it headed back towards the auto-route for the long journey back.

The Englishman led the girls to his truck and opened the back. It was just a normal delivery lorry that you would see in large numbers on any motorway. In the back there was an array of different merchandise, mostly household goods – washing machines, tumble driers, vacuum cleaners and the like.

'Up,' said the Englishman.

There was no ladder, just step bars, and the girls clambered on the back. Delvina helped Edita, who was still struggling with her ankle. They were expecting something similar to the Italian truck but to their horror the Englishman pushed back a pallet of dishwashers to reveal the floor of the trailer. He inserted a large Allen key into a hole in the wood, turned it and then lifted the panel. Below the trapdoor there was a space just about big enough for someone to lie down with about six inches' clearance between their face and the trailer floor above them.

'You, get in,' he said and pushed Edita into the space. 'Lie down and make no noise or you will be fucking dead.'

Edita complied. Sadia started crying. 'No, no I can't,' she said in English.

'Yes you can and you fucking will,' said the Englishman. 'Now get down,' and he pushed her down the hole. Finally, Delvina followed. The three lay side by side, literally like sardines.

'You stay here for short time. Make no noise and you will be ok. Do you understand?'

'Yes,' said Edita.

The trapdoor was closed and the pallet dragged over the top. The girls were effectively in a tomb. They lay there frightened beyond all comprehension, and as the truck started, the overwhelming stench of diesel oil returned. Edita coughed as the toxic fumes attacked the nasal membranes. At this rate they were more likely to be suffocated.

The truck left the industrial estate and made its way towards the docks. Security was extremely tight and thorough searches were the norm. Stowaways were a constant problem and customs officers would randomly use heat-seeking devices to seek out illegal immigrants.

As he approached the checkpoint, the driver was reasonably confident. As a regular through the port he knew many of the officers and had a friendly banter with the latest investigator.

'Bonjour Maurice, comment allez-vous?' he said as the customs officer carrying a clipboard looked up to the cab.

'Oui, très bon, merci, John, et vous?' replied the officer.

'Oui, merci. Et votre famille?'

'Oui, merci,' replied the officer.

John handed Maurice the manifest and the customs officer examined it.

'Ouvrez, s'il vous plaît,' said Maurice.

'Certainement,' said John and he climbed down from the cab

and opened the back of the lorry.

Maurice had no more than a cursory glance.

'Merci, fermez-le,' said Maurice, and John closed up and walked back to the cab with the customs man.

'D'accord, très bon. Vous pouvez aller, bon voyage,' said Maurice.

'Au revoir,' said John.

John eventually completed the rest of the formalities and drove onto the ferry. The journey would take around seventy-five minutes and with the checks on the UK side, it would be sometime before the girls would be freed.

It was gone midnight before the truck was off the ferry and through customs. John was on his mobile, and then headed the truck out of Dover on Jubilee Way, the A2. A couple of miles out there was a large roundabout with a budget hotel set back off the road. He followed the signs to the car park at the back of the hotel. This had been a regular stop.

He got out; there was a minibus parked in the far corner of the car park and someone got out and walked towards the truck.

'Hey John, how ya doin'? Everything ok?' said the minivan driver.

'Hi Col, yeah, cushty mate, cushty,' said John.

John opened the back of the lorry and went inside. There was a torch on the pallet of dishwashers and he lit it up.

'Here, Col, give us a hand to shift these will ya?'

Colin joined John in the back of the truck and moved the pallets. John lifted the trapdoor and shone the torch inside. The three girls blinked bleary-eyed as the light lit their faces.

'Come on, you can get out now, stretch your legs,' said John.

He grabbed Delvina's arms and pulled her out. She lay on the floor of the truck for a moment to catch her breath. Sadia and Edita were extracted in the same way and they too could not stand. John viewed them with the torch.

'They don't look too good, mate,' said Colin.

'Nah, they'll be ok after a bath and some food, you see. Have you got the room key?'

'Yeah,' said Colin.

'Right, let's get 'em inside.'

'Come on girls...! Out,' Colin instructed.

Delvina crawled to the edge of the truck, still taking in oxygen. John and Colin lifted her off the back. It had been the best part of three hours cramped in their makeshift container and her legs could not support her weight. Her knees seemed to just buckle and she fell to the ground, unable to move. The men left her to recover and motioned Edita and Sadia to follow. It was the same result and the three girls just sat on the tarmac at the back of the truck, seemingly immobile.

John looked at the three, then at Colin.

'Come on girls, get up; we need to get going,' said John, and he grabbed Delvina's arm and lifted her to her feet. Edita also needed help; her ankle would not respond to the demands of her brain. Sadia managed to stand on her own, resembling a young foal taking its first steps. She steadied herself for a couple of moments trying to regain equilibrium, and then was sick on the pavement.

'Jesus,' said Colin watching the heaving Sadia.

'Come on,' said John. 'I ain't cleaning that mess up.'

Half dragging, half supporting, the men led the girls to the entrance of the hotel. There was a night porter on duty but not on reception. There was a light on in the office behind the desk with the sound of a TV emanating from it. Colin ushered the girls through the doors and along the corridor to the left where the ground-floor rooms were located.

'Room twenty-three,' he said to John.

The girls were in a total daze, shuffling down the corridor. They waited while Colin opened the door and then led them inside. It was a standard double room with a double bed and a bed-settee which could be used as another.

The girls were still in their tracksuits and sandals, and just stood there waiting for instructions. Edita and Delvina stared at the room and the bed wondering what was going to happen and fearing the worst. Sadia was in a state of collapse; vomit stained her top.

'Ok girls. I've got some sandwiches and you can use the bathroom,' said Colin, and he went to a rucksack and pulled out the food. 'Here,' he said, handing a bottle of water to Sadia. 'Drink this.' She undid the top and started to swig. It was an automatic response; her mental capacity appeared to have closed down.

'There's some fresh clobber an' all. Those tracksuits smell a bit rank.' There was a second, larger rucksack which contained some jeans, tee shirts and underwear.

'Don't know what sizes you are, you'll have to have a shufty through,' said Colin.

Colin put the holdall on the bed and the girls rummaged around and chose suitable clothing.

'You can help yourself to coffee if you want... but it ain't much cop,' said Colin, turning on the kettle on the complimentary tray.

'Right, who wants to go first?' said John. 'The bathroom,' he clarified. 'It's alright, you can lock the door. You'll be ok. You're in England now, you'll be treated well.'

Delvina looked at her sister. 'England?' said Edita.

'Yeah, we'll get you good jobs an' everything... You'll have a good life here. You're lucky, people are selling their daughters to get to England but we've bought you here for nothing. How about that?'

The girls just looked at each other.

'Right, who wants to go first then?' he repeated.

'Edita, you go. We will be alright,' said Delvina in Albanian.

'What'd she say?' said John.

'She say we will be alright,' said Edita.

'Yeah, course you will, love,' said John.

Edita went into the bathroom and locked the door and the shower started running.

'There you are, I said you'd be alright. Here, who wants some food then?' said Colin.

He took out some sandwiches and handed them out, then made some coffee. Delvina started eating; Sadia was still sipping at the water.

It was about an hour before the girls had washed and changed into fresh clothing. It had a therapeutic effect and they were more alert. The girls were sat on the bed, the men on the settee. Edita was still eating her sandwich, her ankle, now a blue colour, still swollen and sore.

Colin spoke. 'Now, I'll tell ya what's going to happen in case you was wondering, like. We stay here tonight. Me and John, here, will be on the sofa; you girls can have the bed... but no funny business, right, or you'll be in deep shit, understand?' They looked at him blankly.

Colin continued. 'In the morning we're gonna take you to another place where you can work and get money. Don't worry, nobody's gonna hurt you. We'll see to that. We're gonna look after ya. Ain't we John?'

'Eh? Oh, yeah,' said John. 'We're definitely gonna look after ya.'

CHAPTER THREE

Friday 14th September 2012, six weeks after the Albanian kidnapping.

Keith Woodley was waiting anxiously in his office. He looked at the desk clock and drummed his fingers. He checked his iPhone again, no messages. 'Come on,' he said under his breath. Then he could hear it; the familiar sound of the Mercedes twenty-six seater as it negotiated the depot entrance. He was always relieved when they returned safely. He watched as the last of his precious vehicles entered the parking bay and draw up next to another single-decker which hadn't been out today. In fact, apart from this one, only the three double-deckers had been in use, the Friday afternoon school run. The remaining fleet lay dormant, like a bunch of discarded toys.

He checked his watch – six-fifteen – and dialled home. Mustn't be late tonight.

It was picked up on the third ring. 'Hi, Jase, can you let your mum know Bruce has just got in? Should be back in half an hour or so. Cheers... Yeah thanks, see you in a bit.'

Keith rang off, left the office and waited outside.

'How did it go?' he said to the approaching driver.

'Aye, it were greet,' said the man in his broad Yorkshire accent. 'But I don't care if I don't hear "She'll Be Coming 'Round the Mountain" again as long as I live.'

Bruce Merryweather was one of the three permanent drivers that Woodley's employed. The rest were self-employed and were used on a 'needs-only' basis. In recent months that hadn't been as regular as in previous years.

'What, you got 'em singing?' said Woodley, smiling.

'Weren't me, I think one or two overdid the gin and tonic at lunchtime. There was this one old girl, used to be a Scout mistress by all accounts, knew all the songs, "Roll Me Over in the Clover", "Wild Rover"; God, we had the lot.'

'How many did you have on?' asked Keith.

'Twenty-three, almost a full bus.'

'Did they pay up ok?'

'Aye,' said Bruce. 'Got it here somewhere.' He rummaged in his trouser pocket and handed over a dog-eared cheque; 'Dunfield Women's Guild', it said.

'Aye, here you go, three hundred and ninety pounds... Mind you, don't think we'll be seeing them again, kept going on about how expensive it was.'

'They've got no idea of the price of diesel,' said Woodley, taking the cheque from the driver and putting it in the side pocket of his jacket. 'It's not really bad value when you think about it.'

'Well, I wouldn't pay twenty odd pounds for a day out in Scarborough,' said Bruce.

'Aye, there is that,' said Woodley. 'Still we've been doing their annual outing for some years; it'll be a shame if they don't come back.'

It wasn't a deliberate underplay; he was considering the repercussions in his mind. Another lost customer; it was becoming a worrying trend.

He walked back through the entrance door of the brick building which housed the administration area, such as it was, a couple of small offices and reception. The walls were littered with notices, schedules and calendars; it reflected the chaos which regularly ensued. There was a welcome desk immediately to the left, although the term would be used lightly; the ambience was anything but welcoming. On the desk there was a small telephone switchboard and, behind, various filing cabinets. His private office was to the right. Keith walked in, followed by Bruce, and he picked up an envelope from the top of his desk.

'There you go,' he said, handing over the weekly wage packet to the driver.

'Thanks... I've cleared t' bus, not much rubbish, tidier than most.'

'Cheers,' said Woodley, but not really concentrating.

'Those bloody football supporters last weekend t'were a nightmare. Took me over an hour to clear up, beer cans, crisps, God knows what else. At least nobody was sick this time.'

It was expected that the drivers would be responsible for the internal appearance of the bus.

Keith followed the driver from the office and locked the door behind him, then keyed in the security code to set the alarm. They left the building together and he locked the entrance door behind them and put the keys in his pocket.

'Not a bad evening,' said Keith looking at the setting sun in a clear sky, just a few clouds.

'You still ok for tomorrow?' he added.

'Aye, it's an early one,' said Bruce.

'Yeah, Birmingham isn't it?' said Keith.

'Aye, Clothes Show at the Exhibition Centre... Oh no, just had a terrible thought, another bus load of women,' he sighed.

'Well let's hope they've got a better repertoire for the return journey,' said Keith. 'By the way, Jack'll be opening up tomorrow. Got a do on tonight, Kathryn's fortieth,' he added.

'Aye, ok. Going anywhere nice?'

'Yeah, there's a charity ball at Hayfield Manor; it's a bit of a surprise. Rodney Baker's the guest speaker.'

'What, the footballer?' said Bruce.

'Yeah,' said Keith. Bruce looked suitably impressed.

'That should be good.'

'Yeah, hope so, cost enough... Anyway, best get off, got a taxi booked for seven-thirty,' said Keith as he walked towards his four-year-old Mercedes parked next to Merryweather's Fiat.

'Aye, see you tomorrow night I expect. Should be back around ten,' said Bruce.

'Yeah, I'll be over to lock up. Take care,' said Keith as he watched him walk towards his car whistling 'She'll Be Coming 'Round the Mountain'.

Bruce left the depot on the outskirts of Aireford and Keith had a last-minute check; sixteen vehicles, liveried with the logo, 'Woodley's of Aireford'. All present and correct. He ignored the rubbish bouncing around the yard in the wind, mostly fast-food wrappers and cartons which were regularly tossed over the wall. Dandelions and other weeds added colour to the tarmac, but also reflected the neglect.

He started the car and drove through the outer gate, stopped, got out and locked the reinforced door. As he got back in, he glanced over the back seat at the package draped in polythene. Hope she likes it, he thought. Then he left for the five-mile drive to Dunfield.

Fifteen minutes later, he pulled up on the drive of the three-bedroomed detached house in a modern development. The twenty-house cul-de-sac was neat and tidy, frontages tended and lawns manicured. Flowers were in abundance, particularly roses, which were probably at their best in early September.

There was a short paved driveway leading to the single garage on the front of the house. Keith took the package carefully from the back seat and draped it over his arm, locked his car and went to the front door adjacent to the garage.

'Hello, anyone at home?' said Keith as he walked into the house.

'I'm up here,' said his wife.

'Hi Dad,' said another voice from upstairs.

'Hi Jase,' shouted Keith.

Keith carefully pegged the garment on one of the coat hooks in the hall, took his jacket off and walked into the lounge. Birthday cards were neatly lined up across the mantelpiece above the gas fire and on top of the wall unit. A banner saying 'Happy Fortieth' was pinned to the wall over the mirror. It was times like this Keith realised just how many friends they had. There was one from his mother, he noticed. 'To My Darling Daughter-in-Law', it said. He picked it up and read it. Must have arrived today, he thought; he hadn't noticed it earlier. A day late; still she did phone to wish her happy birthday yesterday, which was something. Keith could never understand why his mother didn't like Kathryn. 'Could have done a lot better. Should have played the field a bit,' she was always reminding him whenever they went through a bad patch, which over the years had been quite often.

He left the lounge and went upstairs. Kathryn was sat on a stool in front of the dressing table mirror in just her underwear and stockings. There was a fresh smell of body lotion as Keith entered the room.

'Hmm, you smell nice,' he said, and went to his wife, going to kiss her.

'Don't touch my hair!' she said sharply. 'It cost a small fortune. You better get going, you haven't got long... I've hung your dinner jacket and trousers in the airing cupboard. Smelt a bit musty.'

'Thanks, not surprised; haven't worn it for two years,' said Keith.

'Hope you can still get in it,' said Kathryn, staring in the mirror applying mascara.

'Cheeky, I'm as fit as a flea, me,' he said, and headed for the bathroom.

He poked his head around his son's door. 'You ok, son?'

'Yes, thanks,' Jason replied without taking his head from his computer screen.

By seven-twenty Keith had almost finished getting ready.

'Here, can you give us a hand with this, love?' he shouted, trying to tie his dickey bow.

Kathryn was in the next bedroom giving last-minute orders to Jason.

'And don't spend all night on that Xbox,' she said as she left the boy's room and returned to the master bedroom.

'Here, give it me,' she said, moving his hands away.

'This shirt's a bit tight round the neck,' she said as she made the final knot.

'Probably shrunk in the wash... They do you know, I read it somewhere.'

'Yeah, yeah and I'm the Pope,' she said. 'There, that should do it.' She stepped back to admire her handiwork.

'Your trousers look a bit comfy an' all. Your belly's hanging over the top. I said you should've checked it last week. You could've got a new dinner suit. That one must be five years old.'

'Nah, plenty of wear left yet. Can't go chucking good money away,' he said.

'Well it's either that or you go on a diet.'

Kathryn stood there in a low-cut black cocktail dress. In make-up and jewellery she looked the business.

'You look nice,' said Keith.

'Thanks.'

He followed her down the stairs and went into the lounge.

'Ellie's over at Francesca's. I told her not to be late, she's working tomorrow,' she said as she turned off the TV.

She turned around, wondering why her husband hadn't responded.

'Close your eyes,' said Keith from the hallway. He walked in with the polythene wrapper draped over his arms. Kathryn was stood in the middle of the room with her eyes shut. 'Hurry up; the taxi will be here in a minute.'

Keith lifted the wrapper. 'Ok, you can open your eyes,' he said.

For a moment Kathryn just looked at it in disbelief. 'What...? When..? How...?'

Keith removed the polythene completely and held it up. 'Come on, try it on, I'm dying to see what it looks like on you.'

He held the coat open by the top and placed it around Kathryn's shoulders. She pulled it around her and snuggled into it like a comfort blanket.

'It's fabulous... But it cost a fortune. Did you get it from Chloe's?'

'Yeah, I remembered you said how much you liked it when we walked past the place last week,' said Keith.

'I know, but I never meant... I didn't think...'

'It's ok,' he said, cutting her off. 'It looks lovely on you,' he said. 'Happy birthday.'

'Thank you... it's the best present ever.'

She ran her hands down the soft leather and back around the fur neck. It fitted perfectly, fashionably just above the knees, the dark tan colour complementing her auburn hair.

There was a 'toot' from outside.

'That'll be the taxi,' said Keith.

'Where're we going?' said Kathryn. 'You just told me to "posh up".'

'It's a surprise,' said Keith.

Kathryn shouted upstairs. 'We're off now, Jason. Don't forget, don't be late. Ellie said she'll be in around ten.'

'Ok,' shouted Jason.

'Bye son,' shouted Keith.

'Bye Dad,' came the reply.

They walked out of the house to the taxi.

'Hayfield Manor,' said Keith to the driver.

Kathryn pricked up her ears. 'Hayfield Manor? We going there?' she said.

'Yeah, special treat,' said Keith.

'Wow, you really have pushed the boat out.'

'Well it's not every day you have a fortieth birthday,' said Keith.

'I know, but can we afford it?'

'You let me worry about that,' said Keith, and he would, very soon.

He sat in the back of the taxi totting everything up. Coat, eleven hundred pounds; tickets, two hundred pounds, and there were still the drinks to pay for. He hoped the hundred pounds he had in his wallet would be enough. His credit card had reached the £5,000 limit, and his debit card had refused any further withdrawals. 'Refer to Bank' it said when he tried to draw out two hundred and fifty pounds earlier.

Twenty minutes later they arrived at the Hayfield Manor Hotel, a former stately home, now a hotel and conference centre, also a popular venue for dinner-dances and receptions. Tonight was a special charity night arranged by the local Rotary Club. Woodley's Coaches had done work for them over the years and Keith had been able to get tickets through his contact, Phil Dunning. He and Kathryn would be sat on Phil's table with other guests.

The Asian taxi driver got out and opened the door. Keith gave the man a ten pound note. 'See you here at twelve-thirty.' The driver nodded and Keith hoped he had understood.

Kathryn looked up at the magnificent Victorian building.

'Wow, this is great. You wait till I tell Jean about this,' she said, referring to one of her close friends.

Keith watched the taxi disappear down the long drive, and

they made their way to the entrance. Several people in formal evening attire were outside smoking around the doorway. Keith and Kathryn ran the gauntlet and went inside. There was an easel in the entrance lobby with a note written in a marker pen, "Rotary Charity Ball – Curzon Suite". There was an A4 sheet of paper attached with the table seating plan; to the left and right, stairs led down to the ladies' and gentlemen's cloakrooms.

'You better check that in,' said Keith, looking at Kathryn's coat. 'You don't want to get red wine down it.'

'Good idea,' she said, and followed the signs down the steps to the cloakroom.

At the foot of the stairs there was a corridor decorated with red shiny tiles. The lighting was dim and it was quite dark. Women in all there finery were milling about, going in and exiting the wash-rooms; to the right was a small booth where a bored-looking girl was staring into a mobile phone. She looked up as Kathryn approached. Kathryn took off her coat and passed it over. 'Can you look after this for me?'

'Yes... of course,' replied the girl in an Eastern European accent. Without any further acknowledgement the girl handed over what looked like a raffle ticket by way of receipt. Kathryn watched as the girl hung up the coat; there were several rails and most were full, probably a couple of hundred. Kathryn put the orange slip into her handbag. She turned then looked at the girl, who had returned to the delights of her mobile phone.

'Manners,' Kathryn said to herself.

Keith was waiting in the lobby as she returned from the cloakroom. He looked at his wife. They had been childhood sweethearts and even after nineteen years of marriage he couldn't imagine being with anyone else. Tonight she looked glamorous in her posh frock and he noticed one or two heads turn as she walked towards him.

'Everything ok?'

'Yes,' said Kathryn. 'Some people are so rude. The girl looking after the coats never said a word; more interested in her mobile phone.'

'Sign of the times,' said Keith. 'Come on, let's get a drink.'

They followed the signs for the Rotary Club Charity Dinner, up a sweeping staircase to the Curzon Suite. There was a man standing at the ornate entrance door; music could be heard from inside.

'Have you got your tickets please?' he said.

Keith felt his inside jacket pocket and pulled out his two postcard-sized tickets.

'Thank you,' said the man. 'Would you like to enter them for our charity draw? You could win a free weekend stay here. All expenses paid... except meals and drinks,' he added.

Kathryn looked at him. 'That would be nice, wouldn't it?'

'Yeah, go on then,' said Keith.

'That will be twenty pounds, then. Just write your name and mobile number on the back.'

Keith was beginning to worry. It would be another ten pounds for the taxi back and he hadn't bought any drinks yet. He gave the man the money and the tickets were placed in a drum ready to be drawn at some stage during the evening.

They walked through into the Curzon Suite. It was crowded with men in dinner jackets like a colony of penguins, and women in their best outfits. Lively chatter echoed around the room. The lighting was soft, enhancing the decor, and provided a convivial atmosphere. To the right was a bar with probably fifty people trying to get served by three bar staff. The room was dominated by twenty tables, cafe style, all numbered with eight table settings on each. One or two had already found their allocated places and were sat chatting. At the far end of the room there was a parquet dance area and a stage where a disco had been set up; a DJ was playing pre-dinner easy listening music.

Keith looked around to see if he could see his host; then, a shout from the bar area. 'Keith, over here.' He followed the voice with his eyes and spotted him. 'Hiya, Phil,' he replied, and he grabbed Kathryn's hand and went over to meet his friend.

Phil would be about the same age as Keith, in his early forties with dark hair with flecks of grey at the sides. An architect, he had told Keith, he was fit with a trim physique and looked as if he used the gym regularly.

'What're you having?' said Phil. 'James's at the bar, he'll get them in.'

'Pint of lager and a red wine, thanks Phil,' said Keith.

Kathryn was looking around the room; there would be nobody she would know. The professional circuit was not one she frequented. Phil was chatting to another man who was being served at the bar. He started passing drinks back to another couple who were immediately behind them. Then he called to Keith and passed him the lager and wine.

Eventually the melee at the bar subsided and Phil made some introductions. 'Keith, this is my wife Jane,' he said, and Keith shook hands with an attractive woman with bleached-blonde hair in her mid-forties. Her make-up had been expertly applied and she looked as if she could have been a model or a celebrity of some kind, a point not lost on Kathryn, who was beginning to feel inadequate. She wasn't naturally adept at socialising.

'This is my wife, Kathryn,' said Keith, and she shook hands with Phil and Jane. 'This is James and Cynthia, they're on our table,' said Phil, introducing them to the other couple who were on bar duties earlier; more handshakes. Another professional couple, he would also be in his forties, but balding; she, probably younger but bookish-looking with short curly hair.

'Oh, happy birthday, by the way,' said Phil. 'Keith said it was a bit of a celebration.'

'Thank you,' said Kathryn.

'So what do you do?' asked James to Keith.

'In travel... Woodley's of Aireford,' replied Keith.

'Woodley's? Ah, yes, I've seen your coaches around town,' said James as he took a sip from a glass of white wine.

'What about you?' asked Keith, out of politeness, not of interest.

'An accountant,' said James. 'Browns and Easton,' he added.

'James's in our badminton club,' said Phil.

'Do you play at all?' said James.

'No, don't get the time,' Keith replied.

There was a loud rapping on one of the tables as another of the penguins announced that dinner was being served.

'We're on table six,' said Phil as the small group made their way to their seats where another couple were already seated. They got up and shook hands in a familiar way with James and Cynthia

'Kathryn, you're next to me,' said Phil.

'Jane, do you want to sit next to Keith? Cynthia, James, over there,' said Phil, definitely in charge of the seating plan.

'What, no grace?' said James.

'No,' said Phil. 'There was some concern it might offend some of our guests.'

James nodded disapprovingly.

A line of waitresses armed with plates walked in and peeled off, positioning themselves to a table each.

'Soup, who is having?' asked the young lady who had been allocated to table six and who looked like she didn't want to be there. 'Edita', it said on her name badge. She appeared to have a bruise over her left eye.

'Hello, you been in a fight?' said Phil. The waitress ignored him.

'Two here, please,' said the other male guest on the table. Edita attended.

'Hi,' he said looking across at Keith and Kathryn. 'I'm Steve; this is Sonia.'

Keith looked at them both. Definitely money judging by the quality of the man's suit and shirt. He clearly looked after himself, slim and immaculately groomed and with his gleaming teeth he could have been a male model. The woman looked younger and was wearing a low-cut dress and expensive-looking jewellery. He made the introductions.

'I'm Keith, and this is Kathryn, my wife.' There were nods all around.

Introductions over, the discussions started. A wine waiter appeared.

'What shall we have? Four white, four red?' said Phil and seeing there was no dissention made the choices and the wine waiter went away to fetch them.

'That works out at forty pounds per couple... Not bad for this place,' said Phil with the expectancy that cash would be required when the waiter returned.

Sure enough, the bill was presented to Phil, and while the man poured the drinks Keith went to his pocket and produced two twenty pound notes. The other men did the same. Keith was getting really concerned, just thirty pounds left with the taxi to pay for. It would be no use asking Kathryn; Keith had already told her she wouldn't need any money tonight. He hoped he would not be embarrassed.

'What do you do?' said Jane, looking at Kathryn.

'Work in Social Services,' she said, as she finished the last of her pâté.

'Oh,' said Jane, which appeared disparaging although it was

not probably meant to be.

'What part?' picked up Phil.

'Benefits,' said Kathryn.

'That must be interesting,' said Phil.

'Don't know about that but it's busy.'

'So you're not involved in coaches then?' asked James.

'No, that's Keith's. I'm not allowed near it.'

'So how is the travel business?' asked James.

'Oh, you know, steady,' which was Keith's standard response these days. If only they knew. 'Can always handle more,' he added.

Steve looked up from his soup dish. 'So you're Woodley's of Aireford?' he said.

'Yes,' said Keith.

'Do you do airport runs?'

'Yeah, anything, we've got a couple of minibuses as well as the bigger ones,' he replied.

'Hmm, that's interesting. I may be able to put some business your way,' said Steve.

'Great, thanks, let me know. I can do some good deals on regular work. What line are you in?' asked Keith.

'Textiles,' Steve replied.

'He's being modest, Steve owns SBJ Holdings,' said James before Steve could answer. Keith was none the wiser.

'Hyams Fabrics,' said James.

'Really?' said Keith, his eyebrows raised, recognising the name of one of Aireford's largest employers.

'Yes, we get people flying in and out of Manchester all the time. Usually just call a couple of cabs,' said Steve. 'Let me have a card and I'll be in touch.'

'Yeah, will do,' said Keith. 'Thanks.'

This was looking more promising and he was suddenly uplifted from his earlier depression. Kathryn was down her third glass of red wine and chatting easily with Cynthia, James's wife.

The cohort of waitresses reappeared and cleared the starters with military precision. Then they were back.

'Salmon, who is for?' enquired Edita in her imperfect English.

Kathryn, Jane and Sonia responded and were given fish knives.

'Beef?' asked the waitress.

The four men were given steak knives.

'Not meat?' asked Edita, looking at Cynthia, who nodded.

'How long have you been a veggie?' asked Kathryn who was now definitely relaxing.

'Ten years,' replied Cynthia, not rising to any implied criticism. 'I was watching a programme on TV about intensive farming and that was that. No more meat for me,' she said. 'How they treat pigs and chickens... it's scandalous.'

Following the main course, a choice of sweets was offered and Keith chose the sticky toffee pudding. Coffee and mints followed. After a few minutes, the appointed MC on table number one rapped again with a gavel.

'Please be upstanding for the loyal toast,' he announced. 'Ladies and gentlemen... the Queen.'

Everyone stood up and repeated, 'The Queen.'

'There will be a ten-minute break before we start the proceedings,' said the MC.

The strain on Keith's already struggling waistband was making him feel uncomfortable. There was a general exodus as the smokers headed for the front door; others, to the cloakrooms. Keith welcomed the break, a chance to stretch his legs and relieve himself of the earlier lagers and wine. Phil joined him and they walked together down the two flights of stairs, leaving Kathryn chatting to Cynthia. Steve and James had gone to the bar, and Jane and Sonia went outside for a cigarette. Queues started to form down the stairways to the cloakrooms as a hundred people made towards the toilets. Some were going to need more than the allotted ten minutes.

Among the jostle and scrimmaging Keith would not have noticed an attractive, fair-haired girl in a powder-blue mini-dress talking to one of the men on the reception desk.

The break lasted nearer twenty minutes before the gathering had emptied the bar and returned from the toilets.

Another rap on the table and the speeches started.

Keith was feeling mellow from his two glasses of wine on top of the lager, and after a long day he was having difficulty keeping awake. Then his mind quickly returned to the topic it had always returned to over the last couple of years... money. As the distinguished speaker droned on about some Amazonian rainforest trek and how the evening's proceeds would fund the expedition, Keith was beginning to count the cost, not just of the evening but of recent events. The cheque from the Ladies Circle would barely cover the diesel for the Birmingham trip. Still, the travel firm that had organised the Clothes Show excursion was a good payer and he hoped to get another cheque tomorrow night when the bus returned. That should help.

The meeting with the bank manager on Tuesday hadn't gone well. Although he had banked with the same branch for over twenty years, he couldn't argue with the manager when he had presented last year's accounts. The business was losing money, and this year it had been worse, a lot worse. The overdraft of £30,000 was regularly exceeded and only a pleading phone call to the manager had prevented his monthly diesel cheque from being returned. 'If you do that, then the business will go down,' he had said dramatically, but it was not far from the truth. Keith had no savings and the house had been re-mortgaged twice, not that Kathryn would have realised it. The forms that he had presented her for signing were explained away as banking bureaucracy. 'Just some red tape,' he had said.

Keith's thoughts were disturbed when the first speaker finished to generous applause. One or two took the opportunity to nip out for a cigarette or comfort break. A few headed to the bar.

A few minutes later, the MC rapped the table again and formally announced it was time for the finale. Keith looked round the table. Kathryn was down her fourth glass of wine and was chatting with Cynthia. The room went quiet for a moment, then rapturous applause as the guest of honour, Rodney Baker, the former England football international, now pundit and celebrity, stood up to speak.

Keith listened for a while, and then drifted off again, back to the early days. He knew that the career change seven years ago would be a risk but no-one in 2005 could have predicted the banking crisis and the subsequent recession. At thirty-four, after sixteen years in the transport department of the local council, it was time to spread his wings, and when the latest round of redundancies was announced, he had taken the opportunity.

He knew the owner of Fairway Travel Ltd., not well, but the company had worked for the council when some of the education department business was outsourced. Through several meetings and after a great deal of discussion, Keith put a business plan together and went to see the bank manager.

Kathryn was far from enthusiastic about buying the business, even less at using the house as collateral but with his severance money as capital and the property giving sufficient security, Keith convinced the bank to give him a loan.

Keith had no such qualms. He had been responsible for the council's fleet of vehicles for over three years, managing a staff of seventy, so he definitely had the right credentials to run this type of operation. He also had an HGV licence and could help out with the driving if necessary.

As soon as he took over, he changed the name of the business to 'Woodley's of Aireford'. Initially, business was good. Through his contacts in the council he secured several lucrative contracts, including many school runs which he still had today. It was his bread and butter, although now, with the cutbacks, they were fewer in number, and with keen tendering, barely covered the costs. By 2008, he had over twenty buses and employed twelve full-time drivers and five others on call; the subsequent economic climate had changed all that.

CHAPTER FOUR

He suddenly felt a sharp kick on his shins, making him jump. Kathryn was scowling at him. 'You were nodding off,' she mouthed. The rest of the table guests were concentrating on the speaker and hadn't noticed.

There was a rapturous applause as the star of the show finished his presentation. Around the table there was a general consensus. 'Very good,' said Phil. 'Yes, and funny as well,' said James. 'Well, he gets my vote,' said Jane. 'Hot or what?' she said, looking at Sonia. 'That's for sure,' Sonia replied, and licked her lips lasciviously.

'Did you enjoy it, Kathryn?' asked Jane.

'Yes,' replied Kathryn. 'Although I'm not a big football fan,' she added. 'Keith is, aren't you?' she said.

'Yeah,' said Keith. 'Not playing, mind, bit old for that now, but watch the odd game on telly when I'm not working.'

There was another loud tap on the table as the MC announced the prize draw. One of the female guests that most people seemed to know was invited to make the draw. She was wearing a dress that would be more appropriate on someone half her age, but nevertheless performed her duties with much aplomb and handed a ticket to the MC.

'And the lucky winner is.... Tom Spencer,' he announced. Cheers erupted from the gathering and one of the guests on table three walked up and collected his prize. The MC thanked everyone for their generosity.

Shit, forty quid down the drain, thought Keith, and poured another glass of wine.

There was another exodus as the tables were cleared in

preparation for the disco.

'Looking forward to this,' said Kathryn. 'Been ages since we went to a disco.'

Jane responded, 'Phil and I are always at do's, aren't we darling?'

Yes,' replied her husband. 'Especially around Christmas time.'

'It will be even worse next year when he takes over as president, won't it dear?' said Jane.

'Yes, that's for sure... Excuse me a minute,' said Phil, and he got up and walked towards the top table where Rodney Barker was signing autographs. Keith sat looking into his glass of wine.

'Anyone want another drink?' said James. 'I'm going to the bar.'

'Not for me,' said Keith.

'I'm ok,' said Kathryn.

Steve and Sonia had gone to socialise. Jane accompanied James to the bar and linked her arms with his. Cynthia didn't look too happy and picked up the last bottle of white wine and poured herself a large measure.

Keith looked at his watch again – it was ten-thirty. Another two hours, he thought. How on earth was he going to stay awake, he was utterly knackered.

'You alright, Keith?' said Phil returning from the top-table visit.

'Yeah,' said Keith. 'It's been a long day.'

'You want to get over there,' said Phil, nodding towards the top table. 'Rodney's signing autographs. Top bloke, just been chatting to him.'

'Yeah, might do that,' said Keith, but with little enthusiasm.

Before Keith could make a move, the disco cranked up, making any further semblance of discourse impossible.

'Come on Keith,' said Kathryn. 'I want to dance.'

Keith had no idea how he managed to get through another two hours but at twelve-twenty he called Kathryn, who had been dancing with just about everybody. Keith had given up after the second record and had been sat at the table talking to various people trying to drum up some business. He went over to her.

'Need to go,' he said.

She was dancing with Steve, a bit closer than Keith really liked.

'Oh,' she said, grabbing Steve by the waist and pulling him to her. 'Can't we stay a bit longer?'

'Taxi's booked for twelve-thirty,' said Keith.

She looked at Keith in disapproval. 'Oh, alright then,' she said with a feigned pout.

As Keith was walking back to the table, Kathryn, seeing Sonia was chatting to Cynthia and had her back to the dance floor, made an attempt to kiss Steve. Steve responded with a great deal of interest.

'Mmm, I needed that,' she said.

'Plenty more where that came from,' he said.

She looked at him. 'We'll have to see about that then, won't we?' she said. 'Better go,' she added, and Steve escorted her from the dance floor back to the table.

'Hello you two,' said Cynthia. 'You looked like you were enjoying yourselves.'

'Not been dancing for ages,' said Kathryn, not rising to any innuendoes. 'Used to go all the time when I was at school.'

'Keith, don't forget to ring me. Have you got a business card?' said Steve.

'Not on me, but I'll give you my mobile,' said Keith.

He picked up the name card from the table which had been used to indicate the seating plan.

'Anybody got a pen?' he said, and Steve reached in his inside pocket.

'There you go,' said Steve, and Keith tore the card in two and wrote down his number on the back.

'Cheers,' said Keith, handing the card to Steve.

The pen was on the table and with everybody distracted by farewells, Kathryn quickly wrote her mobile number on the remaining half of the card.

'Don't forget your pen, Steve,' said Kathryn.

'Oh, thanks' said Steve as she slipped the pen and card into his hand.

Steve was momentarily confused but quickly twigged.

'We must stay in touch,' she said.

'Definitely,' said Steve, and she looked directly in his eyes before turning her gaze.

'Nice to meet you,' she said to Sonia, and kissed her on the cheek. The pleasantries were exchanged with the remaining guests who were staying for the remaining half an hour, and Keith and Kathryn headed for the exit.

'Well that went ok,' he said as they descended the stairs to the reception area.

'Yes,' she said. 'Really enjoyed it, even the footballer. Thanks.'

'I hope that bloke Steve comes up with the goods,' he said. Kathryn smiled; so did she.

'You know a contract with them could make all the difference.'

They were walking towards the exit door and could see a car waiting outside, 'Shah's Taxi,' it said on the side.

'Thank goodness for that,' said Keith.

'Oh, my coat,' exclaimed Kathryn.

'Jesus, don't forget that whatever you do,' said Keith. 'Here, I'll go.'

'No, it's ok,' said Kathryn. 'I could do with the ladies. You sort out the taxi.'

'Ok, if you're sure,' he said, and watched her walk a little unsteadily towards the stairs down to the cloakroom.

Kathryn completed her toilet trip and freshened up her make-up, then went to the booth where the coats were kept. It was the same girl who was attending earlier. There were not as many coats left now.

'Can I have my coat please?' said Kathryn.

'Of course,' said the girl. 'You have ticket?'

Kathryn opened her purse and rummaged around; the ticket had gone.

'It's here somewhere,' she said, checking each compartment. She looked up.

'Oh, wait a minute, it's over there,' she said spotting the fur collar and pointing to a coat on the end of the second rail.

'This one?' said the girl as she lifted it from its hanger.

'Yes, thank you,' said Kathryn.

The girl wasn't about to argue and gave it to Kathryn without any further enquiry. She was quickly back on her mobile phone. Another couple approached; it would be a short-lived text.

Kathryn walked back up the stairs and out of the building with the coat over her arm; she was still hot from her exploits on the dance floor. The taxi was still there, its engine running, and she got in. The driver didn't bother to get out.

'Everything ok?' said Keith. 'You were a long time.'

'Yes,' she said, without elaboration and the cab pulled away. She put the coat down in the empty space between her and her husband

Another quarter of an hour and the cab pulled up outside their house.

'How much?' said Keith.

'Fifteen pounds,' said the driver.

'But it was only ten going.'

'It's after midnight,' said the driver.

Keith cursed but paid up without a tip and got out. Kathryn, coat over her arm, was already opening the front door.

Inside, Kathryn draped her coat over an armchair and went to the drinks cabinet and poured herself a gin and tonic.

'Thanks for tonight,' she said as Keith joined her in the lounge. 'Do you want a drink?'

'Nah, better not, need to keep a clear head, work tomorrow,' he said. 'Think I'll turn in, it's gone one.'

'I'll be with you in a bit. Just need to wind down a while,' she said.

'Ok, I'll just check on the kids,' said Keith, and went upstairs leaving Kathryn to her gin.

Keith was asleep when he felt Kathryn get into bed. Her hands made their way around his waist and headed downwards.

'Not now, eh, I'm knackered,' said Keith, and he went back to sleep. Kathryn was annoyed at the rebuff, she was far from tired. She was thinking of Steve, wondering if he would call.

Saturday morning, seven-thirty, and seventeen-year-old daughter Ellie knocked on the bedroom door.

'What time is it?' said Keith drowsily.

Ellie put her head around the door, 'It's seven-thirty. I'm off now, see you later,' she said.

'Ok, have a good day,' said Keith.

Saturday morning and Ellie would be catching the bus into town. She had a part-time job at the local pharmacy, and today would be busy. Usually, Keith would drive her in but she had agreed to take the bus today, knowing that it would have been a late night for her parents.

Keith heard the front door close and went back to sleep. It was nine before he woke again, hearing son, Jason, moving about in the bedroom next door.

'Fancy a cuppa?' he said to Kathryn, who was also stirring.

'Hmm, yes please,' she said drowsily.

A few minutes later, Keith returned with the reviving brew.

'What time are you going in?' Kathryn asked as she sat up and took her first sip.

'Said I'd pop in around one... Jack'll look after things till then,' he replied. 'There's only three out today. Bruce is doing the Birmingham job and Dave and Eddie are on the football run.'

'They'll be pleased,' she said in an ironic way.

Keith went back downstairs just as the postman was delivering the mail. He went to the door and picked up the letters before anyone could see, and went into the lounge. There were six today, all addressed to Keith Woodley or Woodley's of Aireford. He opened them one by one and put his head in his hands. Three reminders of overdue payments and two final demands, but it was the sixth that caused him the most concern.

It was headed 'Jackson and Faircroft, Insolvency Practitioners'. The letter went on, 'in the matter of Thomas Foley & Sons Ltd. We regret to advise you that a winding-up order has been issued to the above company by HMRC. You are listed as a creditor in the company records and, accordingly, we would request you to submit your claim to us as soon as possible...'

Keith was momentarily stunned, over two grand; it had been an excursion for an old people's home, two coaches. The invoice had been outstanding for a while but he had spoken to Tom Foley himself only last week and he had promised to let him have the payment by Tuesday, or Wednesday at the latest. The chance of getting anything back now was minimal. He read the other demand letters again - it was almost five thousand pounds. He could never raise that. More importantly, how was he going to explain things to Kathryn? He had told her many times that the business was doing well; he did not want to worry her. If only the bank would help; he was at a loss.

He quickly slipped the letters into his briefcase as he heard Kathryn coming down the stairs.

'Fancy some toast,' she said.

'Yeah, thanks,' said Keith, still thinking about the finances.

'Thanks again for last night,' said Kathryn, and she suddenly noticed the coat draped over the armchair.

She looked at it more closely.

'Oh no!' she exclaimed.

'What's the matter?'

'The coat... this isn't my coat,' she said, holding it up and examining it.

'Are you sure?'

'Of course I'm sure. See... this is marked and it's been worn regularly. Look at the leather and there's a stain,' she pointed out.

Keith joined her in the examination.

'You're right. But how? Didn't you check it when they gave it back to you? What about the ticket?'

'I couldn't find it. I saw that one on the rail and thought it was mine. It looks very similar,' she said. 'And it was quite dark down there.'

Keith was examining the coat.

'What are we going to do?' asked Kathryn.

Keith looked up. 'Well, we'll have to phone up and see if yours is still there.'

'I'll do it now,' said Kathryn.

'Hang on; let's see if there is anything in the pockets. We may be able to contact the owner and apologise. She'll be going mad,' he said.

Kathryn held it up as Keith went through the pockets. He felt a small metal object.

'Nothing,' he said, 'only this.'

He opened his hand and there was a key. 'Looks like it could be from a left-luggage locker or something. Look, there's a number.'

'Oh, yes... sixty-three. Wonder what it's for?' she said.

'I've no idea,' he said. 'You best give the hotel a call. I'll put the key back where we found it.'

Kathryn made the call while Keith made a decision which would change his life; he put the key into his jeans pocket.

'Yes,' she shouted with a sigh of relief. 'They have it; I said that you'd pick it up later. You can take this one back at the same time.'

'Yeah, will do,' said Keith. 'You better check again for the ticket. They might not let me have it otherwise.'

'Yes, good thinking,' said Kathryn, and she went upstairs to fetch her handbag from last night.

'Oh, after all that, here it is, stuck to my debit card,' she said, and handed over the orange slip.

An hour later and Keith was parking up outside Hayfield Manor.

He put the coat over his arm and walked to reception.

'Oh hi,' he said to the girl behind the desk. 'Name's Woodley, my wife phoned earlier. She was given the wrong coat from last night.'

'Just a minute,' said the girl and she went into a back room.

She quickly returned followed by a man, dark, smartly dressed, 'Shalik Aziz, General Manager', it said on his badge.

'I've come about my wife's coat,' said Keith.

'Yes, of course,' said the man. 'Mr Woodley is it?'

'Yes,' said Keith.

'One moment,' he said and went back into the office.

He returned with what appeared to be Kathryn's coat.

'Here we are, sir, my apologies. This should never have

happened, my staff are warned not to give out coats without the correct ticket,' he said.

'Ah,' said Keith. 'That's my wife's fault, I'm afraid. She couldn't find her ticket and pointed it out on the rail apparently.'

The man looked at Keith. 'Nevertheless, it should not have happened. You have the ticket now?'

'Yes,' said Keith and handed it over.

The coat exchange was completed.

'Please pass on my apologies to the owner of that coat. She must have been very worried,' said Keith.

'Yes, she was,' said the manager.

Keith thanked the man and apologised again, then left with Kathryn's coat over his arm.

As he walked back to the car, he suddenly a pang of guilt... the key. He was mulling it over. No-one would ever find out; it could've easily have dropped out of the pocket. Stupid place to put a key anyway, he thought. Someone could even have stolen it from inside the cloakroom. All these thoughts were going through his head trying to help him justify his decision, assuage the guilt. No-one would ever know, he repeated to himself as he walked back to the car.

He opened the door and draped Kathryn's coat over the back seat, then got in and sat for a moment. He leaned forward and put his head on the steering wheel in an apparent aid to the thinking process. He could feel the key in his pocket; it was digging into his thigh, berating him. He considered going back into the hotel and handing the key in. It wasn't too late. He could always say it must have fallen out of the coat pocket and he'd found it in the foot-well of the car.

But what if?

Supposing there was a stash of cash, it could solve all his immediate problems, get the business back on track, and keep the wolves at bay, no-one would ever know and Kathryn would be none the wiser. He had to do something, his world was about to come crashing down – it was only a matter of time. They would lose the house, which would mean he would probably lose Kathryn and the kids. He had no choice. This could be a sign, a change of fortune.

He turned on the ignition and slowly eased the car forward. Then it was as if the car was driving itself, on autopilot; he would drive to the central railway station in Aireford. That would be the logical place to start, just to check; you never know.

It was a warm day for mid-September, the air conditioning on the Mercedes was keeping it cool but he wound the window down anyway; he needed fresh air. Twenty-five minutes later, he managed to find a parking space in the short-stay car park adjacent to the city station. He inserted fifty pence into the ticket machine for twenty minutes, and made his way into the Victorian station building. The left-luggage facility was clearly signed; 'North concourse' it said. He soon found what he was looking for and went to the reception desk.

It was unattended and he rang the bell. Eventually, a man in a dark green uniform with the words 'Secure Luggage' emblazoned in yellow appeared from a back office. 'Yes' he said abruptly.

Keith hadn't thought about his approach strategy and was momentarily off-guard.

'Err, hi. I wonder if you can help me. Can you tell me if this is one of yours?' he said, and pulled the key from his pocket and showed it to the man.

'Nah, we don't use keys, not for ages, mate, everything's scanned,' he replied.

'Oh, right, thank you,' said Keith, somewhat crestfallen, and left the station.

He walked back to the car and sat for a few minutes trying to work out his next move. Then he had an idea and headed off to the precinct. He was working out the story in his head.

He parked up in the multi-storey and walked down the three floors to the shopping mall. There was a kiosk in the mall just a few shops up from the car park entrance, 'Boot & Shoe Clinic, Keys cut While-u-Wait', it said on the signage.

He walked in and there was a man working on what looked like a lathe, tending a lady's shoe. He looked up from his labours over a pair of half-rimmed spectacles, annoyed at the distraction.

'Yes,' he said.

'I wondered if you can help me. My mother's recently passed away and we found this key in her purse. It looks like it could be from a left-luggage locker or something; wondered if you can say where it may have come from,' said Keith.

The proprietor chuntered something to himself about being a charity and made his way to counter.

'Let me see,' he said.

Keith already had it in his hand.

The man examined it closely under his working lamp.

'You're in luck, there's a serial number on the stem. Just a minute,' and the man disappeared into a back room.

Keith looked around the shop. There was a distinctive smell; all cobblers' shops had it, leather, rubber and sweat, not a pleasant odour. There were all kinds of machinery and gadgets which would effect any manner of repairs, watch straps and, behind the counter, an array of blank keys, thousands, of all shapes and sizes. Under the keys, there were dozens of pairs of shoes, tagged and waiting for their owners.

The man returned. 'Just as I thought, it's local. Just looked it up on the Internet... the bus station on Canal Street.'

'Thanks very much. You've been very helpful,' said Keith.

'Would there be anything else, sir, a watch-strap, a key ring, perhaps. I have some new ones just in,' said the man.

Keith felt cornered. He saw the displays of key rings. 'Yes, alright go on then, I'll take a key ring.'

'Any particular sort?' said the man.

'No, any will do,' replied Keith, and the man took a key ring from his display.

'Nine ninety-nine,' he said.

Keith wanted to walk out. He didn't need a key ring, certainly not a deluxe one anyway but there was an expectancy. He handed over a ten pound note. 'Thanks,' said Keith. 'You can keep the change,' and he walked out of the shop. The man muttered something and went back to his lathe.

The good news was that Keith had now identified the whereabouts of the locker that the key would open. Canal Street was only a few minutes' walk away, the other side of the mall. It was the main transport link. He checked his watch, twelve-forty; he would still make it to the depot to relieve Jack, albeit a few minutes late; Jack wouldn't mind. He quickened his stride; he was on a mission.

The mall was busy and stuffy, thousands of people to-ing and fro-ing, many entering through the doors from the bus station, bringing shoppers in from further afield. Keith was going against the stream and dodging the oncoming throng made the walk hazardous. He made the mall exit to the bus terminus. Nearly all the bays were in use, with buses arriving or leaving every few seconds it seemed, disgorging eager shoppers. He looked down the rows and at the far end there was the terminus building which included a cafe. He looked for signs, electronic destination boards at each bay, toilets, information; then he saw it – "Left Luggage". The arrow pointed straight ahead.

Through the terminal entrance, to the left, was a cafe, full with families taking refreshments before entering the abyss that was the mall. It was a bustling place; there was a queue at the information desk and the self-service ticket machine. The 'Left Luggage' arrow pointed to the right. There was a long corridor with metal seating down the middle, most seats were empty but there were a couple of families sorting out shopping. As he walked down, he noticed two men wearing hoodies which, given the temperature, seemed a little incongruous, but Keith paid little attention.

At the end of the corridor, the banks of lockers stretched along the back wall and into an alcove on either side. He could see the CCTV cameras; they were everywhere, which caused him some concern. He didn't want to appear suspicious and attract attention. The lockers were clearly numbered and he followed them along to the right: 125, 126, 127. He changed direction, and about halfway along the middle locker, number 63. He took the key out of his pocket and checked again, 63.

Nervously, he put the key in the lock and turned it, a metallic click; it was open.

He looked inside. There was a large duffel bag, innocuous-looking with a faded tartan pattern. He pulled at the leather-look handles trying to gauge the weight. He didn't want it crashing to the floor when he freed it from the confines of the locker. It moved easily enough, about ten kilos. He slid the bag towards him and took the weight, gently easing it to the floor. He would take a quick peek before deciding what to do. It was not too late; he could still take the key back to the hotel. His hands were shaking as he tried the zip but before he could move it he felt a hand on his shoulder.

His body shook from fright.

The arm went around his shoulder, like a best buddy might. He was wearing a hoodie top, his face obscured.

'Leave the bag and come with us,' an accented voice, possibly Middle Eastern.

He felt a sharp painful prod under his rib cage.

'I have a gun... Do not make this difficult. Walk... this way,' said the man.

Two other men appeared out of the shadows, not English, and approached them. One of them spoke to the gunman. He heard their voices but could not make out what they were saying. Another man also dressed in a hoodie appeared, carrying the holdall and passed it to one of the other men.

There were emergency exits on either side of the bank of lockers. The man walked towards the nearest door with his right arm still around Keith's shoulder; his left, pushing the gun sharply into his ribs. The other hoodie overtook them and opened the glass door.

'There... the van, get in,' ordered the man.

In front of them was an old Ford Transit, parked on a loading bay. Man number two slid back the passenger door and pulled down the seat.

'In,' he barked, and Keith climbed in behind the seat. His new buddy followed.

'Turn around,' said buddy. Man number two had got in the driver's side.

Keith complied and suddenly a scarf or some other blindfold was placed around his head. The fear was overwhelming and he started shaking uncontrollably. 'Keep very quiet,' said a voice.

At one fifteen there was a phone call to the Woodley residence.

Kathryn had been busy washing clothes, son Jason was where he usually was; in his bedroom playing on his Xbox. Ellie was still at work. Kathryn answered.

'Hi Kathryn, it's Jack at the depot. Is Keith still there, only he said he would be here before one?' he said.

'No,' said Kathryn. 'He left ages ago. He had to make a call at Hayfield Manor. I assumed he would go on to the depot from there. Have you tried his mobile?'

'Yeah, that's the thing. It just keeps ringing out. Not like him at all, he always picks it up. No voice-mail either.'

'No, it isn't. I don't know what to say. He's not here. Do you want me to call you if he comes back?'

'Yeah, thanks, if you don't mind. Thing is, I need to get going myself soon, said I'd meet the missus in town at one,' he said.

'I don't know what to say,' said Kathryn. 'Is there anyone else who can take over?'

'Not really, all the drivers are out. I'll have to lock up, but someone will have to open up for 'em when they get back otherwise it'll mean leaving the buses in the street and Keith won't like that'

'No, no, I can see that,' said Kathryn. 'No, you lock up and get off. Keith can always open up when he gets there and if he comes back here first I'll tell him you've had to go.'

'Thanks,' said Jack. 'Give us a bell when he turns up. It's not like him.'

'Yes,' said Kathryn. 'Will do. Thanks, Jack, for calling.'

Kathryn sat down and considered things for a moment, then phoned Keith's mobile from the house phone. Just as Jack had said, it kept ringing out.

Just then she heard her mobile ringtone coming from her handbag. She rushed to the dining room table, opened the bag and answered the call.

'Hello, Keith?' she said. There was some anxiety in her voice.

'Hello, is that Kathryn? It's Steve... from last night,' he explained.

'Oh, hello,' said Kathryn. 'Sorry this is not a good time... I'll call you.'

'Right, ok,' said Steve, and Kathryn dropped the call before Steve could say anything else.

CHAPTER FIVE

Monday 7th August 2012. Travellers Inn Motel, north of Dover.

With three crammed in a double bed plus the additional anxieties of the situation, sleeping was difficult. It wasn't helped by one of the men snoring. Despite the circumstances there would be no attempted escape. Colin had already detailed the dire consequences of causing trouble so, for the time being at least, the girls seemed resigned to whatever fate lay ahead.

It was seven a.m. when Jack woke up. It had also been an uncomfortable night on the sofa; Colin had taken off the mattress and slept on the floor, and was sound asleep.

'Hey, come on Col, get your arse in gear, we got work to do,' said Jack.

Colin stirred.

'Come on, get the girls up, I'm going to get us some grub.'

He left the room and went to the hotel restaurant, and seeing no-one was about, grabbed half a dozen croissants and various pastries, wrapped them in several paper napkins and hid them under his tee shirt which he tucked into his jeans. He then nonchalantly made some toast. When he returned to the room, Delvina was in the shower and the two other girls were sat on the bed drinking coffee. Colin was in charge of the kettle.

'I've made some coffee,' he said when Jack got in.

'Cheers, there's some cake and stuff. That'll keep you going for a bit,' he said, and lifted his tee shirt up allowing the acquired food and napkins to fall on the bed. He gathered up the croissants and pastries and put them on the desk next to the TV.

Colin poured Jack a coffee and distributed the food to the girls.

'Right, as soon as you lot've used the bathroom we'll get on the road,' said Jack, 'and don't be long about it.'

Edita looked at Sadia, who now seemed more coherent at least, and translated for her.

By eight o'clock the group were ready.

'Right girls, we're leaving. Follow Colin and stay shtum, understand?' said Jack.

The girls just looked at each other. Colin had already paid for the room and he led the girls up the corridor and past the reception. Jack followed behind carrying the holdalls. Edita was still having difficulty putting her full weight on her leg, which had stiffened up again overnight. Her ankle was now a dark blue colour. There was one person at the desk busy checking out the four guests queuing, and no-one took any notice as the party left the hotel.

Colin led the group to the car park and opened the sliding doors to the minibus.

'Right girls, get in,' he said. They got into the seats behind the driver. Colin opened the back and stowed the luggage.

'I'll follow you to the compound,' said Colin, and Jack headed for the truck and got in.

After a few minutes the lorry was back on the A2 heading north followed by Colin in the minibus with the girls. It was quiet; the girls just stared out of the windows. Monday morning rush hour and the traffic was horrendous. The truck eventually reached the M25.

Just before the Dartford Crossing Jack turned off the motorway at junction 1a and drove towards Bexley Heath. After a few miles they reached an industrial park and Jack negotiated the truck around the narrow roads, eventually reaching a large lorry compound. There were several other trucks parked up; the tarmac was covered in engine oil, making the surface treacherous. There was a Portakabin in the far corner and Colin followed the truck to one of the parking bays alongside. There was no-one else about and Jack parked and locked up. Then he went to the Portakabin and pushed the keys through the letterbox before joining Colin in the minibus.

Jack turned around. 'Alright girls?' he said. At first there was no reply, and then Edita spoke in her broken English. 'Can I use telephone for my mother please? She will be much worried.'

Jack looked at the three girls. 'Not just now, eh... maybe later.'

Sadia started to cry again, and Edita tried to comfort her.

Colin and Jack were just one component in a large and well-organised enterprise; it was an international operation. The first part was the capture and securing the merchandise – usually girls. Albania was a favourite target due primarily to their relatively lax view on people trafficking, but other countries were also involved. Then there was the transportation – the boat, the Italian truck, and finally the UK leg. Logistically it was challenging but it worked, and this latest was one of many transactions that had been carried out successfully by this gang, with 'cargo' delivered to many places across the country. None of the UK agencies were aware of the organisation.

Colin and Jack headed north in the minibus. They had already received half their fee for the job; the remainder would be paid on receipt.

Delivery this time would be to a house in Aireford, a large city in the north of England with a high immigrant population. It was a journey they had made once before and would take around five or six hours depending on the traffic, which was relentless.

It was mid-afternoon before the minibus arrived on the outskirts of the city. There had been stops on the way and the girls were allowed into the service areas under close supervision. They were even given a burger for lunch and sat at one of the outside tables with the two men, enjoying their first hot meal for four days. For Edita and the girls, fear had been replaced by resignation and acceptance. All fight had gone. It was like being in a state of suspended animation, as the effects of severe trauma took hold. It had become a question of survival.

Most of the journey had been spent in silence, just staring out of the window at the unfamiliar countryside.

'So whereabouts is this place, John? Can you remember?' asked Colin as he followed the signs for 'City Centre'.

'Hang on, I'll get the satnav on the case,' and he proceeded to key in the address into the screen on top of the dashboard.

'Argyle Avenue,' said Jack. 'There you go,' and the map on the satnav sparked into life and highlighted the route.

Colin looked down and started to follow the directions. 'Oh yeah, I remember,' he said, noticing the odd familiar landmark.

'Do you want to give them a bell and let them know we're nearly there?' said Colin.

'Yeah, good call, will do,' said Jack, and he took his mobile out of the pocket of his jeans and keyed in the number.

'Hello, it's Jack. We're nearly there, be with you in five, ten minutes... Right, will do,' he said, and rang off.

'They want us to pull up outside. They're waiting for us.'

Colin nodded 'Yeah got that,' he said.

The girls sensed a change was about to happen; Edita was starting to get worried again.

'Where are you taking us?'

Jack turned around and looked at the three girls. 'Don't worry you'll be fine. They'll look after you. Don't worry,' he repeated.

Jack was far from convincing and Edita grabbed Delvina's hand. Sadia just stared out of the window, the bleak urban surroundings scarcely registering.

They reached the city centre and the inner ring road, past the station and a shopping mall and out into the suburbs. There were no leafy avenues or crescents; just rows of Edwardian and Victorian terraced houses, all identical and soulless.

'Jesus,' said Colin. 'What a dump.'

After a steep rise he glanced down at the satnav.

'Next right, then left,' he said. Jack was looking at the houses. 'Fucking hell, I'm sure it's worse than last time... People actually fucking live here.'

'Here it is, Argyle Avenue,' said Colin.

'Keep an eye out. Number twenty-nine,' he added. 'On the left here somewhere, if I remember rightly.'

Jack was counting up. Even numbers on one side, odd, the other.

'Yeah, you're right... There,' Jack pointed. 'Just by that old Beamer,' said Jack, and Colin pulled up behind a ten-year-old BMW.

'Right girls, stay here,' and Colin and Jack got out.

The front door of number twenty-nine was already open.

'Bring them in,' said a tall, attractive woman in her early thirties.

Colin opened up the side of the minibus. 'Ok girls, out you come. Follow that lady.'

The three girls got out of the vehicle and were quickly ushered into the house. Edita was still limping; her ankle had stiffened up from being cooped up on the journey, but it was less painful than yesterday.

The layout of the house was misleading. It was much bigger inside than it appeared from the exterior. The building had been significantly extended to the back, certainly thirty or forty feet, well into the yard or whatever garden there had been. The front room was now a comfortable lounge area, nicely decorated, with three armchairs and a four-seater settee, a large TV and what looked like a gaming area – there were computer game consoles pointing towards a smaller TV. The decor was bland and functional.

The three girls went into the room and just stood there, totally lost.

'Sit down,' said the lady. 'I will talk to these men, then I will explain to you everything.' She spoke in a strong Eastern European accent.

The girls looked at each other and then sat down. The lady went into another room with the men for a few minutes, and then returned.

'Cheers... Nice doing business with you, Victoria. Aziz knows how to contact Vasyl when he needs another delivery,' said Jack.

'Yes,' said the lady, and Colin and Jack left.

'Cheerio, girls, have fun,' said Jack as he walked past them. The three just stared.

After they had gone, another man entered the room where Colin and Jack had previously been entertained.

'Hello,' he said and he pulled up a dining room chair and sat opposite the three girls.

'My name is Amir and you will be working for me now. This lovely lady is Victoria and she will look after you while you are here. Do you speak English?' asked Amir.

'I do, a little and she does,' said Edita, looking at Delvina.

'What about you?' said Amir, looking at Sadia. She shook her head and shrugged her shoulders.

'You are sisters, I think?' said Amir to Edita and Delvina.

'Yes,' said Edita.

'You look much alike... And what are your names?' asked Amir.

'I am Edita and this is Delvina,' said Edita.

'How old are you?' said Amir.

'Eighteen,' said Edita.

'And you?' said Amir looking at Sadia. Edita translated.

'Sadia,' she said.

'She is fifteen,' said Edita. Amir looked at Victoria and frowned.

'Ok, now you must listen carefully and tell me if you do not understand, ok?' said Amir.

Edita nodded.

'You are very lucky to be here with us. You will make much money and then you return to Albania rich. You will be able to help your families back home and go to university even. How does that sound?' he said.

Edita nodded.

'I supply people to work here in this town and we have many jobs for good girls. Different work... maybe in factory or in hotel and maybe doing other things. You will have much money,' he added.

Edita translated for Sadia. She showed no emotion and just stared at her hands which were resting in her lap.

'We will get you new clothes and you will be well looked after,' he said, and then looked at the girls gravely. 'But you must not try to escape, go to the police or cause any trouble, any trouble,' he repeated. 'Or you will never see your family again, ever. Do you understand?'

Edita translated and Sadia began to cry. Edita held her hand to try to comfort her.

'If you do not cause trouble you will be well rewarded. This I promise,' he said.

'Now I have to go, but Victoria here will explain everything to you,' he said, and got up from the chair and spoke to Victoria out of earshot from the girls. Then he left.

Victoria was a beautiful woman. She was wearing tight black leather trousers, a pair of Jimmy Choo shoes, an expensive-looking blouse with a gold bracelet on her right wrist and a Rolex on the other. Her fair hair had been expertly feathered and her make-up was immaculate. Everything about her suggested money.

She looked at the girls.

'I know you will be scared, but I will tell you a true story. Five years ago, like you, I was brought here from Latvia. I was scared too and could not speak English and had no friends. Now I have all this.' She moved her hands downwards from her head to emphasise her appearance.

'This watch, twenty thousand Euros, this bracelet, ten thousand... I have a flat in town and I drive a Porsche. This could all be yours. Just think what it will mean to your families when you return with enough money to keep them in their old age and ensure you get a good education,' she said.

Edita translated as best she could.

'How long so we have to stay for?' Edita asked the woman.

'I don't know,' said Victoria. 'That depends.'

'Why can't we speak to our families? They will be very worried,' said Edita.

'You will, but first you need to settle here for a while and then we will see. If you cause no trouble and are good workers, then you will be given a phone and you will be able to speak to them.'

Edita translated for Sadia, who appeared to be past caring.

'Now you come with me,' and the girls followed Victoria through the door into the room where the earlier meetings were held between Amir and the drivers. It was like an office with some serious technology. There were six computer towers with wires everywhere, some leading upwards into the ceiling. There were four monitors which were turned off and two large TV screens. LED lights flickered, greens, reds; the room was stuffy and very warm. In each corner there were security cameras. A laptop was open on one of the desks, showing a screen-saver.

The girls took little notice and followed Victoria. There were two doors on the far side of the room. To the left Edita noticed what looked like the kitchen, to the right there was a set of stairs. Victoria led them up to the first-floor landing.

They walked down a corridor towards the back of the house, passing several doors which were closed.

Victoria turned and spoke to Edita. 'There are three other girls here who you will meet soon. They have been here four months and make much money.' At the end of the corridor there was a set of open wooden steps leading upwards. Victoria led the way again.

They were now in the eaves of the house which had been converted into a bedroom area. It resembled an army barracks with two rows of four sleeping bags, each separated by a small cabinet. Three of the sleeping bags had been already assigned. Four sixty-watt light bulbs hung down at regular intervals from the roof suspended by bare flex. At the far end there was a pair of sliding doors which Victoria opened. She switched a light on inside what was a small walk-in wardrobe. There was a rail of clothing, an array of jeans, tops, trousers as well as shoes. There was a separate rail of lingerie and underwear. The girls just looked overwhelmed by the situation.

'Help yourself to anything in here,' said Victoria. She turned again and pointed to the vacant sleeping bags. 'You can have these three,' she added as they walked back towards the exit.

'The bathroom is down here,' she said, descending the steps and opening a door to the left. It was a reasonable size with a separate shower and double washbasin.

They went back to the ground floor and Victoria led them to the main kitchen where there was a fridge, washing machine and dryer and cooker. There was a larder which had an array of food.

'We have stocked up for you. There should be enough for a few days. Then you will need to buy your own from what you earn.'

'But you have not told us what we have to do,' said Edita as they made their way into the lounge.

Victoria looked at the girls. 'You are lucky; we have some work for you which you can start tomorrow. Someone will come for you at seven-thirty. It is not far, you will be working in factory... very good work. Maybe make clothes.'

Edita looked at Delvina. 'But we know nothing about how to make clothes,' she said.

'But they will show you, of course, and we will pay you three pounds an hour.'

'Three pounds an hour?' repeated Edita.

'Yes, don't forget we have had to pay for your transport here.'

Edita looked at Delvina, and then translated for Sadia.

'But you can of course earn lots more money, but I will explain this later. You will be tired from your journey. You should choose some clothes and where to sleep and I will see you down here in one hour. I have work to do,' and the three girls slowly made their way through the computer room and up to the bedroom in the rafters.

Delvina spoke in Albanian. 'I wonder what's in these rooms,' she said as they walked down the first-floor landing. Edita tried one of the doors. 'It's locked,' she said. Then she noticed the security cameras.

'Oh no,' she said. 'I hope they didn't see that.'

Once inside the bedroom the girls started whispering.

'What are they going to do with us?' said Sadia.

'I don't know,' said Edita. 'But we should do what she says.'

The girls went to the wardrobe and started looking through the clothes and eventually chose something suitable but with little real enthusiasm.

Delvina picked up one of the lingerie items and held it up to herself. 'I hope they don't want us to wear these,' she said.

At that moment Edita sensed that they might.

It was nearly five before the girls returned to the ground floor. They had changed and used the shower. Victoria was working at a laptop in the office, and was waiting for them. She stood up as they entered the room.

'Hey, those look ok,' she said as she examined the girls one by one. There was little reaction from the girls.

'Right, you must get food. The others will be here soon, come with me,' and Victoria led them into the kitchen.

She showed them where everything was and told them to help themselves, then left and went back to her laptop.

Sadia spoke to Edita in Albanian. 'I am not hungry.'

'But you must eat. You must stay strong,' said Edita and she put her arm around Sadia and gave her a hug. 'Come on, let's see what there is.'

There was a small table with four wooden chairs in the corner of the room, and the girls found some salad and bread and sat down. The three were locked in their own thoughts eating and said nothing. It was not a comfortable silence. The room was bright and lit from spotlights in the ceiling. There were two small windows but above normal eye-line and they gave little natural light. It seemed to be raining. There was a metal exit door which was connected to an alarm system of some sort. Edita noticed the wiring running down the wall. It felt like a prison.

At just before six o'clock there was movement coming from the lounge. The girls looked at each other... voices.

Footsteps headed towards the kitchen.

Victoria appeared at the door of the kitchen. 'The others are here,' she said, and she stood back to allow three more girls to enter the room.

Edita, Delvina and Sadia looked up from their food and looked at their house-mates.

'Hello,' said the first; a blonde wearing a dark denim jacket, jeans and trainers.

The other two looked at the three new arrivals with a mixture of suspicion and curiosity.

'Hello,' replied Edita in English.

'You will need to eat and change,' said Victoria to the blonde. 'You will be working at seven.'

The blonde just nodded in acknowledgement and the three went to the fridge and started to find some food. For a while there was just the sound of rummaging, rustling and clinking. Then the blonde and her two companions joined the others at the table. Delvina and Sadia stood up to make way for them. The three newcomers started talking in a language Edita didn't understand but thought she recognised.

It was Edita who broke the silence. 'How long have you been here?' she said in English.

'About four months,' said the blonde in more confident English.

Edita caught Delvina's look of horror.

'Where are you from?' asked Edita.

'Macedonia, we are from Macedonia. I am called Marija, this is Elena and Bijana. What about you?' she replied.

'I am Edita; this is Delvina, my sister, and our friend Sadia. We are from Albania.'

Marija looked at the sisters. 'You look so like each other.'

'Yes, we are... how you say...? Twins, yes?' said Edita.

With the introductions over the girls shared their experiences. Marija explained that she and her friends had also been abducted and brought to Aireford but were the victims of a scam, lured with the promise of a better life.

'We were told we were going to Italy,' said Marija. 'But the truck, it kept on going, until we came at the boat to take us to

England. They threatened to kill us and our families if we did not agree to go with them.'

'But what do you do? Have you been able to contact your families?' asked Edita.

'No, we are watched all the time, but we have not been hurt and we have money now... It is not so bad,' she said and looked down.

'But where do you work?' pressed Edita.

'We work in hotel. Every day we clean rooms but it is ok, we have many friends there now. Then we have work here.'

'Here?' said Edita.

'Yes... we chat to people on the Internet and sometimes we make videos... We make more money that way.'

'What sort of videos?' asked Edita, fearing the answer.

Marija looked down. 'We go with boys and they video.'

Edita gasped.

'It is ok, we are used to it and we get good money,' she said, and continued eating.

A few minutes later there were more footsteps and a man entered the room.

The girls looked up to identify the visitor and Marija's eyes lit up.

'Uri!' she said, and left her chair to hug the new arrival.

Edita looked at him. Tall, slim, mid-twenties, long dark hair with a neatly trimmed beard, he resembled a pirate.

'Edita, this is Uri. He is my boyfriend. Tonight we make video.'

Uri looked at the new arrivals. 'Hello,' he said. There was no response.

'Uri looks after us,' said Marija. Elena and Bijana also appeared pleased to see him.

Victoria came into the kitchen and she too greeted Uri enthusiastically.

'You have met our new friends,' she said.

'Yes,' said Uri. 'I hope I will be their friend too.'

'I am sure you will,' said Victoria.

She looked at Edita. 'You will need to go to your bedroom now. We have work to do here,' she said. 'You must be ready tomorrow morning at seven-thirty and you will be taken to where you will work. Marija will explain.'

Edita, Delvina and Sadia followed the other three girls back upstairs to the top of the house and the sleeping area.

The new arrivals had chosen their sleeping bags and sat on them watching Marija and her two companions in the closet. They were choosing lingerie, trying on different outfits, and then applying make-up. Edita was transfixed at the sight.

'What are you doing?' she asked.

Marija was wearing a G-string and negligee.

'Tonight, Elena and Bijana will be on the Internet. I am making video with Uri,' she replied.

Edita had difficulty speaking. 'And... this is ok?'

'Yes, yes, it is good. We work till eleven o'clock and then other girls come and work until in the morning four o'clock. This is very busy time. The Americans are very good customers.'

Edita tried to take it all in as Marija explained the extent of the operation.

It was a reasonably new but growing feature in Internet porn. The "chat rooms" were open from seven in the evening until four a.m. using live Internet streaming. For a monthly fee members could log on to the website, Camgirls.com, which gave them unlimited access to the girls. They would request them to pose or act out their fantasies for them over a video link. There was also a 'private' facility where, for another fee, girls would be connected to a member on a one-to-one basis.

It was extremely lucrative. The website hits were up to a

hundred thousand a week, with over a thousand members online at any one time, on a Saturday it was often as high as six thousand. The income generated was substantial, with monthly subscription of thirty dollars a time. Then there was tipping. If the viewers were particularly pleased with a performance they would give the girls tips ranging from $5 to $30, although sometimes it was considerably more. The money was taken direct from the member's credit card. This was a real incentive and the girls were now expert in extracting as much money from the members as possible. It took striptease to a new level. The girls shared the tips 50/50 with Victoria.

Marija continued giving Edita some background.

She told Edita that Victoria was in charge of the Internet work. The chat room operation was set up less than a year ago; before that it was just videos and Victoria was a regular performer. She had become an Internet celebrity with her own website and fan page. Joining her members' centre cost twenty-five dollars a month, giving access to video downloads and pictures. She had almost ten thousand members and the money from this enterprise she kept. There was a hint of pride in Marija's voice as she described Victoria's achievements.

Victoria had, however, been grooming Marija since her arrival. In fact, this was Victoria's strength; befriending the girls and acting as their protector. It had made them dependent on her and they were now totally compliant.

Victoria was also a partner in a recruitment company, Azure Recruitment Services, run by Amir Aziz; on the face of it, a legitimate business supplying low-skilled workers to various places. One of the regular recipients of workers from Azure was the Hayfield Manor Hotel which was owned and run by Amir's brother, Shalik. Despite the government crackdown there were still opportunities to exploit vulnerable people, particularly illegal immigrants.

Edita was translating for Delvina and Sadia as much as she could. The thought of following the Macedonian girls into the world of chat rooms and videos filled them with dread.

'Well I won't do it,' said Delvina. 'Nor me,' said Sadia.

Marija looked at the three. 'That is what I said at first but it was ok. Victoria showed me what to do, and now... well most times it is nice. Especially with Uri, he is gentle and loving,' she said. 'And the money is good, very good. They let us go shopping and to McDonald's.'

'Why do you not run away?' asked Edita.

'And go where? The authorities? The police? They do nothing and if they find you are an illegal you will go to prison. Anyway, where could we earn this money in Macedonia?' said Marija.

Edita just looked at her.

'Victoria said that one girl did try to escape but the police just brought her back again,' said Marija.

'What happened to her?' asked Edita.

'Two days later she left and then no-one has seen her,' said Marija, dropping her eye contact.

Edita just stared.

'We must go now, but do not worry. Everything will be ok, you will see,' said Marija, and the three Macedonian girls, who were now very scantily dressed, walked down the steps, leaving the Albanians with a great deal to think about.

CHAPTER SIX

Delvina and Sadia looked at Edita.

'What are we going to do?' Delvina always sought the counsel of her sister when dealing with problems. Up until now it was what dress to wear or whether she should see a certain boy but this was a different situation entirely. Edita was also at a loss.

'I don't know. We are prisoners here and at the moment we must try to stay strong.'

'But I don't want to go with boys.'

'I know,' Edita leaned across and cuddled her sister. Sadia joined them in a three-way hug.

She looked at Delvina. 'Marija and her friends seem ok,' she tried to reassure her sister.

'But they are doing what they are told to do,' said Delvina.

'I know,' said Edita. 'I know.'

Sadia just sat staring ahead.

Eventually, the three went to their respective sleeping bags and tried to get some rest. They were disturbed just after eleven by Marija and her two companions returning from their night's work. There was excited chatter and giggling.

'You are asleep?' asked Marija as she walked towards the closet to change.

'No,' said Edita.

'Do not worry, everything will be fine. Tonight I make good video with Uri. It was nice... He is a good boy. If you go with him it will be fine; he will look after you.'

'I don't want to go with anyone; anyway I thought he was your boyfriend.'

'He is, but he has to go with the other girls to make money. I do not mind. When we have enough he is going to take me away with him and we will live in the country, in Ukraine, where his mother lives. He says it is beautiful there.'

Edita thought about this. 'Do you do videos with other boys?'

'Sometimes, but Uri is best. Sometimes we have older men with fat bellies. That is not so nice; they do not treat us so well.'

This did little to provide Edita with any comfort.

By half past six the following morning all the girls were awake and getting ready. Marija, Elena and Bijana would be taken to the hotel. Edita watched them. They looked slightly older than her and her sister, early twenties, maybe. Marija was blonde but the others darker and shorter and it was clear who the dominant character was. They were wearing no make-up and dressed casually in trousers, trainers and tops; looking at them, they just seemed like any other girls you would see walking down the street.

The six girls eventually went downstairs and into the office where another young man was working on a laptop.

He looked up and greeted Marija warmly.

'This is Nicolai,' said Marija. 'He makes the videos.'

'Yes, I am editing the one from last night... very good. Should make much money,' he said. He turned to Edita. 'Hello,' he said. He would be about the same age as Uri, early twenties and judging by his accent, a fellow countryman. He had long scruffy hair and was wearing a tee shirt and very distressed jeans.

'Victoria will not be here until tonight. I will take the new girls to the factory. Amir will take you to the hotel,' he said, looking at Marija.

There was a 'toot' from a car horn. 'That will be Amir,' said Nicolai, and the three Macedonians headed for the front door. 'See you tonight,' said Marija. Edita just looked at her; words would not come.

Nicolai led the girls into the lounge. 'We will go now,' he said.

'Where are you taking us?' asked Edita

'Do not worry, it is not far. You will make money, yes?' he said.

Delvina and Sadia seemed in a state of shock and hid behind Edita as they walked out of the house. Edita's ankle had continued to improve but she was still limping and couldn't put her full weight on it.

It was dry and quite warm, a nice summer's day; but for the girls, anything but.

Nicolai followed them and locked up.

'In here,' he said, and opened the rear door of the BMW that was parked outside the house when they arrived.

The girls got in the back seat and Nicolai shut the door. There was a click as he engaged the child safety lock from the driver's seat.

'It is not far,' he said again.

Ten minutes later they arrived on a large industrial complex. It was surrounded by a ten-foot-high brick wall. Over the entrance there was a large sign: "Hyams Fabrics". To the right there was a gatehouse with a barrier, and Nicolai waved to the attendant, who waved back. The barrier was raised.

The main building was a throwback to sixties design, and looked drab and uninspiring. People were going about their business. Vans and delivery wagons moved slowly, avoiding staff on the way to their work. The front entrance looked like offices and the car went past and down the service road at the side to the rear of the factory; forklift trucks zigzagged about the yard with pallets of merchandise. There was a large car park, which Nicolai ignored, and he stopped on a visitor's bay at the side of the factory.

The girls looked wide-eyed at the building, wondering what lay ahead.

Nicolai turned around and spoke to the girls. 'You will work here, it is good money and they treat you well. Amir told me to say for you to remember what he tell you.' Edita was struggling with the translation.

'You must not run away or tell anyone where you live. You tell them you are happy to be working here and trying to make for you a better life,' he said.

Edita looked at him. 'Yes,' she said. 'But what about papers, you need papers to work here, yes?'

'You do not worry, Amir, he sees to everything. It is done.'

Azure Recruitment Services as an agency would be responsible for all documentation, and Amir had already provided Hyams with work permits and passport details, albeit forged. Unbeknown to the girls, even their names were different, but there would be no checks, it was just bureaucracy. Steve Jones, the MD, was an important client of Azure and Amir would do whatever it took to provide him with what was required.

It was a successful relationship; although Hyams did not presently have any of Azure's people working there. The previous batch, again three girls, was employed in the spring for six weeks and after the contract was up they were collected by the same people who had brought the Albanians and taken to London. Amir had no idea what had happened to them; they would disappear into the system.

Edita, Delvina and Sadia would be on temporary contracts, not that they would see one, to cover seasonal peaks. The company was gearing up for the Christmas orders and needed extra hands. They would also not see any pay. Azure would invoice Hyams.

Nicolai got out of the car and opened the back door. 'You, come,' and he led the girls through the works entrance.

The girls gasped as they entered the factory, a mixture of anxiety and trepidation. The scale of the place was difficult for them to take in. It was a hive of activity with over five hundred people beavering away at their allotted tasks.

They followed Nicolai down a corridor into another area where items were coming through on conveyor belts and being packed into boxes by around twenty people; all but one were women.

A large woman in her forties wearing a "Hyams Fabrics" overall approached Nicolai.

'Hiya Nicolai, good to see you again. These the girls?'

'Yes,' he replied. 'I will stay with them so they know what to do.'

'Well if they are as good as the last lot I'll be very happy.'

'Yes,' said Nicolai. 'They will be very good.'

'Ok girls, you come with me and I will show you where everything is,' she said.

She walked around the work area to a door on the other side and the girls followed. There was a small staff room with a self-service coffee machine and a small sink unit. Along one of the walls there was a row of metal lockers and next to that, perhaps a dozen coat pegs. Most had jackets but three of them had Hyams overalls hanging from them.

'This is where you hang your clothes and these are your overalls,' she said,

Edita translated and they went to put on their work-wear.

'Very smart,' said the supervisor after the three were suitably attired. 'I'm Gina, by the way.'

'I... I am Edita, this... my sister, Delvina... this, our friend Sadia,' replied Edita nervously.

'Yes, I can see you are,' said Gina. 'Such alike... are you twins?'

'Yes,' said Edita.

Gina looked at them approvingly. 'Right, we better get on, there's plenty to do,' she said, and led the girls back to the production area.

It was noisy and Gina had to shout above the cacophony of the clanking of the machinery, the incessant chatter from the workforce and a radio blaring out pop music. Some of the people were singing along.

Gina went to the line and spoke to one of the women and then to Edita.

'This is Sheila; she will show you what to do.'

Nicolai was stood against the wall, watching proceedings.

Sheila spoke to Edita. 'It is very easy; you will soon pick it up.'

'Here we are doing men's shirts... They come down that chute and onto the belt. You just fold the shirt like this, pin here and here. Put them in the box and stack them here. You have to watch the sizes and make sure the right size goes in the right box. You check the label here,' she said.

The girls watched attentively as Sheila demonstrated with exaggerated movements. Edita struggled with the translation and had to ask Sheila to slow down her instruction.

'See, it's easy, that's all there is too it. Now you have a go,' she said.

Edita took a shirt and started to fold it as she had been instructed. 'No, that sleeve goes there,' said Sheila as she corrected an error.

By the third shirt Edita got the hang of it and Sheila seemed very pleased. 'That is very good, you learn quickly.'

Edita felt strangely good about this accomplishment, a sense of satisfaction. She began translating for Delvina and Sadia. Nicolai applauded from his vantage point.

'Very good,' he shouted.

Within an hour the three girls had mastered the packing process and delighted Sheila.

There was a break at nine-thirty and she took the girls to the staff room and got them a drink from the vending machine. 'Just water,' said Edita. Delvina and Sadia had the same.

Gina joined them.

'You are doing very well,' she said. 'I wish the local girls would pick it up that quickly; thick as planks some of them.' Edita just looked at her sister, none the wiser.

Nicolai came into the staff room to check everything was ok and appeared to be very satisfied with the feedback from Sheila. He took out a twenty pound note from his pocket and gave it to Edita.

'Here, you will need to get some food. There is a place here, Gina will show you,' he said.

'We stop at twelve for lunch. I'll take you to the canteen,' Gina said. 'And you can meet some of the other girls.'

'And Ronnie, don't forget Ronnie,' said Sheila.

'Oh yes,' said Gina. 'He's almost a girl anyway, nice lad.'

Sheila laughed; the meaning was lost on Edita.

After their break Nicolai left them. 'I go now. I will be back for you later when you finish, outside where we stopped,' he said.

'Ok,' said Edita.

At twelve o'clock, the shift stopped and everybody left the conveyor belt and headed through the door to the main factory. Sheila went up to Edita. 'Come with us, love, you and your friends. I'll show you where to go.'

The girls left their workstation and followed Sheila through the main factory which still appeared to be working at full pace, and into an office area at the front of the building. To the right was a wide stairway, busy with people seeking sustenance. There were pictures up the wall with nondescript landscape scenes designed to brighten up the drab decor. The smell of food permeated the area as they reached the first-floor landing and a set of double doors. Sheila led the way.

'Gina will join us later, she has a meeting with her manager,' she said, as they walked towards the serving area. There was a range of hot food on offer, with serving staff waiting eagerly with utensils, ready to dish out the required fare.

Edita looked at all the different meals on offer, most of which they didn't recognise. She looked at Delvina and Sadia and spoke in Albanian. 'We need to eat something.'

Then she spotted a beef burger which they were certainly familiar with. Edita looked at Sheila. 'We will have a McDonald,' she said, pointing at the pile of burgers.

'Three burgers, chuck,' said Sheila to the girl behind the counter, and the meals were duly dispensed with a good portion of chips. Sheila handed Edita three trays. 'You will need one of these,' she said.

'What about drink?'

'Just water,' said Edita.

'Over there,' said Sheila pointing to a water cooler at the far end of the canteen.

Edita, Delvina and Sadia followed Sheila, who had chosen sausage and chips, to the cashier.

'You pay here. Have you got money?' she said rather belatedly.

'Yes,' said Edita and produced the twenty pound note that Nicolai had given them.

'The food here is really cheap. That will last you a few days,' said Sheila.

Edita gave the note to her.

'Take for these three with this, chuck,' said Sheila to the cashier handing over the note and pointing to the three trays containing the burgers.

The cashier gave Sheila fourteen pounds change, which she passed to Edita, who viewed it with uncertainty.

The canteen was set out in long rows of tables and there were clusters of staff separated by empty seats. It appeared the different teams ate together and did not mix with other groups.

'We're over here,' said Sheila, and led the girls to a row at the far end near the water cooler.

'You can get your water there,' she said, pointing to it.

Although the girls had been working all morning there had been little chance for any interaction with their co-workers due to the close supervision and training by Sheila and Gina. There was naturally curiosity as they sat down.

As they made themselves comfortable the questions started. 'What's your name, where're you from?' the first. Edita was not ready for any social discourse and wasn't sure how to respond. Sheila intervened, seeing that Edita was uncertain.

'This is Edita, Delvina and Sadia. They're agency girls,' she said, avoiding the question of nationality. Edita looked at the inquisitor. 'Hello,' she said.

The interest was short-lived and after more introductions the conversation returned to more usual topics – celebrity gossip, soap operas and reality TV.

The girls finished their burgers and after freshening up made their way back to the packing shed with the rest of the team.

At four-thirty, Gina approached the three girls, who were still folding and bagging men's shirts.

'It is time to stop now,' she said. 'You can go. You have done well today. Tomorrow we will have other jobs for you.'

The girls finished bagging their last shirt of the day and went to the staff room to change, and then it was outside to meet Nicolai who was waiting in the BMW with the engine running.

The girls got in and once again the doors were locked.

'So, it was good, yes?' asked Nicolai.

Edita looked at Delvina. 'Yes,' she said. 'The people were very nice.'

'I told you not to worry; everything will be fine for you.

You will make much money... You will be RICH,' he said in a bellowing voice, and laughed.

Edita smiled for the first time since the disco. Today had not been what they had expected and there was almost a sense of achievement. Even Sadia was more animated and the three talked readily on the way back to the house. There had been no thoughts of escape or running away; as Marija had said, where would they go?

Victoria was waiting for them when they returned to the house and greeted them in the kitchen. She was dressed in a different outfit from the previous day but was still very stylish.

'How was your first day?' she said.

'It was ok,' said Edita.

'You are not walking so well, I notice. Your leg, it is ok?' said Victoria.

'It is ok,' said Edita. 'It is nothing.'

'Good,' said Victoria. 'I have something for you,' and handed them a small notebook each.

'These are yours, they will show you how much money you have. I will keep them for you,' she said.

Edita opened the first page. It was laid out like a cash-book; the date, then an 'in' column, an 'out' column, then 'balance'.

'Today you each have twenty-one pounds, less seven pounds each for the money Nicolai gave you for food,' she said.

Sure enough, Edita's cash column showed a £21 credit and a £7 debit, balance £14. Delvina and Sadia showed the same. They had no idea what that meant; there was no means of converting it to Leks, the Albanian currency, but Edita realised it would not last long when compared with what they had paid for their lunch.

'You can have this money at any time. Me, Nicolai or Amir will give you cash and write in your book. I will keep them safe for you. Understand?' she said.

Edita translated for Delvina and Sadia. 'Yes,' said Edita.

'Now, you will need some food soon and someone will get what you need. You will just need to make a list and give it to me or Nicolai. The money will come from your books. If you want to buy more things when you have enough money we can go to the shopping mall and Nicolai will pay. Then he will take it from your books.'

The girls looked at each other.

'Understand?' said Victoria.

'Yes,' said Edita.

'Ok, now you go and change and shower and then you can eat,' said Victoria.

The girls walked through the office and up the stairs. Nicolai was back on his laptop.

In the bedroom, Edita was examining her ankle, which, although still painful, had continued to improve.

'How is your leg, Edi?' asked Delvina.

'It is much better,' Edita replied.

'Let me see,' said Delvina, and Edita raised her leg. Delvina started to massage it.

'Ow,' Edita winced. 'Not too hard.'

'Stop complaining,' said Delvina. 'This will help to make it better.'

By six o'clock the girls were back in the kitchen and exploring the fridge and cupboards and choosing food. Victoria noticed a marked change in the atmosphere; there was more chatter.

Footsteps from the lounge heralded the arrival of the Macedonian girls. They were carrying bags which looked like they had come from a boutique. Marija went over to Edita and hugged her. 'How was it for you today? Was it ok?' she said.

Edita was a bit taken aback with the affection. 'Yes, it was ok.'

'We will be down in a minute, we will eat with you,' she said, and she led her group up to the sleeping area.

When they returned they were dressed in what looked like cocktail dresses.

'We have been shopping with the money from last night. Do you like it?' said Marija, noticing the interest from Edita.

'Very nice,' said Edita.

'Yes, we will be wearing them in the chat room tonight. We will make much money,' said Marija.

Victoria came into the room with a carrier bag.

'I think this calls for a celebration,' she said, and produced six bottles of wine.

She went to one of the cupboards and took six glasses and opened two of the bottles.

Marija took one of them, unscrewed the top and poured out the wine into three glasses.

'We do not drink,' said Edita.

'But you must try. This is very good,' she said, and Elena and Bijana joined her, soon emptying their glasses. Victoria had already opened a second bottle.

'Here, you try,' she said, and poured three more glasses.

Edita sipped at the Merlot.

'It is good, yes?' said Marija.

'Yes, it is good,' said Edita, and Delvina and Sadia started drinking.

'I have not had wine before,' said Sadia in Albanian, which was the first time Victoria had heard her speak.

'What did she say?' asked Victoria.

Edita provided the translation.

'I sveikata,' said Victoria, and held up her glass. 'It is what we say in Latvia.'

Edita raised her glass. 'Shëndeti tuaj,' she replied. 'We say in

Tirana.'

Despite their earlier resolve, Edita, Delvina and Sadia had entered into the spirit of the moment and were soon on their second glass.

Marija looked at Victoria. 'Has Nicolai finished the video?'

'I think so. It is going on the website at seven,' Victoria replied.

'That is good, can I see it?' she said.

'Of course,' said Victoria, and she went into the office.

Marija turned around to Edita. 'Do you want to see?' she said. Delvina looked on disapprovingly.

'Ok,' said Edita, and she got up from the table, leaving her sister and Sadia with their drinks and, somewhat unsteadily, followed Marija to the office where Nicolai was on the laptop.

'Marija and Edita want to see the video,' said Victoria as she saw the girls approach.

'Sure,' said Nicolai. 'It is finished; I have put it on the website. Already many hits,' he said with some satisfaction.

'Let me see,' said Marija, and with Edita and Victoria they watched the screen as Nicolai played the video.

Edita watched Marija and Uri perform. The wine was starting to make her feel light-headed and looking at the video it didn't look so bad, and Uri... he seemed a really nice boy, certainly very good looking. Back in Tirana she would have jumped at the chance of going with him if he had asked her out.

After twenty minutes the video finished. Marija was thrilled with the result. 'That is very good,' she said.

'Yes,' said Victoria. 'The best you have done, I think.'

'How many hits?' asked Marija excitedly.

'So far...? Over one thousand, in half an hour,' said Nicolai.

'Very good,' said Victoria. 'You have done well. I will speak to Amir. Maybe he will give you more money.' Edita was listening to the conversation.

'How much money to go with Uri on video?' asked Edita.

Victoria looked at her. 'On video we pay fifty pounds. Chat room it is thirty.'

Edita thought for a moment; over twice what they would get at the factory.

She weighed up the consequences. The money would help support Delvina and Sadia; she felt it was her responsibility.

'Ok, I will go with Uri,' she said. 'When can I do it?'

Victoria looked at Marija. 'Uri will be here later,' she said.

'Ok, I will do it then,' she said.

Marija went to Edita and hugged her. 'It will be good,' she said. 'Uri is a good lover. He will make you very happy.'

'You do not mind?' Edita said.

'No, you are my friend now. It is good,' she said.

Victoria smiled. 'I have a better idea, Marija,' she said. 'Why don't you join in? You and Edita with Uri. You can show her what Uri likes.'

'Yes, I would like that. What about you, Edita. We can both love Uri together,' said Marija.

'I don't know,' she said.

'We pay more for three,' said Victoria. 'They are very popular... seventy-five pounds.'

'Uri will be a very happy man,' said Marija, and laughed.

'Ok,' said Edita. 'I will do it.'

Edita went back into the kitchen, spoke to Delvina and explained her decision to go with Uri and Marija.

'No, no you cannot,' said Delvina.

Sadia took another sip of wine.

'It will be fine and I will earn enough money to buy us nice things,' she said.

'But I don't want you to,' said Delvina.

'Don't worry,' said Marija in English. She could not understand the Albanian language but she could see Delvina's concern. 'I will look after her,' she said, and hugged Edita. 'We will be very good friends,' she added. Sadia suddenly had a fit of the giggles; a mixture of nerves and alcohol.

The group stayed in the kitchen drinking wine under the watchful eye of Victoria. She didn't want Edita to become incapable; there was a good night in prospect and a very remunerative one, such was the demand for threesomes on their website.

With Marija on video call again it was just Elena and Bijana who were on chat room duty, and they returned to the kitchen ready for action just before seven. Elena spoke to Delvina, her English too was limited.

'Chat room is very good, very easy, you watch you see,' she said.

'Yes,' said Victoria. 'You can see what happens.'

So at seven o'clock, while Elena and Bijana went to their chat rooms, the remaining girls went into the office where Nicolai was setting up the Internet feed. There were two monitors and the group watched as Elena and Bijana took up their positions.

'The girls both have computers and they watch the messages. Also we can see here. They do not reply, it is either me or Nicolai, we pretend to be the girls,' said Victoria.

Within seconds of the lines opening, messages started coming through from the members as they logged on from around the world.

Sadia suddenly put her hand to her mouth and rushed back into the kitchen and was sick in the sink.

Edita went to her. 'You have had too much. You drink water now. It will be ok.'

Sadia was recovering and breathing heavily. 'Here, drink this,' said Edita.

'Is she ok?' asked Victoria, who had followed Edita. Delvina was still watching the antics in the chat room on one of the monitors.

'Yes, she is not drinking before. She will be ok,' said Edita.

Victoria went to the fridge and gave Edita a litre bottle of water. 'Here, she should drink, and you also,' she said.

Edita took a gulp and passed the bottle to Sadia; then returned to the monitors. Nicolai was typing away on the keyboard and Delvina was watching as the girls performed for the camera.

'I cannot do that,' said Delvina.

'It is ok,' said Edita. 'I will make enough money and you won't have to do anything.'

Victoria intervened. 'Edita, why don't you go upstairs with Marija and choose some clothes for your video. Uri will be here soon.'

'Yes, come on, it will be fun,' said Marija.

'Ok,' said Edita, the alcohol had now deadened any pain from her bruised ankle... or from the consequences of what she was about to do. The four girls went upstairs, Sadia was still very unsteady on her feet but Edita had now pretty well sobered up, contemplating what lay ahead. She was starting to feel nervous.

Delvina and Sadia lay down on their sleeping bags while Marija was helping Edita in the closet. There seemed to be a lot of giggling.

Eventually they came out wearing very revealing outfits.

'What do you think?' said Marija to Delvina as Edita paraded her costume. 'I think Uri will like, yes?'

Delvina did not answer and turned her head away.

Edita went over to her. 'Do not worry. It will be fine,' she said. She looked across at Sadia; she was fast asleep. Delvina hugged her sister. 'You do not have to do this.'

'It will be ok,' she said, and followed Marija downstairs. She did not hear Delvina sobbing.

Down in the office there was much excitement. Amir had arrived and was watching the chat room feed on the monitors. He checked the hits. 'Very good,' he said to Victoria. 'Very good.'

'Hello,' he said to Marija as she and Edita entered the room. 'And Edita... your first time I think, yes?'

'Yes,' said Edita.

'Do not worry. Uri is a good boy. You will be fine. Here, I have something for you,' and he took his wallet from his jacket pocket and handed Edita a twenty pound note.

'That is from me,' he said. Edita looked at him and Victoria.

'Don't worry, you will still get the money I promised,' she said. 'Here, I will look after it for you. Uri is in the kitchen, why don't you go and say hello?' she added. Edita gave Victoria the twenty pound note and followed Marija into the kitchen where Uri was drinking a glass of wine.

'Hello,' said Marija, and she went over and hugged him. 'You remember Edita?' she said.

'Yes of course,' he looked at Edita. 'Very pretty,' he said, admiring the skimpy outfit. 'We will make good love tonight, I think.'

CHAPTER SEVEN

Edita picked up one of the empty glasses and poured herself another glass of wine.

Marija noticed her hands shaking. 'Do not worry, we will look after you, won't we Uri?' she said.

'Yes of course, it will be very nice. We make good video. We make good love,' he said.

Victoria came in from the office. 'Nicolai is ready,' she said. 'Do you want to go upstairs?'

Edita gulped down the rest of her wine. 'Ok, we will do it,' she said with an air of defiance.

The three of them went to the first floor and Marija opened the first door. 'This is where we make video. The others are chat room.'

The room was just like any bedroom with a large double bed, dressing table and wardrobe. The three walked in followed by Nicolai with an expensive-looking portable video camera.

Edita looked at Marija. 'It is ok. Nicolai will take the pictures. He is very good,' Marija said.

Victoria was downstairs with one eye on the video monitor as she replied to the chat room feeds that were coming in. It was very busy. Amir sat on the desk in front of a laptop, waiting.

In the bedroom Nicolai switched on the camera 'Ok,' he said.

Edita took a deep breath as Marija slowly started to undo her top.

The video session was over in half an hour and when the three participants and Nicolai returned to the office there was much excitement. For Edita it had been an experience of mixed emotions. She had only been with one boy before, Agim, one of her classmates. What started as nothing much more than a fumble at the back of the school field turned into her losing her virginity, over twelve months ago. This was altogether different.

'Very good,' enthused Amir.

'Yes, that was very good,' said Victoria. 'I can't believe it was your first time.'

Marija hugged Edita. 'I said it would be good,' she said.

'Yes,' said Edita. 'It was not what I was expecting.'

'You seemed to be enjoying yourself,' said Victoria.

'It was different,' said Edita.

'Here, give me your book.'

The three cash-books belonging to Edita, Delvina and Sadia were on the table by the laptop and Edita picked them up and gave them to Victoria. She started to write seventy-five pounds in Edita's.

'No,' said Edita, 'twenty-five for Delvina and Sadia.'

'Are you sure?' asked Victoria.

'Yes, it is what I want,' said Edita, and Victoria updated the books accordingly.

She put the books back in the drawer in the desk underneath the laptop. 'You will earn much money here,' she said. 'You have very good body. Many boys will want to make love with you. You will become famous video star.'

Edita just looked down and made no comment.

Victoria poured Edita another glass of wine and she was deep in thought as she took a drink. For a few minutes she had lost all control and been swept away in the moment; it was a new experience. She told herself it was just about the money and protecting her sister and Sadia. In reality she wasn't sure how she felt, but part of her had been excited by it.

Uri came into the kitchen and helped himself to a glass of wine.

'So Edita, it was good, yes?' he said.

'Yes,' she said, and took another sip of wine.

By ten-thirty Edita was suffering the effects of the wine and adrenaline, and was exhausted. Amir had gone but Victoria was still monitoring the chat room feed with Nicolai. She walked up to Victoria. 'I go to bed now,' she said.

Victoria hugged her. 'Don't forget this,' she said, and handed her the twenty pounds that Amir had given her earlier. 'Sleep well... it was good tonight.'

Edita considered the remark, left the kitchen and made her way to the sleeping quarters. The chat rooms were still doing great business and all kinds of noises were coming from the rooms as she walked past.

Delvina was awake when she approached her sleeping bag and got up.

'Edita,' she said. 'I have been so worried.'

'I am ok. I just need some sleep,' she said as her sister hugged her.

The following morning, Wednesday, the girls were up at six-thirty and preparing for work. Sadia was suffering the mother of all hangovers and nursing a major headache. Marija was talking to Delvina about how good the video had been and that Edita would make much money. Delvina felt the pressure growing.

The girls went their separate ways again with Amir taking the Macedonians to the hotel; Nicolai chauffeured Edita, Delvina and a worse-for-wear Sadia to the factory. Again, it had been a successful day in the packaging department and the girls were starting to make some friends.

Given her experiences the previous day, there had been no pressure on Edita to repeat her video performance that evening and the three Albanians spent the time watching TV.

Friday morning, the three girls had been at the house since late

Monday afternoon and were becoming acclimatised to their new circumstances, although the atmosphere of threat was never far away. Edita was desperate to contact her parents yet her requests were politely but firmly declined. 'Let's see how things go,' said Victoria when quizzed by Edita the previous evening.

They arrived at the factory as usual and were told they would not be needed until Monday. With the weekend approaching there was a joyous atmosphere among the workers and people were singing and joking which uplifted the spirits of the girls, except Sadia. She had been drinking wine again and although the hangover had more or less cleared, Edita was concerned about her. She had gone quiet again and seemed locked in her own world.

Nicolai collected them from the factory at four-thirty and they arrived back at the house at five o'clock. Victoria was at the laptop when they walked into the office.

'Hello,' she said to them. 'I have been seeing the hits for the video from Tuesday night, Edita, over four thousand. That is very good.'

'Very good,' said Nicolai.

Edita looked at Victoria, then Delvina, but said nothing.

Victoria had their cash-books in her hand. 'Here, I have your books,' and she gave them to the girls. Edita looked at the items. There was the money carried forward from Tuesday of £14, then the £25 from Edita's video. Victoria had added three days' wages of £21, then deducted £40 – "rent" and another £40 "food and travel", it said in the "particulars" column, leaving them with just £22 each.

'What is that?' asked Edita, pointing to the item marked "rent".

'We have to pay money for the electricity and taxes,' she said. 'Every week.'

'And that?' asked Edita.

'That is for food and the wine and also for the journey to work.

Gas is very expensive here,' said Victoria.

Edita looked at Delvina. Sadia had not understood and just stood there.

'Do not worry, if you like you can make more money tonight and then tomorrow Nicolai will take you to the mall. You can buy nice things. Marija can go as well, she has much money,' she said.

Edita looked again at the book, then at Victoria. 'How much money?' she asked.

'The same,' said Victoria. 'Delvina and Sadia could make money as well.'

Sadia became agitated. She had caught the meaning and shouted in Albanian. 'I cannot do that. I cannot do that.'

'It is ok, Sadia,' said Edita, trying to calm her down. 'You do not have to do anything. I will see to it.'

'What is wrong with her?' said Victoria.

'It is ok. I will speak to her,' said Edita. 'She is scared. That is all.'

Victoria looked at Sadia. 'Do not worry, it will be ok,' she said, but did little to convince her.

The girls went to the kitchen and started preparing food. Nicolai was back on the computers setting up for the evening's sessions. Victoria brought in another two bottles of wine. 'You will need more food tomorrow I think,' she said. Edita looked at Delvina.

'Ok,' said Edita. 'I will make video again tonight.'

'Ok, that is good,' said Victoria. 'You will make money. I will tell Amir, he will bring someone to make video with.'

'But what about Uri? I want Uri,' said Edita.

'Uri is working with other girls tonight but you can meet Victor. He is a friend of Uri's. Very handsome, all the girls like him,' said Victoria.

'You cannot do this,' said Delvina in Albanian. Sadia was just sat at the table staring down.

'Yes, it will be fine,' said Edita.

'Then I will do it too. You cannot do it by yourself,' she said.

'No, Delvina, no, you don't have to, I will do it. I will make enough money for all of us. You have not been with a boy,' said Edita.

'Then it is time I did,' said Delvina.

Delvina was like her sister and could be stubborn at times. She looked at Victoria, and before Edita could stop her, said in English, 'I want to make video.'

'Excellent,' said Victoria.

At six o'clock, Marija and her friends returned with Amir and the office was crowded. Edita's video was being shown on one of the monitors. Victoria and Nicolai were watching.

Marija spotted Edita in the kitchen and went to see her. Elena and Bijana joined the others at the monitor.

'Edita,' she said, and hugged her. 'Are you ok?'

'Yes, I am fine,' she replied.

'The video has many hits,' said Marija.

'Yes,' said Edita.

'You are doing another, yes?' said Marija.

'Yes,' said Edita, 'with Victor.'

'Oh, you will like Victor, very nice. Very big,' Marija said, making hand gestures to emphasise, and started to laugh.

'And you, Delvina?' said Marija.

'Yes,' replied Delvina.

'That is good. You will have good time,' she replied. She noticed Sadia sat at the table drinking from a bottle of water, staring at the wall.

'What about her?' said Marija.

'No,' said Edita. 'She is too young.'

'But she could make much money. Schoolgirls very many

hits,' she said.

'Not yet. We will look after her,' said Edita.

Victoria came into the kitchen. 'I have spoken to Uri and I have changed things. He will be here for video with Delvina. It will be better,' she said.

Edita put her hand out to Delvina and held her hand. 'Are you sure? You do not have to do this,' she said.

'Yes,' said Delvina. 'You should not have to do this for me.'

'Have you seen Edita's video?' said Victoria.

'No,' said Delvina. 'I do not want to.'

'Ok,' said Victoria.

So by seven o'clock Elena and Bijana were in the chat rooms and Edita and Delvina were getting changed preparing for their video performances. Marija had made suggestions on outfits and they were sat applying their make-up.

Amir, Uri and Victor had arrived and were in the kitchen drinking beers. Victoria had suggested that Marija would supervise the sessions. So while Nicolai was videoing, Marija would be out of camera shot choreographing the action. The sound would be dubbed on later so she would be able to give audible instructions. It would also be support for the novices.

Sadia was sat on her sleeping bag when Edita and Delvina were ready to leave. 'Do not worry,' said Edita, and she went to her. 'Everything will be fine. Delvina and me will make enough money. We will be ok.' Edita bent down and hugged Sadia but there was little response.

'We will see you later. Try to get some sleep,' said Edita, and the two girls walked down the two flights of stairs to the kitchen. Victoria was chatting to Uri and another young man.

'Ah, there you are,' said Victoria as they appeared. 'You look very nice. This is Victor; you have met Uri.'

Victor did not disappoint. Almost six feet tall, slim with dark curly hair and ubiquitous designer stubble. The boys kissed their respective partners. Uri turned to Victor. 'You will love Edita, she is very good,' he said. 'And Delvina, I am looking forward to being with you. You look so like your sister,' he added. Delvina just nodded and offered a nervous smile. Victoria poured the girls a large glass of wine which they both consumed very quickly.

'Delvina, why don't you come into the office and watch? You will see what to do,' said Victoria.

So, reluctantly, Delvina followed Victoria to the office and sat down in front of a blank monitor while Victor and Edita, followed by Marija and cameraman Nicolai went up to the video room.

The monitor sprung into life and the makeshift bedroom came into view.

Delvina watched as the action unfolded; Uri was stood behind her caressing her shoulders and providing a commentary.

For Delvina it was not a comfortable experience watching her sister in these circumstances. They had been close all their lives and shared many things but this was different. As before, the session lasted less than half an hour. Edita had put on a dressing gown and returned to the office to warm applause from Victoria and Amir.

'Bravo, bravo,' said Amir. 'Very good, you will have many hits I think.'

It was Delvina's turn and she was shaking. Edita hugged her.

'Do not worry, it will be ok,' said Edita. Marija will be with you.

Delvina followed Uri up to the bedroom, again with Marija and Nicolai.

Edita was watching on the monitor; Victor was having another beer in the kitchen.

Again the action unfolded and straight away Edita could sense

Delvina's fear, but then Marija came into shot and just like the previous evening took charge of things.

Edita watched as she expertly guided Delvina and within half an hour the video was complete.

Delvina returned to the office with Uri, Marija and Nicolai. Edita went to her sister and hugged her.

'Are you ok?' she said.

'Yes, I am ok,' said Delvina, but Edita could sense that wasn't the case.

As Nicolai started the editing process, the rest of the group returned to the kitchen. Victoria went to the fridge and produced a bottle of champagne. 'Another celebration I think,' she said, and passed the bottle to Uri to open. There was a "pop" as the cork flew across the room, then he poured out the drinks.

Amir looked at the two girls and raised his glass.

'Very good Edita and Delvina, you will make lots of money,' he said.

Victoria nodded with a degree of satisfaction. For Delvina, however, the experience had been traumatic and she couldn't share in the excitement. Edita was more pragmatic and would play the game. There would be opportunities to escape, she was sure of that. She just had to keep things together.

The group stayed in the kitchen finishing the champagne while Victoria and Nicolai kept up with the endless Internet feed for the chat rooms; it was another busy night. Every so often Victoria would check the membership figures on the laptop and the account where the money was rolling in. Just under a thousand new members in two nights, the cash flow was relentless.

At ten-thirty, Edita said she was going to check on Sadia who had been left on her own in the attic bedroom. Delvina wanted to sleep, so the sisters said goodnight and headed upstairs.

They reached the top floor and Edita went to Sadia's sleeping bag; it was empty.

'Sadia,' called Edita.

'I'll check the closet,' said Delvina. 'She's not here,' she said, opening the sliding doors.

'Sadia,' called Edita again.

A quick sweep of the rest of the top floor also proved fruitless.

'Where could she go? She can't have gone downstairs, we would have seen her,' said Delvina.

'What about the bathroom, maybe she's having a shower?' said Delvina.

'Come on,' said Edita. 'We'll check.'

Edita tried the door; it was locked from the inside.

'Sadia,' called Edita and knocked on the door. There was no reply. She banged her fist. 'Sadia, open the door.'

Edita turned to Delvina. 'Go downstairs and get help, something is wrong.'

Delvina went downstairs to the office; Victoria and Amir were on laptops monitoring the chat room feeds. They could see she was agitated.

'Delvina, what is wrong?' said Victoria.

'Help please,' she said in Albanian.

There were confused looks. 'Sadia, help please,' she repeated in English, pointing upstairs.

Victoria left the desk and followed Delvina back upstairs.

Edita was still banging on the door.

'What is the problem?' said Victoria as she reached the bathroom door.

'Sadia is in here I think. She will not answer,' said Edita.

'Sadia, come on, open up,' said Victoria. 'Wait here,' she said to Edita, and went back downstairs.

Moments later, Amir appeared with Victoria. 'What is the problem?' he said.

'It is Sadia. She is inside I think. The door, it is locked,' said Edita.

Amir knocked and shouted but still no response. He pushed Edita to one side and shoulder-charged the door. It was a small bolt designed to show that the room was occupied rather than to keep anyone out and it gave way on the first attempt. The momentum caused Amir to stumble as the door flew open.

Edita followed behind and gasped in horror. Sadia was laid in the bath with her head submerged. There was a serenity about her, her body almost bleached white apart from her lips which were a bluey/purple colour. Tracks of red oozed from her wrists, staining the water.

'Quick, help me,' said Amir, and Victoria grabbed two towels from the rail and helped Amir lift Sadia out of the water and onto the floor. Her wrists were still bleeding, but just a trickle. Victoria noticed a pair of scissors on the floor.

'They are from the office,' she said to Amir, who was blowing air into her mouth. He made no acknowledgement.

'It is no good, she is dead,' he said to Victoria. 'Help me cover her.'

Edita put her hand to her mouth. 'No, no,' she said.

'You go to your room, now!' said Victoria. 'We will see to this.'

Edita turned around and hugged Delvina, then slowly went up the open stairs to their billet.

In the bathroom there was great concern.

'What are we going to do?' said Victoria.

'We will see to it,' said Amir. 'Get some more covers.'

Victoria went downstairs and returned a few minutes later carrying a sheet. Uri and Victor followed.

'We need to cover her well and clean everything. There must be no trace,' said Amir. 'Go and get her sleeping bag,'

Victoria went upstairs and retrieved Sadia's sleeping bag. Edita and Delvina were huddled together trying to comfort one another.

When she returned to the bathroom the men had swaddled Sadia's body. 'Open the bag,' said Amir. Victoria unzipped the sleeping bag and Amir and the boys gently rolled her inside and zipped it up. The top was still open. 'We must seal this,' said Amir.

Victoria went back downstairs and returned with a large stapler.

'We try this,' she said, and Amir bent the top of the sleeping bag back.

'This is no use. It will not work,' he said anxiously, as he tried in vain to secure the end.

Uri was looking on. 'Do you have, how you say?' he said. He made a gesture that looked like he was tying something.

'Rope?' said Victoria.

'Small,' said Uri.

'String?' said Victoria.

'Yes, I think,' said Uri.

'Yes,' she added, and went back down to the office. She returned with a ball of standard office string.

'Yes,' said Uri. He picked up the scissors and made a hole through the sleeping bag and threaded the string through.

'Yes,' said Amir. 'That is good.'

Further holes were made and the top of the sleeping bag was duly sealed.

'What do we do now?' said Victoria.

'Do not worry, we will see to it,' said Amir.

'It is ok,' said Uri. 'I know a place. She will never be found. Victor and me will take her.'

'Ok,' said Amir. 'Are you sure?'

'Yes, it will be good,' said Uri.

Uri, Victor and Amir carried the sleeping bag downstairs. Amir opened the front door and checked the coast was clear, then opened the boot to the BMW. Victor and Uri carried the bundle out of the house and dropped it in.

'The keys,' said Amir as he handed them to Uri. 'And drive slow, ok. No Polici.'

Uri and Victor got in and pulled away.

'What has happened?' asked Marija when Victoria came downstairs. 'What was Uri doing with that sleeping bag?'

'It is Sadia,' said Victoria. 'She has died. We cannot keep her here. Uri has taken her away.'

Marija put her hand to her mouth in shock. 'I must see Edita,' she said, and went upstairs.

Back in the car, Uri was driving down the back-streets of Aireford, avoiding main roads.

'Where do we go?' said Victor.

'It is not far,' said Uri and eventually they arrived at a building site across the other side of town from Argyle Avenue. It was a cul-de-sac and Uri parked up at the end of the street; the area was deserted. He looked around; there were no CCTV cameras.

'Here?' said Victor.

'Yes, it will be good. I work here,' said Uri.

Uri was a bricklayer by trade and knew the site well. He went to the entrance, which was padlocked, but around the corner was an open field and along the side the fencing to the site was less secure. It would mean they would need to take the sleeping bag from the car for a short distance but it was a risk worth taking.

Uri and Victor took the bundle from the boot and carried it around the corner of the fencing. With no street lights it was pitch dark and it took a moment for their eyes to adjust. The ground was wasteland and littered with all sorts of debris, creating additional hazards, but after a few minutes they came to a gap in the fencing. Uri went first and he dragged the sleeping bag through, then Victor followed.

'Here,' said Uri.

In the distance an arc light shone to illuminate the main work area. On the periphery, foundations and footings were being constructed and although not in direct light, it was easier to see the outline of the new construction. Uri guided Victor across more builders' waste to a brick outline. In between the footings there was a shaft, dropping about fifteen feet to the foundations.

Uri and Victor manhandled the sleeping bag to the edge of the brickwork and let it fall to the bottom.

'Tomorrow it will be filled,' said Uri.

Back at the house there was a state of panic. Victoria was in discussion with Amir, considering the ramifications.

'What about Hyams?' she said.

'We will just tell them she has returned home. We will soon find someone else for them,' said Amir.

'What about the other two?' said Victoria.

'We will need to watch them,' said Amir.

Meanwhile, Marija was upstairs trying to comfort Edita and Delvina. Elena and Bijana were still entertaining the World Wide Web in the chat rooms oblivious to what had happened. Nicolai was managing the feeds.

Sadia's death had had a big impact on Edita and Delvina; they had been through a lot together and had come to view her almost as a younger sister. Edita had done what she could to protect her but it hadn't been enough. Eventually, the two girls from the chat rooms joined them. Marija told them of the tragedy. There was an initial disbelief but after the realisation, a feeling of deep despair.

'They will never let us go now,' said Delvina. 'They will kill us.'

'No, no,' said Marija. 'They need us.'

'They soon get other girls,' Delvina replied. 'We know too

much.'

Edita was thinking and shared her sister's fears, but was wary of saying anything in front of Marija and her companions. She was not sure if they could be trusted.

'I will speak to Victoria. She will look after us, I am sure,' Marija said.

Sleep had been almost impossible for the sisters. Delvina was sharing Edita's sleeping bag for comfort. Seeing the other girls were asleep, she whispered to her sister.

'What are we going to do?' She spoke in Albanian to avoid any possibility of the others understanding.

'For now...? Nothing, we wait for chance to escape,' said Edita.

'But we know everything. They will kill us,' said Delvina.

'No, I don't think so. Not while they still need us. They won't want to lose the money but we need to be clever. Make them believe everything is ok. At the moment we don't know where to go.'

'But the factory, we could tell them,' said Delvina.

'But they will do nothing and they would tell Amir and then...' Edita tailed off but the meaning was clear.

'The police, then,' said Delvina.

'No, Marija said that we would be put in jail; we are illegal immigrants. The police won't help us. No, we will wait. There will be a time,' said Edita.

'But I don't want to make video,' said Delvina.

'No,' said Edita. 'I will do them.'

Delvina hugged her sister and eventually they drifted off to sleep.

The following morning, Victoria was downstairs waiting for the girls when they came down for breakfast. All five were together and were still in a distressed state; it was eerily silent as they prepared their food. Things were different now and Victoria had a lot of repair work to do.

She looked at the group. 'Listen, I have some news,' she said. 'I know it has been difficult but I have spoken to Amir and we are going to give you some money and you can go to the mall. Nicolai will take you.'

Edita and Delvina showed little interest but the Macedonian girls were more enthusiastic having been many times before.

It was Marija who responded. 'Yes, that will be good,' she said. 'Come on Edita, we will buy nice things, make you happy.'

Edita thought for a moment, and then looked at Delvina. 'Yes, we should go,' she said.

Delvina's reluctance was obvious but Edita had an idea, it would give them a chance to check the lie of the land. They still had no real idea where they were, just a town somewhere in England that they had never heard of before.

'Ok,' said Victoria. 'I will give Nicolai some extra money but you can use your books as well if you would like.'

By nine-thirty Nicolai was driving the five girls to the shopping mall; the BMW was cramped. Edita asked to sit in the front and no-one seemed to mind. As the car headed out towards the mall, Edita was watching. Road signs, direction indicators but none of the names registered; she had only heard of London. She knew they were in Aireford – there were many signs. She noticed a bus, "Woodley's of Aireford", it said.

As they arrived in the multi-storey car park there was excited chatter among Marija and her companions; Edita and Delvina just stared out of the window at the drab, featureless interior; concrete and row upon row of cars.

Nicolai parked on the sixth floor and the group took the lift to the shops. He was keeping a close eye on the Albanians.

The group spent over three hours trawling through clothes and shoe shops. It was clear that Marija, Elena and Bijana had plenty of money to spend and they made the most of the occasion. The sisters were careful and just spent the fifty pounds from Victoria that Nicolai gave them.

'Don't forget you will need some food,' said Nicolai as he watched the girls on their spending spree.

On the way back to the house Nicolai called in at a large supermarket to replenish the foodstuff for the week. The amount was shared between the girls and deducted from their cash-books. Nicolai made the changes; Edita's showed a balance of £35.

Back at the house, Amir and Victoria were waiting for the girls to return.

CHAPTER EIGHT

Victoria heard the BMW pulling up outside the house and opened the front door to greet them like a concerned mother. There was an air of excitement and giggly banter between Marija and her two companions as the girls went to the boot of the car to retrieve their purchases. Edita and Delvina were more subdued. Nicolai locked the car and followed them into the house.

Edita felt nervous as she sat on one of the sofas in the lounge wondering what was going to happen. She had the carrier bag with the top she had bought on her lap; Delvina was sat next to her. Marija and her companions were busy comparing their purchases.

'Can you three leave us? I want to speak to Edita and Delvina,' said Victoria, looking at the Macedonians. Marija led them into the kitchen. Amir was sat on one of the chairs and just watched.

Edita was anxious wondering what was going to happen; the threat had returned. Victoria looked at the sisters. 'Look, I know it is hard but we need to go on.'

'But we want to go home, to our family,' said Edita. Delvina started to cry.

'I know, but it is not possible at the moment. It would cause much trouble and we do not want that... Soon you will go home and with much money. You have seen Marija and the girls they are happy and have money, enough to return and pay for university.'

Edita looked down and said nothing.

'We have looked after you well,' continued Victoria. 'When I came here they hurt girls but we will look after you if you do not cause trouble.'

'We will not cause trouble,' said Edita, looking up at Victoria and Amir.

'Good, good,' said Amir. 'That is settled, then.'

Victoria looked at Amir, then back at Edita. 'Tonight if you want to make video we will pay seventy-five pounds, but if you do not, that is ok; we have other girls who can come.'

'Ok,' said Edita. 'But not Delvina.'

Delvina looked at her sister and spoke in Albanian. 'No, you can't do it on your own. I won't let you.'

'I will be ok. Tonight I will do it. You should not,' said Edita.

'You could do chat room,' said Victoria. 'We pay thirty pounds.'

Edita looked at Delvina. 'I don't know what to do,' said Delvina.

Victoria intervened. 'We will show you. It is easy. You can watch Marija, she is very good. She makes much money, gets many tips.'

'Ok,' said Delvina.

'Tonight I will help with video. I have not been with Victor for a long time. We will be three, Edita, yes?' said Victoria.

'Yes,' said Edita.

So, later that evening Edita was ready in her costume to record the video with Victoria. Victor and Uri had both arrived. Uri had agreed to do the camera work. Delvina was with Nicolai watching the monitors as Marija and her companions performed in the chat rooms. Saturday night and the calls were relentless; the girls had trouble keeping up with demand. The virtual tills were ringing.

Victoria was in the kitchen finishing her make-up and Edita was sat opposite doing the same, but Victoria could see she was anxious. She rummaged in her handbag and pulled out a small polythene bag containing some white powder. 'Here, try some of this,' she said to Edita. 'It will help you relax. You will feel good.'

'What is it?' asked Edita.

Victoria ignored the question and went back to her handbag, took out a compact and opened it up, and then tipped a small amount of the powder onto the mirror. She took out a straw from the handbag and sniffed it up until it had gone.

'Here, you try,' she said, and Edita took the straw and Victoria placed another portion onto the mirror and Edita sniffed as Victoria had done. She immediately sneezed but within a few minutes began to feel the effects of the hit; a floating sensation, not unpleasant.

So with Uri in control of the camera, Victoria, Edita and Victor went to the video room and performed.

After it was finished, they returned to the office where Amir and Nicolai had been watching. Delvina was concentrating on the chat room activity.

'Bravo,' said Amir. 'That was special. We will have many hits.'

Monday 2nd September, four days before the dinner-dance; there was an important meeting at the house. It was mid-morning and the girls were all at work. Amir had been speaking on his mobile. He finished the call and spoke to Victoria.

'That was our friends in London. They want to pick up the cash for the Albanian girls this week. I said we can arrange it for Friday. Can you get the money together by then?' said Amir.

'Yes,' said Victoria. 'One hundred and fifty?'

'Yes,' said Amir.

'I will start drawing from the banks tomorrow,' said Victoria. 'Did they say how they wanted it delivered?'

'Yes they suggested using the safety deposit box again. It worked well last time,' said Amir.

'I said you will meet Oleksi at the hotel on Friday night and give him the key,' he said.

'Oleksi? Oh I think I will give him more than that,' said Victoria. 'We had a good time when he came before. I think I can put a smile on his face.'

'It is good to keep them happy. They bring us good girls,' he said.

The people-trafficking enterprise was controlled and run by a group of Ukrainians based in London. From their sleazy office above a kebab shop they coordinated the trafficking and supplied the "cargo" to clients around the country. It was a well-organised set-up, not just in the logistics of the transportation but in the method of payment. Using bank accounts was way too risky and the vast majority of transactions were made in cash. The process of exchanging the money was carefully thought-out; two parties being caught handing over substantial amounts of money would always lead to questions being asked. The left-luggage drop was a relatively risk-free means of delivery. The traffickers were able to siphon the money through a variety of retail outlets, restaurants and even launderettes.

Azure Recruitment Services had their headquarters in a smart office complex in the centre of the city and employed ten people. Both Amir and Victoria, who was now a partner, divided their time between the office and the Argyle Avenue house. As well as their private residences, the partners owned two other properties close to Argyle Avenue. Victor and Uri lived in one of them; the other was used as a base for the girls who provided the chat room entertainment from eleven till four a.m. Two of them were from the Czech Republic, two from Russia and another two from Lithuania, who had originally came to the UK with Victoria. They had arrived on student visas and not returned home, but it was through choice and not coercion that they stayed. They were free to leave whenever they wanted but even after paying their rent, the money they were earning was a great inducement to stay; far more than they could ever hope for in their own countries.

The accounts would show that Azure Recruitment Services Ltd earned its income from normal recruitment activities and from rents, as well as "consultancy fees", much of which originated from the lucrative porn venture; it was a complex organisation. The business had accounts with all the major local banks.

The three shareholders, Amir, his brother Shalik, who was General Manager of Hayfield Hotel, and Victoria had personal accounts scattered across the city. The hotel, which was also owned by Azure, was a valuable asset in disguising payments and contributed significantly to the company's cash flow. It too had its fair share of illegal money passing through its tills and would provide some of the cash for the transaction. The money for the exchange would be drawn over a period of days to avoid arousing any suspicion.

There was one particular account, however, held at one of the few overseas banks in the city which would be the main source of funds. There was a high-interest account where the income from the website and chat rooms was collected. Substantial balances, often in excess of one million pounds, accrued. Amir had a special relationship with the local manager who was regularly entertained at the hotel with one of the girls. Transfer or withdrawal of funds was never questioned and money was interchanged across the businesses, making it extremely difficult for any tax authorities to track.

Amir called the Ukrainians back and confirmed that Victoria would meet Oleksi at the hotel on Friday night around nine-thirty to make the exchange. He would be driving up from London and Shalik had reserved a suite for their VIP guest. Victoria would be providing the entertainment.

Since their arrival five weeks ago, Edita and Delvina continued their daytime jobs at Hyams; the Macedonians were at the hotel. The evening work carried on unabated and the cash-books were beginning to look reasonably healthy, despite the frequent deductions. Delvina was now a regular in the chat rooms and had already acquired a fan following, but Edita's dalliance with cocaine had escalated and her habit was beginning to affect her mood as well as her cash-book; Victoria deducted half of Edita's video fee to cover the cost. Sadia's suicide was a thing of the past.

Far from being a reluctant participant, Edita was now starting to request video work. Delvina was becoming increasingly concerned for the well-being of her sister.

That evening, the girls arrived back to the house at the usual time; Nicolai continued as chauffeur. Victoria was in the office with Amir, preparing for the night's entertainment.

'Hello Edita, Delvina,' she said. 'I have a new person for you tonight, Edita.'

'That is good,' said Edita.

In the short time that Edita had been making videos she had become something of a star. Her videos were by far the most popular on the website and she was attracting a large following. Downloads were in the thousands and new members had almost doubled in four weeks. Her popularity had not gone unnoticed by Victoria, who herself was no stranger to male fan worship. She was keen to cash in on the momentum and a web-based marketing campaign featuring Edita, who was now known as Fallen Angel, was beginning on Saturday night. As a result, Edita had been promised more money – her payment for the cash-book was now seventy-five pounds or one hundred for a threesome. She regularly worked with Marija and, occasionally, Victoria.

Edita had convinced herself that she was still playing the game but such are the subtleties of conditioning that she was becoming 'normalised'; the pattern of their daily routines was becoming a way of life. For Delvina, who was nowhere near as strong a character as her sister, it was more a question of survival; most of the time she was just frightened and went along with whatever she was asked to do.

The new partner arrived at eight-thirty and Edita was shocked when she saw him sat on the sofa in the lounge. He was much older than her previous liaisons, fat and balding. Edita went up to Victoria, who was in the office with Nicolai. Delvina was in one of the chat rooms.

'I do not like him,' Edita said. 'I do not want to go with him.'

Victoria took Edita into the kitchen, out of earshot.

'But you must; he is an important man for Amir, and Shalik.'

'But he is ugly,' Edita replied.

Victoria thought for a moment, and went to her handbag again. 'Here, you can have some of my special magic. You will not notice,' and Victoria handed over a small bag of white powder. 'And we will pay you one hundred pounds. It will be just you and him, no video.'

Edita looked at it, then at Victoria. 'Ok, I will do it but I will make it not last long and then I leave him.'

Victoria smiled. 'Yes, that will be good,' she said.

Karim Farhat was an Iranian businessman and used the Hayfield Manor for numerous functions and meetings. He was considered a friend of Shalik Aziz and someone who was important to the hotel. It was Shalik who had contacted Amir about pairing him with Edita; he had seen one of her videos and was a big fan. He was aware of the connection and asked Shalik if he could arrange it and had offered two thousand pounds for the opportunity. Edita would see a mere fraction of this fee.

Edita had taken Victoria's special magic and was feeling more relaxed about her evening's mission; it was just another job. The sooner she got on with it, the sooner it would be over.

Victoria led her into the lounge where Karim was drinking whisky.

'Oh, you are even more pretty than in the films,' said Karim as he was introduced to Edita.

Edita smiled. 'Thank you,' she said.

'Why don't you take Karim to the room?' said Victoria.

At Victoria's suggestion Edita had chosen a mini cocktail dress which she knew the Iranian would like.

For some reason Edita was on alert. Although the heroin was deadening her emotions, there was something about this man she did not like; her instinct told her to be careful.

She led him upstairs. Meanwhile, Victoria had switched on the monitor to the video room. Although there was no video camera she wanted to make sure Edita was giving her best. If necessary she would join in. Nicolai was on the other monitor looking after the chat rooms.

As the action was about to start, Amir joined them at the monitor. He had been to the nearby off-licence to buy more whisky. Karim had an appetite for it.

Victoria could see straight away that Edita was not comfortable but she appeared to be coping. Karim was sat on the bed while Edita stripped off. She then started undressing the Iranian. He looked like a beached whale lying on the bed naked, and Edita almost laughed in derision at the thought. Unfortunately, despite her best efforts the Iranian's manhood failed to respond and just lay there flaccid almost hidden by the overhang of his belly. He became more and more frustrated, then angry and started shouting at Edita.

'You whore, bitch, you are no good to me,' and suddenly he hit Edita with a backhand slap across the face.

Victoria saw what was happening.

'Quick, Amir, he is hurting Edita. Get up there now,' she said. Nicolai watched on the monitor.

Amir was through the door and up the stairs. Along the first-floor corridor, third door on the left.

He opened the door. The Iranian was starting to use his fists on the defenceless girl.

Amir grabbed him by the shoulders. Karim was sweating and Amir had difficulty holding onto him. He turned around and snarled at Amir.

'Leave me alone, you bastard, I paid much money. I will have my time with this girl,' he said.

Before Amir could respond, Karim head-butted him, splitting his nose open and spraying the floor with blood. He fell to the floor. Edita, meanwhile, was in the corner of the room watching proceedings, clutching her clothes. Karim walked towards her. 'Now my pretty, it is time for you to earn your money. Come here,' he ordered.

Edita looked at him. Bizarrely he was now fully erect, fired up by the conflict and violence. She was shaking with fear but suddenly she could see Amir behind him getting up from the floor. Karim was watching Edita. 'Come on my pretty, on the bed,' he barked.

Amir picked up the chair from the dressing table and charged at the Iranian, bringing it down on him.

Karim fell to the floor, clutching his head. Nicolai appeared at the door armed with a knife. Amir was breathing heavy, his bloodied nostrils flared like a rampant stallion. Edita ran out of the room, still clutching her clothes, and downstairs into the arms of Victoria who had seen it all on the monitor.

'Help, help me,' said Edita, her make-up hideously smeared across her face, her left eye swollen and her lip bleeding.

'It's ok, everything will be ok,' said Victoria. 'Go into the kitchen and get dressed, I will be with you in a minute.'

Edita did as she was told and started dressing; Victoria ran upstairs to the video room. The floor was covered in blood and Karim was on his knees still holding his head.

Nicolai handed the knife to Amir.

'Right you bastard,' he said in Farsi. 'You will not treat my girls in this way. Get dressed and out of the house, now.'

Amir had the knife pointing to Karim; Nicolai was also poised for trouble. Victoria came into the room and started remonstrating with him. 'I should cut your balls off,' she said.

Karim looked at the three and started picking up his clothes, cursing vehemently in his native language. Amir was still holding the knife towards him and was ready to use it if necessary.

The Iranian got dressed and walked unsteadily down the stairs with blood seeping from a head wound, and was escorted out of the house by Nicolai. He turned at the doorway and spoke to Amir. 'You have not heard the last of this.'

'I hear your wife is a dragon, Karim. Go home and hope she does not hear about tonight,' responded Amir.

Karim skulked away and got into his car, still cursing.

Back in the kitchen, Edita was now dressed and sat quietly at the table, traumatised. The chat-room girls had no idea what had happened. Victoria went to her. 'He is gone. It will not happen again, I promise,' she said, and hugged Edita. Amir joined them. 'How are you?' he said, looking into her face. Her left eye was starting to close and her lip was swollen.

Victoria looked at Amir who had a handkerchief over his nose to stem the bleeding.

'Well there will be no videos for a while and I don't think she should be at work tomorrow. There will be too many questions,' she said.

'Yes, I agree,' he said.

'You need to see to your face,' she said, looking at the bloodstained handkerchief.

'It is nothing; it will be fine,' said Amir, and he walked upstairs to the bathroom.

Victoria went back to the lounge and came back with a bottle of brandy.

'Here, drink this,' said Victoria as she poured a measure into a glass and handed it to Edita.

She took the glass and sipped, then winced as the alcohol stung her swollen lip. Victoria looked at Edita's face. 'I have something that will help with that,' she said, and went to one of the cupboards and produced a box containing basic medical aids – plasters, cotton wool and so on. She took out a bottle of witch-hazel, poured some onto some cotton wool and proceeded to dab it on Edita's bruised eye. Edita winced again.

'It will stop hurting soon,' Victoria said.

Amir walked into the kitchen. 'I have had a thought; maybe Edita could help at the hotel. Shalik, he always wants people...' He thought for a moment. 'I know we could swap with Elena or Bijana and send them to the factory. Marija can show Edita what to do,' he said to Victoria.

Edita heard and looked up. 'I will not go without Delvina,' she said.

Victoria looked at Amir, then at Victoria. 'No, that is alright, we will change and you can both go to the hotel.'

Amir looked at Victoria. 'We need to speak,' he said, and went out of the kitchen with Victoria. In the office the chat rooms were still busy and Nicolai was running the keyboard commentary for the girls.

Edita was sat at the table in the kitchen sipping her brandy; her eye was starting to hurt now. This evening's trauma had been a wake-up call and her thoughts again turned to escape. She would not be anyone's punch-bag ever again.

Amir spoke to Victoria out of Edita's earshot. 'I am worried about the girls. They might try to escape after what has happened. We should keep one of them close,' he said.

'But they will be ok at the hotel. Marija will watch them and Shalik is there as well. I think it will be fine. I will speak to Edita.'

'Ok,' said Amir. 'But we <u>will</u> need to watch them.'

Victoria went back into the kitchen where Edita had finished her brandy and was sat staring down at the table. She looked up at the approaching Victoria.

'That is settled,' she said. 'Tomorrow you and Delvina will go with Marija to the hotel and work there until you are better. Tomorrow night you can help Nicolai and me with the chat room calls if you like. I will pay you twenty pounds.'

Edita looked up but was not really focusing. 'We will talk about it tomorrow,' Victoria said.

At eleven o'clock, Delvina and the others had finished in the chat rooms and been replaced by the late shift. They returned to the kitchen and saw Edita sat talking to Victoria.

'Edi!' exclaimed Delvina when she saw her sister and went to her.

'What has happened?' she said. She sat down next to Edita and put her arm around her in comfort.

'She had a bad time,' said Victoria. 'But it is ok now. It will not happen again.'

Marija was also concerned and Victoria explained what had happened, then outlined the change of working arrangements.

'Tomorrow, Elena and Bijana will go to the factory with Nicolai and Edita and Delvina will go with Marija to the hotel. Amir will take you,' she said.

There was a look of resignation on the girls' faces, but Victoria could see the change was not welcomed. 'It will be fine. We will telephone the factory and explain everything. When Edita has recovered we will change again.'

Delvina was still fussing over her sister and eventually the girls made their way up to the sleeping quarters. Delvina and Edita shared the same bed again to give each other comfort.

The next morning, as arranged, Nicolai took Elena and Bijana to Hyams while Amir drove Marija, Edita and Delvina to the hotel. Edita's eye was not as swollen but was turning black. As Victoria had said, any new video presentations would have to wait. There were plenty in stock, however, and downloads were selling well.

Once again, an air of uncertainty hung over the Albanians; anything out of routine spelt potential danger. The car was quiet on the way to the hotel but as they pulled up to the house Edita couldn't help staring at the magnificent building. Amir drove the car around the back to the staff entrance and the girls got out. Amir locked up and followed them into the building; he had business to discuss with his brother, not least the issue of Karim Farhat.

Marija took the two girls to the ground-floor staff quarters where they would be given overalls and their duties explained. They would report to Anna Dyszatow, their Polish supervisor and House Manageress. She greeted them with some surprise, no-one had told her of the new arrangements. She was a striking girl, mid-twenties, with an almost white complexion and black hair that went down to her waist which she was tying up under a protective bonnet. In front of her was one of the trolleys which was used to carry cleaning materials and toiletry refills.

Marija explained the situation. 'I will show them what to do,' she said. Anna went to Edita. 'Hello, I am Anna... What has happened to your eye?'

'I fell,' replied Edita. Anna was far from convinced. 'Ok, Marija will show you what to do. You will start on the third floor,' and that concluded the induction process.

Edita and Delvina were given their uniform and trolley and followed Marija through the staff quarters and down the corridor to the lift. They had to take it in turns to ride to the third floor; the lift wouldn't take two trolleys.

Meanwhile, Amir had met Shalik in the General Manager's office. He explained the situation regarding Karim. 'You will need to be careful with him. He was very angry, but he will not be allowed to hurt my girls.'

Shalik nodded sagely. 'It won't be a problem. I can deal with him if necessary.'

'Victoria will be collecting the money today and tomorrow for the meeting with Oleksi on Friday,' said Amir.

'Can you let her know I have twenty-five in the safe here?' said Shalik.

'Of course,' said Amir.

They finished their discussions and Amir returned to the Azure office in town. Victoria was already working and Amir briefed her on the discussions with his brother.

Friday 14th September, the day of the dinner-dance

All week Edita and Delvina had been at the hotel working as chambermaids under the supervision of Marija. Victoria had asked her to keep a close watch on them. In reality it had actually been a good break for the Albanians, and they much preferred their new vocation to working in the factory. There was less pressure and the surroundings and conditions were far more pleasant.

Edita was gradually recovering from her earlier ordeal and was more like her old self. However, the experience had, if anything, made her more determined to try to get away. It was a case of finding the right opportunity. The thought of a prison cell, or worse, being returned, scared her more than their present situation; going to the police was not an option. It would have to be another way. But there was no immediate hurry; for the time being at least they were still being reasonably well looked after.

With Edita's bruise still visible she had not been asked to perform in videos; her back catalogue was still proving to be a money-spinner in any case and, in the circumstances, Amir and Victoria were more than happy to give her a break. This had implications with their cash-book balances, however, which were starting to dwindle without the extra income. Delvina had done a couple of evenings in the chat room and Edita, without the video work, had stopped taking the heroin, which had helped.

At lunchtime, the girls received a visitor while they were taking their break; it was Shalik. He spoke to Marija. 'Tonight we have a big function and I am short of staff to be waitress. I have spoken to Amir and he said you can work. I will pay twenty pounds.'

Marija looked at Edita who had translated for Delvina. Edita shrugged her shoulders in a non-committal way.

'Yes, that is ok,' said Marija. 'But someone will have to show us what we do.'

'That is ok. I will get someone to do that. It is not hard to do,' he replied.

So at four-thirty the girls finished their cleaning and reported to Mario, the head waiter in the large function room. There were four other local girls supplied by Azure who would supplement the regular waiting staff. Tonight was a "big do", Mario explained. He was a large man, dark hair, mid-forties and already attired in a black dinner jacket and dickey bow, reflecting his status as maître-d'. He spoke in a strong Italian accent, which the girls struggled with at times, but after an hour or so's coaching everyone seemed happy with their roles.

They were told to report back at six-thirty.

CHAPTER NINE

Victoria, meanwhile, had collected all the cash that would be needed to pay for the girls, fifty thousand pounds each. There would be no rebate for the unfortunate Sadia. The Ukrainians were also out of pocket having lost one of the girls on the boat, and questions were being asked of their Romanian suppliers.

After a detour to her regular salon to have her hair cut and styled, Victoria returned to Argyle Street with the remaining money; it was six o'clock. Amir had collected the cash from the hotel, and after a final count, one hundred and fifty thousand pounds in fifty pound notes was packed into a large holdall. 'I will take you to the bus station,' said Amir.

'Later,' replied Victoria. 'It will be quiet. Then you can take me to the hotel... I have to sort things out here. We need to arrange the chat room now that Shalik has three of our girls.'

The evening was set. Victoria drafted in a couple of girls from the late shift to work the chat rooms, Nicolai would look after monitoring the Internet feed. She showered and changed into her outfit for the evening which she was sure would meet with Oleksi's approval; a low-cut powder-blue mini-dress which she had bought earlier from her favourite boutique, and black shoes with five-inch heels. She walked into the lounge where Amir was waiting for her. He looked up and down at her rather skimpy attire. 'You will need a coat,' he said. 'It will be cold later.'

'Yes, I have one,' she replied, and went into the kitchen. The short-brown leather coat with fur collar was draped over one of the chairs. She put it around her shoulders and picked up her handbag.

'Can you take the money?' she said to Amir, who duly obliged.

So after checking with Nicolai that everything was running well, they left the house. Amir opened the car door for Victoria and then deposited the holdall into the boot. It was gone nine o'clock as they headed towards the bus station. It was quiet with only three bays occupied with empty buses waiting for their time slots. Amir parked behind the building in a service bay and Victoria got out of the car, carried the holdall into the main hall and followed the signs to the left-luggage facility.

Having used this drop once before she was familiar with the layout and soon found the rows of lockers. It was a straightforward process. She opened up one of the lockers and deposited the bag inside, closed it and inserted a pound coin into the coin slot, releasing the key. She looked at it, number 63, and dropped it into the pocket of her coat, then headed back to the car.

'Everything ok?' asked Amir. 'You have the key?'

'Yes, fine. Now I will meet Oleksi,' she said, and Amir drove off towards the hotel.

As they entered the hotel driveway the main hotel car park was overflowing and cars were strewn down both sides of the road. Amir went up to the front entrance and stopped in the drop-off zone. 'I will see you in the morning?' said Amir as a question.

'Yes, I do not expect to be returning tonight... I will telephone when I want you to pick me up,' she said, and left the car.

She was glad she had taken Amir's advice; it was a chilly night and she welcomed the warmth of her coat. The hotel was packed and Victoria ran the usual phalanx of smokers congregating outside the front entrance. She was aware of being ogled and some wag proffered a wolf-whistle. She ignored the ribaldry and headed for reception.

Inside there was a considerable hustle and bustle as men in dress shirts and dickey-bows and women in their best finery headed downstairs to the cloakrooms and back upstairs to the conference room, like soldier ants scurrying from their nests to a food source.

'Hello Victoria,' said Ingrid Jansen, the duty receptionist.

'Hello Ingrid. Is Shalik about?'

'Yes, he is in the office. Do you want to go through?' replied Ingrid, and she opened the entrance hatch at the end of the reception desk so Victoria could enter.

She walked through a door immediately in front of her. It was a small office, cluttered with filing cabinets, computer screens and other office paraphernalia. There was a man who was part of the security team watching various monitors, and a young woman entering data onto a laptop. Shalik was talking on his mobile but rang off when he saw Victoria enter.

'Victoria, my dear, you look beautiful,' he said, and walked towards her. 'That was Oleksi on the telephone; he will be here in about twenty minutes.' He kissed her on both cheeks.

'Here, let me take your coat,' and Victoria slipped it from her shoulders and handed it to him. 'Can you look after this, Grianne?' he said, and passed the coat to the Reception Manager.

'Yes, of course,' she said in her strong Irish accent. She got up from her computer and received the coat from Shalik.

'Would you like a drink?' said Shalik. 'We can wait in the bar.'

'Yes, thank you,' she said, and Shalik led the way from the office and back out into reception.

On the ground floor to the right of the lobby there was a small cocktail bar, and Victoria followed Shalik inside. It was like an oasis of quiet; soft background music and just a few couples talking intimately and enjoying a nightcap before retiring to their rooms.

A waiter came over immediately and took the order, a tonic water for Shalik and for Victoria her favourite cocktail, a Southern Screw, one part vodka, one part Southern Comfort with a dash of orange juice.

'I am sorry about Karim,' said Shalik. 'I have seen your girl who is working here. She is getting better I think. I have spoken to her.'

'Edita?' said Victoria.

'Yes, I think that is her name. I told her it will never happen again.'

'Have you spoken to him?' asked Victoria.

'No, but I spoke to his brother and told him what had happened. He has shamed his family. He will not trouble us again,' he said. Victoria smiled.

'You wait till you see Amir, his eye it is black from Karim. He hit him,' she said.

'Is he alright?' asked Shalik with some concern.

'Yes, he will be fine.'

Shalik sipped his tonic water and thought for a moment, then looked at Victoria.

'The girls, they do well,' said Shalik. 'They learn very quick. I will keep them here if Amir agrees.'

'Yes, that will be better for them I think,' said Victoria.

As they continued chatting Shalik had difficulty in keeping a professional tone to the conversation as his eyes were attracted to Victoria's legs and deep cleavage. She was used to it and just ignored the surreptitious glances. Then Grianne entered the room and spotted them in the corner; she went up to them.

'Mr Bolyk is here,' she said.

'Tell him to take a seat. We will be with him in a moment,' said Shalik.

Grianne returned to the lobby while Shalik and Victoria finished their drinks.

A couple of minutes later, Shalik and Victoria entered the lobby to be greeted by the pounding sound of a disco coming from the main conference room upstairs.

Oleksi saw them approaching and got up from his chair and

greeted them warmly. 'Shalik, my good friend, it is good to see you again and Victoria, you look so beautiful,' he said, and kissed her on both cheeks. He had a small overnight carry-on bag with him, which he pulled along as they walked.

'How was your journey?' asked Shalik.

'It was ok,' he said, 'much traffic.'

'You must be tired,' said Shalik. 'Have you eaten?'

'Not for a while,' said Oleksi.

'Ok, so why don't you and Victoria go to your suite and I will send up some food, and a bottle of champagne,' he added.

'Thank you,' said Oleksi.

'Victoria will show you,' said Shalik.

'Where is my coat?' asked Victoria. Grianne had heard. 'Don't worry it'll be fine, I've taken it to the cloakroom.' she said.

Shalik noticed Victoria's concern. 'It will be ok. You can collect it in the morning. It will be quite safe,' he said. Shalik was aware of the cash exchange but had not been party to the precise methodology; Victoria trusted no-one.

It was Oleksi who was looking impatient and put his arm around Victoria's waist. 'Come, show me the room, my dear, and you can tell me your news.' Oleksi had expectations.

Oleksi was short in stature, and Victoria with her heels now appeared to tower over him, but what he lacked in height he certainly made up for in physique. He had short curly fair hair, swarthy, with a face that did not naturally default to a smile. He also had a rose tattooed on his chest, the image of someone associated with the Russian Mafia.

The suite was on the top floor and the noise from the disco was confined to the rhythmic bass lines of the songs. Oleksi pushed the swipe card into the slot, a small green light flashed and the locked door clicked open.

'After you, my dear,' said Oleksi, and he moved to one side to allow Victoria to pass.

It was a large room with a separate bedroom and bathroom. Victoria sat on the four-seater leather sofa.

Oleksi took his jacket off and placed it over the back of one of the chairs. He was wearing a two-piece suit with a white open-neck shirt.

'You have the key?' asked Oleksi.

'Of course,' said Victoria.

There was a knock on the door before the conversation could develop further. Oleksi answered it and a waiter entered pushing a trolley containing a selection of cold platters. The waiter walked over to the dining table and set out the food and cutlery, and then produced an ice bucket with a magnum of champagne and two glasses.

'Anything else you need, please ring reception,' said the man, and he turned and left.

'Will you join me?' asked Oleksi.

'Yes, thank you,' said Victoria.

Oleksi watched as she got up from the settee. 'You look wonderful, my dear,' he said.

'Thank you,' she said, and smiled.

Oleksi opened the champagne, poured out the glasses and handed one to Victoria. He pulled back one of the chairs from the table for Victoria, then sat opposite her.

'Help yourself,' he said, and Victoria served herself with a selection, then Oleksi followed.

'You like the girls we sent?' said Oleksi.

'Yes,' said Victoria. 'Very nice, they work well.' She said nothing about Sadia.

'That is good. That is good,' he repeated. 'I have some more due in at the end of the month. You must say if you want anymore. I have many customers.'

'I will speak to Amir,' she said. 'We may need another two or three. I will let you know.'

The small talk lasted until the end of the meal.

'Shall we take the champagne into the bedroom?' said Oleksi.

'Yes,' said Victoria, and he led the way to the four-poster.

He took off his shoes and lay on the bed while she slowly undid the zip to her dress and let it fall to the floor.

For Victoria, it had been a torrid night. Oleksi was insatiable in his sexual appetite and not a gentle lover. She was glad when he eventually fell asleep. She got out of bed at just turned seven and ran a shower. Without a change of clothes she dressed in her outfit from the previous evening. Oleksi was just waking when she returned to the bedroom.

'Victoria, where are you going? I have not finished with you yet,' he said, trying to sit up.

'I have much to do today, Oleksi,' said Victoria. 'I will get the key so we can finish our business.'

She left the bedroom and could hear Oleksi calling her, but she ignored his remonstrations and left the suite. She took the lift to reception and it was the duty manager, Jan Croote, who welcomed her.

'Hello Victoria. Shalik said you might be around today,' she said from behind the desk. A couple of guests walked up to Jan to check out. 'Won't be a minute,' she said to Victoria.

Victoria felt somewhat under-dressed in her evening outfit, and although it seemed a fine day outside, there was a cold draft coming from the open main door which caused goosebumps on her bare arms. She rubbed them to keep the circulation flowing.

With the guests suitably attended, the manager opened the hatch and let Victoria through into the office. Jan followed. Another assistant was processing papers onto a computer.

'You must be cold in that dress,' said the manager, suitably attired in her corporate uniform, a smart blouse and business suit with her name badge prominent on her lapel.

'Yes, I have come for my coat,' she said. 'I left it with Grianne last night.'

Jan looked around. 'Well it's not here,' she said.

Victoria looked around slightly concerned. 'I think she took it to the cloakroom,' said Victoria as an afterthought and feeling slightly relieved.

'I'll just go and check,' Jan said. 'It will be locked.'

Jan went to one of the drawers and hunted around among numerous keys.

'Ah, here it is,' she said, pulling out a key with a label, "Ladies' Cloakroom", attached.

Victoria sat down and waited patiently. The assistant got up twice to check out guests on the desk. It was a good ten minutes before Jan returned.

'Is this it?' said Jan. 'It's the only one left.' Jan looked at it. 'It's beautiful, must have cost a fortune.'

Victoria looked at it. 'No, there must be a mistake. That is not mine,' she said.

Jan looked concerned; Victoria, more so. 'Are you sure there are no others?' said Victoria.

'Yes, certainly, it was on its own. There are no others,' said Jan.

Victoria looked at it. 'It is like mine, but it is new; mine is older,' she said.

'I don't know what to say,' said Jan.

'I need to speak to Shalik. I need my coat, it is very important,' said Victoria.

'He will be here at nine o'clock,' said Jan.

Victoria checked the time; three quarters of an hour. She hoped Oleksi had gone back to sleep.

Just past nine o'clock, Shalik came into the office and was immediately confronted by Victoria.

'Shalik, my coat, it has gone. It has been taken,' she said, now in a desperate state. Oleksi had not yet appeared but she knew he could walk in at any moment wanting the key. She had not yet called Amir but would have to if the coat did not turn up soon.

Shalik could see her anxiety. 'When did you have it last?' he said.

'You know when,' she retorted. 'Last night, you remember. You gave it to Grianne to look after.'

'Ah yes, she took it to the cloakroom.'

'Yes, but it is not there now and this one is. Look, it still has a number. It is not mine. Someone has my coat,' she said, beginning to rant.

'Ok, do not worry. We will find it,' said Shalik. 'I will give Grianne a call.'

Shalik left the office and keyed a number into his mobile. Victoria was now extremely concerned.

'I have spoken to Grianne and she says she left it with the attendant in the cloakroom. I cannot contact her at the moment, she is not answering her phone,' said Shalik.

This news had done nothing to diminish Victoria's anxiety.

Then the phone rang and Jan answered the call. A smile lightened her face and she mouthed to Victoria, 'someone has your coat.'

Victoria breathed a sigh of relief. Jan put the phone down and highlighted the news.

'That was a Mrs... Woodley,' she said, reading her handwriting. 'She says she was given another coat last night by mistake and didn't notice till this morning,' said Jan.

'What?' said Victoria. 'How can that be?'

Shalik looked at her. 'I do not know. I will look into it but I think I will need a new cloakroom attendant, that is certain.'

'So what is happening? When can I have my coat?' said Victoria.

'She said her husband will be in to exchange it later,' said Jan.

'When?' said Victoria.

'She just said "later".'

Victoria started pacing the office. Oleksi still hadn't shown but it wouldn't be long. For a minute she thought of returning to the room and entertaining him for a bit longer to delay the inevitable enquiry. She still had not divulged the importance of the coat to Shalik.

Another call came to reception, this time it was internal. The call was answered. 'That was Mr Bolyk in the James Suite wanting breakfast. He asked if you were available to serve it to him,' said Jan to Victoria.

Victoria was in a dilemma. She couldn't reasonably refuse but she wanted to be around for when the coat arrived. 'Ok,' she said. 'Let me know when it is ready.'

Twenty minutes later, a waiter from the restaurant knocked on the office door to say the breakfast was ready to take up.

Victoria looked at Shalik. 'Ok, I will take it,' she said. 'Just make sure you look after my coat,' she said sternly, and left the office.

The waiter was at the lift with the breakfast trolley laden with a variety of cereals, juices and a pot of freshly brewed coffee. There was a plate with a metal lid over it containing a full English fry-up.

'I will take it,' said Victoria to the waiter, who appeared transfixed at her revealing outfit.

She took the lift to the top floor and wheeled the trolley to Oleksi's suite. She knocked on the door and looked around. Seeing the corridor was deserted, she quickly unzipped her dress, stepped out of it and placed it on the empty bottom shelf of the trolley. She stood there in just a thong and her shoes. She had been left with no alternative but to employ delaying tactics.

The door was opened and Oleksi stood there open-mouthed.

'Breakfast is served, sir. I hope you enjoy the menu,' she said with a fake smile.

Oleksi moved to one side to let her in and closed the door.

At around ten-thirty the bell sounded on the reception desk; Jan attended. It was a man carrying a coat.

'Oh hi,' said the man. 'My name's Woodley, my wife phoned earlier. She was given the wrong coat from last night?' he said with an inflection.

'Just a minute,' said Jan, and she went into the office.

She quickly returned, followed by Shalik.

'I've come about my wife's coat?' said the man in what appeared to be a question.

'Yes, of course,' said Shalik. 'Mr Woodley is it?'

'Yes,' he replied.

'One moment,' he said, and Shalik went back into the office.

He returned with another coat.

'Here we are, sir, my apologies. This should never have happened, my staff are warned not to give out coats without the correct ticket,' said Shalik.

'Ah,' said Keith. 'That's my wife's fault, I'm afraid, she couldn't find her ticket and pointed it out on the rail apparently.'

Shalik looked at him. 'Nevertheless, it should not have happened. You have the ticket now?' said Shalik.

'Yes,' and handed it over.

The coat exchange was completed.

'Please pass on my apologies to the owner of that coat. She must have been very worried,' said Keith.

'Yes, yes she was,' said Shalik.

'Thank you,' said Keith. Then he apologised again and left the hotel with the coat over his arm.

Shalik went back into the office carrying Victoria's coat.

'Thank goodness,' said Jan. 'It's a lovely coat but... I don't know, Victoria seemed extremely wound up about it,' she said.

'Yes,' said Shalik. 'She did.'

It was gone eleven before Victoria returned to the office.

'Is my coat here?' she said.

'Yes,' said Shalik. 'The man returned it about half an hour ago.'

'Thank goodness,' said Victoria. 'Here, give it to me,' she ordered.

Jan handed it over and straight-away Victoria started going through the pockets; the right one, nothing, empty, and then the left, again nothing.

'No, no this cannot be right,' she said, and tried again. Still nothing, both pockets were completely empty.

'What's the matter?' said Jan, seeing Victoria getting more and more stressed.

'It is not here,' said Victoria.

'What isn't?' said Shalik.

'The key... it is not here,' she said again.

'What key?' said Shalik.

Victoria looked at Jan. 'It's ok, I'm needed on reception,' she said, sensing a confidential moment was required. She left and shut the door.

'I left the money... at the bus station in a, how do you say...? A locker. I put the key in my pocket, in my coat,' she said.

'A locker? You mean... you put the money for Oleksi in a luggage locker?' he said incredulously.

'It has worked before. It is very safe,' said Victoria, sensing a degree of criticism in the tone of his voice.

Shalik thought for a moment. 'There must be ways of getting it,' he said.

'I don't know without the key,' she said. 'I will need to speak to Amir.'

'He will not be pleased,' said Shalik.

'I know,' said Victoria.

'What about Oleksi?' he said.

'I will have to tell him what has happened. He will be down soon,' she said.

While Victoria was speaking to Amir, Shalik took the key to the cloakroom and had a search around.

He returned to the office. Victoria saw him. 'I have spoken to Amir, he is coming,' she said.

'Ok, I have looked again, there is nothing in the cloakroom,' he said.

'They must have duplicates,' said Shalik, 'at the bus station.'

'Yes,' said Victoria.

It was quarter to twelve before Amir arrived and entered the hotel just as Oleksi came out of the lift and headed for reception. Victoria was waiting anxiously in the office. Jan recognised Amir and let him in. Shalik greeted his brother and looked at his face with some concern. 'Your eye, it is ok now?' he said.

'Yes, it is nothing, it will be fine,' he said.

Oleksi stood at the desk. 'I want to speak to Victoria,' he demanded.

'I will just get her,' said Jan.

Having been told of Oleksi's presence, Victoria came out of the office. 'Come through,' she said and she held open the hatch for him to go through to the office.

'Would you like some coffee?' said Shalik when Oleksi appeared.

'Thank you, no. I just need the key and I can get back to

London; Vasyl will be waiting.'

Shalik looked at Amir. 'Actually there is a problem,' said Amir. 'The key is missing.'

'What do you mean, the key is missing?' said Oleksi.

'Tell him,' said Amir, looking at Victoria, and she explained what had happened.

'I cannot believe you have been so stupid,' he said. 'I will need to speak to Vasyl, but I will not leave here without the money.'

'Of course,' said Amir. 'We are working on it.'

Oleksi left the office and reception and walked towards the front door with his phone fixed to his ear.

Meanwhile, inside, some tough talking was taking place. 'What do we do?' asked Shalik. 'We can't replace the money today. We have to get that key.'

'Or get into the locker,' said Amir, deep in thought.

Victoria entered the debate. 'What if the key has been stolen?'

Amir looked at Shalik, then back at Victoria. 'What do you mean?' asked Amir.

'What if the key was stolen from the coat?' she clarified.

'But who would do that...? And why? No-one knows what the key would open,' said Amir.

'No, that is true, but maybe they could find out,' said Victoria.

'You don't think it could be the Ukrainians,' said Shalik.

Amir looked at him in disbelief.

'That makes no sense. It is their money,' said Amir.

'But if they stole the money they could say we hadn't paid and we have to pay again,' said Shalik.

Amir recognised the tenuous logic but dismissed it. 'Well it is possible but I don't think so. We work well with them,' said Amir.

'Do you trust them though?' said Shalik.

'Yes,' said Amir. 'I think so. They have always delivered.'

A similar conversation was taking place in the hotel grounds between Oleksi and Vasyl Hudzik, his boss in London.

'Do you trust them?' said Vasyl, who had been remarkably calm about the whole thing. Oleksi knew that this was not necessarily a good sign. Vasyl would regularly appear to be thinking things through then inexplicably explode into a vicious rage. He recalled one basement incident where Vasyl was interrogating a suspected informant who was trussed up in a chair. He appeared to be discussing the situation quite rationally with the informant, and then suddenly plunged a knife into the man's right thigh. After the screams had died down, he repeated the sadistic act on the unfortunates left thigh. Then after the man had confessed, Vasyl took out both the man's eyes before plunging the knife into his ribs.

The ferocity had frightened Oleksi and the two other gang members that were present. They knew not to get on the wrong side of Vasyl Hudzik.

'I trust no-one,' said Oleksi. 'I will stay here until we get the money.'

'Yes, that would be sensible,' said Vasyl. 'Call me when you have it.'

The line went dead and Oleksi contemplated the discussion and what he would do as he walked back to the hotel.

Back in the office, Victoria returned to the theft possibility.

'If someone had stolen it and found out where the key belonged, they would go to the locker, wouldn't they?' she said.

That got Amir's attention. 'We should get down there,' he said. 'I will call Uri and Victor, get them to meet us at the bus station.'

'But if it is not, you could be waiting there for nothing,' said Shalik.

'Yes, that is true, but we can ask about lost keys. People lose keys, it must happen,' said Amir. 'If not, we will break it open.'

'That will be dangerous. There will be many cameras,' said

Shalik.

'Yes,' said Amir. 'Let us hope it does not come to that.'

Jan had let Oleksi through and he came back into the office.

'So what have you decided?' asked Oleksi.

'We are going to the bus station,' said Amir, 'to try to get the money.'

'I hope you are successful,' said Oleksi. 'It will be a pity to upset our good relationship.'

'Yes, we will not do that. You will get your money. I promise that,' said Amir.

'I have spoken to Vasyl and he has told me I cannot leave here without it so I will stay here until you have it. Maybe Victoria can keep me company, yes?' said Oleksi.

Victoria was in a corner. She was beginning to despise the man and his sexual preferences.

Amir looked at Victoria. 'Of course, Victoria would be very willing to keep you company. Won't you dear?'

Victoria feigned a smile. 'Of course,' she said, but her body language this time was far from convincing.

'Excellent,' said Oleksi.

Victoria picked up her coat and followed him out of the office. 'You will let me know when you have the money?' he said as he walked away. 'There is no hurry,' he added, and patted Victoria's bottom.

'Wait,' called Amir. Victoria returned to the desk.

'What is the number?' he said. 'You know it?'

'Yes,' said Victoria. 'Sixty-three,' she whispered and turned back.

Amir watched the couple head towards the lift.

Amir looked at Shalik. 'I don't like him. I am worried about Victoria.'

'What choice do we have?' said Shalik.

It was twelve-fifteen and Amir and Shalik left the hotel and walked to the car park.

'I said we will meet Uri at the bus station. I told him to bring the gun,' Amir said as he got in the BMW.

CHAPTER TEN

It was around twelve-forty when Amir parked up in the multi-storey and he and Shalik descended the three floors to the pedestrian exit. Victor and Uri had arrived in their Ford Transit and were waiting by the car park entrance; they were both wearing hoodies despite the mild weather. At Amir's suggestion they had parked in one of the service bays directly behind the bus station, in case they needed to leave in a hurry, he had said. Another white van would not cause any concern.

It was Amir who outlined what he planned to do.

'We will wait for a while and if no-one comes, we will open the locker. You have something, Uri?' asked Amir.

'Yes,' said Uri, and opened his jacket. There was a jemmy protruding from his inside pocket. 'Victor has the gun,' he added as the four walked towards the terminal building. Early afternoon and the whole area was teaming with people heading to the shops or returning with their goods. Buses were leaving or arriving in a continuous stream.

They walked through the automatic glass doors and into main the building. The quaintly named "Haven Cafe" on the left was doing a roaring trade and the nauseous smell of processed food filtered through into the walkway. To the right, destination boards flashed details of arrivals and departures. Anxious passengers scanned them seeking their ride. Children were running around, out of control. Down the corridor, towards the lockers, Amir noticed the deserted left-luggage information kiosk; it closed at twelve-thirty on Saturdays it said on the notice.

'That answers that question,' said Amir to Shalik. Victor and Uri were walking a couple of paces ahead of them. 'We will have to force it open.'

The lockers stretched before them, left and right in banks of three. They followed the numbers and found number sixty-three down the left-hand annex on the right. The area was deserted.

They examined it closely. 'Seems ok, it is still closed,' said Shalik. 'Yes,' said Amir.

The lockers worked on a default 'open' when not in use.

'What do you want us to do?' said Uri.

'We will split up. You and Victor go back up the corridor, get a sandwich or something, and wait. There are some benches there. If anyone comes, keep an eye on them,' said Amir.

'But what if no-one comes?' said Shalik.

'We will wait for one hour, then break it open,' said Amir.

'What about the cameras?' said Uri.

'We will wait over there by the door,' he said, nodding his head in the direction of the emergency exit. 'There are no cameras there. Remember, just act normal. It will be ok,' replied Amir.

Uri and Victor were retracing their steps towards the cafe when Uri noticed a man walking towards them. He seemed anxious, looking around as if checking the CCTV cameras and appeared to be hiding his face when he spotted one.

The man walked past and Uri attracted Victor's attention.

'Did you see that man?' said Uri.

'Yes,' said Victor. 'We follow I think.'

They turned and watched as the man appeared to be looking at the lockers. He went right and Uri and Victor followed close enough to keep him in sight. The man was following the numbers and didn't notice them. He walked down the left-hand aisle and stopped immediately in front of locker sixty-three. Amir and Shalik had also seen the man and walked towards him from the opposite direction.

'It's him,' whispered Shalik to Amir, 'the one who returned the coat.'

He seemed to have difficulty inserting the key but after a couple of goes managed to open the lock. Uri watched him make a grab for the holdall and drop it to the floor. He had his hands around the handles as if he were trying to open it. Victor was on him and placed a hand around the man's shoulders.

'Leave the bag and come with us,' said Victor.

Uri watched Victor discretely take the gun from his jacket pocket and thrust it into the man's body.

'I have a gun. Do not make this difficult. Walk this way,' said Victor with his right arm around the man's shoulder in a friendly manner. The gun was in Victor's left hand, pushing discretely into the man's ribs. Uri picked up the holdall and handed it to Amir, who had now joined them.

'Take him to the hotel. I will meet you there,' Amir whispered out of earshot. 'Cover his eyes, make sure he cannot see,' and he and Shalik walked back into the main building. Amir had taken charge of the holdall.

Victor walked towards the emergency exit where Amir and Shalik had been waiting, with his right arm still around the man's shoulder; his left pushing the gun sharply into his ribs. Uri overtook them and opened the frosted-glass door. The Transit was parked in a loading bay to the left, about twenty feet away.

'There... the van, get in,' ordered Victor.

Uri slid back the passenger door and pulled down the seat.

'In,' Victor barked, and the man climbed in behind the seat. Victor followed. Uri was in the driver's seat and passed Victor a scarf from the door storage well.

'Turn around,' said Victor.

The man complied and suddenly the scarf was placed around his head, denying him any visual sense. The fear was overwhelming and the man started shaking uncontrollably.

'Keep very quiet,' said Victor. He started checking the man's pockets and found his mobile phone.

'I will take that,' said Victor.

He slid open the back of the phone, took out the SIM card and passed it to Uri, who wound down the window and threw it away. Uri started the Transit and headed out of the bus station, then took the road back to the hotel.

The man was still shaking. 'Where are you taking me?' he said, his voice quivering. 'I'm sorry about the bag. I just wanted to see what was in it. I wasn't going to steal it, honest.'

There was no response. 'Look, I have a family, they'll be worried,' he said.

'Be quiet,' said Victor.

Meanwhile, Amir and Shalik had returned to the hotel with the money. Jan was still on reception and she opened the hatch for them. 'Where is Oleksi?' Amir asked her.

'Still in his room I think,' she said.

Amir went into the office and picked up one of the phones and dialled.

'Oleksi? I have your money,' Amir said.

Amir looked at Shalik. 'He is coming,' he said.

Ten minutes later, Oleksi was at reception. Amir handed over the holdall with the money.

'Sorry you have been waiting, I hope everything is ok now,' he said.

Oleksi felt the weight of the bag.

'Yes, everything is... how you say? Cool,' he replied. 'And Victoria has been most accommodating so the time, it was not wasted. Vasyl, he will be in touch,' he replied, and walked off through the swing doors of the front entrance.

Amir looked at Shalik and breathed a sigh of relief.

'We still have a problem to resolve,' said Shalik. Amir looked quizzically. 'The thief...? What do you intend to do?'

'Ah, I am not sure. Let's wait and see what he has to say,' said Amir.

A few minutes later, Uri arrived at reception. Jan went into the office and reappeared with Amir.

Uri looked around to make sure no-one was listening. 'We have the man.'

'Ok, we will let you in the delivery door around the side. We will take him down to the basement,' Amir replied.

Uri went back to the van which was idling outside the main entrance and drove it around the side of the hotel to the small maintenance door used for deliveries of laundry and produce. It was not in regular use and was also alarmed from the inside.

Amir and Shalik walked through reception and along the corridor past the lifts. To the right was another short passageway and a glass door at the end. There was a set of stairs to the left with a notice 'private, staff only' appended. There was a keypad which disarmed the outside door and Shalik punched in the code and held it open. Uri drove the van as close as he could get – it was only a matter of a couple of feet to the entrance. Victor slid the van door open.

'Out,' he said, and Keith moved forward.

'I can't see,' he said.

Victor guided him from the van and pushed him quickly through the open service door. Amir grabbed him and bundled him down the flight of concrete steps to the right. Uri locked the van and he and Victor followed them. Shalik closed up and went back to reception.

Keith in his blindness was stumbling down the stairs; fear had restricted his motor responses. Victor was supporting him, Uri in front and Amir brought up the rear.

There was a storeroom at the bottom of the steps with a wooden door and small grilled window. Amir pushed in front and opened it.

'In here,' he said.

The room was empty awaiting renovation, pots of paint, ladders and other decorating material were scattered about, stored for their next outing. The stench of paint and cleaning chemicals was almost overwhelming. The man started to gag.

In the corner was a dining room chair with the seat in need of a new covering. The red faux-leather covering looked as if it had been slashed with a knife and the stuffing was hanging out.

Uri dragged it into the centre of the room. Victor led Keith forward. 'Sit,' he ordered as if he was training a dog. Keith felt for the seat and complied. There was a roll of electrical wiring on a drum next to one of the ladders and Uri picked it up and started unwinding a twenty-foot length. On the floor next to the wire was a pair of pliers. He picked them up and cut off the piece and passed it to Victor, who started to wrap it around the unfortunate thief.

'What are you doing?' he started remonstrating again. 'Ow!' he exclaimed as the wire bit into his flesh. He started hyperventilating; beads of sweat rolled down his forehead and were absorbed by the material of the scarf.

'Be quiet,' said Victor.

'Search him,' said Amir.

Uri checked his jacket pockets and pulled the contents; keys, handkerchief, wallet.

Uri passed the wallet to Amir. 'Let's see who we have,' said Amir, and he started going through the contents.

'So, you are Keith... Woodley?'

'Yes,' said Keith weakly.

'Hmm, nice children,' Amir said looking at a small family photograph which was inside one of the leather pockets of the wallet. 'How old are they?'

'Seventeen and thirteen,' said Keith.

'And what are their names?'

'Ellie and Jason.'

'Nice, nice names. The girl, she is very pretty,' said Amir.

'Yes,' Keith said.

'She would make men very happy.' He passed the photo to Uri.

'Very pretty,' said Uri. 'I would like to make love with her. It would be very sweet.'

'Leave my kids alone,' said Keith.

'You have a wife... Keith?' said Amir, deliberately using his name.

'Y... Y... Y... Yes,' stammered Keith.

'Is she pretty?' asked Amir. 'You don't have a picture. She is a dog, yes? Woof, woof,' he said. Uri and Victor laughed. Keith said nothing.

'What is her name?' asked Amir.

'Kathryn,' said Keith.

'And you live in Dunfield, it says here, yes?' said Amir, reading from his driver's licence.

'Perhaps we should pay them a call and ask them to join us; the girls anyway. Not the boy, we should shoot him. He would not want to live anyway when he finds out what we have done to his sister and mother.'

'No, no don't hurt them, kill me if you have to, but leave my family alone. They haven't done anything,' Keith pleaded.

'Well, that is true,' said Amir.

'Look, I didn't mean any harm. I was just curious. I didn't know what was in the locker. I found the key, that was all,' Keith said, his voice hardly registering.

'And where did you find the key?' asked Amir.

'It was in the coat pocket.'

'And you decided to keep it?' said Amir.

'Yes,' said Keith. 'And I'm sorry. I didn't know what I was

doing. My mind was all over the place. I am not a thief. I was desperate, that was all. I made a mistake, I'm sorry.'

'Why are you desperate, Keith?' asked Amir.

'Money, my business is about to go under.'

'You do have problems, Keith, don't you?' said Amir. Keith was barely functioning. 'And what sort of business do you have?'

'Coaches, I run coaches,' said Keith.

'Coaches,' said Amir. 'Hmm, yes the cost of fuel it is bad, yes?'

'Yes,' said Keith.

Amir was still rummaging through the wallet; he found a business card. 'Woodley's Coaches?' he said.

'Yes,' said Keith.

'I know your coaches. I have seen them. You have many,' said Amir, putting the business card in his pocket.

'No, not many,' said Keith.

Amir looked at Uri and Victor. 'We will leave you for a minute while you consider your position,' said Amir.

The three men left the room with Keith trussed up in the chair like a Christmas turkey, shaking uncontrollably.

Outside the door Amir spoke to Uri and Victor. 'I have an idea.'

'I thought we were going to kill him,' said Victor.

'I have a better idea. I think he could be useful,' said Amir.

Uri looked at Victor. 'Useful?' said Uri.

'Yes, we have transport problems, yes? Either me or Nicolai has to drive the girls every day to the factory and the hotel. We could get him to do that.' Amir stopped for a moment, letting his train of thought run like a fish on a line. He reeled in his thoughts.

'Yes... and maybe we can even get our own girls,' he said.

'But Oleksi's people do that,' said Uri.

'And it is very expensive, and dangerous. Sooner or later they will be caught and we will be in trouble too. They will find us,' he said. He paused for a moment. 'The more I think about it the more it makes sense.'

'How will we do that... get our own girls?' Uri clarified.

'FaceBook... Internet chat rooms, wherever the young people are... Hmm, yes, I will speak to Victoria,' said Amir.

'But what about the man?' said Uri. 'Surely we have to punish him.'

'We will, we will, but while he is useful to us we would be foolish not to use this to our advantage.'

Uri looked at Victor and shrugged his shoulders. 'If that is what you want,' said Uri.

'Yes it is. We will speak to Mr Woodley,' said Amir.

The door opened and Keith jumped. He was still blindfolded and had no idea what was happening.

'I have been discussing your situation with my colleagues and we have a proposition for you,' said Amir.

'Yes,' said Keith, who was prepared to do anything to make it all stop.

'You have coaches?' said Amir.

'Yes,' replied Keith.

'We need transporting things. You will work for us and take people where we need them to go,' said Amir.

'I don't know if I can. If I don't get some money soon I won't have a business,' said Keith. His head was bowed, drooping towards his chest. He had lost the will to live and seemed resigned to whatever fate awaited.

'We will pay you and there could be bonuses for certain work,' said Amir.

Keith lifted his head. He still couldn't see but it was a sign of interest.

'What do you mean?' asked Keith.

'As I have said we could have some business for you. I will discuss with my associates but we will need you every day and if it works out well, some special work... in Europe,' said Amir.

'I can do that,' said Keith in desperation. 'Anything, anything you want, I will do it.'

'There will be some conditions,' said Amir. 'Our arrangements will be between us. No-one else must know, and of course there will be serious problems if you contact the police. We will kill you, and your family, make no mistake. From now on we own you.'

'You have my word; I will do as you say. Just tell me what you want me to do,' said Keith.

Amir looked at Uri and Victor, who looked somewhat perplexed.

'You will be driven back to the car park... You have a car there, yes?'

'Yes,' said Keith.

'Where are your coaches?' said Amir.

'I have a depot in Aireford, on the Industrial Park,' said Keith, and he gave details of the location.

'Yes, I know it,' said Amir. 'I need to discuss arrangements with my associates. So tonight at nine o'clock we will meet you there and tell you what we need,' said Amir. 'You say nothing, to no-one... Understood?'

'Of course, of course, I won't say nothing, promise,' said Keith.

'Just to be sure, two of my associates will be close to your home. Just as insurance until we know we can trust you,' said Amir.

'You won't have a problem, you have my word.'

'Good, until tonight then,' said Amir, and nodded to Uri and Victor.

Victor placed his hand on Keith's shoulder and he froze; he thought he might die, but he felt the tension of the electrical flex slacken. Uri grabbed him. 'You... stand,' and Keith complied. He was trying to get the circulation in his legs and arms working and Victor and Uri had to almost drag him off the chair.

'You, come,' said Uri, and Victor led Keith through the door of the storeroom and up the stairs. Amir opened the emergency exit and Keith was bundled into the back of the Transit. Victor followed.

Keith sat there in silence, still traumatised as the van made its way back into town to the multi-storey car park. As they pulled into one of the service bays at the back of the bus station, Victor loosened the scarf and as the Transit drew to a stop, slid open the side door, removed Keith's blindfold and pushed him out. Keith lurched forward, his hands breaking his fall. The van drove off, leaving Keith sat on the tarmac, still getting his eyesight focused and checking the grazes to his palms which were bleeding. First priority, find a gents.

Amir, meanwhile, had returned to the office in the hotel where Shalik was sat talking to Victoria and outlining what had happened to the key and the capture of the thief. She was still wearing her powder-blue mini-dress, and whilst she had showered in the hotel room, she was desperate to return to her flat and change.

She was relating her experience with Oleksi. 'Never again,' she exclaimed, sipping on a glass of water. 'That man is an animal.'

Amir explained his plan regarding the coach business. 'Shalik said you were going to kill him,' said Victoria.

'Yes, I considered that, but this is better. We can have our own operation and not worry about Vasyl and Oleksi.'

'They won't be happy,' said Shalik.

'So?' said Amir. 'That is their problem. I have a plan to get our own girls and if we can collect them it will save much money and be safer.'

'But how will we get them?' said Victoria.

'We will use the Internet. We will offer them work... and love.

We will not have to use drugs like Vasyl. They will come willingly. I have been thinking... Nicolai, Victor and Uri, they can be boyfriends. Yes?' said Amir, becoming increasingly enthusiastic about his new plan.

'We will meet at the house and talk later. We can use the girls as well,' he said.

Victoria looked at him; she could see the logic.

'I don't know about Edita and Delvina... but they have seemed better these last two days. I think the change to the hotel was good. I will ask one of them to do the chat room tonight. I don't know about a video, Edita still has marks,' she said.

'You could hide them with make-up. She is very popular, she gets many hits,' said Amir.

'I will talk to her. Now Amir, can you take me home, please?' said Victoria. 'I will come to the house later to arrange tonight's work.'

'Yes, of course. I am meeting with Mr Woodley later. I will tell him what we need him to do,' said Amir.

Keith reached the gents, his legs still shaking, and he sat in one of the cubicles trying to come to terms with what had happened. It was not a prescient he had considered in any shape or form. He started to recover his senses and afterwards washed his face with cold water to get rid of the sweat, and bathed his hands. His whole body felt sticky and there were deep welts in his wrists where they had been confined by the electrical cable.

He started to get his thoughts together more rationally. First thing, get to the office; it was gone four and he would be missed. He was thinking of ways to explain his absence; Kathryn would be worrying and he had no phone. He reached his car and anxiously searched his pockets. His keys and money were still there so he would be able to get out of the car park and into the depot. He would call Kathryn from there.

It took twenty minutes through the busy afternoon traffic to reach the coach park, his mind racing with the recent course of events. As he approached, he could see two single-deckers were parked in the street nearby. Jack had obviously parked them and locked up. He got out of his car, opened the main gate and drove through, then parked in front of his office. He unlocked the door and disarmed the alarm, made for his desk and dialled the number; he had thought of an excuse.

It rang and rang. 'Come on,' he said to himself, then the pickup.

'Hello,' said Kathryn.

'It's me,' said Keith.

'Keith!! Where have you been...? We've been worried sick. I was about to call the police. I've phoned all the drivers. Jack had to leave to pick up his wife. I told him to lock up... Where have you been? What's happened?'

She spoke quickly in a mix of relief, anger and confusion.

'I'm sorry I haven't been able to get in touch. I was mugged.'

'What!?' she said in horror.

'Well not mugged exactly. I wasn't beaten up or anything.'

'What happened? Are you alright?'

'Yeah, I'm ok, just a bit shaken. After I dropped off the coat at the hotel I went into town... I wanted to do a bit of shopping before I went to the depot. While I was there I popped into the coffee shop at the bus station. You know the one, by the front entrance, The Haven or something it's called. Anyway, I had my phone on the table while I was drinking my coffee, checking some emails, and this bloke came up and just snatched it as bold as you like, and took off.'

'That's terrible. So what happened, did you catch him?' said Kathryn.

'No, I chased him into the mall but it was packed; he'd gone. So

I found one of the security guards and told him what had happened and he calls the police, didn't he? So I've been stuck at the central police station, you know, the one on Park Street, waiting to give a statement. Apparently there are gangs going around snatching bags and phones... immigrants, they said, and they want to get them. I had to give descriptions and everything. Took ages,' he said. 'I couldn't phone or anything.'

It seemed plausible and Kathryn was gradually calming down. 'Thank goodness you're ok. I didn't say anything to the kids. Didn't want to worry them; they're both out.'

'Ok, good, look I'm going to get the buses in the yard and tidy up a bit, then I'm going to need to sort out a new phone, so I'll have to pop back into town. I'll be in by six I hope,' he said.

'Ok, I'll get the dinner on for then. Do you need to go out later?'

'Yes, Bruce's got a bus out to Birmingham expected back about nine-ish.'

'Can't you get someone else to lock up, after what you've been through?' said Kathryn.

'There isn't anyone... Anyway, I'll be alright.'

'Ok, see you later,' said Kathryn, and she rang off.

Keith exhaled, hoping his lie would hold. It was the best he could come up with.

As he sat at his desk, the shock was beginning to overwhelm him; he found it difficult to concentrate and his hands were shaking uncontrollably. He needed a stiff drink, something to make it go away, but that was not an option. Suddenly his financial worries were the least of his problems.

He shook himself. 'Come on, come on,' he kept saying as if by way of motivation; no-one else was going to put the buses to bed. He managed to get himself out of the chair and exited the office. After putting the coaches in their bays he locked up the compound and headed back into town to get a replacement phone. That was another lengthy process. Explaining what had happened to the phone shop people had been difficult but after ranting at the poor assistant he was eventually able to get a replacement straight away. The old one had been blocked. He was given a new number which would mean getting in touch with all his friends and business contacts to advise them of the change, more hassle. As he drove away his mind was again racing. He blamed himself for his stupidity and this was someone's punishment, he had decided. It would never happen again he told himself. Then there was the meeting; he was dreading that. He would not say anything to anyone.

It was just turned six before he was able to return to Dunfield. Kathryn was waiting anxiously for him, peering out of the window every time a car went by.

Hearing the car pull up, she opened the door for him. Kathryn's new coat was still on the back seat and Keith carried it carefully into the house and handed it to her. He looked at it; it had caused him a lot of problems. She put it over the arm of the settee and gave him a hug.

'I was so worried,' she said. 'I really thought something had happened to you.'

Keith considered this; something, of course, had, but he would say nothing to alarm her. It was his problem and he would deal with it.

CHAPTER ELEVEN

Victoria returned to the house in Argyle Avenue around six-thirty, having changed into something more comfortable, and warmer. Amir had explained to Nicolai that he was getting someone to ferry the girls every morning and was sharing his plan of attracting girls via the Internet.

'We can then go and collect them rather than use the Ukrainians,' said Amir.

'How will you do that?' asked Nicolai.

'Ah, let's just say we have a new associate who will help us,' said Amir. Nicolai was intrigued but knew better than to pry further.

'What do you think, Nicolai?' said Victoria, who had overheard the conversation as she walked into the office. 'Could you set something up... on the Internet, so we get girls to want to come here?'

He looked at her with a degree of enthusiasm. 'Yes, I know how to do that; I can open up some accounts tonight and get started.'

Edita and Delvina were in the kitchen, the Macedonians were in the sleeping quarters getting ready for the chat room duties.

Victoria took off her jacket and joined the two girls in the kitchen.

'How are you today?' she asked.

'OK,' said Edita unenthusiastically. 'We sleep this morning. Last night, it was late. Now it is just so boring we have nothing to do.'

Victoria had forgotten they had been working at the hotel the previous evening. Nicolai had collected them at two a.m. The boredom was a major issue but she was not prepared to let them go out on their own, not yet anyway. She had a thought.

'I was going to ask if you feel like making a video again... with Uri or Victor. There will not be anyone else after what has happened. I promise. I will pay one hundred pounds. I will give you some of my magic powder if you wish.'

'No it is not necessary,' said Edita. 'I am ok.'

Having not done any extra work for almost a week their cash-books were getting low and Edita had already considered the prospect. 'Ok, I will do it,' she said.

'I want to do it also. We need money,' said Delvina. 'Is that ok?' she added, looking at Victoria.

'You don't have to,' said Edita.

'No, I want to,' said Delvina.

Victoria looked at her. 'Are you sure?'

'Yes, for one hundred pounds,' she replied.

Victoria thought about the proposal for a moment. 'Hmm... both of you? That is a lot of money.'

'It will be worth it,' said Delvina, looking at Edita.

'Ok, I will phone Uri and Victor. They will be happy I am sure.'

Edita and Delvina were engaged in some urgent discussion but Delvina was adamant she would participate.

So that was the business side completed. The Macedonians would do the chat rooms, Edita and Delvina would film a video with Uri and Victor. Nicolai would be the cameraman and Victoria would look after the Internet feed.

Victoria went back to the office and explained the plan to Amir.

'Excellent,' he said. 'We need new material, our customers they expect it. We should get many hits tonight.'

Amir walked into the kitchen to talk to the girls and turned to Victoria. 'I will be going out later with Uri so Victor can do the video and then Uri can do his when we return.'

At eight-thirty, with the house a hive of activity, Amir and Uri left to go to the coach depot and their meeting with Keith. Amir outlined his ideas to Uri, which were taking a definite shape.

'Yes, that is good,' said Uri.

It took about twenty minutes to reach the Woodley's bus garage. The main gates were open and they drove through and parked in front of the office. Keith had heard the car draw up and was starting to shake again. The earlier fear had returned.

He opened the door and let the two men in. 'This way,' he said, and took them into his office.

Amir and Uri sat down without being invited; Keith sat opposite, behind his desk, trying to maintain an air of control.

He looked at the men: Amir, resembling a terrorist, with a short black beard and thick dark hair which cascaded in waves to his collar; and Uri, shaven-headed like some sort of Russian enforcer. It was just as he had envisaged them, which did nothing to alleviate the threat he felt.

'You said you had a proposition,' said Keith, with about as much authority as he could muster.

'Yes,' said Amir.

'Ok, I'm listening,' said Keith, trying to give the impression that there was some room for negotiation. There wasn't.

'I have discussed your situation with my business associates and we want to... how can I say this? Utilise...? Is that the right word?' He looked at Uri, who smiled. 'Yes, utilise, I like that word... utilise your operation.'

'What do you mean... utilise?' said Keith.

'As I explained earlier, we have need of transportation and you have what we need,' said Amir.

'You mean you want to take over my business?' said Keith.

'No, not at all, not that; just use your services. I do not have the time to run your business,' said Amir.

'I'm listening,' said Keith, which sounded more confident than he was feeling.

'We will pay well for the service. You need business, yes?' said Amir.

'Yes,' said Keith looking down at his desk.

'There will be... how you say...? Conditions. We will want you to do the driving for us... You drive, yes?'

'Yes,' said Keith. 'That won't be a problem.'

'You will tell no-one about our arrangement. Is that clear?' said Amir.

'Perfectly,' said Keith.

All this time Uri just watched Keith, and the attention was spooking him. Keith shifted anxiously in the chair, uncomfortable with the scrutiny.

'How will this work?' said Keith.

'I have a company called Azure Recruitment Services. They will contact you and arrange everything. We will need you to go in Europe as well from time to time. You can do that?' said Amir.

'Yes, but I'll need another driver. It's the law,' said Keith.

Amir thought for a moment. 'Ok, I will get one of my associates to go with you. But I will let you know about that when we are ready.'

'You mentioned payment,' said Keith.

'Yes,' said Amir.

'You know the business is in trouble. If I can't pay for fuel it will close and there's nothing I can do about that,' said Keith. 'It's the recession.'

'We need to make sure it doesn't then,' said Amir. 'I might even be able to put more business your way.'

Keith looked up at the two men, trying to work out the motive. This afternoon, he had been sure they were going to kill him, and now they wanted to save his business?

'When will you want me to start?' asked Keith.

'Monday, just a short journey... we will pay your normal rate plus we will give you some more. You tell us how much.'

Keith looked at Amir. 'Why would you do that?'

'To ensure you have a business we can use. It is in both our interests, and there will be a bonus for the overseas work,' said Amir. He looked at Keith. 'The other condition is straightforward. You know what will happen if you say anything or cause us problems?'

'Yes,' said Keith.

'Make no mistake. You have been very fortunate today, but you are on trial, ok? If it goes well then you will have paid your debt, but if not, then...' Amir's face reflected the seriousness of the message. 'We will kill you and your family,'

'Yes, I get that,' said Keith, looking down at the desk again. This was clearly no reprieve.

Amir looked at him. 'You have a phone number where we can call you?'

'Yes,' said Keith, and he gave Amir the number of his new mobile.

'Expect a call tomorrow. We will need to take some people to work, that is all. You have a small bus?' said Amir.

'A minibus you mean?' said Keith.

'Yes,' said Amir.

'Yes, I can let you have one of those. We use them for some school runs. What time?'

'We will let you know,' said Amir. 'Early.'

Keith looked at the men and was asking himself what on earth he had got into here; a simple decision, ill-judged, born out of desperation, and only now were the repercussions beginning to emerge.

'We have finished here,' said Amir, and he and Uri got up. 'We will call you tomorrow,' he said, and walked out.

Keith stayed in his chair and did not stir for several minutes; when he did his movements were laboured. Everything seemed so much effort. A thought crossed his mind; the ultimate way out, then all his problems would be gone. He jumped as the phone on his desk rang and snapped him out of his ruminations.

'Hello,' he said, picking up the receiver. 'Oh, hi... no, Bruce shouldn't be long though. He said about ten. I'll give him a call and see how long he is going to be. Yeah, ok.'

He replaced the receiver. He wished he could tell Kathryn what was happening but she would only worry; he was on his own.

He picked up the phone again and dialled the driver's mobile. All the large coaches were fitted with hands-free phone kits. The call connected. 'Ten minutes,' said Bruce in answer to Keith's enquiry.

Just a few minutes after ten the coach pulled into the depot and Keith went out to meet it. After a short exchange Bruce gave Keith a cheque. 'Thanks, any problems?' asked Keith.

'No 't'were fine, no singing thank goodness. Think they were too knackered after traipsing around the NEC all day.'

'Thanks Bruce, see you Monday,' said Keith.

The driver got in his car and drove away, and Keith went back to his office and locked the cheque in the petty cash tin ready for banking on Monday. He closed up and left the depot. Sleep would not come easily tonight.

Later, at Argyle Avenue, it was a busy Saturday night. Delvina and Victor were at the monitors watching Edita shooting her video with Uri. Amir was chatting with Victoria who was updating him on the new social media enterprise. 'Nicolai has been very busy,' she said. 'Victor and Nicolai have their own pages and already attracting many girls,' she said. 'Uri will have his when he has finished the video.'

'That is good,' said Amir.

'How long before we can get some girls here?' said Victoria.

'I don't know, maybe one month. We will have to see but soon I hope,' replied Amir. 'Next week I will speak to Mr Jones and see what he needs.'

Sunday morning in Dunfield, and Keith was in the kitchen making a cup of tea. It was six-thirty a.m. He had had little sleep and had got up to avoid disturbing Kathryn. His head was all over the place and suddenly his financial worries seemed a minor consideration. The fact that the new business opportunity might just save his livelihood was of little comfort if he was going to be living in fear for the rest of his life. But there was no alternative; what's done is done.

Keith mooched about the house for a while, walked in the garden, and then sat at his desk in his small den, staring at his computer screen and trying to do some admin. Concentration levels were non-existent. Kathryn came down the stairs about eight o'clock.

'I wondered where you were,' she said. 'You ok?'

'Yeah,' said Keith.

'You're not worrying about that mugging are you?'

Keith had to think for a moment. 'Mugging...? Oh... no, no nothing like that, just trying to work out some new work rotas. I'm going to be doing more driving, save some money. Can't be stuck in the office all day.'

'It is ok is it...? The business, I mean. You're not in any trouble or anything are you? Only I know that it's been quiet recently. One of the driver's wives was telling me the other day,' she said.

'Who was that?' he asked.

'Brenda Shawcroft, Dave Shawcroft's wife I bumped into her

in Tesco's and she was telling me,' she said. 'I told her you never tell me anything.'

'Nah, it's often quiet this time of year. It'll pick up now the schools are back. In fact, I'm starting a new contract next week which will help, and if it works out we should pick up more work on the back of it,' he said, trying to deflect the earlier question.

'As long as you're ok... Do you want a cup of tea?'

'Yeah, thanks, and don't worry, everything's fine,' said Keith, and he was back on the computer aimlessly tapping the keys.

Keith couldn't settle and at eleven o'clock headed off to the depot. There were no runs today but he could do with the peace and quiet. Ellie and Jason were up and the house had begun to sound like a mobile disco.

He was in the depot checking one of the coaches when he got the call. It was a woman's voice, not English.

'Hello, I am calling from Azure Recruitment. You are helping us with some taxi, yes?'

'Yes,' said Keith.

'You will take people from a house in Argyle Avenue to Hayfield Hotel and to Hyams factory tomorrow at quarter to seven and seven-thirty. Is that possible?'

'Argyle Avenue, that in Aireford?' he said.

'Yes.'

'Whereabouts?' he said.

She gave him directions. 'Yeah, I know roughly. Could be tight, that time of day, rush hour,' he replied.

'You will do it?' she said.

'I'll give it a go, tomorrow, quarter to seven, Argyle Avenue?'

'Yes, to hotel then you come back and take more to factory,' she clarified.

'Yeah, I'll be there,' he said, and rang off.

He considered the brief. Hayfield Manor Hotel, now that was a coincidence. He shivered at the memory. The coat; it's where it all started. It gave him a weird feeling of déjà vu.

He had another call about twelve-thirty from Kathryn to see if he wanted any lunch. 'No ta, I'll get a sandwich,' he said; he needed to be on his own.

Back at home, Kathryn was concerned about Keith; she hadn't seen him so distant. With the children visiting friends, she had the house to herself and was deep in thought. Cleaning didn't appeal and now it was her turn to feel restless. Then suddenly there was a buzzing noise coming from her handbag; it was her mobile phone. She considered possible callers as she reached to retrieve the phone. She looked at the screen... number withheld.

She pressed the call button. 'Hello.'

'Hi, Kathryn?' said the caller.

'Yes.'

'It's Steve. Is it convenient to talk?'

Kathryn didn't immediately register. 'Steve...? Oh, hi, yes, yes, sorry.'

'You ok? You sounded a bit stressed yesterday.'

'Oh, yes, sorry about that, Keith got himself mugged. It was all a bit frantic.'

'Mugged? Is he ok?'

'Yeah, someone grabbed his phone, that's all... wasn't hurt or anything.'

'Oh... right, as long as he's ok... Look I was just ringing to see if you wanted to go out for a drink sometime. I enjoyed your company on Friday.'

'That's a nice thought Steve, but... I'm not sure that's a good idea.'

'It could be fun.'

'Hmm fun, remind me,' said Kathryn.

'I would love to show you,' said Steve.

'Let me think about it,' said Kathryn. 'Give me your number. I'll give you a call.'

'Ok,' said Steve, and he gave Kathryn the number. 'I don't give up easily.'

'Pleased to hear it,' said Kathryn. 'I'll call you.'

'Make it soon,' said Steve, and he rang off.

Kathryn looked at her phone for a moment and put the piece of paper with Steve's number on it into the side pocket of her purse. Much to her surprise the call had given her a much-needed boost; it had been a long time since she had been propositioned. She suddenly felt more energised. The oven cleaning beckoned; she would take out her frustrations on the cooker.

Back at the depot, the office phone rang. Keith thought it would be Kathryn again.

'Hello,' he said, without the normal business courtesies.

'Is that Woodley Coaches?' said the caller.

'Sorry, yes. Keith Woodley here.'

'Hi Keith, it's Steve, Steve Jones.'

There was a pause. 'Of course... sorry Steve, I've got my head in paperwork. What can I do for you?'

'It was about the discussion we had on Friday. Got a couple of airport pick-ups this week, wondered if you would like them.'

'Yes, yes, that would be great,' said Keith, remembering too late to stop himself from coming across too enthusiastically. 'Bugger,' he said to himself.

'Let me have the details,' said Keith, and Steve explained his requirements.

'I'll have some more coming up. There are some pick-ups at Heathrow as well. Do you have a limo as part of your fleet by any chance?' said Steve.

'No, but I can get hold of one,' said Keith. 'I've got a driver I use sometimes for prestige clients.'

'Excellent,' said Keith. 'I'll get someone from the office to confirm over the next couple of days,' said Steve.

'Cheers,' said Keith, and Steve rang off.

Keith sat for a moment, hardly able to take in the change of fortune, on the business front at least; just maybe there was a chance.

By four o'clock he was becoming weary of the office; the walls were starting to close in. He shut down his computer and locked up. Kathryn was in the lounge watching TV when she heard his car pull onto the drive.

'Hi, you ok?' she said as Keith came in and took off his jacket.

'Yeah, managed to clear a pile of paperwork,' which was a bit of an exaggeration, his productivity level had been minimal. 'You never guess what, I had a call from that Steve bloke, you know, the one from the dinner on Friday.'

Kathryn was on alert. 'Steve...? Oh, yes I remember. What did he want?'

'Well, you remember on Friday he said he wanted to use us for airport runs an' stuff but I didn't think anything would come of it but it just goes to show? Wants two pick-ups next week, with more to come.'

'Well that's good, isn't it...? Would you like a cup of tea? I was just about to make one,' she said, changing the subject.

'Yeah, thanks,' said Keith, and he sat down, picked up the Sunday paper and started to read.

Sunday in Argyle Avenue, Victoria had arrived early to oversee the new Internet campaign to attract young girls. Victor and Uri were also in and working the social media sites, trying to attract new friends and nurturing existing followers. Nicolai was opening new accounts and registering aliases – Victor and Uri now both had three accounts in different names in an effort to attract more followers.

Victoria, however, wanted the girls out of the way, the less they knew about the new enterprise the better.

'Nicolai, how would you like to take the girls to the mall today? I think they have deserved a treat.'

Nicolai looked up from one of the screens. 'Sure, I'll take them.'

So when Edita and Delvina came downstairs around nine-thirty, Victoria posed the question. 'How would you like to go shopping today?'

Edita's enthusiasm was only lukewarm. 'Yeah, ok.'

'You and Delvina did well yesterday, you have money now you can spend,' she said.

Edita looked at Delvina. 'When can we phone our parents?' she said.

'Soon, very soon,' Victoria replied.

Delvina was in tears and Edita hugged her.

'I'm sorry,' said Victoria, seeing Delvina's distress. 'It won't be for much longer.'

Marija, Elena and Bijana came into the lounge and Victoria announced the shopping trip; there was more enthusiasm. The girls looked at each other with big smiles. 'Are you coming?' she asked Edita.

'Yes,' she replied.

Monday morning, six-thirty-five a.m., and Edita, Delvina and Marija were waiting for their lift to the hotel. They were wearing new clothes.

The Sunday shopping trip had proved to be a useful distraction and with money available the girls had spent most of the day at the mall. The exhilaration of Marija and her two friends as they went from store to store trying on outfits was contagious, and soon

Edita and Delvina were caught up in the excitement. It had served to lift the depression that had been hanging over the Albanians like a dark cloud, retail therapy in every sense. They returned to the house carrying carrier bags of clothes and chatting animatedly as they swapped experiences.

There was a surprise waiting for the girls when they returned from the shops. While they had been away Victoria had acquired a TV for their bedroom. She thought that it would help dispel the boredom, idle hands and all that; it might also help to improve their English. Nicolai was tasked with setting it up in the attic, a two-minute job for the savvy Ukrainian. Edita and Delvina made the most of the new acquisition and spent most of the evening watching unfamiliar programmes, continually switching channels to find something they could understand. There was nothing in Albanian. Chat-room duties, meanwhile, had been undertaken by the Macedonians, who were only too pleased to replenish their cash-books after their spending spree.

Right on time there was the sound of a vehicle pulling up outside the house, followed by a knock on the door. Keith had arrived to take the girls to the hotel. As this was the first journey, Amir had insisted that the girls were accompanied and Nicolai would do the honours. He led the three to the minibus and opened the door to the passenger seats behind the driver, and they got in. Nicolai got into the front next to Keith.

'Hayfield Manor Hotel?' said Keith.

'That is right,' said Nicolai.

Keith couldn't pinpoint the accent exactly, but it sounded Eastern European. He set off.

'My name's Keith by the way,' he said, trying to engage with his new client.

'Yes,' said Nicolai. 'I know.'

That killed off any chance of banter. The girls also said nothing.

They arrived at the front entrance of the hotel just after ten past seven and Keith got out and opened the door for the passengers. Nicolai shouted to them. 'We will be here at five o'clock.'

'Ok,' said Edita.

Keith headed back to the house.

'We're gonna be cutting it a bit fine,' he said.

Nicolai didn't understand the colloquialism.

'What do you mean?' said Nicolai.

'The traffic... it may be gone seven-thirty when we get back,' he said. 'There's nothing I can do.'

'It is ok,' said Nicolai. 'We have time.'

'Ok, you're the customer, but don't say I didn't warn you,' said Keith.

Keith hadn't slept well again, wondering what this new partnership would entail. He considered all kinds of possibilities; drugs were the favourite, and he wrestled with his conscience but he knew he had little choice in the matter; the threat for non-compliance was real. The irony was that it might just save the business, and for that he would deal with the devil himself. So far the trips to and from the house were easy money, no sign of narcotics; it was just like a school run. A taxi service, that was all; that did get him thinking. As he was driving he had a brainwave, a new business model. Given the slowdown in coach hire he could sell some of his surplus single-deckers and lease a couple more minibuses. That would release some cash and reduce his outgoings. If his new partners wanted minibuses, then they would have minibuses. Then there was Steve and his airport runs; he couldn't use coaches... or double-deckers, plain daft. Yes, that makes a lot of sense.

He pulled up outside the house again; it was turned seven-forty.

'Well we're back. It's the best I could do. You've seen the traffic,' he said to Nicolai.

'It is ok,' said Nicolai. 'Wait here.'

Nicolai went in and returned a couple of minutes later with Elena and Bijana. There had been words; they were unhappy with having to return to the factory, especially as Marija was still at the hotel. Nicolai promised to speak to Victoria, which placated them for the moment.

They climbed into the back, with Nicolai back next to Keith.

'We go to factory,' said Nicolai.

'Hyams?' said Keith.

'Yes,' said Nicolai, and that was it. Keith dropped the girls off just before eight, and then returned with Nicolai back to the house. On the way back Nicolai gave Keith instructions for the return trip that afternoon. The hotel pick-up was at five, Hyams at six.

'Same time again tomorrow morning,' said Nicolai as he got out. Keith whispered something under his breath which sounded like 'ignorant pillock', but the Ukrainian wouldn't have heard.

Keith headed back to the depot, happy with his morning's work. He made a mental note of the fare, and then added the twenty per cent. He would start the invoice as soon as he got into the office. For the first time for a while he felt motivated. If that's all his new business partners needed, it was going to be a doddle; somehow, though, he thought it might not be.

Jack Clayton was already at the depot and was walking towards the office when he saw the minibus arrive. He waited for Keith to stop and went over to greet him.

'Hiyup,' he said as Keith got out. 'You're an early bird.'

'Aye,' said Keith. 'Got a new contract; started today.'

'That's good news, boss,' he replied.

'Yes... Have you got a minute? I need to discuss something with you,' said Keith. He saw Jack's reaction. 'Don't worry, it's good news for a change.'

'Aye,' said Jack, and followed Keith to the office.

'What happened to you on Saturday?' said Jack as he sat down opposite Keith's chair.

'Saturday?' said Keith with a look of surprise. 'Oh, yes, Saturday... I got mugged.'

'Mugged?' said Jack, and Keith outlined the same story that he had told Kathryn as he boiled the kettle and made two coffees.

He then went on to explain his idea to streamline the business.

'We can't afford to have twenty-six seaters lying empty and I'm not sure about the double-deckers either. We make next to nothing on the school runs,' said Keith.

'We're under contract,' said Jack.

'We can give a month's notice,' said Keith.

'Can't see you getting anymore council contracts if you do that,' said Jack.

'Not bothered,' said Keith. 'More trouble than they're worth. We can get rid of the double-deckers and replace them with the new Merc Execs,' he added.

'What, the nine-seaters?' said Jack.

'Yeah, we can charge premium prices. I was speaking to Steve Jones on Friday, he owns Hyams.'

'What, Hyams Fabrics?' said Jack.

'Yeah, we're going to be doing some airport runs and some exec chauffeuring.'

'But that's great... Well as you say, it makes sense,' said Jack.

So having bounced the idea off his trusted works manager, Keith spent the morning setting his plan in motion. He had not felt this enthusiastic since he started the business.

Back at the hotel, things could not have been different. Edita was beginning to despair of their situation. Despite promises, they had not been allowed to contact their family, who would be frantic with worry. If only she could contact them.

The opportunity happened quite by fortune. She parked her cleaning trolley outside room 208 and, as usual, she knocked on the door and opened it with her master key card. 'Room Service,' she called as she had been trained to do.

There was no reply and she walked in with her bucket and cloths in one hand, dragging the vacuum cleaner in the other. No-one was in but straight away she noticed something on the desk opposite the bed. Someone had left their phone charging. Now was the chance.

CHAPTER TWELVE

Edita looked at the phone, and then shut the door which would normally be left open while the rooms were being cleaned. She plugged in the vacuum cleaner, trying to decide what to do. If she were caught there was no comprehending what might happen; she could even be killed. She put her cloths down on the desk and stared at the phone again for a moment; then picked it up and examined it. It was not the same model as her own, but back home she was always texting or emailing friends so was completely familiar with the functions. The main problem would be if it was password protected. She pressed the call button and the screen saver appeared. She was in luck, there was no password.

She knew the family phone number but was desperately trying to remember the international dialling code for Albania. Earlier in the summer she had travelled with her family to Croatia for the holidays and had called her friends a couple of times. Her parents wouldn't allow regular calls, it was too expensive. She tried it once, 00335. A discordant noise emanated from the phone. She switched off and tried again... the same.

She wracked her brains; she was sure that was right. She held the phone in her hand and started to dial again, a different number, 00355; the charging lead trained back to the plug socket. Her hands started to shake and she had difficulty in keying in the digits but then the number was completed. She pressed "call". The international ringing tone sounded. After three rings it was answered.

'Mammi?' said Edita.

'Edita...? Edita...? Is that you,' said the voice.

'Yes, please help us. We are safe but we have been kidnapped. We are in England.'

Suddenly there was a noise outside; it made her jump. Edita quickly rang off and put the phone down on the desk where she found it and switched on her vacuum cleaner, trying to look as relaxed as possible, but feeling far from.

The door opened and a man in a smart business suit walked in.

'Sorry,' he said and smiled, 'forgot my phone.' He was shouting over the sound of the cleaner. Edita switched it off.

'Forgot my phone,' he repeated and walked to the desk, unplugged it from the charger and put the phone in his pocket. 'Thank you, have a nice day,' he said as he walked back to the door.

'Thank you,' Edita managed to reply.

It closed automatically behind him and suddenly Edita felt sick. She rushed into the bathroom and vomited into the sink. She turned on the tap and cleaned the basin, then filled one of the plastic glasses with water and gulped it down. She just hoped the man would not check his call log any time soon.

Edita gradually composed herself and continued with her cleaning duties. When she had finished the room she went to find Delvina who was further down the corridor. There was no-one else on the floor. Anna, the house manager, was in a meeting. Seeing the coast was clear, Edita went into the room where Delvina was working.

'Hello,' said Delvina. 'It is break already?'

'No... I needed to see you. I have just spoken to Mammi.'

'What?! How?' said Delvina.

'I used a phone someone had left in the room,' said Edita.

'How is she? What did she say?' said Delvina animatedly.

'I couldn't say much. The man came back. I just told her we had been kidnapped but we were safe,' said Edita. 'I told her we were in England.'

'Did you say where?' said Delvina.

'No, I didn't have time,' said Edita.

'I just wanted to let her know we were ok,' said Edita, and she started to cry.

Delvina put her arms around her. Edita quickly composed herself.

'We will talk later, I must get back before I am missed.'

Mid-morning, back at the house, Nicolai and Victor were chatting to their "friends" on the social media sites they had targeted for potential new recruits. Uri was working on the building site. At Amir's suggestion, Victoria had taken time off from the office to oversee the operation. Nicolai had collected her in an old Ford Escort they used; she would never park the Porsche in Argyle Avenue.

She was stood behind the lads watching the feeds coming in, drinking coffee and advising on replies she thought would attract girls.

Victor had already made contact with seven possible targets; he was posting under the name of "Tyler".

'Have you seen this one?' he said to Victoria.

She looked at the stream with someone called 'Portia'.

Portia - 'Hi Tyler how R U'

Tyler - 'Good thnx U'

Portia - 'Can't wait 2 C U Pls send pic'

Tyler - 'Ok, wait'

'What are you going to do?' asked Victoria.

'I will send her one of my video stills,' said Victor.

'Not too sexy,' said Victoria.

'I know,' said Victor, and he scanned his picture library and chose one he thought she would like.

The picture took a minute to upload. The streaming continued.

Portia - 'Wooooow U R a hunk'

Tyler - 'Thx'

Portia - 'Wait I will send U'

The picture started to download, and then appeared. It was a 'selfie', a young woman, late teens, standing in what looked to be her bathroom with a mobile phone pointing at the mirror. She was naked.

Tyler - 'Woooow, U R butifl'

Portia - 'Thnx'

Tyler - 'U R so sexy'

Portia - 'U 2'

Victoria watched the online courting ritual take its course in front of her eyes.

'Where is she from?' asked Victoria.

'Latvia,' said Victor.

'That is good. If we can get more from Latvia we can collect them in one journey. See if she has any friends,' said Victoria. 'We can get them fixed up with Uri when he gets in.'

'Yes,' said Victor.

The Internet chat continued and Victor/Tyler was able to get more information on the unsuspecting Portia. Victor told her that he was working in the UK and doing really well, making lots of money and saving so he could return to Ukraine and continue his education at university, which as it happens was not far from the truth. In reality, both Victor and Uri were illegal immigrants from Ukraine and, like many others, had arrived on a forged student visa and not returned. The London gang, controlled by Vasyl Hudzik, had arranged their transportation for a significant sum and had put them in touch with Amir; the rest was history.

Both were qualified bricklayers and Uri particularly had been in great demand. There were plenty of construction sites only too happy to turn a blind eye to the laborious paperwork and pay cash in hand. Victor was also regularly employed but with the money he was earning from the videos he was less inclined to spend his time humping bricks. He much preferred his evening activities.

Back at the depot, by lunchtime things were happening. Keith was sat in his office contemplating his first morning run for Amir and was beginning to think he had won the lottery. The phones had hardly stopped ringing; Azure Recruitment certainly had a lot of connections. For the first time in a long while he felt his luck was beginning to change. Finding the coat was a sign; it was meant to be. He was back on top.

Maggie Jevons, the bookkeeper cum receptionist, bought him in a sandwich and his fourth mug of coffee. She was a stout woman, in her mid-forties with a reputation for straight talking. She was adept at fielding enquiries from creditors regarding overdue payments.

'By 'eck, I'm rushed off my feet I am,' she said. 'Don't know what's happening today, t'phone's hardly stopped ringing.'

'Aye,' said Keith. 'Happen business has turned the corner, I think... Taken more orders this morning than the last two months. This week's almost full... Mind you I need to sort out the fleet; we're getting bookings for minibuses. I've had to use the twenty-six and forty-two seaters. Short distances mostly, mind... couple to Newcastle, one to Liverpool and another to Birmingham.'

'That'll cost. Hope you remembered the extra diesel,' she said.

'Aye, I've added a bit on, like... Strange that, now you come to mention it, nobody's haggled. All new people, don't know where they came from, asked for a price, I told 'em and they just said "yes"... just like that,' and he started wondering.

Maggie broke his concentration.

'Oh, nearly forgot, had someone on from Hyams earlier, summat about a couple of pick-ups from Manchester Airport and an executive run from Heathrow?' she said with an inflection.

'She said you knew about it, summat about a discussion with Steve Jones.'

'Aye, that's brilliant. Aye, he's the owner, met him at the dinner-dance on Friday. He said he would get someone to ring. That's great news. Did they say when?'

'Aye, they're in t'diary... Manchester runs are Wednesday and Thursday. Heathrow's next Monday, I think. I'll check. I thought Dave Shawcross could do 'em. He looks more the part than Bruce, and Jack can be a bit... you know.'

'No, that's great. You'll need to ring Ted Avis, see if you can get hold of one of his limos... but watch him on price. I need fifty per cent on this,' said Keith.

'Don't worry I'll soon sort him out,' said Maggie, and smiled. Keith chuckled to himself. Ted Avis won't know what's hit him, he thought. He looked at Maggie.

'Well that's great, let's hope it continues. It'll be nice to get some payments out on time for a change,' she said.

'Aye,' said Keith. 'That it will... By the way, did you bank the cheques?'

'Aye, first thing. That'll keep the wolf from the door for a bit.'

'Well you know what to do. Priority must be the diesel, without that we can't work,' he said, and looked at her.

'Aye, I know the drill.'

'Oh and remind me to speak to Reg Ainsworth at the council tomorrow I need to give notice on the school runs.'

'What?' said Maggie.

'Don't sound so surprised,' said Keith. 'We've been losing money on 'em for years.'

'I know but even still... they won't like it.'

'Well unless they can increase the contract by thirty per cent then they go, and I can't see 'em agreeing to that,' he said.

'Aye, can't argue with that,' she said, and left him to his

sandwich.

As she went back to her office, she looked back at Keith. He seemed different somehow... more in control.

By late afternoon he had arranged to meet his leasing agent to order new buses and dispose of some of the existing fleet. The meeting would take place tomorrow at ten o'clock. He had decided to sell his three double-deckers, one of his twenty-six seaters and one forty-two seater. In their place he would order three Mercedes Executive nine-seaters. The financing was complicated but the agent had worked out some figures and had emailed them to Keith. Even better news; there was a saving on his monthly contract which left him feeling even more elated. He was upbeat and whistling 'She'll Be Coming 'Round the Mountain' as he locked the depot at six o'clock and headed home.

Earlier, around three o'clock, Kathryn Woodley was taking a break from the incessant queues at the benefits office and went to the staff room. As she would do at every break time, she picked up her phone from her handbag to check her FaceBook posts. There were three missed calls and a text. She opened up the message.

'Hi should have been playing golf tonight but called off. Bit of a loose end, fancy meeting up for a drink? Steve.'

She suddenly felt her heart skip a beat, like a schoolgirl getting her first love letter. Something took hold of her. She texted back.

'Ok, when? Where?'

She went to the coffee machine in the corner and put a twenty pence coin into the slot. Although there was a sink, fridge and kettle, she couldn't be bothered with making a fresh cup; at least the machine brew was just about drinkable.

No-one else was in the rest room, several other colleagues were out the back tugging on cigarettes. Kathryn could see their shapes through the frosted glass. She went to one of the five tables and picked up a dog-eared newspaper which had been discarded unceremoniously in the centre and started to read the headlines. She heard the 'ping' of a text and looked at her phone while taking a sip of coffee.

'8.00 Hayfield Manor?'

She thought for a moment, her pulse was off the scale as she texted back... 'Ok'

'GR8 C U there' was the response.

Kathryn switched off her phone and put it in her bag. She was suddenly racked by guilt. She went back to her desk and opened the window to her till. Three people from an adjoining line jostled for positions. Kathryn's concentration levels had dropped considerably and for the rest of the afternoon she was on autopilot.

She returned home around five-thirty, her head still in turmoil, and parked her five-year-old Renault Clio on the narrow drive, leaving just enough room for Keith to park his Mercedes.

'Hi, I'm home,' she shouted, to no more than a cursory response; Ellie was in her room, Jason on his Xbox. She changed into her round-the-house clothes, and then started preparing the evening meal. She took the food from the fridge and started chopping vegetables. As she peeled the potatoes, she was mulling over her decision to meet Steve. She had not felt this excitement for as long as she could remember – never, probably. She was trying to justify her actions to herself. She was always unappreciated, taken for granted. The children, she could accept, but Keith was just as bad; she did everything for him with little in return. Yes, there was the coat but before that...? It was a nice thought but it was only because it was her birthday; it would soon be back to the usual routine: work, cooking, cleaning, ironing, never any "me" time.

All these thoughts were playing in her mind. Life was passing her by, she decided. Didn't she deserve some happiness, some excitement in her dull and drab routine? Not that anything would happen of course, her and Steve; she was only meeting him for a drink after all. It might even help Keith with the business... playing up to Steve Jones. He might put more work our way.

She hadn't heard Keith return from the depot and jumped hearing the keys entering the door; it was as though she had been abruptly wakened from a dream.

'Anyone home?' Keith called from the hall.

'In the kitchen,' shouted Kathryn in response.

Keith went into the kitchen and pecked Kathryn on the cheek.

'How was your day?' she asked.

'You'll never guess. It's been brilliant. The best day for... I don't know how long. The phone's been going berserk. New business coming out of our ears... At this rate we'll have to take on some temps. That bloke Steve... you know, from the dinner on Friday, turned up trumps an' all.'

Kathryn's ears pricked up again, but she carried on stirring gravy.

'That's great,' she said, and Keith continued to detail his day's successes. Kathryn was sort of listening; not once had he asked about her day.

Keith went to the kettle and made himself some tea, continuing his outpourings excitedly. He took his first sip which gave Kathryn the chance to interrupt. 'I'm going out tonight. You don't mind do you?'

'No, course not... Monday night? You don't usually go out on a Monday.'

'Phyllis called,' she said hesitantly. 'She's got a spare ticket for a cosmetics evening at Hayfield Manor,' she said, still stirring the gravy and not making eye contact, hoping the lie wouldn't show.

'Oh right,' said Keith, somewhat surprised. 'Yeah, course that's fine, I'll keep an eye on the kids. Need to catch up on paperwork anyway so I won't be going out. What time'll you be back?'

'Not sure, shouldn't be too late though.'

'Ok, I might be in bed if it's after ten, got an early start in the morning with this new contract.'

He took his mug of tea into the lounge and picked up the paper. She didn't respond; she was still stirring the gravy; any traces of lumps had long since disappeared.

The family sat down to their shepherd's pie and Keith was effusively explaining his day to Ellie and Jason. They were wrapped up in their own world but pleased to see Dad happy for once. It made a change from his usual complaints... the government, cost of diesel, potholes, grumpy drivers and even more grumpy passengers.

Keith was on his laptop when Kathryn came down from the bedroom. Her perfume preceded her.

He looked up. 'Mmm, you smell nice.'

Kathryn thought quickly, she didn't want Keith thinking that she had made any sort of special effort, might raise suspicions. She would need to play it cool.

'Thanks... Well it is a cosmetics evening.'

He looked at her in her smart blouse, which he did not recognise, and short skirt. She was carrying her new coat.

'You're not taking your coat are you?'

'Why not...?' she said.

'Oh, nothing... Just don't go leaving it behind.'

'No chance, not after last time,' she replied.

There was a moment of silence as she looked around the room. She was desperately trying to avoid any further interrogation.

'Right, I'm off then... See you later.'

'Ok,' said Keith. 'Make sure you've got your keys.'

'Yeah, got them,' she said, then pecked Keith on the cheek and left the house. Keith was back on his laptop.

She breathed deeply as she walked towards the car, aiming the fob at the Clio. The four indicators responded as if welcoming her, beckoning her, reassuring her; she opened the door and got in. She sat for a moment; it wasn't too late to back out.

'Sod it,' she said to herself in an air of defiance, and started the engine.

Steve Jones had arrived at the hotel earlier, at five o'clock; he had a meeting with Shalik and Amir. He walked into reception and Amir was waiting in one of the leather armchairs opposite the desk. Steve saw him and was greeted warmly.

'Steve, it is very good to see you,' said Amir, standing up and shaking hands vigorously with the visitor.

'Shalik is in the office, he will be joining us shortly. Come through to the terrace, I will get some coffee for you.'

'Thanks,' said Steve.

The two men walked past reception and down the corridor to the Terrace Bar which overlooked the golf course.

'Sorry to hear about your game,' said Amir.

'Can't be helped,' said Steve. 'Partner's pulled a muscle in his back or something so he'll be out of action for a week or so... still, it's given us a chance to check on business.'

'Yes,' said Amir. 'Everything is going well, the recruitment agency, it has really been busy.'

'Good to hear it,' said Steve.

'You mentioned you would be looking for more girls,' said Amir.

'Yes, another three I think. No, make that four... I've had very good reports about the Albanians you sent us... and the Macedonians as well... so much better than the local girls. I'd swap the whole lot of 'em if I could.'

'Yes,' said Amir. 'They are good girls, work hard.'

'When will you be able to let me have them?' said Steve.

Amir stroked his chin. 'We are working on that, maybe one month. We are going to pick the girls up ourselves,' he said. 'Save much money.'

'Yes, I can see that,' said Steve. 'Not too long though, eh. I'll need them for the Christmas orders. We'll start getting them out at the end of the month. We'll be very busy.'

'Yes,' said Amir. 'We are working on it.'

Steve looked up and could see Shalik enter the Terrace Room looking for them. He was older than his brother, clean-shaven and taller. He was extremely smart, as befitting a hotel General Manager, his typical Middle Eastern dark hair swept back and starting to fleck with grey, rather distinguished-looking, like a younger Omar Sharif. Steve put his hand up to attract his attention.

Shalik acknowledged and went to join them. Steve stood up and shook hands with the new arrival.

'Steve, how are you?' said Shalik.

'Shalik, my friend, great to see you, Amir has been bringing me up to date... says business is going well,' said Steve.

'Yes, hotel it is very busy,' said Shalik.

'Yes,' said Steve. 'I was here for a function on Friday. Packed out it was.'

'Yes,' said Shalik. 'I heard you were here. I am sorry I wasn't able to meet you... As I said we were very busy.'

'No, you're alright Shalik. I had guests to entertain... Talking of which, have you got a spare room for a couple of hours tonight? Meeting someone... may need a bit of privacy,' said Steve.

'Of course, it will not be a problem. We are not full tonight, I will ask Ingrid to let you have a key. She is on duty,' said Shalik.

'Cheers,' said Steve. 'I owe you one.'

Steve was an important client. As well as the recruitment agency, the hotel was regularly used by Hyams' for their clients from all over the world. Shalik would of course look after their every need, including the occasional request for a girl for a VIP visitor.

Having agreed on Steve's resource needs, the three discussed his room requirements for forthcoming visitors in more detail and Shalik made notes. Steve was a shrewd operator and keen negotiator; he would always get a good deal. It was gone six by the time they had concluded their business and Amir got up to leave. 'Must get back,' he said.

He shook Steve's hand and kissed his brother, then said something to him in Farsi.

Shalik got up. Steve looked at his watch, six-twenty, plenty of time.

'Any chance of a sandwich, Shalik?' he said.

'Of course, it will be my pleasure. I will get someone over to take your order,' said Shalik.

'Cheers,' said Steve. 'You can put it on my account.'

'Of course, and I will get Grianne to email you confirmation of the dates and rates we discussed,' said Shalik.

'Thanks for that. A pleasure doing business with you,' said Steve.

'The pleasure is mine,' said Shalik, and bowed his head reverentially.

Steve watched as Shalik walked away, pleased with his transactions. A few minutes later a waiter took his order and Steve watched the news on one of the TVs on the wall while he waited for the food. His mind started to wander and his thoughts were now firmly fixed on his date. He had told his wife he was meeting a client, which was a regular happening; sometimes he was, sometimes... like tonight. Sonia wasn't concerned, she was too well looked after to rock the boat. Her monthly clothes and beauty allowance was more than most people's salary.

The anticipation grew as the time approached. Eight o'clock,

Steve was sat in reception watching the people coming and going. He wondered whether he would recognise her again; it was dark on Friday and a lot of alcohol had been consumed. Ten past and he was starting to think she might not show. Then there she was, walking up the steps towards the entrance. She looked incredible and memories from their previous meeting came into his mind, the close dancing, the gaze in her eyes that definitely said, 'I am interested'.

It had taken Kathryn just over twenty minutes to reach the hotel; at a couple of roundabouts she considered going all the way around and heading home. She asked herself 'what are you doing?' on more than one occasion, but something spurred her on; she was committed. She drove through the hotel gateway and headed for the car park. One last check in the mirror and she locked up and walked towards the entrance, her coat draped casually over her shoulders. She scanned the reception area bustling with people registering and seeking information. Then she saw him; he waved to acknowledge her presence.

As he walked towards her, it was her turn to think back to their previous meeting. Comparisons between Steve and Keith were pointless, but she couldn't help herself. Steve would be two or three years younger, he was immaculately dressed, sports jacket, slacks, loafers, colour coordinated and expensive. Trim, she noticed, with a lean physique; he obviously looked after himself. Keith's exercise regime meant walking to the car and his "muffin-top" stomach was a regular source of cruel jibes in the household.

As they met in the middle of the reception area they kissed cheeks formally, as if in a business meeting.

'Glad you could make it,' said Steve with a degree of confidence.

Kathryn wasn't sharing the same level and was distinctly nervous.

'That's ok,' she said.

'Can I take your coat?' he asked.

'It's fine, thanks,' she said, and subconsciously held the lapels of the coat and pulled them together, hiding her blouse.

'Shall we go to the Terrace Bar?' he said. 'It's a beautiful evening and there are some great views across the grounds.'

'Ok,' said Kathryn. Inside, her stomach was doing cartwheels, a mix of excitement and apprehension.

There was a spare table in the corner with two comfortable armchairs positioned next to each other facing it... ideal. Steve walked towards the table and waited while Kathryn made herself comfortable. She draped her coat over the arm of the chair and sat down. The seat was slightly lower and her skirt rode higher than she had intended, almost to 1960s level. It did not go unnoticed. Kathryn tugged at the hem self-consciously.

'You look fabulous,' said Steve.

'Thank you,' said Kathryn.

A waiter appeared.

'What would you like to drink,' he asked.

'Just an orange juice,' she said.

'Are you sure? I can't tempt you with something a bit stronger? A cocktail perhaps,' said Steve.

'Better not, I'm driving.'

'Well, one won't hurt.'

Kathryn was in a quandary. If truth were told she could murder a drink right now, something just to calm her nerves.

'Aye alright, go on then. I'll have a gin and tonic,' she said.

'Large gin and tonic and a half of lager,' said Steve to the hovering attendant.

'Yes sir,' he said, and headed back to the bar.

Steve looked at Kathryn; he could smell her perfume. She could feel his eyes sweeping her body and she suddenly felt unsure of herself; this was new territory.

'So how was the benefits office today?' he said, trying to make conversation.

In the light of the situation, it was an incongruous question but it was neutral ground.

She almost laughed.

'It was fine, thanks,' she said. 'Busy.'

'Yes, I expect it was,' said Steve, which concluded that area of conversation.

He tried another tack.

'We've been in contact with Keith today; he's doing some airport runs for us.'

'Yes, he mentioned it,' she said.

'Do you get involved with the business?' he asked.

'No, not at all, don't have the time,' she replied.

The waiter returned with the drinks and Steve signed the tab.

'Thanks,' she said as the waiter poured the small bottle of tonic water into the rather large measure of gin.

'I imagined you being the power behind the throne,' said Steve with a smile.

'You've got to be joking; I've got no interest in buses. I've enough to do without running after drivers and greasy mechanics,' she said and laughed.

Steve picked up his lager and took the first sip, leaving a film of froth on his top lip. He picked up one of the napkins beside his glass and dabbed the offending moisture. Kathryn stifled a laugh; Keith would have used his sleeve. The gin was starting to work its magic.

He continued his courtship with more polite questions, which she answered in monosyllables, and after ten minutes of what seemed to be a cat-and-mouse game, he raised the stakes.

'I was discussing our transport needs with my finance director earlier and I may have a proposition for Keith, could be worth a lot of money.' He let the words sink in.

'Keith will be pleased,' he said.

Steve continued.

'Yes, well just between you and me, we've been thinking about outsourcing our delivery section for some time. It's a big operation but I don't think it fits our business model and I can see possible savings in using an outside contractor. What do you think?'

'About what?' she said. 'I don't know anything about it.'

'Of course, but is it something that you think Keith would be interested in, do you think?' he pressed.

'Yes, yes I'm sure he will be,' she said, and took the final sip of her gin and tonic.

'That's good, I'll ring him tomorrow,' he said.

Steve noticed the drink. 'Can I get you another?' he asked.

'Just an orange juice,' she said.

Steve looked towards the bar and raised his arm. The barman acknowledged and a waiter was duly dispatched. Steve ordered the drinks.

'An orange juice, please.' He was not going to push another alcoholic beverage on Kathryn. 'And half of lager.'

'Just popping to the men's room,' he said as the waiter wandered back to the bar.

While he was gone, Kathryn took stock. The gin and tonic had certainly helped calm the nerves and she was starting to feel more relaxed in his company. She looked out across the grounds and watched the last of the golfers heading back to the clubhouse. It was starting to get quite dark and only seasoned players would still be out on the course. It was a strange atmosphere, not romantic exactly but... she couldn't decide. Dangerous? Impulsive? Adventurous? Words that she would not readily associate with herself; but exciting, yes.

After five minutes Steve returned, and as he sat down his hand rested momentarily on Kathryn's. She didn't move it and taking this as a sign he started stroking the back of her hand. Kathryn again didn't move. He slid his hand under hers and folded his fingers around it. She responded. She felt like that schoolgirl again. It was the back row of the movies, young sweaty palms playing finger wrestling, not sure what to do next. It was like being hit by a series of electric shocks. Other parts of her body, more intimate parts, were also beginning to awaken. She started to flush. She hoped he wouldn't notice. Now she wanted the ladies, but decided to wait... to see what would happen next.

Steve turned to her and looked her in the eyes.

'You are so beautiful,' he said. 'I fancied you the moment I saw you on Friday.'

'Really,' she said, sipping slowly on her orange juice.

'I couldn't stop thinking about you on Saturday. I wanted you so badly,' he said.

'Well, we'll have to do something about that, won't we?' she said, and looked at him under her eyebrows, an unwittingly sultry expression.

Steve wasn't sure if he was making his move too early, but as he had found in business, fortune favours the brave, and he made his play.

'Well, I do happen to have a room available,' he said.

She looked at him. 'That was a bit presumptuous,' she said, but not as sharply as she might have done, and smiled; she wanted to make a point.

'No, no,' said Steve, probably too defensively. 'I had a meeting arranged after my golf match but, as you see, I haven't been able to use it.'

She looked at him with her orange juice poised at her lips.

'It would be a shame to waste it, then,' she said.

There were so many emotions; she was in uncharted waters but having set sail she would go where the wind blew her.

CHAPTER THIRTEEN

Steve squeezed her hand. 'My thoughts exactly... Shall we go?'

Kathryn was looking into his eyes, still holding her drink to her lips. No reply was necessary.

Steve got to his feet and Kathryn knocked back the remainder of her orange juice and stood up. She picked up her coat from the chair, and then followed Steve out of the Terrace Bar. They walked past reception to the lift.

There were two lifts; the one on the left was on the fourth floor according to the indicator, the one on the right responded to the call and started to descend. Steve was fiddling with the key card in his pocket as they waited for one to arrive.

There was a ping as it reached the ground floor; it opened and a couple emerged, totally oblivious to the two people waiting.

'After you,' said Steve, and Kathryn got in. Steve followed.

'Fourth floor,' said Steve, and Kathryn pressed the fourth-floor button.

It was just the two of them and Steve pulled Kathryn towards him. She looked into his eyes and any thoughts of resistance just melted away. Their lips met, then a feeding frenzy of tongues as the emotion rose to the surface.

There was another ping as the lift reached its destination.

They disengaged as the door opened. Steve checked the key card again.

'428' he said, and they followed the signs halfway down a long corridor.

'Here,' said Steve.

Kathryn had wrapped the coat around her shoulders again and watched Steve negotiate the entry. There was another entry she was even more interested in; she could feel herself becoming aroused.

They went inside and the door shut behind them. Steve looked around, he was familiar with the layout; the rooms were very similar. There was a slot to put the key card in to engage the electrics. He slid in the card and the room was bathed in a warm light from a large brass standard lamp in the far corner of the room. Kathryn went to the window and admired the view; it was pretty dark now, with just a hint of orange in the sky to denote the end of dusk and the arrival of night.

She closed the curtains and turned and looked at the bed. A shudder went through her body.

'I need the bathroom,' she said, not intending to break the spell, just being practical.

'Sure,' said Steve. 'After you.'

The bathroom was just by the entrance door. It was a good size and Kathryn looked at herself in the large mirror, checking her make-up before taking a pee.

She wiped herself with a piece of toilet paper then went to the sink and rinsed out one of the flannels. There were two containers of soap and hand cream just below the mirror. It was expensive stuff with a nice smell and she washed between her legs and dried off. Then she had a thought. She put her knickers in her handbag. She had a feeling she wasn't going to need them.

As she came out, Steve went in, and she sat on the bed waiting for him to finish. She heard the toilet flush and she could feel the excitement rising; the anticipation of what was going to happen.

Steve had taken off his jacket and went to her. She stood up and they started kissing again as intense as in the lift.

'God I want you,' said Steve.

'Better do something about it then,' said Kathryn again, and her right hand moved downwards and found the belt to his trousers. She negotiated the clasp with one hand and pulled the belt from its holds and dropped it on the floor. She found the fastener on top of his chinos and pulled it open with an impatient jerk, then tugged at the zip. She slipped her hand down the front of his boxer shorts... the promised land; hard, firm, ready for her. He groaned. She squeezed it gently and started rubbing it up and down. Steve started to undo Kathryn's blouse and she let go of Steve for a moment to help it to fall from her shoulders and join Steve's belt on the floor. He gasped at the sight of her breasts encased in a half-cup bra. Kathryn put her hands behind her and unclipped it. Steve was on her, devouring her breasts.

Kathryn found her interest again and pushed Steve's trousers and shorts down and could see his hard penis in her hand. She wanted to eat it.

Steve, meanwhile, had discovered her little secret.

'Wow, no knickers, now that is sexy,' he said, and their tongues locked again.

He gently rubbed her between her legs and Kathryn thought she was going to explode.

'Let's get into bed,' she said. 'I want you naked.'

It was like a scene from her favourite erotic novel; the one she kept in her locker at work which her husband knew nothing about. She was playing out the role of a high-class hooker; for now she was Belle.

Steve stripped off as he was told, lifted the covers and got in.

Kathryn did the same.

'Hold me for a minute,' she said.

They lay there, hands gently exploring. Steve started stroking Kathryn's breasts, her breathing started getting heavier.

'Now,' she said.

Steve rolled on top of her and Kathryn guided him in. She opened her legs to let him go deeper and he started his thrusts.

'Not yet, not yet,' she said as she could see Steve's eyes. He held on for as long as he could.

'Now,' she said, and Steve erupted into her.

She let out a scream and her hips bucked to meet his last push.

Nothing was said, they just lay there. Kathryn had never experienced anything like it before; she never knew it could be like this.

They disengaged and Steve leaned over and held Kathryn close to him.

'Wow,' was all he said, but it was what she too felt at that moment.

Their breathing slowed and they lay there recovering, each in contemplation.

After a few minutes it was Steve who broke the silence.

'What time do you have to get back?' he said, which brought Kathryn back to earth.

'About eleven.'

The romance of the moment had been replaced by the reality of the situation.

'I need the bathroom,' she said, and got out of bed.

As she cleaned herself down, all kinds of emotions were coursing through her mind. The guilt started surfacing but she quickly put it to one side; she would deal with it. Tonight was just for her.

She checked her watch, it was ten-fifteen, and as she returned to the room, Steve was getting out from the other side of the bed.

'Won't be a minute,' he said, and he went into the bathroom. Kathryn got back into bed.

A few minutes later they were locked in each other's arms.

'Can we do this again?' said Steve.

The question caught Kathryn slightly off-guard; she hadn't considered any continuing arrangement... or the consequences.

'I'd like that,' she said.

'Good... I was hoping you would say that,' said Steve.

'I'd better get going,' she said, and started to search for her clothes, which seemed to be scattered across the room.

Steve watched her as she started to dress and was admiring her body.

'God, you look so good,' he said as she stood up and positioned her bra and clipped it in place. Kathryn had a good figure but it had been a while since it had been acknowledged by anyone, at least directly.

'Thanks,' she said.

After a few minutes they were both dressed and ready to leave. Kathryn checked herself in the mirror and applied a hint more make-up. She could smell Steve's aftershave and hoped it would go.

Steve kissed her. 'Thanks for tonight... it's been really special.'

Kathryn thought for a moment. 'Yes it has,' she said.

They left the room and took the lift to reception. There was no passionate kissing, despite the lift being empty.

'You better go ahead,' said Steve as they reached the ground floor.

'Ok,' she said.

'Thanks,' said Steve. 'I've enjoyed tonight.'

'Yes, me too,' she said, and she stepped out of the lift, wrapped her coat around her shoulders and turned left past reception into the evening air without a backwards glance.

Earlier that evening, back at Argyle Avenue, Victoria was monitoring the Internet traffic with Nicolai, Uri and Victor.

'How is it?' she asked.

'Good,' said Uri.

Although the chat rooms were live, Victoria was taking more interest in the latest social media project. Uri had returned from bricklaying and had joined Victor updating his posts. He was also attracting female admirers.

'How many followers now?' asked Victoria.

'Fifty-one,' said Uri, who had adopted the name Faron for his profile page.

'Eighty-three,' said Victor, and pulled a gloating face at Uri.

'I will soon catch you,' said Uri.

'Never mind who has the most,' said Victoria. 'I want you to watch for girls in Latvia and see if we can get them here. What about that Portia girl you were talking to this morning, Victor?'

'Yes, she is online now,' said Victor.

'Does she speak good English?' said Victoria.

'Yes,' said Victor. 'She is replying in English... it is good I think... She has a friend, Vaira, at Riga University, who wants to come to England.'

'Excellent,' said Victoria. 'See if we can get some more.'

Just then Amir arrived. He had been home and eaten and had returned to the house to update Victoria.

'How are things?' he said.

'Good,' said Victoria. 'Victor has two girls from Riga that could be interesting.'

'That is good,' said Amir. 'I have spoken to Mr. Jones. He wants four girls as soon as we can arrange. We need to work on this.'

'Yes,' said Victoria. 'If they have passports we will not have to make them. They can work here without visa, no problem.'

'Yes,' said Amir. 'I know someone who will make passports, but it cost much money.'

'Yes, if we can get them from Latvia it will be good,' she said.

By the end of the evening Victor had managed to get Portia and her friend Vaira to agree to come to the UK. They just needed two more to make the trip viable and deliver Steve Jones' requirements, but with the success of the chat rooms there was always a demand for new girls. Victoria and Amir continued to watch the Internet feed with growing interest.

Upstairs, Edita and Delvina were watching TV, they were not needed this evening in the chat room, but Edita was still upset following her brief discussion with her mother. Hearing her voice brought thoughts of home very much to the fore, the pain almost unbearable. Delvina had been in tears for most of the evening and Edita was unable to answer her question. 'What are we going to do? When will they let us go home?'

Tuesday morning, and at six forty-five Keith was at the house, engine running, waiting for the girls to take them to the hotel. Nicolai was at the door and led them to the waiting minibus. Keith slid open the door and Edita and Delvina got in. Keith waited expecting Nicolai to join them but instead he walked up to Keith. 'You know where to go. Be back at seven-thirty for factory,' he said.

'Yeah, ok mate, I'll do my best but depends on the traffic. You saw what it's like,' said Keith.

'Yes, quick you go now,' said Nicolai.

'Right,' said Keith, slid shut the door and got in.

He checked his rear-view mirror and could see one of the girls crying.

Keith steered the minibus between the parked cars towards the main road. He checked his mirror again.

'You ok, love?' he said, seeing Delvina still crying.

'She is ok,' said Edita sharply.

Keith turned right and immediately joined a queue of traffic snaking its way into the city centre which he would have to negotiate. He turned the radio on but wasn't able to concentrate. His thoughts turned to the business of the day; contact the council, sort out the new buses, lots to do.

He eventually got through the city centre and headed out towards the hotel. He was distracted again by the girl in the back who still appeared to be crying.

'My name's Keith,' he said, trying to make conversation.

No reply.

'What are your names?' he asked.

No reply.

'Sorry, just trying to be friendly,' said Keith.

'We are not your friend,' said Edita.

'Ok,' said Keith. 'Just concerned about your friend. What is it, boyfriend trouble?'

'It is not your concern, and she is not my friend, she is my sister,' said Edita.

'No, I know... sorry, just don't like seeing anyone upset, that's all. No man's worth that, love. There's plenty more fish in the sea,' said Keith.

'You know nothing,' said Edita.

'I guess not,' said Keith.

Delvina had started to calm down but her eyes were red and her body occasionally convulsed from crying. Edita was speaking to her in Albanian.

'So where are you from?' said Keith, not recognising the language.

Edita wasn't used to this enquiry and was nervous about speaking to a stranger, but there was something about Keith; he seemed... honest.

'Albania,' said Edita.

'Long way from home,' said Keith.

Delvina looked at Edita, understanding the remark, but she was cried out.

'Yes,' said Edita.

There was another queue at a set of traffic lights, another ten minutes if he was lucky with the lights, thought Keith.

'So how long have you been in the UK?' said Keith.

'Not long,' said Edita.

'So what do you do at the hotel... work I mean?' said Keith.

'We clean,' said Edita.

Keith was through the lights and not far from the hotel. Edita was staring through the window; Delvina just looking down at her hands, totally dejected.

Five minutes later, Keith pulled up to the front of the hotel and let the girls out.

'See you at five,' said Keith. There was no acknowledgement and Edita and Delvina went round to the service entrance to sign in. Edita reflected as she walked; it was the first time anyone had shown them any real kindness since they had been in the UK.

Later that morning, back at the depot, Keith had just finished his call with Reg Ainsworth, the head of transport at the city council.

'How did it go?' asked Maggie Jevons when Keith walked through into the reception.

'Well let's put it this way, we won't be top of the list for any future tenders,' said Keith.

'I said he wouldn't be happy,' said Maggie.

'Aye, that's putting it mildly. He weren't best pleased. I told him he's been getting us on the cheap for years.'

'He's just worried about what he'll have to pay on a new contract,' said Maggie.

'Aye, that'll be interesting,' said Keith.

'Oh, nearly forgot, Steve Jones from Hyams rang. Can you call him back?' she said.

'Aye, just get a coffee. Have you got his number?' said Keith.

Maggie passed him a Post-it sticker with a number written on it.

'There you go. I'll make you a coffee if you give us a minute. I'll bring it in for you.'

'Cheers,' said Keith, and went back to his office.

Keith looked at the yellow note, checked the number and started to dial. It was picked up on the second ring.

'Steve Jones,' came the stern response. Keith had his direct line.

'Steve, it's Keith... Woodley, you rang earlier.'

'Oh, hi Keith, sorry... how are you?'

'Fine Steve, fine... business is really picking up,' said Keith.

'Pleased to hear it... That's what I wanted to talk to you about. I might have another proposition for you, if you're interested,' said Steve.

'Always interested in business,' said Keith.

'Good... Look, are you free for lunch? I know it's short notice but I'd like you to meet my Finance Director and Operations Manager.'

'Well, yes,' said Keith. 'Where? What time?'

'Can you get across to the works, say twelve-thirty? I've got a lot on today so I'm having a working lunch,' said Steve.

'Aye,' said Keith. 'I'll be there.'

'Great, see you at twelve-thirty,' and he rang off.

Steve put down the receiver and checked his mobile phone for the umpteenth time, looking at the text messages... the one at nine o'clock.

'Thanks for last night. Special x'

Reply: 'Yes'

'Can we do it again?'

Reply: 'Yes'

'Soon?'

Reply: 'Yes'

'Friday?'

Reply: 'Have to check.'

'Let me know'

'Will do x'

'xxx'

Steve read the message again, checking for any nuances, any indications of how she felt, although why that was important to him he hadn't considered.

'Steve... Amir Aziz wants a quick word, are you free?' said Patsy Grove, his attractive thirty-year-old PA. The intervention made him jump.

'What? Oh... yes, send him through. See if he wants a drink and can you get me a coffee? Thanks.'

A few minutes later, Amir was escorted through into Steve's office by Patsy who was carrying a mug of coffee and a bottle of mineral water. She put them down on the conference table where Steve was waiting to greet his guest.

'Hi Amir,' said Steve.

'Hello,' said Amir.

'Wasn't expecting to see you... any problems?' said Steve.

'No, no,' said Amir. 'Just wanted to let you know we have found the girls you wanted. I didn't want to talk over the phone.'

'Ok,' said Steve. 'So when can I have them?'

'Two weeks, I hope,' said Amir.

'That's fine,' said Steve.

Amir looked down and appeared anxious. 'I want to speak about the payment.'

'Oh,' said Steve. 'What about the payment?'

Azure Recruitment did not make a large profit in providing workers to Hyams. In line with most agencies, there was an initial fee equivalent to three months' wages, then the weekly rate of six pounds an hour which of course was less than the minimum wage but double what the girls actually received for their labour. The real money was in the chat lines and videos which were raking in a fortune. Despite losing Sadia, Edita and Delvina's video work had already more than paid for their transportation. The need for girls therefore was a continual process to keep the customers happy; the more chat lines, the more revenue.

'We would like you to pay the fee soon to help for the journey,' said Amir.

Steve looked suitably concerned at being asked this favour.

'So you want me to subsidise your new arrangements?' said Steve.

'Help with the cost... It is very expensive, the petrol, and the ferries,' said Amir, 'and we can keep the weekly payments the same. I have done some calculations. We get you four girls, the fee is... just a minute I have it here.'

He rummaged around in his pocket and produced a scrap of paper.

'Yes, four girls, it will be eleven thousand, five hundred pounds... yes, just over,' said Amir.

'I'll take your word for it,' said Steve.

'We would do a discount if you could help us. Ten thousand pounds, then no fee, you save much money,' said Amir.

'So if I pay you ten grand upfront, you will not charge a fee and you'll supply me with four girls?' said Steve, summarising as much for his own benefit.

'I'm not happy about paying upfront. What's wrong with our existing arrangements?' said Steve.

'It is as I said, it will help with the costs,' said Amir.

One of the problems that he and Victoria had worked out when they had decided to transport the girls themselves was the travel cost. Using the London gang had meant there was an element of credit in that they did not have to make payment for a few weeks after receipt, which gave them time to raise the money. Now there was no such facility; petrol, hotels and ferries would need to be covered and having just paid Vasyl for the three Albanians, raising that amount of money would take time.

Steve looked at Amir.

'What is my guarantee?' said Steve.

'What do you mean?' asked Amir with a look of surprise.

'Ten grand is a lot of money... How do I know the girls will be any good?' said Steve.

'They will be... We will check and we will return money if you are not happy,' said Amir.

Steve was making a point, he had some specialist contacts who were adept at getting money from unwilling payers and there was no doubt he could recoup his investment if necessary.

'Alright,' he said. 'Let me know when you need it and I'll get the money for you. Cash I take it?' said Steve with a smile.

'Cash is best,' said Amir.

Steve stood up; the meeting was concluded. Amir had not touched his water and the bottle was still on the table, unopened.

'Phone me when you are ready,' said Steve, and Amir shook his hand.

'Thank you. It will be good. You will see,' said Amir.

Steve opened the door to his office and into a small reception area where Patsy the PA was sat with her head in a laptop.

'Can you see Mr Aziz out, Patsy? Thanks,' said Steve, and Patsy got up from her desk and walked along the long corridor, escorting Amir to the lift to the ground floor.

It was just before twelve-thirty when Keith arrived at Hyams and parked in one of the vacant visitors' bays. Having dropped the Macedonian girls off earlier, this was his second visit of the day.

As he walked towards the main entrance he noticed a Middle Eastern man coming in the opposite direction. Instinctively he ducked behind another parked car and watched the man get into a BMW and drive away.

'Well, I wonder what that's all about?' he asked himself, recognising his new employer.

Lunchtime at the benefits office, and Kathryn was sat reading a book on her e-reader in the staff room. It had been a Christmas present from Keith and had proved invaluable, with over fifty titles stored. Two other members of staff were also taking their break but there was no conversation, both were on social media sites on their mobile phones, totally unaware of Kathryn's present novella. When asked, she was strangely evasive... just a chick-lit, she would say. Erotic novels had been her preferred genre ever since she downloaded her first book. It took her away from her humdrum routine and into a world of passion and romance; something missing in her life for so long. She never in a million years imagined she would be living that dream, but here she was. The words were hardly resonating, and Kathryn had to reread paragraph after paragraph.

Last night had been special, but she would never let on. Colleagues had commented on her apparent distance, but she just dismissed the enquiries. She kept thinking back, rerunning every move, every position. She could feel Steve's hands as they explored every inch of her; it made the hairs on her arms stand. Then the text; the re-run... did I want to do it again...? You bet! But she wasn't going to make it too easy.

It was just turned ten past eleven when she had got back from the hotel the previous evening. The house was eerily quiet, everyone in bed. She had checked the children before changing into her nightclothes and washing off her make-up. It was strange getting into bed next to Keith; he was lying on his back, dead to the world and snoring his head off.

She nudged him, there was a snort, cough and a fart and he turned over. She just lay there for what seemed to be hours, locked in a myriad of emotions.

At Hyams, meanwhile, in the upstairs reception area to the executive rooms, Keith was greeted by Patsy, the PA.

'Keith Woodley, for Steve Jones,' he confirmed. Patsy picked up one of three phones on her desk and dialled two digits.

'Keith Woodley for you, Steve,' she said.

'Go through, Mr Woodley, they're waiting for you... first door on the left.'

As he approached the door, it opened, and Steve greeted the arrival.

'Keith, glad you could make it. Come in, I want you to meet a couple of my team.'

Keith walked into the boardroom, according to the name on the door. Two men in smart suits were sat on the opposite side of a long walnut table.

'Have a seat and I'll do the introductions,' said Steve.

Steve sat at the head of the table, indicating his position of power; the two men were to his left and Steve indicated for Keith to sit on his right. There was a tray of sandwiches, crisps, samosas and some fruit together with four bottles of water and four glasses.

'Keith, this is Gary Knight, my Finance Director,' said Steve.

A tall, angular man, completely bald, apart from a band of dark hair which appeared to go around his head, resembling a monk's hairstyle, but lower; he epitomised an accountant. It was as if they were cloned in some way. He acknowledged with a nod of the head.

'Hello,' he said. Keith acknowledged.

'And this is Pete Squire, Head of Operations.'

The head nodding ritual continued. Keith looked at man number two, more his kind of man, certainly not comfortable in a suit, Keith could tell.

'Ah do,' he said in a broad Yorkshire accent.

'Hi,' said Keith.

Steve handed the platter of sandwiches to Keith together with a plate and napkin, then a bottle of water.

'Cheers,' said Keith.

Steve started the discussion.

'The reason I've asked you to pop in Keith is I have a proposition for you.'

'Go on,' said Keith.

'We've been looking at our operations and want to make some changes,' said Steve. 'We're looking to outsource our delivery operation.'

'Pete, do you want to explain?'

'Aye,' said Pete. He wiped his mouth, having taken a large bite of a sandwich. He looked at Keith and cleared his mouth.

'The operation isn't large, about twenty trucks and vans. Most of our deliveries go directly to our distribution centre near Rugby. That's got its own distribution network and we won't be changing that. It's just here, in Aireford. We're going to expand the factory which means shutting the truck depot. The space'll be used to build new dyeing sheds...the ones we've got are donkeys years old, and out of date.'

Keith could see the passion from the man as he explained the rationale in detail.

'So we're looking for someone to house the trucks and basically run that side of the business for us,' said Steve, interrupting Pete.

Keith was almost speechless. 'Aye, I can see the logic,' he said. 'So how do I fit in?'

'Well I hope you'll be able to accommodate our wagons and run the deliveries. We'll pay you a monthly rent and of course cover fuel and labour. All our drivers are self-employed so there won't be a lot of admin. We'll continue the day-to-day running from here.'

Keith couldn't believe his luck.

'Gary's done some costings. Do you want to go through these with Keith?' said Steve.

The accountant looked at Keith and in what seemed to be a foreign language outlined the proposed cost structure, admin fees, labour, fuel and so on. 'We've worked out what we think is a generous rate,' said the finance man.

Keith nearly fell off the chair when Gary suggested the amount.

'When are you thinking of moving on this?' said Keith, trying to avoid showing his excitement.

'Next month,' interjected Steve. 'If we can get everything arranged.'

'Well, as it happens I've been reviewing our own business model,' he said, trying to impress his audience with some business-speak. 'I'm in the process of selling my double-deckers and two of my singles and leasing some nine-seaters to cater for some of the new contracts. It'll give us much more flexibility and free up some space...' He paused as if giving himself thinking time.

'I'll need to chat to my operations chap but yes, I think we should be able to accommodate your wagons,' said Keith.

'Excellent,' said Steve. 'I'll arrange for Pete to go across to your depot tomorrow and sort out some more details.'

'Yes, that'll be great,' said Keith.

After finishing their lunch, Steve stood up and the three followed. He shook hands with Keith.

'It's been a pleasure doing business with you,' he said.

'Likewise,' said Keith, and the team left the boardroom to their various duties. Keith was escorted to the lift again by the ever-attentive Patsy.

As he descended the two floors, Keith was trying to take it all in.

CHAPTER FOURTEEN

As Keith walked to the car, he thought about the earlier sighting of Amir. He detested the man, he gave him the shivers and for a moment Keith wondered what he was doing there, but of course he supplied people to the factory so it made sense he would have some connection with Hyams. What did that say about Steve Jones' integrity, he wondered. He pondered that for a moment before getting into his car, but he was soon thinking about more pressing things.

He headed back to the depot but was not really concentrating. He couldn't believe the transformation in just a week, and, it seemed for the better. Business was coming in thick and fast and even his dealings with the gang had not been as onerous or as threatening as he first feared. He was obviously being useful to them and he hoped would soon have paid back any indebtedness. The incident with the coat had changed everything.

He couldn't wait to get back and tell Kathryn all about his latest news. He keyed in a number on the hands-free phone set up in the car.

'Woodley's,' came the reply.

'Maggie, it's Keith, can you get Jack in the office for me if he's about? I don't think he's out this afternoon, probably in the service bay. I'll be back in about ten minutes; I need to have a chinwag. Aye, ok.'

Keith dropped the call; all sorts of ideas were going through his mind, all positive. He was on a roll.

It was over an hour before he finished the meeting with Jack Clayton, his longest-serving employee, works manager and trusted friend. He knew he would get straight answers from him and expected the usual nay-saying, but to Keith's surprise Jack was as upbeat as he always was and was keen to start doing measurements. Keith gave him Pete Squire's phone number.

'He'll give you any information you want. He's coming over tomorrow to have a look round and go over the detail,' said Keith.

'Cheers,' said Jack, and he left Keith's office whistling 'She'll Be Coming 'Round the Mountain'.

At twenty to five Keith was on the road to get to the hotel to pick up the two Albanian girls. He'd had his meeting with the leasing guy and concluded the arrangements for his buses and the new vehicles, with delivery in three weeks.

He pulled up at the service entrance around the side just after five, and Edita and Delvina were stood there waiting, still looking utterly dejected.

He got out and slid open the side door and the girls got in.

'Hi girls, had a good day?' he said as he drove off.

Delvina was staring out of the window, Edita looking straight ahead.

'Why do you ask us?' said Edita sharply.

'Ok, ok, I get it, you don't want to talk,' said Keith.

'We are not allowed to talk to you,' said Edita.

'What do you mean?' said Keith.

'They will punish us if we talk,' said Edita.

'What do you mean? Who will punish you?' said Keith.

'I cannot say,' said Edita.

'That Nicolai bloke from yesterday?' said Keith.

'I cannot say,' said Edita.

'Well don't you take no notice, if you want to talk it's fine by me; I'm not going to say anything.'

There was no reply and Keith could see the girls in his mirror, whispering to each other in Albanian.

He was crawling through the town centre; the traffic was bumper to bumper, and started heading up the climb towards Argyle Street.

'Look, it's none of my business girls, but are you in some sort of trouble?' said Keith.

More whispering, sharper this time.

'We will be punished if we say,' said Edita.

'Well, as I said, I'll say nothing. I just drive the taxi that is all. I don't work for them.'

There was no reply and they were approaching the end of the road.

'Right, ok girls, we're here. I'll pick you up same time tomorrow but remember what I said. If you want to talk to me it's fine; it won't go no further. You have my word,' said Keith as he parked up.

The door opened and Nicolai was there, stood at the entrance.

Keith got out and slid open the door on the driver's side, out of view.

As the girls got out, Edita looked at Keith. 'Thank you,' she whispered. Keith nodded. 'It's ok,' he mouthed.

'Just fetch the others from Hyams,' shouted Keith to Nicolai.

'Yes,' he replied, and ushered the girls in and shut the door.

Keith drove on to the factory, wondering about the girls.

It was gone six by the time Keith had delivered the Macedonians back to Argyle Street and picked up his car from the depot. It was strange; he noticed the factory girls seemed far livelier than the ones from the hotel. They were busy chatting between themselves in the minibus, but making no attempt to engage with their driver. Keith decided not to say anything.

As he reached home, Kathryn's Clio was on the drive in its usual place.

'Hi, I'm home,' he shouted to anyone who would listen.

'In the kitchen,' Kathryn called back.

Keith went into the kitchen and picked up a mug from the rack and started making a tea. Kathryn was peeling potatoes by the sink, dressed in her round-the-house clothes, jeans and top. He went over to her and pecked her on the cheek.

'How was your day?' she asked, and it was like opening the floodgates as the words gushed out. Keith explained the goings-on with great enthusiasm. Her ears pricked up as soon as Steve's name was mentioned.

'Couldn't believe it,' he said. 'Right out of the blue, calls me up and says he wants us to take over his delivery business. Just brilliant, looks a right earner as well.'

The outpourings took another fifteen minutes, with hardly a word from Kathryn apart from the odd acknowledgement. The conversation was broken by Jason coming into the kitchen.

'How's it going son?' said Keith as he approached.

'Cool,' said Jason. 'When's dinner, Mom? I'm starving,' he added.

'Won't be long... Have you finished your homework?' said Kathryn.

'Nearly,' said Jason. 'Finish it off after tea.'

Twenty minutes later the family were sat around the table, and Keith continued to tell them about his plans for the business.

There was a break in conversation while Keith ate some of his quiche.

'I'm going out on Friday,' said Kathryn.

Keith looked up from his plate.

'What's this, a hot Friday night disco?' said Keith jokingly.

'No, no,' said Kathryn. 'One of the girls at work is leaving. She's having a do, that's all. I said I would go... unless you're out.'

'No, I wouldn't think so. I've got to take one of Steve's bigwigs to the airport on Saturday morning so I'll be in bed early anyhow... Wants a limo,' said Keith. 'Still, he's paying well so can't turn it down.'

Kathryn felt her tummy turn at the mention of Steve's name.

'What time will you have to leave...? Saturday I mean?' said Kathryn.

'I've got to pick him up from the hotel at five-thirty,' said Keith.

'Which hotel?' said Kathryn.

'Hayfield Manor... does a lot of work there apparently,' said Keith.

Kathryn's appetite had totally disappeared and over half of her meal was still on her plate as she cleared the dishes; no-one noticed. There was no more interrogation about her night out so Kathryn didn't press it further. Friday night was on, and she couldn't wait.

After finishing the washing-up, Kathryn went into the garden. Keith was on his computer sorting out some admin. Out of sight, she took out her phone from the pocket of her jeans and accessed her text messages. She reread Steve's earlier message, then sent a text.

'Ok, Friday,' it said.

She waited to see if there was any response. She paced around the lawn, pulled up a couple of weeds that were protruding between the paving slabs, still nothing, then, just as she was about to head indoors, there was a ping from her phone. She looked at the screen.

'Great, same place?'

Kathryn was having trouble with the small keyboard, and her shaking fingers.

'Yes'

'Shall I book a room?'

Kathryn shivered. 'Yes'

'8.00'

'Yes'

'Can't wait xx'

'Yes'

She turned off her phone and went inside.

At Argyle Street, there was a lot of excitement as Victor and Uri continued the quest to attract female admirers. There was an air of competitiveness. Victoria smiled at their banter and antics, most of which was carried out in Ukrainian, which she didn't understand.

Edita and Delvina were upstairs in the attic but both were listless. Victoria had noticed their demeanour and had commented. Reluctantly and despite protestations from Delvina, Edita had agreed to make a video with Uri. Nicolai would carry on the FaceBook feeds and Victoria would be behind the camera. Edita was past caring; at least it would top up their cashbooks. Afterwards, Victoria noticed the lack of enthusiasm in the performance; it was as though Edita was going through the motions. Unfortunately, her mood had translated onto the screen and Victoria wasn't sure if they could use the video.

As Edita returned downstairs to the kitchen, Victoria had a word.

'Are you ok, Edita? You don't seem to be enjoying yourself as usual.'

'I am fine,' said Edita sharply. She took a bottle of water from the fridge and brushed past Victoria.

'I am going to bed,' she said.

Victoria looked at Nicolai. 'Keep an eye on those two,' she said. 'Something isn't right.'

The following morning Keith pulled up outside the house at

the usual time, the girls were waiting. Despite Victoria's warning, Nicolai was not going to accompany the girls to work; he had more important things to do. It would be eight-thirty in Latvia and he was keen to get back to the social media chat lines. Two of the girls they had targeted were already online.

Keith drove away down Argyle Street to the T junction. He looked in the mirror and the girls seemed less upset.

'How are you girls this morning?' he said.

'We are ok,' said Edita.

'Keith... you can call me Keith,' he said.

'Yes,' said Edita.

There was some discussion between the girls in Albanian. Then Edita spoke to Keith.

'Can I have your phone please to call my mother?'

Keith was a bit taken aback by the request.

'Where does she live?' said Keith.

'In Albania,' said Edita.

'Phew, not sure about that, costs a fortune on the mobile,' said Keith.

'Please, please, we will pay you,' said Edita. 'Our mother, she is very worried.'

Keith was in a good mood and feeling benevolent. 'Aye, go on then, but make it quick, eh?'

He took the phone from the dashboard holder and waited for a stop at a set of traffic lights to key in the password. He passed it behind him and Edita took it. She looked at the screen then started to dial. Keith could see Edita with the phone at her ear waiting for it to connect. Then animated chat in Albanian. Edita handed over the phone to Delvina, more chatter. Back to Edita and after a couple of minutes she hung up and passed the phone to Keith. Delvina was crying again.

'Thank you, thank you,' she said.

'That's ok,' said Keith, who was starting to work one or two things out.

'You're illegals aren't you?' said Keith.

Edita look at Keith in the mirror and could make eye contact.

'We were taken... from our home, and brought here, yes.'

'Jesus,' said Keith. 'What, from... where was it? Albania?'

'Yes, they gave us drugs,' she said.

'Why don't you go to the police?' said Keith.

'The police, they will do nothing,' said Edita. 'Then the people, they will kill us.'

'Jesus,' said Keith again. He was starting to realise what he had got into.

'Maybe you can help us,' said Edita.

'I don't know about that. They'll kill me an' all,' said Keith.

It went quiet and Keith drew up outside the hotel. He slid the doors open and the girls grabbed their stuff and got out.

'Look, I can't promise anything, but sit tight and I'll try to think of something,' he said.

'Thank you,' said Edita.

The morning was busy again back at the depot. The promised visit by Pete Squires had taken place and Keith had left him with Jack Clayton to show him around and discuss logistics. Maggie came in with yet another coffee. Keith looked at her as she handed him the mug.

'Do you know,' she said rhetorically. 'Tomorrow all the buses are out... if you include the school runs with the double-deckers. I've had to call in all the temporary drivers; can't remember the last time that happened.'

'That's great,' said Keith. 'Oh, did you manage to get the limo for Saturday?'

'Yes, one of Ted's guys will drop it round Friday night about six,' said Maggie.

'That's great. Hope you got a good deal,' said Keith.

'Well, I managed to get him down to one fifty. Wouldn't budge further,' said Maggie.

'That's ok. I quoted Steve Jones four hundred,' and he looked at her and smiled.

Keith was still on a high when a call came through which would alter things.

'Keith I have a Mr Aziz for you... wouldn't say what it was about, quite rude in fact,' said Maggie.

Keith's disposition changed. 'You better put him through,' said Keith, and he cleared his throat with a cough.

'Keith Woodley,' he said.

'It is Amir.'

'Yes,' said Keith, not wishing any long conversation.

'I have a new job for you. I will come at six tonight and tell you what you will do... yes?' he said.

'Yeah,' said Keith. 'What sort of job?'

'Tonight at six,' said Amir, and he rang off.

Keith sat for a moment; a touch of reality had set in. He thought for a moment and then picked up the phone. The call rang out, no reply; he left a message.

'Hi, it's me. I'll be a bit later tonight, some business at the depot. I'll call you when I leave.'

Keith rang off. He didn't know when Kathryn would pick up the message but it would be in time for her to rearrange the catering arrangements.

Maggie soon noticed the change in demeanour.

'You ok? You look like you've lost a pound and found a sixpence,' she said.

'Eh, oh... yes,' said Keith. 'Nah, I'm ok.'

But he wasn't; he had a bad feeling about the meeting.

By five forty-five the depot was quiet. There were a couple of buses out plus a minivan on one of Steve's airport runs. Keith was sat in his office on his own, deep in contemplation. He had picked up the Albanians earlier and there was only polite conversation and nothing related to the morning's discussion.

Then the door opened, making him jump, and Amir and Uri were stood there.

'Didn't hear you knock,' said Keith, irked by the bad manners.

'We didn't,' said Amir.

'You better sit down then,' said Keith, and the two visitors pulled up two chairs and sat close to the table, which he found very intimidating.

'You mentioned something about a job,' said Keith.

'That is why we are here,' said Amir. Keith looked at them, trying to maintain some sort of composure, but failing. There was a rank smell; one of them had a halitosis issue.

'Next week you will drive for us,' said Amir.

'Ok, where to?' said Keith, who had discovered the source of the breath problem.

'Latvia, we have some passengers to bring here,' said Amir. Uri was sat slightly behind Amir eyeing Keith up. Keith was very uncomfortable.

'Latvia... but that's...'

'Yes,' said Amir. 'About four days there and back. You have... how you say? A small bus. We will have five people I think.'

'A minibus you mean, yes, but I can't do that on my own, it's illegal,' said Keith, who was trying to look away when Amir was speaking.

'You will not go on your own. I will go with you,' said Amir.

'Ok,' said Keith. 'That's alright then,' he added with more than a hint of sarcasm, which Amir didn't pick up.

Amir had no choice. When he and Victoria discussed the trip it was obvious he would have to go. He was the only one who had a valid passport.

'What about the ferry and everything?' said Keith.

'We will sort everything out. Someone will call you and get the information. We go Monday,' he said.

'What about the diesel?' said Keith. 'It's gonna cost a bit.'

'We will pay for that?' said Amir.

'What about the hotel and factory runs?' said Keith, putting as many blocks in the way as he could think of.

'You have another driver I think?' said Amir.

'Yes,' said Keith.

'That is ok then. You tell me who it will be and I will tell Nicolai,' said Amir.

'Right,' said Keith.

'I will call here Sunday five o'clock with the papers you will need. That is all,' he said, and he got up from the chair and walked towards the door. Uri did the same.

He turned around. 'You will tell no-one about our journey, you understand,' said Amir.

'But I have to say something; I can't just leave...' said Keith

Amir cut in. 'I am not concerned, it is your problem. I will be here Sunday, five o'clock.'

He turned and walked out.

Keith went to the window and opened it as wide as it would go. He could see the two men walking to a large Mercedes. Amir was driving and Keith watched them leave the depot.

'Shit,' he said. Four days in close proximity with this man was not a pleasant prospect.

He sat at his desk thinking of how he could explain away his absence. Then a thought occurred to him – there had been no mention of payment. He would have to negotiate something on

Sunday. If there was no invoice it would certainly alert Maggie, who was a stickler for paperwork, and saying it was a 'cash job' would not help much either; she would want it to bank. He put his head in his hands and groaned. He was now pretty clear on what he was caught up in, but how he would ever extricate himself from it was another matter entirely.

It was gone seven before he arrived home, and the family had eaten. Kathryn was washing the dishes when he walked in. He went to the kitchen, straight to the fridge and took out a bottle of lager.

'Not a good day then?' said Kathryn. She knew the signs.

'Nah, it was ok... Got to go away next week... Latvia of all places,' he said, and drank a large mouthful of beer straight from the bottle.

'Well that's good, isn't it?' she said.

Actually, from an outsider's perspective it would appear very good. He backtracked.

'Err, yes, yes... just with all this business coming in, I could have done without it,' he said.

'I hope they're paying well,' she said as she put the last of the saucepans on the drainer.

'Err, yes, should be a good earner,' his favourite phrase.

'Your dinner's in the microwave. Just needs heating up,' she said. 'Kids are doing homework,' she added, noticing that Keith had made no enquiry.

'Oh good,' said Keith, negotiating the timer on the microwave.

Kathryn went into the lounge. Jason and Ellie were upstairs in their rooms doing homework. She put on the TV but was not concentrating. Her phone was in her hand. Steve had texted.

'Can't wait to see you again,' was the message timed at five forty-five p.m.

She replied, 'me too.'

It was seven-thirty and she wasn't expecting a response, just hoped. She tried to watch the TV but her mind was elsewhere.

Five minutes later, a message. 'Can't stop thinking about you.'

She replied again, 'me too.'

'I want to touch your breasts, your pussy.'

She nearly dropped the phone. She felt like that naughty schoolgirl again and had to stifle a laugh. She looked at the screen. Did he really say that? She was not sure how to respond. 'Sexting' it was called, wasn't it? She'd read about it in the papers. Kids were doing it, apparently, and that's how she felt, like a kid. She giggled to herself. She looked to make sure no-one was watching.

'Yes,' she replied. She couldn't think of anything else.

A minute later there was another message.

'God, I want you so bad,' it said.

'Me too,' she replied, 'got to go.'

She wanted to say more but any minute Keith or the kids would be in to watch TV.

She had one last look. A message had arrived again; 'xxx' was all it said.

She read the earlier message again and felt a warm tingle inside, just below her tummy.

Thursday morning, six-thirty a.m., Keith was waiting outside the Argyle Street house. He watched Edita and Delvina approach the minibus and he slid open the door for them to get in. Nicolai was watching; Keith acknowledged and drove off.

'How are you two today?' he said, watching them via the rear-view mirror. Delvina was looking out of the window but Edita returned the eye contact.

'We are ok,' she said.

There was an exchange in Albanian.

'Can we have your phone again to call our mother?' said Edita.

'Not sure about that,' said Keith. 'It's a bit pricey phoning abroad, you know.'

'We will pay you... You want sex? You can have sex, yes?'

'No, no,' said Keith. 'No, you're alright, love. Here, have the phone but don't be long, eh?'

The traffic was crawling along and Keith managed to disengage the phone from its holder and enter the password. He passed it to the girls who were soon chatting animatedly into the handset.

'Hey girls, finish now eh? It's gonna cost me an arm and a leg,' he said.

More chat, then Edita passed the phone back to Keith.

'Thank you, thank you. You have been very kind. We give you good sex if you like.'

'No girls, it's fine. Thanks anyway,' he said.

Edita was back chatting with Delvina, seemingly quite upbeat.

About five minutes away from the hotel Edita leaned forward.

'Can you help us... to escape?' she said.

Keith considered the question. 'Don't know how I can, love. Like I said yesterday, they'll kill me if they find out. They won't be too happy I've been letting you use the phone,' he added.

He saw Edita's face in the mirror, so much sorrow. He was being torn. 'Look, ok, ok,' he said. 'You sit tight, keep your head down and I'll see what I can do.'

'Thank you, thank you,' said Edita, only translating part of the response, and she turned to Delvina and smiled.

After he had completed the morning's runs Keith was back at the depot working out how he was going to explain away Latvia to Maggie. She was going to be more of a problem than Kathryn.

He called her in.

'Have a seat,' he said, which immediately had her on full alert.

'What's up? You're not going to give us the push, are you?' she said.

'What? No, no, don't be daft. No, I just wanted you to know we've had a new job come in, last night... for those Azure Recruitment people.'

'What, the hotel and factory lot?' she replied.

'Yeah, dropped in last night, only want me to go to Latvia,' said Keith.

'Latvia... Latvia? That's Russia isn't it? Why d'they want you to go there?'

'Pick up some tourists and bring them back to the UK, they said,' replied Keith. 'I'll need one of the nine-seaters.'

'For how long? They're like gold dust at the minute,' she said.

'Five days I reckon. Can you juggle the runs around?'

'S'pose I'll have to,' she said. 'Hope they're paying you well.'

'Aye,' he said.

'Who're you taking with you? You'll need two drivers for that. We're a bit thin on the ground, you know. We'll have to get in one of the temps.'

No, no that won't be necessary. They're providing one,' he said.

This was of course all true, but Maggie was a bit uncertain.

'All seems a bit strange to me; what about the ferries and hotels?'

'They're seeing to all that as well,' he said.

'Well you're the boss. I'll see what I can do... but it won't be easy,' she quickly added.

'Thanks,' said Keith. Another hurdle crossed.

With another mug of coffee on his desk Keith started looking up possible routes on the Internet. Then his thoughts took a different direction. He keyed in a search option... 'Trafficking'. He scrolled down all the options on the first few pages. Nothing obvious, mostly drugs. He refined the search, 'Trafficking people'.

He became so engrossed with some of the stories, some horrific, that he lost focus for a time. Then he searched again, 'Trafficking people Albania'.

Then he discovered something, a refuge centre in London. He read the 'home page' of the website.

'A safe haven for girls', it said, exactly what he was looking for. He made a note of the address and telephone number on a scrap of paper.

At Argyle Street, although arrangements appeared to be progressing well, there was a sense of anxiety as this was the first trip they had tried themselves, but so far, so good. There were four "definites", girls who were desperate to work in the UK. Victoria had checked their pictures and profiles and they seemed ideal; two were at college, one at high school, the other at Riga University, all intelligent girls. The other thing was that they were, or at least appeared to be, quite uninhibited; all four had posted raunchy pictures to Uri and Victor. This would make it easier to persuade them to work the chat rooms and do videos, Victoria had said.

Ideally they wanted two more, as the accommodation Amir had arranged would easily take six and they could certainly make use of them given the present demand for material. Victoria was considering a twenty-four-hour operation, given the worldwide clientele. Amir owned another house in the area which was leased, and he'd given the tenants a week to make alternative arrangements in preparation.

Uri was working on the building site, but Nicolai and Victor continued searching for other girls who would be interested in joining the bus to the UK and nurturing the definites.

At Azure Recruitment, Victoria was putting together an itinerary, booking ferries and hotels along the way. Logistically, the home leg was more complex as they had no details of the returning cargo. She made provisional bookings for eight.

Keith was waiting outside the hotel again for the Albanians. They were late but after a few minutes they came around the corner, walking quickly. He opened the door to let them in and pulled away.

'How was your day?' he said.

Edita was beginning to feel more relaxed with Keith.

'Ok,' she said. 'Hotel, it is very busy, clean many rooms,' she said.

Keith put his hand in his pocket and pulled out the scrap of paper.

'I don't know if this will help, love,' he said. 'I've been making some enquiries. This is the address and phone number of a place in London that looks after girls who have been kidnapped and sent to the UK from Albania. They will get you home.'

Edita took the piece of paper and translated for Delvina.

'Thank you,' she said. 'Thank you... but how far is London? How can we get there?'

'Your best bet is to get to the station and get a train,' he said. 'It's about three hours.'

Edita looked at Delvina and translated.

'But we have no money,' she said. 'We cannot buy a ticket.'

Keith was thinking. What if one of the girls had been Ellie, his daughter, in a similar situation? He would want someone to help her, wouldn't he?

'Ok, listen, I can't promise anything, ok,' he said. 'I can't do anything just now and I'm away next week, but when I come back, I'll see what I can do.'

Edita looked at Delvina and back at Keith.

'You will help us, yes... that is wonderful. Thank you, thank you,' she said.

'I will try, I said. When I get back,' said Keith.

'Yes, thank you... Keith. You are a good man,' she said. The irony was not lost on Keith given his pending journey.

CHAPTER FIFTEEN

Friday morning, and by seven-thirty Kathryn was already washed and showered. She had hardly slept and got up as soon as Keith had left for the hotel and factory runs. She checked her phone. There were four messages from Steve; the excitement was growing.

Keith was outside the Argyle Street house at the usual time, with Edita and Delvina waiting at the entrance. He opened the minibus doors for the girls, and then went to Nicolai who was stood watching.

'You know about my trip next week?' he said.

'Of course,' said Nicolai.

'Well Amir said to get one of my other drivers to take over the hotel and factory run while I'm away,' said Keith.

'So?' said Nicolai.

'You need to know his name. I'll get him to do tonight's run and you can meet him. I've got a lot of preparation to do,' said Keith.

'Ok, what is his name?' said Nicolai.

'Jack, Jack Clayton. He's my number two, good as gold. Won't be no trouble.'

'That is good,' said Nicolai. 'Jack... Clay...ton. That is right?' said Nicolai.

'Yes, he will be here tonight. I've told him where to be and who he will be picking up,' said Keith.

He went back to the minibus and set off. Edita and Delvina seemed happier and were chatting together. Then Edita leaned over to speak to Keith. 'Is it ok to use your phone again...? Please?'

'Aye, go on then,' he said, and passed the phone across. 'Don't be long though, eh?'

Edita dialled and more chat in Albanian. This time more excitedly.

After a few minutes, Edita rang off and handed back the phone. 'My mother said she is praying for you for helping me and Delvina. She says you will have a place in heaven.'

Keith suddenly felt very humble, and guilty. He hadn't done anything yet and wasn't sure what, if anything, he was going to be able to do. Much would depend on the trip to Latvia. But now he felt a strong sense of obligation.

'That's ok love. As I said, I'll try to sort something out when I get back,' he said.

'Oh, nearly forgot, you'll have a new driver tonight. His name is Jack and he's a good guy. You be nice to him, eh?' said Keith.

'You want us to have sex with him?' said Edita.

'Good God no... no,' said Keith, and burst out laughing. 'Wouldn't be capable, love anyhow. No, I just meant don't give him a hard time,' he added, still chuckling.

Edita made the translation. 'Yes, I understand,' she said.

'When will you be back?' said Edita.

'Week on Monday,' he said, and then uttered under his breath, 'if we don't get fucking arrested.'

'Ok,' said Edita. 'I hope you are safe.'

'Cheers,' said Keith, recognising the sincerity.

They arrived at the hotel and Keith let them out. 'See you a week Monday. Just sit tight till I get back.'

'Oh nearly forgot, Jack'll be driving the same bus, this one, and I'll tell him to wait at the usual place,' he added.

'Thank you, you have been very kind,' said Edita, and she led Delvina around to the service entrance of the hotel ready to start another day.

Keith was back at the depot by eight-thirty and wandered into the service bay where Jack Clayton tended to hang out when not on a run. He was examining the inner workings of one of the nine-seater minibuses, holding a spanner like a surgeon with a scalpel.

'Hi Jack, thought I would find you here,' he said. 'Problems?'

'Eh, aye up Keith. Nah... I've put this one by for you, just thought I'd give it a bit of a service like. It's the best one here... It's the one I'd choose if I was making t' trip next week. Just put in a new set of plugs. It'll run like new.'

'Cheers,' said Keith.

Jack stood there wiping the oil from his hands with a rag that appeared to be adding to rather than alleviating the problem.

'You will be ok... with this run I mean? It's been a while since we've been on't Continent,' he said.

'Aye,' said Keith. 'Maggie's getting me a few Euros but they're paying for all the fuel as we go along.'

'What about the route?' said Jack.

'Had a look last night, seems straightforward enough. Rotterdam, Berlin, Warsaw, then through Lithuania, that's what it said,' said Keith.

'Are you sure you don't want me or one of the lads to go with you?' said Jack.

'Nah, you're ok, Jack, thanks. The guy who's paying for it says he can drive. We'll have to keep the rest of the seats free for the passengers.'

'How many are you bringing back?' asked Jack.

'At least four they said,' replied Keith.

'And they're coming on holiday?' said Jack.

'That's what he said,' said Keith.

'Why would anyone come all that way on a coach to Aireford...? I mean it's not your usual holiday resort,' said Jack.

'Aye, that's for sure,' said Keith. 'Still they're paying for it. It's up to them.'

'What about the return trip?' said Jack?

'Didn't mention it,' said Keith.

'Oh... right,' said Jack. 'All seems a bit strange to me,' he added.

'Well, can't turn down good business,' said Keith.

'Aye, too right there,' said Jack.

'By the way,' said Keith as he was about to walk away and leave Jack to his surgery. 'I thought you could do tonight's run, the hotel and factory, and then if there're any problems you can let me know.'

'Aye, right you are,' said Jack, and Keith explained the arrangements and where to pick up the girls.

At Argyle Street, Victoria was overseeing the Internet exchanges, with Victor and Nicolai having taken the day off from the office. She had worked out all the timings, booked the ferries and hotels and calculated that they would be in Riga sometime on Wednesday night so the pick-up would need to be Thursday morning.

'Tell the girls to be at the bus station in Riga at seven-thirty on Thursday, the Pragas Iela one; it is very close to the train station. They will know it; I used it all the time when I lived there,' said Victoria.

Nicolai and Victor wrote it down and contacted the girls. The four were already online and appeared excited at the prospect.

'See, this one,' said Victor, having given the pick-up details. Victoria looked at the messages.

'Yes, I know it well. I will be there,' said Portia. 'I have a friend also who will come.'

'That is good, very good,' said Victoria. 'That will be five. Try to get another one if you can. Don't forget to tell them they will need their passports.'

Amir walked in to check on progress.

'How are things?' he said.

'Good,' said Victoria. 'We will arrange to pick them up on Thursday. Have you spoken to Mr Jones about the money?' she added.

'Yes, he will pay. I will call him now... We will need the money on Monday,' he said.

Amir moved into the kitchen away from the noise of the computer room and dialled Steve Jones' direct line.

'Jones,' was the reply after the third ring.

'It is Amir. We have the girls arranged... We will need the money on Monday as you agreed.'

'Monday!? That doesn't leave much time,' said Steve.

'But it will be ok, yes?' said Amir.

'Yes, ok. Let me check my diary... no, it's fine,' he said. 'I'll call at the hotel about eleven.'

'Excellent,' said Amir.

Later that afternoon, Maggie appeared at Keith's desk with yet another coffee. It had been so busy he had hardly had a break. Pete Squires from Hyams had called about transferring the haulage work and Keith had passed it on to Jack; he had enough on his plate at the moment.

'Just had Ted Avis on the phone; he'll be here about six-thirty with the limo,' she said.

'Oh right, thanks Maggie. That's a bit late... said he would be here for five... Not to worry, better let the wife know,' he said, and took out his phone and sent a text.

'Will be back about seven,' it said.

Kathryn was still at work and had heard the ping of the text from her handbag. She hoped it would be Steve again; this would be number six.

There was a lull at the desk and she took out her phone and had a peek. She read the note.

'Damn,' she said to herself. She quickly returned a message.

'Don't forget going out', it said.

Keith read the reply; he had completely forgotten.

'OK,' he replied.

By six o'clock, Jack had returned from the hotel and factory run and reported to the office.

'Hi Jack, how did it go?' said Keith as he walked in.

'Aye, no problem. Nice girls,' he said.

'Did you meet the guy at the house?' said Keith.

'Oh aye...'t were fine. Told him I'd be there Monday, quarter to seven,' he said.

'Cheers,' said Keith. 'You get off, Jack, I'll close up. I'm waiting for Ted Avis; he'll be a while yet. I can catch up on some bits and pieces.'

'Aye, right you are... By the way, been meaning to ask, did they ever catch anybody about your phone?' said Jack.

Keith had to think for a minute.

'Oh, err, no... Not heard a dicky bird,' said Keith.

'Aye, better things to do I expect, the police. Right see you tomorrow. What time will you be back from t' airport?' said Jack.

'About eight-thirty, nine I expect. Traffic shouldn't be too bad Saturday morning,' said Keith.

Jack left the office and Keith was on his computer. Maggie had already left. At six-thirty, he checked his watch and looked out of the window into the depot. His buses were all neatly lined up waiting for their next outings. Keith looked at his watch again. Kathryn would not be best pleased.

It was ten to seven before the Daimler pulled up outside the reception area. Keith was stood waiting.

'Hiya Keith,' said Ted as he got out of the car. 'Sorry it's a bit late, traffic's a nightmare.'

'No problem,' said Keith, accepting the keys from him.

'D'you think you could do us a favour and run us back, like?' said Ted. 'Only I couldn't arrange a lift.'

Keith was in a dilemma; the clock was ticking. He pondered for a moment.

'Sorry, Ted mate, wife's expecting me back... but, look, I've got a better idea. Why don't you take my Merc and drop it back tomorrow morning and we can swap back?' he said.

'Aye, go on then,' said Ted.

'Wait there, won't be a moment,' said Keith, and he went back into the office.

'There you go,' said Keith, returning with a set of keys for his Mercedes.

'It's just over there,' said Keith, pointing to his parking spot just beside the office.

In the Woodley household things were getting fraught. Kathryn had already had a go at Ellie and Jason for seemingly minor indiscretions and both were in their respective bedrooms taking out their frustrations on social media posts.

It was nearly twenty to eight and she was pacing up and down in the lounge. She checked herself in the mirror for the umpteenth time. She had had an extended lunch hour and paid a call to the hairdressers. She was wearing her 'night out' gear; white blouse, short grey skirt, hold-ups and heels. 'Come on,' she muttered under her breath.

Just then, the Daimler pulled up on the drive. Kathryn went to the door, had one final check and left the house.

'Sorry I'm late, love,' said Keith as he got out of the limo.

'Well, I can't stop, gonna have to go or I'll be late. See you tomorrow sometime,' she said, and kissed Keith on the cheek as she walked past him and to the Clio. She flicked the key fob and opened the door, put her coat on the back seat and started the engine. Then she looked over her shoulder and reversed out of the drive. She was gone.

Keith just watched feeling suitably admonished, and guilty. He trudged into the house.

Kathryn was still putting her seat belt on. She looked down, her skirt was almost at the top of her hold-ups and the belt was pushing her chest upwards. She shivered.

It was five past eight as she parked the car at the back of the hotel. It was almost full and she had to go to the overflow area at the far end before she could find a space. She checked herself again in the mirror and undid another button on her blouse.

She picked up her coat from the back seat, locked the car and headed for reception. The car was parked on gravel and she cursed as the stones and uneven surface impeded her progress. 'Shit,' she muttered as she nearly lost her footing. Her shoes would be scratched to pieces at this rate, she thought. As she reached the swing doors, she paused briefly trying to compose herself, then went inside and looked around.

Steve was waiting in the same place and got up and walked towards her; Kathryn smiled more than she had intended. He kissed her on the cheek as he had done the last time.

'Do you want a drink?' he said.

'Yes please,' she said, almost too quickly.

'We'll go into the Terrace Bar, it's quite busy tonight.'

Funnily enough, she had hardly noticed the hubbub in the reception area; she had eyes for only one thing.

She followed Steve along the corridor to the bar and watched his slim hips move in his grey chinos, he was carrying a grey sports jacket casually over his shoulders; involuntarily she bit her bottom lip.

The bar was busy with guests and golfers who had finished their rounds and were enjoying a 19ᵗʰ tee tipple. It was a warm night and the Terrace Bar patio doors were open with chairs and tables set up outside to allow an al fresco experience. There was a table in the corner, away from the window, and Steve headed for it. Kathryn felt conspicuous walking through the bar, and for a moment the thought of discovery went through her mind.

'What would you like?' said Steve as Kathryn settled in her seat.

'Gin and tonic please,' she said.

A waiter approached them. 'Large gin and tonic and half of lager, please,' said Steve.

'You look stunning,' said Steve as the waiter went to dispense the drinks.

'Thank you,' she said.

'I haven't been able to concentrate on anything this week,' he added.

'Yes,' said Kathryn.

'Sorry about some of the texts,' he said. 'Couldn't help myself.'

'That's ok,' said Kathryn. 'They made me laugh.' They had also done other things but she kept that to herself.

The waiter brought the drinks and Steve signed for them.

Kathryn took a sip. 'Can we go?' she said. 'I feel a bit conspicuous here.'

'Yes, of course,' said Steve. 'We can take our drinks up.'

Steve led the way. Kathryn picked up her coat and handbag and followed.

'Four, three, four,' said Steve as they got to the lift.

The door opened and they both went in. Kathryn was nearest the buttons and pressed for the fourth floor.

Steve leaned across and kissed her. With her gin and tonic in one hand and her coat and handbag in the other, responding as she would have liked was not that easy. She was trying desperately not to drip her drink over her blouse.

The lift stopped with a judder and it took all Steve's powers of balance not to spill his lager. Kathryn saw the funny side and giggled.

They soon found the room and Steve negotiated the key card. As before, he opened the door and inserted the card into the slot to turn on the electrics. He put the lager on the side next to the TV and Kathryn put her drink next to Steve's. Then she threw her coat over the back of one of the armchairs and suddenly all the pent-up emotions of the last few days were unleashed.

The slow uncertain moves of the first time were replaced by an urgency. With their lips seemingly locked together, Kathryn peeled off her blouse and unclipped her bra; then pushed Steve's shirt over his shoulders, letting it fall to the floor. She pulled down the zip on the side of her skirt while Steve unfastened his trousers. Kathryn broke away and sat back on the bed in just her knickers and hold-ups; Steve removed his socks and lay beside Kathryn in his shorts.

Then it was just a morass of hands, fingers and tongues. Steve turned her over on her stomach and was in her, doggy style. Kathryn thought she was going to faint, Steve was taking her to places she had only read about in the pages of her lunchtime read. It didn't really happen, not in the real world. It was just fantasy, but here she was playing out her wildest imaginations. She screamed as she reached orgasm, Steve followed and they just lay together, their bodies rising and falling in harmony.

'God that was so good,' said Steve, and he looked across at her and he could see she was crying.

'Are you ok?' he said.

'Perfect,' she said, and she leaned over and kissed him.

They lay there for a while, and then Steve got up fetched Kathryn's drink,

'Thought you might need this,' he said.

Saturday morning, four-thirty a.m., the buzzer on the bedside clock inflicted torment on Keith's ears and he awoke startled. He pressed the silent button and let out a soft groan. He looked across the bed; Kathryn was laid with her back to his. He carefully slid out of bed; Kathryn stirred momentarily. He had not heard her come in, but it must have been quite late. It was gone eleven-thirty before he set the alarm and turned out the light.

He quickly showered and went downstairs. Kathryn's coat was draped over the arm of the sofa and her shoes were on their side in the middle of the lounge. He picked them up and placed them neatly next to the shoe rack in the hall. He checked the clock, five a.m., just enough time to grab a slice of toast and a cup of tea. He reversed the Daimler out of the drive; it was a tight manoeuvre, a good foot wider than his Mercedes.

Kathryn was restless. Keith's departure had disturbed her sleep and she was having difficulty returning to her slumber. She could feel Steve's hands all over her body replaying every move. She had never made love continuously like that, not even on her honeymoon. It was with some reluctance when she had called time; it was gone midnight.

'Can I see you again?' Steve had said. Truth was she didn't want to leave him.

It was almost one o'clock by the time she had parked up back at the house, but she didn't feel in the slightest bit tired; she was still on a high. The place was eerily quiet as she put her coat over the sofa and kicked off her shoes. She went to the kitchen and poured herself a glass of water before going upstairs. She could hear Keith snoring before she had reached the bedroom door. This wasn't what she wanted, she decided, she needed something else.

Kathryn tossed and turned, trying to make sense of the miasma in her head. She couldn't remember if she had gone back to sleep after Keith had left, but she didn't think she had. She eventually dragged herself out of bed at seven-thirty. Instinctively, she picked up her phone on the bedside cabinet and checked; a text message from Steve. 'A night I will never forget xx', it said. It was an hour old but she returned the message. 'Me too x.'

Jason and Ellie were always out on Saturdays; Ellie with her part-time job, Jason, playing football. So by ten-thirty she had the place to herself. She put a load of washing into the machine but it was as though she was on autopilot, her mind was somewhere else.

Keith, meanwhile, was back at the depot and had watched nearly all his buses leave, some day trips, a couple of football specials. Jack had held back the nine-seater which he would be using on Monday. Inside he was starting to have a really bad feeling, not just about the journey but about the whole thing. He had no doubt that it was some kind of people-smuggling racket and here he was actively participating; of course, though, he had little option. However, he had decided he would do something for the Albanians; it would at least assuage some of the guilt.

He looked at the office wall clock and cursed to himself. He had forgotten to call Kathryn; he had been distracted. He picked the receiver up from the desk phone and dialled. It rang out but there was no reply; he would try again later.

Kathryn did hear the phone ring, she was just getting dressed, but when she saw the number she let it go to answer phone; she did not feel like talking to Keith.

In Argyle Street, the activity was frenetic. As it was Saturday

Victoria had asked Marija, Elena and Bijana to work the chat rooms in the morning to catch the last of the American traffic. The demand was continuing to increase together with the income stream.

Edita and Delvina were in their rooms watching TV. The previous night, Edita had done another video with Uri, and with their cash-books refilled, the two had decided to go into town in the afternoon. Nicolai would be chaperoning. With Keith's offer to help and the opportunity to speak to their mother they were feeling more positive and there had been a noticeable change in their demeanour. Victoria was beginning to think they were at last settling down in their environment and she felt quite relaxed about them going into town, as long as they were accompanied. The main focus of attention, though, was the pending visit to Latvia and the recruitment of the new girls.

Uri and Victor were preparing the new house in Sutherland Close, an adjoining road. It was a question of a few minor repairs and adding some furniture acquired from a second-hand shop. They were in the bathroom fixing a blocked sink. Uri had something on his mind; it had been bothering him for some time.

'What do you think of the new plan?' he asked Victor.

'What new plan?' replied Victor.

'Getting the girls from the Internet,' said Uri.

'It is good,' said Victor. 'We have seen many nice girls, pretty girls.' He moved his arms up and down in an hourglass fashion and smiled.

'But what about Vasyl?' said Uri.

'What about Vasyl?' said Victor.

'If he finds out that we have been bringing in girls, what will he do?' said Uri.

'I don't know, I just do as I'm told,' said Victor.

'He will be angry,' said Uri.

'But why, it will not affect them?' said Victor.

'Of course it will... Amir won't have to pay them for girls now,' said Uri. 'They will lose much money and Vasyl will not like that,' said Uri.

'What are you saying?' said Victor.

'Vasyl helped us to get here, yes, and get job. You know what he told us about calling him if there was trouble?' said Uri.

'But this is not our problem, it is Amir... Anyway we paid them for our passage,' said Victor.

'Yes, but if he finds out that Amir is bringing in girls and we knew and didn't tell him... what then?' said Uri.

'He would probably kill us,' said Victor.

'Exactly,' said Uri.

'So what do we do?' said Victor.

'Nothing for the moment, we wait for the new girls. If we say something now, Amir will just call us liars,' said Uri.

'Then Amir will kill us,' said Victor.

'Yes,' said Uri.

The pair got on with the sink issue but were deep in thought.

Late afternoon, Kathryn had finished the washing and was making herself a drink when her phone beeped. It was a text from Steve. 'Can you talk?' it said.

She looked at the screen and reread the message. The kids were still out and Keith was at the depot.

'Yes,' she replied.

A minute later her phone rang.

'Hi,' said Steve.

'Hi,' she replied.

'God, I've missed you,' he said.

'Missed you too,' she said.

'Can you get away for a while tonight...? Just a couple of

hours,' said Steve. 'Sonia's going to her mother's and won't be back till around ten.'

'What about the kids?' asked Kathryn.

'She's taking them with her,' he said.

'I don't know,' said Kathryn. 'I haven't seen Keith since last night. What had you got in mind?'

'Well I won't have time for the hotel but we could go for a drive somewhere. Find a pub or something,' said Steve.

'Sounds nice,' said Kathryn. 'What time... if I can get away?'

'Sonia's going out about seven... back about ten.'

'Not much time,' said Kathryn.

'Yes, sorry, it was all I could manage. I was going crazy not being able to see you,' said Steve.

'Yes, I know what you mean.' She paused for a moment. 'Look, I'll see what I can do, but I can't promise. I'll text.'

'Ok,' said Steve. 'Hope to see you later.'

'Yes, gotta go.'

Kathryn hung up and started working out possibilities. It all depended on what time Keith got back, and that could be anytime if recent events were anything to go by. She looked at her watch, ten past four.

She picked up the phone and dialled.

'Hi,' said Keith, picking up his mobile from his desk. 'I've been trying to ring you. I tried a couple of times,' he said before she could speak, in case she was angry for the apparent snub.

'Oh, I've had the Hoover on, didn't hear it.'

There was a slight pause. 'What time will you be home tonight?' she added.

'Don't know; it's been chaos here. We've had most of the buses out. Last one's due in around seven,' said Keith.

'Ok, well I may be out if you're late,' she said, and waited for the response.

'Out again? You're getting a real party girl.'

'I wish,' said Kathryn. 'Jane Fraser... she's one of the supervisors, was taken into hospital this morning, suspected gallstones. Deborah Johnson, you remember her, don't you? She phoned this morning, asked if I fancied visiting her then popping out for a drink afterwards.'

'Well, it sounds like it's all arranged,' said Keith.

'No, it's not. I said I'd speak to you in case you'd arranged anything... There's nothing on the calendar, thought you'd probably be busy.'

'What about the kids?' said Keith.

'They'll be alright till you get here and they've got my mobile if there're any problems,' she replied. 'I won't be late.'

'Well, I'll see you when you get back then,' he said, and hung up.

He looked at the phone and wondered if he had done anything to upset her but was interrupted by his mobile phone ring.

'Hello,' he said, and listened.

'Shit... Where...? M1, Sheffield? No, ok. Have you called Spicers...? Good... Ok, sit tight, I'll be there as soon as I can. How many have you got? Ok, there's a twenty-four-seater just come in, I'll be in that... yeah, about six-ish. I'll give you a call on the road,' he said, and rang off.

Keith got up and went into the yard. Dave Shawcross was cleaning out the bus he had just returned in from a shopping trip to Leeds. He saw Keith approaching.

'Hi boss, everything ok?' he said, seeing a look of exasperation on Keith's face.

'Nah, Bruce just called in. Broken down on the M1 north of Sheffield,' said Keith.

'What, the Meadowhall crowd?' said Dave.

'Yeah, just got on to the motorway and the clutch went... I'm gonna have to pick 'em up. Bruce's called Spicers... the breakdown gang,' he clarified. 'They're on their way.'

'Do you want me to fetch 'em?' said Dave.

'You can't, you haven't got the hours,' said Keith. 'But you could hang on here and man the switch for us for a bit if you're ok.' Dave had been trained in using the phone switchboard. 'Just in case we get any more calls,' said Keith.

'Yeah, no problem... nowt planned tonight,' said Dave. He looked around at the yard. There were still six vehicles out.

'What're you gonna use?' said Dave.

'I'll have to take this one. Bruce has got twenty on,' said Keith.

'They're not gonna be too happy,' said Dave.

'Aye, you can say that again,' said Keith.

'I'm just about finished here. I'll fill her up for you,' said Dave.

'Cheers,' said Keith, and he went back inside the office to lock up.

Ten minutes later, Keith was on the road heading for the stricken vehicle with twenty irate customers and a frustrated driver on board. He was heading out of town when he had a sudden thought.

'Shit,' he said to himself, and pressed the speed dial on his phone.

'Hello,' she said.

'It's me. Look, I've got a breakdown with one of the buses,' he said. 'I've got to go and pick up the customers.'

'What time will you be back?' said Kathryn, trying to hide her frustration.

'No idea. It'll be gone six by the time I get down there. Then I'll have to get back to Aireford and do the drop-offs. Nine, half past, something like that,' he said.

'Can't someone else do it?' said Kathryn.

'No, there's no-one else in apart from Dave Shawcross and he hasn't got enough hours left; he's already been out today,' said

Keith.

'Well, I'm not letting Deborah down. I've already said I would meet her,' said Kathryn.

'No, no of course not,' said Keith. 'What about the kids?'

'Ellie's ok, she staying in tonight. She can look after Jason. They'll be fine,' said Kathryn.

'Yeah, ok, can't do much about it, sorry,' said Keith. 'See you when I get back.'

'Yeah,' said Kathryn, and rang off.

CHAPTER SIXTEEN

Keith snaked through the Aireford traffic heading towards the motorway, while Kathryn went to Ellie's room to explain the evening's arrangements.

'That's cool,' said Ellie. 'I'm watching "Cribs" at eight-thirty.'

'Ok, but no arguing,' said Kathryn.

'Jase is in his room glued to his Xbox, so no chance,' said Ellie.

'Ok, I won't be late and your Dad said he would be back around nine-ish... You've got my mobile number, haven't you?' said Kathryn.

'Yesss,' said Ellie, and went back to her iPad, getting frustrated at the third degree.

At just turned seven, Kathryn was on her way to meet Steve, casually dressed in jeans, top and flat shoes.

'The Royal Oak' was about five miles away and a pub that Kathryn knew well, although she hadn't been there for some time. She parked up and went inside. It had changed a lot since her last visit, with a new carvery and bar set-up. It took her a few moments to get her bearings.

There was an alcove away from the restaurant area and Steve was sat, also dressed in jeans and a designer shirt, and appeared to be anxiously looking out of the window. He turned and saw Kathryn and got up to meet her.

'You look fabulous,' he said. 'What would you like?'

'Now that would be telling,' she said, and smiled.

'To drink,' he clarified, and smiled back.

Kathryn was much more confident now with Steve. In fact, she was more confident in general; she would never have been that forward normally, not with anyone. But here she was, self-assured and totally in control of her feelings.

Steve went to the bar and ordered soft drinks for both of them while Kathryn made herself comfortable in the alcove. She looked around just to check, but it was still relatively early and the bar area was not that busy. Steve returned with the drinks and sat close to her. He took her hand.

'Be careful,' she whispered. 'Someone might see.'

'Sorry,' said Steve, and let go.

There was polite chatter for about twenty minutes, and Kathryn was starting to relax. Steve kept looking into her eyes and a frisson ran through her body.

'Do you want to go somewhere?' said Steve.

'Yes,' said Kathryn, and poured back the rest of her mineral water and put her glass down on the table.

Keith followed suit and he got up and led the way.

Three cars down from Kathryn's Clio was a top-of-the-range Range Rover with personal number plates, SBJ 10. Steve aimed the fob and the lights flashed and there was a click as the door locks disengaged.

'We can leave your car here and go in mine.'

'Great,' said Kathryn.

She climbed in and looked at the leather seating and walnut dashboard. 'This is nice.'

Steve reversed from the parking space and the car glided across the uneven surface of the car park and turned left into open countryside.

'I'll find somewhere to stop?' said Steve.

'Yeah, ok,' said Kathryn, and she unzipped her jeans, slid them down and took them off. She was sat in her knickers

Steve nearly lost control. He regained his composure, looking left and right for suitable privacy.

'What about there?' said Kathryn, pointing to a farm track leading to a dilapidated barn.

'Yes,' said Steve, and he turned right and parked behind the ruin. Perfect.

It took Keith over an hour to get down the motorway. He spotted the broken-down bus on the north-bound carriageway but, travelling south, he had to go to the next junction to turn back. The Spicers' breakdown truck was in front of the coach ready to hitch up. The driver was sat in his cab eating a sandwich. Keith pulled up behind the coach and he could hear muffled cheering coming from inside.

Bruce was wearing a hi-viz jacket and got out to meet Keith. 'Am I glad to see you? The folks are getting a bit restless. Police stopped an' all... wanted all my docs and everything. Took a good look inside; I think they were checking for illegals,' he added. Keith winced.

The guy from the breakdown truck joined Keith and Bruce, and between them they worked out a safe routine for getting the passengers off the first bus and into Keith's replacement. Although not a regular event, it was not the first time and within a few minutes twenty tired but relieved passengers were heading back to Aireford while the breakdown truck, with Bruce on board, followed towing the broken-down bus. It would drive back to the depot ready for the mechanics who would work on it on Monday. Bruce would supervise the parking.

By the time Keith had dropped off all the passengers it was nine-thirty. Most had demanded their money back but instead Keith had managed to negotiate a twenty per cent discount off their next outing at Christmas, which they seemed reasonably happy to accept. He was quite pleased with his negotiation skills as he would merely increase the price by twenty per cent so they would end up paying the same. Despite the recent upturn in business, he was still not out of the woods financially.

Bruce was waiting for him; the breakdown truck had arrived safely twenty minutes earlier and the broken-down bus was outside the service bay ready for repair.

'How did you get on?' said Bruce.

'Fine,' said Keith. 'Think they were too knackered to complain too much. Said I would give them a discount on their next outing.'

'You did well there then, I thought there was going to be a riot at one stage... Anyway, if there's nothing else I'll get off and see if the missus still remembers me,' he added.

'Cheers,' said Keith. 'Thanks for hanging around', and Bruce got into his car and drove away.

Keith's stomach growled. He'd eaten nothing since his lunchtime sandwich, so with his Mercedes returned by Ted Avis, he locked up the depot and headed for the nearest fish and chip shop.

Next to the derelict barn, it had been a torrid time. Kathryn was trying to remember the last time she had had sex in a car, and thought it was in Keith's old Escort before they were married, when privacy was at a premium. She remembered it being a very cramped affair and not particularly enjoyable. This was completely different. The naivety of youth had been replaced by the knowledge of experience. That and the fact the Range Rover seemed twice the size, and with reclining seats, was just like a double bed.

Steve looked at his watch; it was nine-thirty and pretty dark. He switched on the interior light which seemed to shine like a beacon and would attract attention despite their remote location. What he didn't need was some farmer checking out possible trespassers.

Kathryn was dressing and applying fresh make-up in the

courtesy mirror underneath the sun visor.

Steve looked at her. 'I love you, you know,' he said.

'Yes,' said Kathryn. She thought before responding. 'I love you too.'

He leaned over and kissed her. She wiped some lipstick from his face. 'That would be a give-away,' she said.

He looked at his watch again. 'Better get you back to the pub,' he said, and started the car.

There was silence as he drove the short distance to the Royal Oak. Much needed to be said but neither wanting to say anything.

There was a quick exchange in the car park. Ensuring no-one was looking; they stole a kiss before heading their separate ways. 'I'll text you,' said Steve.

Kathryn felt empty as she drove home; she was battling a range of emotions that was tearing her apart. She loved her family but Steve had unleashed some incredible feelings that she never knew existed. She was in agony.

Back home, Keith had got in and was eating his fish and chips on a tray watching TV when Kathryn pulled the Clio onto the drive next to the Mercedes. She picked up her jacket from the back seat and let herself in. The smell of vinegar greeted her.

'Oh, you're not eating fish and chips in the lounge are you? It'll stink for days,' she said as she walked into the room.

'Sorry, love, only just got in myself; it's been a pig of a day. I'll go in the kitchen.'

'Too late now,' she said, and went to hang her jacket on the peg in the hall.

'I'm going to have a shower... Kids' ok?'

'Yeah, nothing's broken that I can see so they haven't been fighting. They're both in their rooms,' said Keith.

He carried his tray back to the kitchen, suitably admonished, where the discarded fish and chip wrappers were scattered over the draining board. He screwed them up and tried to force them into the pedal bin, which was already overflowing.

He sat down and slopped on more tomato ketchup to his meal. He looked at the plastic bottle, there was a large blob of congealed sauce on the top which he scraped off with his knife and put on the side of his plate. The chips were going cold and greasy and despite his lack of food he was not feeling all that hungry. Tomorrow's meeting with Amir, which he had managed to put to one side during the day, was coming back to centre stage in his mind. He was not looking forward to that one bit.

By ten-thirty, Kathryn was showered and changed into her nightie and dressing gown. She had talked to the kids and went back downstairs. Keith was asleep in the chair with the football highlights on the TV. She turned off the set and went back upstairs with a book, leaving Keith to his slumber.

Kathryn woke around seven-fifteen, still thinking about Steve. Keith was lay next to her, snoring. She had no idea what time he had come to bed.

Sunday morning, seven-thirty a.m. in Argyle Street and the computers had been in operation all night. Nicolai had been supervising but with only two hours' sleep he had gone to one of the video rooms to get his head down for a few hours. Uri and Victor had stayed until two when they left to get some sleep. Uri had made another video with Marija. The online library was now well stocked.

Victoria had arrived at six-thirty and was managing the early morning social media feeds. She checked again with the four girls who were due to be picked up on Thursday. They were all online and there seemed no lack of keenness. On the contrary, the words 'can't wait to see you, be with you' were dotted among the messages; Portia particularly seemed besotted with Victor, or his alter ego, Tyler. She was in for a surprise.

With two shifts of chat room entertainment, plus the online videos, there was now constant traffic to the website and the cash was continuing to roll in. The problem of getting at it was starting to cause problems, however. Using the recruitment business and the hotel to launder the money was proving insufficient. The account was showing a balance of over half a million pounds. Amir, however, had a plan.

During his many discussions with Steve Jones he had discovered that among his many business interests, Steve owned an investment company which bought land for development, obtained planning consent and sold it on to property companies. Steve had told him of the tax advantages but, importantly, moving money was reasonably straightforward. It was where Steve would get the cash to pay Amir for the girls. He would discuss it with Steve when he met him on Monday.

Edita and Delvina were still in the attic; another Sunday and boredom was already setting in. During the week it wasn't so bad, both of them quite liked the work at the hotel and they had started to make one or two friends. But the only thing really keeping them going was the thought that their ordeal could soon be over. They were relying on their new friend Keith to help them get away.

In the Woodley household, there was a tense atmosphere. It was eleven o'clock before Keith stirred; he wasn't going to the depot till later for his meeting with Amir. Kathryn was trying to do housework but her mind was elsewhere. There had been three texts from Steve, each one seemingly more desperate than the last, and which had not helped her mood. She had responded in equally emotional terms.

Jason had been picked up by one of his friend's parents to take him to football practice at nine-thirty, and Ellie had left to go into town to meet up with her girlfriends, leaving Kathryn and Keith on their own.

Keith had showered and Kathryn was reading the Sunday papers on the dining table with a coffee when he came downstairs. The smell of last night's fish and chips still hung in the air. She looked at him with an empty stare. He rubbed his face with his hands, still apparently suffering from sleep deprivation; he made a groaning sound.

'Urgh, I think I must've fell asleep, it was gone two before I woke up.'

'Yes, you were dead to the world in front of the TV when I came down. I left you to it,' she said without making eye contact.

'Yes, sorry about that, it was a pig of a day... Any coffee going?'

'Yes, kettle's boiled,' she said, making no attempt to get up.

Taking the hint, Keith went into the kitchen and made himself a drink.

'So, how did it go?' he said.

'What?' said Kathryn.

'Last night,' said Keith.

'Oh, fine,' she said.

'How's your friend?' he said.

Kathryn looked up. 'What friend?' she said.

'The one in hospital,' Keith clarified.

'Oh fine,' she said, and her eyes returned to a Sunday supplement.

'Are you ok?' said Keith. 'You're not angry with me or anything? Only you seem... I don't know... a bit distant.'

'What?' she said, and looked up. 'Oh... no, no... Everything's fine.'

'Good, anyway I've got to go to the depot.'

'Don't know why you don't move your bed there,' said Kathryn sharply.

'So that's it,' said Keith.

'What?' said Kathryn.

'The reason why you seem a bit... off.'

He sat down on the opposite chair. Kathryn looked up.

'Look, I know it's been a bit difficult recently but I <u>will</u> make it up to you, promise. But with all this new work coming in and, well, yesterday's breakdown, it's taken up my time... You know how it is,' said Keith.

'Yes, I know,' said Kathryn. 'And you're still going away tomorrow I presume. You've not said much about it,' she reposted.

'Yes, yes,' said Keith. 'That's why I've got to go out later... See the bloke who's organised it.'

'That's all right then,' she said coldly, and looked back down at her magazine.

The fact was that Keith hadn't talked about the trip in any detail for two reasons. One, he felt his stomach churn every time he thought about it, and two, she didn't seem particularly interested, despite the fact it was the first time in years he had done any trips to the Continent. Either way, he had avoided any real discussion on the subject.

Keith got up and went into the kitchen to get some breakfast.

'I'm going out,' shouted Kathryn from the lounge. 'Be back later.'

Keith walked back to the lounge. 'Where are you going?'

'Supermarket... we need some bits and pieces.'

She picked up her handbag and car keys and left. Keith stood and watched confused and concerned at her behaviour.

It was two hours before Kathryn returned, during which time she had managed to speak to Steve who was also out "shopping". Keith was watching football on the TV when she returned with a carrier bag of produce.

'You were gone a long time,' he said.

'I bumped into one of the girls from work and we went for a sandwich,' she said.

'Oh, right,' said Keith. 'Well, I've got to go in a few minutes. Shouldn't be late.'

'Dinner's at seven so if it's after that it'll be in the oven,' she said as she went into the kitchen and started to pack away the shopping.

'Ok,' said Keith, and he got up and picked up his jacket. 'See you later.'

'Yes,' she shouted from the kitchen and made no attempt to see him out. The door slammed behind him.

As he drove to the depot he started thinking things through. Yes, he had been distracted by work, he realised that, but he had made it up to Kathryn, surely. The new coat, the dinner-dance was proof he wasn't neglecting her. He would think of other ways of making things up to her; maybe a short break, perhaps, after his trip; he would have a bit of money after all. He would mention it when he got back.

There was much to do in the depot. Emails hadn't stopped despite it being Sunday, and there had been several new enquiries for work. Suddenly Keith became engrossed in the business and any thoughts of the discord at home, for the time being at least, had gone.

Six o'clock, Keith was sat at his desk anxiously awaiting the arrival of Amir with some trepidation. He heard the car pull up and braced himself for the entrance. As before there was no courtesy, Amir just walked in with Uri and sat down at his desk opposite him.

'You are ready for tomorrow?' said Amir. A statement phrased as a question.

'Yes,' said Keith.

'Good,' said Amir. 'I have map and ferry and hotel is booked. We leave tomorrow at six o'clock to drive to the ferry.'

'Hull, I take it?' said Keith.

Amir considered the colloquialism for a moment. 'Yes it is Hull. Eleven o'clock, the ferry it goes, but we should be there at eight. That is enough time, I think.'

'Aye should make it in two hours; straight down the M62,' said Keith.

'You have good... eh... bus?' said Amir.

'Yes,' said Keith. 'Nine-seater, like you said.'

'Good, that is good,' said Amir.

Keith was maintaining his composure and despite any inner feelings was trying to maintain a semblance of control

'What about payment?' said Keith. 'You said you would pay me when I work for you.'

'Yes... yes, I did say that,' said Amir. He thought for a moment. 'Ok I will pay you two thousand pounds. That will be enough I think.'

Keith tried to look calm as though he was considering the proposal. He knew that room for negotiation would be minimal in any case.

'Aye, that should cover it.'

'We will pay when the passengers are here with no trouble,' said Amir.

'Cash?' said Keith.

'Of course,' said Amir.

Uri continued to stare menacingly at Keith, which was unnerving him.

'Good,' said Keith. 'Was there anything else?' he added, trying to draw the discussion to a conclusion.

Amir looked at Uri. 'No we are done here,' he said. 'Uri will bring me tomorrow at six o'clock. Then we leave.'

Amir and Uri left without ceremony and Keith got up from his chair and watched them go to their car from the window. They appeared to be chatting animatedly.

Keith sat down in his chair, his stomach threatening to overspill. He went to the water cooler in the corner of the office and helped himself to a paper cup, trying to stem the nausea. He knew the trip was almost certainly illegal and he had no idea whether he had outlived his usefulness to the gang or not. If so, once he had completed the journey, what would they do? Maybe that's what they were talking about. Keith felt the need to relieve himself of his lunchtime sandwich.

He looked at the clock, it was six-thirty. At least he would make the dinner deadline; although his appetite would be non-existent.

There were no buses out, and having checked around, Keith locked up the depot and headed home.

He parked up on the drive. The curtains were open and he could see the family in the lounge through the window; there appeared to be a discussion going on. He opened the door and straight-away could hear raised voices.

He walked into the lounge and Ellie was in a heated argument with Kathryn.

'Dad, you tell her,' Ellie said, pointing at Kathryn.

'Hang on, hang on... tell her what? What's going on?' said Keith.

'I just told her she can't go out to see Charlotte tonight. She's got school tomorrow,' said Kathryn.

'It's so unfair,' said Ellie. 'I want to talk to her about my project.'

Keith looked at Kathryn, then at Ellie. He was caught in the middle.

'How long will you be?' said Keith as he was taking his jacket off.

'I'll be back by ten at the latest,' said Ellie.

'Seems fair enough,' said Keith, looking at Kathryn.

'I knew you would take her side. She can wrap you around her little finger,' she said angrily to Keith.

She turned to Ellie. 'Well, you do what you want. It's your life but don't come looking to me when your grades aren't good enough to get to university.'

'That's not fair,' said Ellie. 'I am working hard.'

'Oh yeah, spending all day on bloody FaceBook more like,' said Kathryn.

'I do not!' said Ellie.

Keith intervened. 'Hey guys stop, stop. Ellie you go round to Charlotte's but be back by ten... Come on let's all calm down, it's Sunday and we don't need all this rowing and arguing.'

Ellie looked at Keith. 'Thanks Dad,' and went to get her coat, totally ignoring Kathryn.

'What about your dinner?' shouted Kathryn.

'Don't want any,' said Ellie, and slammed the door behind her as she went out.

'Well thank you <u>very</u> much,' said Kathryn sarcastically. 'The dinner's in the oven. Help yourselves,' she added, and got up from the table and went upstairs.

Jason was sat at the table watching the goings-on. 'Come on son. Let's get some dinner, eh?' said Keith.

Keith went to the kitchen and dished out two portions and returned to the table. 'There you go, son,' he said. 'Don't worry about those two... it's a girl thing,' he said, and Jason smiled. Keith felt better. 'We need to stick together us blokes, eh?'

'Thanks Dad,' said Jason, and started tucking in to his roast.

Monday morning at Argyle Street; final preparations were being made for the trip to Latvia. Both Uri and Victor had been chatting regularly to the four girls who they considered "definites" for the journey. There was another who was "probable" and another "possible". Nicolai was working on those two. A free trip to the UK to meet their lovers and start a new life was proving to be very popular. Each girl had been sworn to secrecy. Amir didn't want anyone alerting the authorities and he also didn't want a stampede. There could be all kinds trying to get on the bandwagon.

If things worked out there would be other opportunities, Amir had said. He hoped that this would be a regular occurrence. He envisaged a trip every couple of months to supply Hyams, the hotel and anyone else who needed cheap labour, and of course it would ensure the chat rooms and video feeds were maintained.

Uri, however, had expressed concerns about Keith, which was the topic of conversation when they left the depot. 'I do not trust him,' said Uri. 'We should have killed him like we said.' Amir was more sanguine. 'He will be fine. We will try this one, and then we will see.'

At ten-thirty, Amir left the house to meet Steve at the hotel to collect the cash. He had a chance to catch up with his brother before the meeting. Amir brought Shalik up to date with the journey, promising another two girls if everything went to plan.

Steve arrived at eleven o'clock and was greeted like royalty by Shalik, who made sure that he was suitably supplied with coffee, water and biscuits. 'I will have it sent up,' said Shalik after he had taken the order.

Steve went upstairs to the mezzanine to meet Amir in one of the conference rooms overlooking the golf course. It was just the two of them.

After the normal pleasantries, Amir noticed Steve's briefcase.

'You have the money for us?' he said.

Steve opened the valise; it was filled with rows of £50 notes.

'It's all there,' said Steve.

'Yes, I am sure,' said Amir, and he picked up the briefcase and moved it to his side of the table.

There was a knock on the door and a waiter arrived with Steve's coffee, a tray of biscuits and a jug of iced water and two glasses.

'Put them on the table,' ordered Amir, and the waiter duly obliged and then left.

'While we are here, Steve, I wanted to ask about another proposition you mentioned before,' said Amir.

'Which one?' said Steve as he took a sip of his coffee.

'Your investment plan,' said Amir.

'What, the property company?' said Steve.

'Yes,' said Amir.

'I haven't got any projects at the moment, but possibly at the end of the month,' said Steve.

'That is ok,' said Amir.

'Ok,' said Steve. 'Tell you what I'll do. When we have more news I'll give you a call and we can discuss it.'

'Yes, that will be good,' said Amir.

Steve took another drink of his coffee, contemplating the offer. Although he had mentioned the investment business to Amir previously, it had not been with a view of attracting a potential partner. Steve had no desire to do anything that would link him directly to Amir. Supporting his recruitment business was to his benefit and was low risk, but anything else would need careful consideration.

'So when can I expect the girls?' asked Steve.

'Next Monday,' said Amir.

'Ok I will let my admin people know they will be getting four more agency staff next week. Let me know their names as soon as you can,' said Steve.

'Yes,' said Amir, and after finishing his coffee, Steve concluded the meeting and left. Outside the hotel he sat in his car and sent

Kathryn another text.

Amir followed Steve down to reception with the briefcase and went into the office to talk with Shalik. Grianne was working at the computer and Shalik asked her to leave. The brothers spoke in Farsi.

Amir opened the briefcase and counted out three thousand pounds. He would convert this to Euros for the journey. The rest he put into the hotel safe. 'If everything goes to plan I will pay Mr Woodley two thousand pounds,' said Amir.

'But why?' asked Shalik.

'Because he could be very useful to us. We can use his business to move the girls without suspicion. We may even be able to put money through it... Maybe buy a few buses,' he said and laughed. Shalik laughed.

'Yes, that is good,' said Shalik.

By four o'clock Keith was really getting anxious about the trip. He had been unusually quiet all day; it hadn't gone unnoticed.

'What's the matter with you? You look like you've got the troubles of the world,' said Maggie as she brought him his second mug of coffee.

'Oh... nothing, just thinking about the trip, that's all.'

Maggie went through a checklist with him, which brought more focus and helped calm him down. 'Passport, documents, Euros, tickets,' she said.

'They've got all the tickets apparently,' said Keith.

After an hour sat answering phone calls and emails he decided to go to the service bay and speak to Jack Clayton. Jack was working on the stricken bus from Saturday.

'How's it going?' asked Keith as he entered the bay.

'Ok... it was the clutch. New one'll take a couple of days... It's going to cost a bob or two,' he added.

'Yeah,' said Keith. 'I should have some money from this trip which will cover it.'

'Right,' said Jack. 'Just thought you should know, I'll let you have the exact cost when I get the invoice.'

'Everything set for the minibus?' said Keith.

'Aye, it's as good as I can get it. Should be fine,' he said.

Four o'clock and Keith drove home to pick up the clothes and toiletries he would need for the journey. Kathryn would not be in until half-five but he would wait for her to return. Both Ellie and Jason had returned home from school and were in their rooms finishing homework. They were both diligent workers and doing well at school. They preferred to get their homework done before dinner if possible, giving them the evening to do their own things.

Keith had packed his overnight holdall and was sat at the table in the lounge reading the paper when he had a text from Kathryn. 'Sorry, held up at work, will be in later. Have a good trip.'

Keith read it with an air of disappointment and wondered if she was still mad at him.

He went upstairs and said goodbye to the kids and left to get back to the depot.

As six o'clock approached Keith was getting more and more anxious. Jack had filled the minibus with diesel and parked it outside the office next to Keith's car. There was an update on the broken-down bus which was ready to receive its new clutch, Jack reported. Keith was giving him some last-minute instructions. 'Oh, and don't forget to keep in touch with Pete Squires at Hyams about the delivery business while I'm away.'

'I'll be glad when you're gone, you sound just like my missus,' said Jack before leaving for the day.

With all the buses back in the depot, and Maggie having left at her normal time of five o'clock, Keith was on his own. He made a final trip to the toilet, and then heard a car draw up. He looked through the window, saw Amir get out and the car drove off.

Keith checked around, took a deep breath and locked the office. He saw Amir with his phone, taking a picture of the bus.

'What are you doing?' asked Keith reaching the man.

'It is for the passengers. They will know which bus,' he said.

Keith shrugged his shoulders and opened up. His bags were already on board and Amir threw his holdall on the seat immediately behind the front passenger seat and got in.

'We go,' said Amir, and Keith drove out of the gates, locked the depot and headed for the motorway. He looked across at his passenger. He had a black eye, he suddenly noticed; he hoped someone had hit him.

CHAPTER SEVENTEEN

While Keith was on his way to the ferry, Kathryn was sat in Steve's Range Rover straightening out her clothes after a second visit to the disused barn. She had received the text from Steve around four to see if she could meet him at the Royal Oak as they had on Saturday. She knew full well that they would not be going to the pub. The words "meet at the Royal Oak" had taken on a different, secret connotation and it made her shiver.

Kathryn sent some quick texts to the kids saying she was working later and that she would bring some pizzas for tea, which would be well received by Ellie and Jason. She also sent a message to Keith indicating she wouldn't be there to see him off.

Steve was already waiting in his Range Rover when she pulled into the car park and waved her over. She got in and Steve set off.

An hour later, as she was re-applying her make-up, Steve needed to mention something.

'I couldn't put it into a text but I've to go away for a few days,' he said. 'Sorry.'

She turned around and looked at him.

'Where?' she said.

'Abu Dhabi,' he replied.

'When do you go?'

'Tomorrow, two o'clock from Manchester, one of Keith's guys are taking me to the airport.'

'He didn't mention it. When will you be back?' she asked, trying to apply her lipstick and speak at the same time.

'Saturday,' he replied. 'I'm going to miss you so much.'

'Yes, I'm going to miss you too,' said Kathryn.

He could see her disappointment and felt guilty. He looked at her; her head was down.

'I know,' he said. 'I've just had an idea. I'm off to Dubai in a couple of weeks. Why don't you come with me?'

She turned and looked at him.

'Dubai...? How long for?'

'Five days... Monday, back Saturday.'

'How can I?' she said.

'I don't know... Get some time off work.'

'I can't just leave the kids for that long and expect Keith to baby-sit. He's working all hours,' she said. 'He's off to Latvia today of all places.'

'Oh... I didn't know,' said Steve.

Steve thought for a moment. Latvia? Then he twigged, of course, Keith must be making the run for Amir. He knew he was doing some work for Amir but not specifically the Latvian trip.

He leaned across and kissed Kathryn.

'That's a shame... it's a six-star hotel. The bed is enormous.'

'Don't tease,' said Kathryn. She thought for a moment. 'But how will we be able to do it? I mean don't they have laws out there about unmarried people sleeping together?'

'Yes,' said Steve. 'But it won't be a problem, I know the hotel owner very well, they tend to turn a blind eye these days... it will be fine.'

He could see the look of uncertainty on her face.

'Well at least say you'll think about it,' he said.

'Oh, believe me, I'll think about it all right, but I can't see how I can get away.'

Keith had made good time along the M62 motorway, the weather was fine and the traffic, once they had got past the M1 junction, was running well. Inside the bus the atmosphere was decidedly frosty. Amir just looked ahead at the road as if in a trance and made no attempt to make any conversation. Keith couldn't think of anything to say and just drove; the sooner this was over, the better.

They arrived at the ferry terminal in Hull just after eight and registered at the gate. They were ushered into a parking bay where the documents would be checked before they would be allowed on board. The formalities were surprisingly quick. Amir produced the tickets and his documents; Keith, just his passport, and after half an hour or so they followed the rest of the vehicles onto the car deck. Keith noticed that despite his appearance and lack of English skills, Amir had a UK passport. He wasn't about to question its authenticity. Amir was also beginning to realise that using Keith had been a shrewd move. The minibus, suitably emblazoned with "Woodley's of Aireford" on the side, and with an English driver, had definitely expedited the process.

The ferry was very busy, with trucks from all over Europe returning home having deposited their goods across the UK. Others were fully loaded, exporting cargo in the opposite direction; then probably fifty private cars, tourists of many nationalities.

'We have two rooms,' said Amir, and Keith breathed a sigh of relief. A shared compartment was going to be very unpleasant.

They made their way to the accommodation deck and found their cabins, which were next to each other.

'I will see you in the morning,' said Amir, and handed Keith a folder. 'You will need these I think. It is where we will stay and where we need to go.'

Keith unlocked his cabin door and looked around; it resembled a prison cell, about the same size, but it was comfortable and there was a TV so he would have some entertainment at least until they got into open water. He put his bag next to the bed, took out his phone and dialled home.

Jason picked up the call.

'Hi Dad, how was the journey?'

'Fine thanks, son. Is your mum there?' said Keith.

'Yeah, she's just here,' he replied, and he could hear muffled voices. 'It's Dad,' he heard Jason say.

'Hello,' said Kathryn.

'Hi, how's it going?' said Keith.

'OK, how was the trip?' she said.

The questions went backward and forward but there was little proper dialogue, and after a few minutes of this cat-and-mouse game Keith called it a day. 'I'll call you tomorrow evening sometime,' he said.

He had had nothing to eat since lunch and decided to check out the restaurant. There was still an hour to go before the ferry was due to sail but the gates were closed. Everybody that was leaving was on board.

It was heaving with people and the restaurants were busy; Keith had to queue to get his food. At eleven o'clock, he was having a beer in one of the bars and there was a cheer as he felt the vessel starting to move. After his nightcap he decided to return to his cabin and try to sleep; tomorrow was going to be a long day.

He spent some time studying the map and itinerary that Amir had left with him before turning out the light. Ahead lay a journey of around nineteen hundred kilometres; the first stop was just south of Berlin, about eight hundred kilometres away from the ferry port at Rotterdam.

Back home, Kathryn couldn't settle; her world had been turned upside down in just a few days. All she could think about was how she could get away for a week to accompany Steve to Dubai, but all avenues seemed to draw a blank.

With Keith away and the kids in bed there were plenty of opportunities for text messaging to Steve. He was in his den at home ostensibly doing paperwork, but like Kathryn, concentration had been impossible. Text messages were in full flow. For both of them, emotions had reached the 'red zone' and words like 'can't imagine life without you' were starting to appear.

At four-thirty, Keith was in a deep slumber when the ship's tannoy announced that breakfast was available in the restaurant. He looked at his watch and groaned. It was another two hours before the ferry was due to dock. He struggled out of his bunk. There was a small bathroom with just enough space for a sink and shower. With it being gravity-fed there was very little pressure, but it did the job. He was just drying off when there was a loud knock on the door. Keith opened the door with a towel wrapped around his waist; it was Amir.

'We go now, eat,' he said.

'Give us ten minutes, eh,' said Keith.

'I go to restaurant... you come soon, there is much to do,' said Amir.

Keith shut the door. What did he mean by "much to do"? He couldn't think of anything.

By five-fifteen Keith had made his way down the two flights to the breakfast area and saw Amir at one of the tables. He went over and sat adjacent rather than facing Amir; he wanted as little eye contact as possible.

Amir turned and looked at him. 'So what's this "lots to do"?' Keith asked.

'You know where to go?' said Amir.

'Yes, I've seen the route... but you'll be there to direct me if need be,' said Keith.

'That is good, then. Yes, I will have map. We will find it,' said Amir.

'Good...was there anything else?' said Keith.

'No, that is all,' said Amir. Keith wondered what all the

urgency was for.

'Ok, I'm going to get some breakfast,' he said.

The restaurant was self-service and Keith helped himself to a cooked breakfast; he had no idea when he would be eating again. He returned to his seat and tucked into his fried bread.

'We must go to bus and put in our things,' said Amir as Keith finished his food.

'We can't go to the car deck yet,' said Keith. 'They'll tell us when we can go. It'll be another hour yet.'

Amir looked around and fiddled with his fork. There were the remains of an apple and orange on his plate; not much of a breakfast thought Keith. He'd done this journey several times before and was familiar with the routines and then he started to realise something. Amir was also anxious about the trip. Maybe he was an illegal immigrant on a forged passport; perhaps that was it. Keith perked up at this discovery; Amir hadn't a clue what he was doing. It was Keith who was in control.

After finishing his breakfast Keith turned to Amir. 'I'm going back to the cabin for a bit and freshen up. Listen out for the announcement, <u>then</u> we can load up the bus,' he said with some authority.

'Yes,' said Amir. 'That is good.'

It was just before six when the passengers were told to return to their vehicles and prepare for disembarkation. Keith had packed his holdall and left the cabin. Amir was waiting and looked rather anxious.

'Follow me,' said Keith. 'We've got plenty of time.'

Keith led Amir down to the car deck and stowed their gear in the minibus, then sat inside waiting for the ferry to dock; by six-twenty they were driving to the customs hall.

Amir looked distinctly uncomfortable as the uniformed officers checked the vehicle and documents but the formalities were fairly routine and by ten to seven Keith was heading out of the docks and heading for Utrecht, then the German border.

Keith drove carefully, particularly at junctions; it had been a while since he had driven on the right-hand side of the road. Amir sat impassively in the passenger seat, merely confirming directions, when they reached an intersection. Once they had reached the main route, the A1, which would take them most of the way, Keith pulled into a service station to get a coffee.

'Why have we stopped?' said Amir sharply as Keith made the turn into the facilities. 'I did not say to stop.'

Keith ignored him. 'I need a break and a piss if that's alright with you,' he said. 'Are you coming or staying here?'

'I stay,' said Amir.

'Suit yourself,' said Keith, and made his way to the cafeteria and toilets. He had taken the keys to the bus with him; he didn't want Amir driving off.

After twenty minutes Keith was back in the minibus and Amir was fidgeting. 'We must go, you drive, now,' he said as Keith got in.

'I don't know what your problem is; we've got loads of time,' he said.

'We stop when I say,' said Amir.

'Yeah, ok,' said Keith. 'When do you want to take over?' he added.

'What do you mean, take over?' said Amir.

'You, doing some driving,' said Keith. 'I can't do all of it. It's illegal.'

'I do not drive. I pay you to drive,' said Amir.

Keith turned and looked at him. 'What do you mean, you don't drive? I asked you if you can drive and you said you could.'

'Yes, I can drive a car but not bus. I pay you to drive,' Amir repeated.

'Shit,' said Keith under his breath. 'Well if we get stopped or we have an accident and the police find out there'll be trouble.'

'Why will they find out?' said Amir.

'Let's hope they don't,' said Keith.

He was concerned. Today's drive was about 800 kilometres, around 600 miles, and, without much sleep, keeping awake was going to be a big challenge. He stared at the autobahn stretching out in front of him, mile after mile of soulless concrete.

As the minibus ate up the miles, Amir seemed more accommodating and the stops became more frequent. Keith had made his point and they eventually arrived at the motel Victoria had booked on the autobahn, just south of Berlin, at five-thirty.

Keith was shattered and hobbled off the bus; his legs had stiffened. Amir went to reception to present the booking documentation and after a few minutes he handed Keith the room key.

'Tomorrow we leave, seven... be ready then,' he said, and walked off to his room.

'Goodnight to you too, tosser,' said Keith under his breath. 'Yeah, ok,' he said more audibly, and followed the signs along a corridor to find his base for the night.

Keith put his holdall on the floor and collapsed on the bed, exhausted; within minutes he was asleep. It was gone seven before he woke up and he was momentarily disorientated. He went to the bathroom and washed his face to freshen up. Then he left his room to find the adjacent restaurant, past reception and to the right. It was full of truckers and tourists from many nationalities and the menu catered for all tastes. Keith chose a veal schnitzel with vegetables. After his meal he was sat at his table relaxing with a small glass of beer. He took out his mobile and phoned home.

Again, the call was picked up by his son. 'Hi Dad,' came the happy voice, which lifted Keith's spirits.

'Hi son, you ok?' said Keith.

'Yeah, where are you?' said Jason.

'Germany, near Berlin somewhere,' said Keith. 'Is your mum there?'

'Yeah, I'll put you on, just a sec,' said Jason. There was a pause as the phone changed hands.

'Hello,' said Kathryn. 'In Germany, I hear.'

'Yeah, not far from Berlin.'

The conversation that followed was brief and lacking in any emotional tones. 'Are you ok?' said Keith, eventually picking up on the apparent coldness.

'Yeah, just a rotten day; I think I'm going to go to bed in a minute,' she said.

'Oh, ok,' said Keith, and after the "goodbyes", rang off.

He sat at the table looking around at the number of single men just sat playing with their phones, or other mobile devices; some were reading but all were socially disengaged. He contemplated his conversation with Kathryn and couldn't understand why he still seemed to be in the doghouse. Tomorrow he would mention a break together, maybe that would cheer her up.

The following day was a long hard slog for Keith. They had left the motel in Germany at seven o'clock, as Amir had demanded, and Amir had barely said a word the whole day apart from barking orders of when to stop, and the occasional direction when they reached an intersection. Keith had had to use all his powers of concentration to stay awake.

The landscape changed dramatically as they crossed the Latvian border. The country has one of the highest densities of forests in Europe and the road was soon enveloped in trees, which cut out light and impaired any views. He breathed a sigh of relief as they reached the outskirts of the Latvian capital, but it took another half an hour to find their lodgings; traffic was busy in the city even outside the rush hour.

They eventually pulled up outside a modest backstreet hotel just after nine o'clock, eleven hundred kilometres, over six hundred and seventy miles. It was not far from the bus station which would be tomorrow's pick-up point.

It was comfortable enough, but the way Keith was feeling he would have slept anywhere. This time Amir did join Keith for a meal in the restaurant to detail the following day's arrangements. He produced a city map of Riga.

'We are here,' he said, pointing at the street where the hotel was situated. 'We go... here,' he indicated the short distance with the sweep of his finger. 'Not far... ten minutes,' he said. 'We leave tomorrow seven o'clock, be ready,' he said, before leaving Keith to his mobile phone.

He checked for a signal. It would be expensive calling the UK, but he needed to connect with his real world for a while.

He dialled the number and this time it was Kathryn who answered. There was a two-hour time difference and Kathryn was just tidying up after dinner.

'Oh, hello,' she said as the call was answered. 'I thought it might be you. It said "international" on the phone... How was the journey?'

'Ok,' said Keith. He decided not to say anything about his driving solo.

After a short catch-up, Keith raised the question. 'I was thinking, when I get back, perhaps we can get away for a weekend, just the two of us. Leave the kids with your mum. What do you think?'

This caught Kathryn off-guard; she was still trying to work out how she could get to Dubai with Steve.

'What...? Oh, yes. I don't know when though. Got a lot on at the moment,' she said, applying delaying tactics.

Keith was disappointed at her apparent lack of enthusiasm. 'Well, it was just an idea, see what you think.'

'Yes we can chat about it when you get back,' she said. 'Anyway, this must be costing you a fortune. Do you want to call again tomorrow? No... I'm not going out,' she added, sensing a hint of sarcasm in Keith's enquiry.

Seven-fifteen, the central bus station at Pragas Iela in the heart of Riga, close to the Daugava River, and Keith pulled into a parking bay. Amir had been anxious since leaving the hotel, but then there was a lot riding on the next few minutes.

'Wait,' he said, and got out and walked towards the terminal building. He had details of the girls and copies of their pictures and looked around to see if he could see anyone resembling them. It seemed an impossible task; it was incredibly busy. The rush hour was in full swing and there were hundreds, maybe thousands of people crossing to and from the nearby railway station and their onward connections.

Victoria was also waiting anxiously back in Argyle Street, where it had just turned five a.m. She had Portia's mobile number and sent her a text explaining where the bus was parked. Keith was sat in the driver's seat when there was a knock on the window, making him jump. Two girls about the same age as his daughter were stood on the pavement. He got out to see what was happening.

'You are to UK?' said one of them. She showed Keith a picture of his minibus.

'Yes,' said Keith.

'You take us, I think,' she said.

For a moment he thought about warning her but he could see Amir walking towards him with two other girls.

Amir looked pleased as he approached them.

'Hello,' he said. 'I am Amir.'

This was a very different Amir, suddenly effusive with all the charm of a slime-ball.

'Beautiful girls, you will be so happy in UK. What are your names?'

Keith watched the transformation. His dislike for this man had increased even further, if that was possible.

'I am Brigita and this is my friend Daina,' she said.

Brigita had long dark hair, Daina was shorter with fair hair; both looked like students and were carrying bulging rucksacks.

Amir fawned again. 'You must meet Portia and Vaira, they are students. They are coming to the UK also,' and the two girls with Amir acknowledged them. They spoke in Latvian and then all four began to giggle.

'You must get on bus now, there is far to go,' said Amir.

Keith took their luggage and stowed it at the back of the bus; there was plenty of room with the empty seats.

The girls got on board; Amir looked at his watch, not quite seven-thirty. The four "definites" were finding their seats.

'How many more?' asked Keith.

'Maybe two more, I am not sure,' Amir said.

He sat in the passenger seat at the front and started texting Victoria. 'We have four, what news of others?' it said.

Moments later there was a return text. 'Two more said they would be there.'

Amir looked again at his watch. 'There should be two more,' he said.

It was seven-forty.

'Do you want me to drive around? They might see the bus. It's going to be nigh on impossible to spot them with all this lot,' said Keith.

'Yes, you drive,' said Amir. He spoke to the passengers. 'There are two more girls. We look for them.'

Keith pulled away slowly and Amir was stood up looking around. Keith did another circuit of the parking bays and was about to leave the terminus when he spotted two girls waving franticly at the bus. Keith drove towards them and pulled up alongside. Amir opened the door. 'You are for UK, yes?' he said.

'Yes,' said a girl with bleached-dyed hair and a stud through her nose. 'I am Alise, this is my friend Velna,' she said, pointing to a studious-looking girl with spectacles.

Amir checked his list. 'Yes, Alise and Velna,' he said, and looked at Keith. 'That is it, we go now.'

The two girls got on and this time Amir took their baggage.

Keith pulled away and followed the signs for the motorway. Amir was in the back chatting to the girls and there was a great deal of excited chatter. He was pleased that he had Victoria; she would be able to translate when they got back to Aireford.

'You have your passports. I will need them for when we cross the border. I will look after them,' he said. There was much rustling around in bags but each produced their documents and handed them to Amir without much concern. It would be the last they would see of them for a while.

Amir went back to the seat next to Keith and supervised the directions, although the signage was clear and made any intervention superfluous. The return would follow the same route and Keith was faced with another laborious drive. This time, with the background chatter of the girls, the journey was easier. Fortunately, the border crossings – Estonia, Poland, Germany and Holland – had all gone without a hitch, much to Amir's relief.

Victoria had booked the same truck-stop near Berlin for the return journey stopover. The services were just off the autobahn and served both carriageways. It was gone nine o'clock as the minibus pulled into the car park. Amir turned around and made an announcement to the passengers.

'We stay here tonight. You wait, I will see to everything.'

When Amir returned with the keys Keith noticed there were only three.

'Where's the rest?' he said.

'What do you mean...? The girls, they share,' Amir replied.

'Well that's not going to be any good; they'll never all fit into one of those rooms.'

'It will be fine. I have nice room for them,' said Amir.

'Suit yourself,' said Keith, and the passengers started to disembark.

Amir led the way like the Pied Piper, with the six girls trailing in a line behind. The earlier excited banter had gone, overtaken by exhaustion. Through reception and down a corridor, Amir opened one of the doors for the girls and handed them the key.

'This is your room, nice room,' he said.

The girls looked around. There were two double beds. He could see the girls looking at each other.

'It is nice, yes?' he said.

'It is small for all of us,' said Portia, who seemed to have taken over as leader. Her English was almost fluent.

'Well, you can share with me if you wish... or Keith here,' Amir said.

Portia looked at the other girls and spoke in Latvian.

'No, it's ok, we will manage,' she said.

'That is good,' said Amir. 'You can buy food down there,' he added, pointing in the opposite direction towards the restaurant.

'We will need our passports,' said Portia.

'No, it is fine. I have them safe. If there is a problem you tell me.'

Portia spoke to the girls and there were some concerned looks which Amir picked up.

'It will be fine, I have them if you need them, you just tell me,' he said. He didn't want them to feel there was any threat, certainly not at this stage of the operation.

'Ok,' said Portia, and the girls went inside and shut their door. There was much discussion going on.

'Here, this is yours. We leave tomorrow at seven,' said Amir, and handed Keith the next-door room key.

He took it from the Iranian and went inside; he was exhausted. There had been breaks every couple of hours or so, mainly for the girls, who seemed to be continuously drinking cans of Coke which in turn led to the need for more stops. In the brief exchanges they seemed bright intelligent girls just seeking some kind of adventure; he had no idea what was in store for them; neither did they. Despite his fatigue he needed to eat and went down to the restaurant; it was open all night and was again busy with truck drivers and tourists.

After his meal he called home; it was answered by Kathryn.

'Hi,' he said.

'Oh, hi,' she said. 'Wasn't expecting to hear from you.' This confused Keith; he always phoned when he was on the road on a long trip. It was a routine from the very early days.

'Why wouldn't I?' he said.

'I thought it might be too expensive,' she said.

'No it's fine... How are you?' he said.

'Fine,' she said.

'And the kids?'

'Yes, they're fine,' she replied.

'Did you think any more about what I said about going away?'

'What...? Oh, no,' she said. 'We'll talk about it when you get back.'

'Yeah, ok,' said Keith, detecting a reticence.

'Where are you?' said Kathryn.

'In that truck-stop just outside Berlin.'

'Oh, right... when do you think you will be back on Saturday?'

'Don't know exactly, but if everything goes ok about ten, eleven o'clock-ish I guess.'

'In the morning?' she asked.

'Yes... if all goes well.'

'Oh, ok,' she said.

After a couple more minutes of catch-up of daily goings-on, Keith rang off. He was too tired for any meaningful conversation.

Kathryn and Steve had continued their text traffic while Steve was in the Middle East. The messages had become more and more urgent as the week had gone on and Kathryn was desperate to see him again. Steve was due back into Manchester Airport early morning Saturday after an overnight flight, and the pair were discussing ways of meeting up. A 'Royal Oak' was definitely on the cards.

The following morning, Keith was helping the girls load up for the penultimate leg of their journey; the run down to the ferry. With the end in sight, and the benefit of a good night's sleep, Keith was in a fairly buoyant mood. Amir was in the seat next to him but keeping up the charm offensive with the passengers. The girls seemed to be in good humour; they had joked about the accommodation and it appeared that alcohol consumption had been involved.

The journey was long and boring but also, thankfully, uneventful. Keith managed to stay awake as Portia was sat behind him and kept up a regular dialogue. Amir was dozing for much of the journey and took little notice. As well as speaking excellent English, he found out she was at university in Riga and came from a wealthy family. It appeared that her move to England was an act of defiance against her parents. She had always wanted to see England and thought this would be an ideal opportunity. She also said she was looking forward to meeting Tyler with whom she had been in contact in England, and who had arranged the trip. Keith had no idea who Tyler was but guessed it would be one of Amir's people.

They arrived at the Europort terminal at five-thirty, in good time for the ten o'clock departure. The formalities at customs again went without a hitch and as Keith drove the minibus onto the car deck, the girls were giggly, excited at the prospect of landing in England.

CHAPTER EIGHTEEN

Everyone exited the minibus and followed Keith to the reception area where they would pick up their cabin keys; or at least Amir and Keith would. The girls would have to make do with recliners in the public lounge. The budget wouldn't stretch to more accommodation.

As it happened the girls didn't seemed too concerned. Once the ferry was underway a disco started up in one of the lounges and they were very happy to spend most of the night dancing and having a great time.

In his cabin, Keith collapsed on the narrow bed and for the first time in five days started to relax. His mind retraced the journey. When he closed his eyes he could see road signs, brake lights, and mile after mile of road. He was asleep for over an hour before he woke with what felt like a hangover, his head heavy and his mouth dry. He went to the bathroom and washed his face, then picked up his mobile and called home.

Jason answered again. It was seven o'clock UK time and the conversation was light and uplifting; finished homework, one of his pals had got detention, things that were important to a thirteen year old. Keith's difficulties were put into some kind of perspective; everyone has issues.

'Is your mum there?' he asked after five minutes of adolescent download.

'No, she's out,' said Jason. 'She's gone to see Nana Anderson.'

'Oh, ok,' said Keith. 'Tell her I called, will you? I'll see her tomorrow.'

'Yeah, ok,' said Jason. 'What time will you be back?'

'Don't know, about half-ten, eleven,' said Keith.

'Ok,' said Jason. 'Bye.'

The call was disconnected and Keith was momentarily consumed with sadness; he was desperately missing his family.

Back home, however, Kathryn would not be reciprocating those feelings; her vision, totally myopic, consumed by the intense passion she had found with Steve. Her absence from the household was not, this time, to see him; he was on his way back from Abu Dhabi. She wanted to raise a question with her mother.

June Anderson lived five miles away with her husband Peter and they enjoyed a good relationship with their daughter, and doted on the grandchildren. Kathryn had phoned earlier from work and asked if she could call in on her way home.

'Of course, my dear, it will be lovely to see you. What a nice surprise,' June said.

It was just turned six by the time Kathryn arrived at their bungalow in nearby Calverley Park, a prosperous community about seven miles from Aireford.

There was the usual catch-up when she arrived; 'How's Keith? How are the kids?' the usual kind of questions. There was a discussion about his trip to Latvia. 'How exciting,' said June. 'I've always fancied a cruise to the Baltic States but you're not keen, are you dear?' she said. Her question was aimed at Peter, who was sat in front of the TV trying to watch a quiz show. 'What?' he said, one eye still on the TV.

'Won't get any sense out of him till six-thirty, thinks he's cleverer than any of the contestants. Come on, we'll go into the kitchen.'

They took their tea and sat at the small breakfast bar.

'I wanted to ask a favour,' said Kathryn.

'Of course, dear, anything,' said June.

'I've got the chance of a week in Dubai, a week on Monday. Wondered if you could keep an eye on the kids and maybe look after their meals; Keith is so busy at the moment so I can't rely on him being in,' said Kathryn.

'Dubai! Wow that sounds amazing, I've always fancied going there but your father doesn't like anything to do with the Middle East. I think he's allergic to sand,' she said, and laughed. 'Of course I will. How did you manage that?'

Kathryn had been rehearsing a story.

'One of the girls at work was offered a free ticket, all expenses paid, but her mother's ill and she can't go so she offered it to me,' said Kathryn.

'That's fantastic,' said June. 'Of course, you must go. It will be a trip of a lifetime. Just let me know what you want me to do.'

Kathryn breathed a sigh of relief, just one more hurdle and she was home and dry. Steve was in for a nice surprise tomorrow in more ways than one.

Saturday morning, and the ferry was heading down the Humber. It was cool with just a hint of the approaching autumn and Keith was on the outside deck in his jacket getting some fresh air before the final leg of the journey. It was five-thirty and once again an early breakfast was the order of the day. Despite the movement of the ferry he had slept surprisingly well, exhausted from his efforts of the last few days. He was deep in thought as he watched the industrial skyline of the city environs go by as the vessel sailed towards its terminus in Hull.

He was disturbed by an announcement asking all drivers to "proceed to their vehicles", and he made his way inside carrying his holdall. Amir was waiting by the reception area with the girls who looked decidedly worse for wear and in need of a good night's sleep.

'Where have you been?' said Amir. 'I wait for you.'

'Just on deck, come on let's go,' said Keith, not fazed by the

Iranian's apparent aggression.

Again, the border controls were completed without any difficulties and Amir looked relieved as Keith headed the minibus out of the docks towards the motorway.

Portia was sat behind Keith again and started talking to him.

'I can't wait to see London,' she said.

Amir interjected before Keith could answer.

'You will, soon, you will see,' he said. 'We have a very nice house for you to stay while you are here. You will be able to do many things, earn much money.'

Keith said nothing.

At just after ten o'clock, they reached the outskirts of Aireford and Amir gave Keith directions to Sutherland Close and the house they had prepared for the girls.

'Yeah, I know it,' said Keith.

The girls watched out of the windows as the minibus made slow progress through the grey city streets. Aireford was not at its best on a cold, drab late-September morning. There was however some excitement as they went past the shopping mall and cinema.

Sutherland Close was just a few blocks away from Argyle Street and was similar in design, a three-bedroomed terrace property. Within a few minutes Keith was parking up outside. Amir had phoned ahead and Victoria was waiting on the doorstep.

Portia got out first, carrying her rucksack. She looked at the grim facade; it was not what she was expecting. The rest of the passengers got out and looked up and down the street.

Victoria walked towards them and welcomed them in Latvian. They were delighted to hear their native language and Victoria kissed them on the cheeks individually and led them indoors. 'Hello, it is so good to see you at last.'

'Where is Tyler?' said Portia. 'Is he here?'

'No,' said Victoria. 'But you will meet him later. I am here to look after you. I will explain everything.'

Amir watched them go indoors, and then got back in the minibus.

'You take me to other house,' he said as he got in.

'Argyle Street?' said Keith.

'Yes, we go, now,' said Amir, and Keith complied, eager to get rid of his unwanted passenger.

The girls seemed happy with their new accommodation despite the hint of fresh paint and soon were bombarding Victoria with questions; how had she got here, what was it like, what did she do, and so on. Victoria gave them a brief tour of the house, explaining where everything was; with three bedrooms the girls would pair up and all seemed well.

After settling in, the girls sat in the lounge drinking Coke from the well-stocked fridge and Victoria addressed them. 'Tonight we have arranged a party for you to welcome you here. I will tell you everything, what will happen, where you will work. You will also meet the boys,' she said, and winked. 'But now you should rest. I will be here with you all today,' she added.

Victoria knew that this was the most important time and was the same for all new arrivals. She didn't want them feeling that there was any threat. The party would be an important part of the induction procedure.

A few minutes later Keith pulled up outside the Argyle Street house

'What about payment?' said Keith as the Iranian was about to get out. 'You agreed.'

'Yes,' said Amir. 'I will call tomorrow, at your office, six o'clock. I bring it.'

Keith was not in a strong position to argue. 'Right, ok... Only I'll need that money... if you're going to want me again,' he said.

'Yes, I will pay,' said Amir, 'tomorrow.'

With that Amir walked towards the front door with his luggage and let himself into the house without a backwards glance.

'Bastard,' said Keith under his breath, and pulled away; he was relieved to see the back of him. The sooner he was out of their clutches the better, but he had no idea when that would be. Then a thought hit him; he was now directly involved in people trafficking, an accomplice no less, and could face a prison sentence if he were caught. His anxiety quickly returned.

He tried to put the consequences at the back of his mind and arrived back at the depot just after ten-thirty. He breathed deeply as he entered the compound. There were a few buses parked but more were out. The three double-deckers were still there but the new buses would be arriving next week, so their days of ownership by Woodley's of Aireford were numbered.

Jack Clayton had seen the minibus pull up and came out to greet him.

'Hi boss, how did it go?' he said as he approached Keith to shake his hand. He was pleased to have him back.

'Aye, great,' said Keith. 'Ran like a dream, no problems.'

'That's great... coffee's on,' he said.

'So what's been happening?' said Keith with his hand on Jack's shoulder in a brotherly fashion, as they walked inside to the office.

He was surprised to see Maggie sat at her desk.

'Maggie? What are you doing here?' said Keith.

'Well we were so busy this week I thought I would come in and lend a hand.'

'Thanks,' said Keith. 'Really appreciate it.'

'Only till one o'clock mind. I do have another life you know.'

Keith smiled. 'Of course,' he replied.

There was a hot cup of coffee waiting on his desk and Keith was almost overwhelmed by the loyalty of his people.

'How did you get on with the clutch repair?' said Keith as he started opening some personal letters.

'Oh, fine,' said Jack, pulling up a chair and sitting opposite Keith. 'It's back on the road... good as new. Not seen the invoice yet.'

Jack started recounting the week in minute detail. 'Oh, and everything's going ahead with the Hyams delivery business, Pete says they'll have contracts by the end of next week, all being well.'

'That's great news,' said Keith,

After another half an hour of catch-up, Keith needed to get back home; he was looking forward to seeing his family again.

Back in Dunford, Kathryn was also waiting for Keith's return but with a completely different agenda. She had heard from Steve, who had arrived back from Abu Dhabi, and the "Royal Oak" was on for tonight; she couldn't wait. She also needed to raise the tricky subject of Dubai. She had no idea how he was going to react; it was new territory, she had never been abroad without him before. She rehearsed her story again.

She heard Keith's car pull up onto the drive and felt a twinge of nervousness. The keys turned in the lock and she went into the kitchen to make a drink, not wishing to confront him immediately he came into the room.

'Anyone home?' he shouted in a light-hearted manner; his normal greeting.

Kathryn came out of the kitchen holding a mug of tea.

'Hello,' she said, and Keith went to kiss her.

'Be careful,' she said as she moved away from him to protect her drink. She pecked Keith on the cheek as you would a favourite elderly aunt. 'How did it go?' she said, and sat down on one of the dining chairs.

'Not bad,' said Keith, putting his holdall on the floor. 'A long haul though, I'm absolutely knackered.'

'I'm not surprised,' she said. 'Do you want some tea? The kettle's just boiled.'

'No, you're alright, thanks. I'm caffeined out... Kids about?' he said.

'No, Jase is playing football, Ellie's at work,' said Kathryn.

'That's handy,' he said. 'We should make the most of the time.'

'What do you mean?' said Kathryn.

'Well... you know... I've been away for nearly a week. The soldier's greeting.'

'What, you want a shag?' said Kathryn.

'Well I wouldn't have put it that bluntly.'

'Sorry, I've got loads to do. You'd better let me have your dirty washing, I was just about to put a load on,' she said, which definitely killed any moment.

'Yes,' said Keith. 'I suppose you will be.'

'Take your bag upstairs and bring down anything you need doing.'

This was not the homecoming Keith was hoping for, and he skulked off upstairs.

After sorting out his bag he came down with a hand full of clothes.

'Stick them in the kitchen. I'll sort them out later,' she said, and picked up the newspaper to read while she finished her tea.

'So, how's work?' asked Keith.

'Fine,' said Kathryn.

'And your friend in hospital?' said Keith.

'What?' said Kathryn, and looked up. 'Oh, yes she's on the mend. I was thinking of going to see her again tonight... won't be late.'

'Oh, right, ok,' said Keith.

'Are you going back to the depot later?' said Kathryn.

'Yeah, about four, got a lot of work on today.'

'Oh ok, I'll leave you something in the microwave if you're not in when I go out.' she said.

'Right,' he said. There was a pause. 'I'm just going to get my head down for a while.'

'Ok,' she said, without looking up from her paper.

Keith went upstairs, undressed and got into bed, still wondering what he had done to upset Kathryn. He would mention the weekend away later and see if that would cheer her up.

Downstairs, there was another ping on Kathryn's mobile. It was Steve.

'You still ok for tonight?'

She texted back 'Yes, can't wait. Might have some news.'

'What?'

'Can't tell you, a surprise.'

'Tease.'

'It'll be worth it.'

'Hmm sounds interesting.'

'It will be. 7.00?'

'Yes.'

'See you there xx'

'xxx'

That was the message trail. Kathryn was smiling.

It was gone two o'clock before Keith woke up. Jason was in his room playing on his computer and Keith put his head around the door.

'Hi Jase, you ok?' he said.

'Hi Dad,' Jason said. 'Come and have a look at this.'

Keith went in and watched as Jason demonstrated his dexterity on the latest online game craze.

Kathryn was ironing in front of the TV in the kitchen when Keith got downstairs.

'Any chance of a cuppa, I'm gasping?'

'Kettle's not long boiled, help yourself,' she said.

Keith moved past her and switched it on. 'Do you want a cup?'

'Not long had one, thanks,' she said, seemingly engrossed in the TV.

Keith recognised that any chance of a conversation was minimal so he went into the lounge and started reading the newspaper. Kathryn was trying to time her run to broach the topic of Dubai.

She folded away the ironing board and unplugged the iron to let it cool before returning it to the cupboard. Here goes.

'I've got some news I've been dying to tell you.'

Keith looked up from the paper. 'What's that, love?' he said.

'If everything goes ok, I'm off to Dubai next week,' she said, deciding that attack was the best option.

This had Keith's immediate attention.

'Dubai...? How? Who with?'

Kathryn sat on the dining chair opposite him and spun the same story that had worked with her mother. Someone at work has offered her a ticket if she wanted it, a group of girls she loosely knew, all expenses paid, etc., etc. She waited for a reaction.

'What about the kids?'

'I've spoken to mum, she was over the moon. She said she would come over in the afternoon and cook some dinner for you and the kids. She was so pleased for me.'

'What about the expense, you'll never be able to afford it. It costs a fortune out there.'

'Everything's paid for, flight, hotel and meals. Just need some spending money and mum's given me a couple of hundred towards it.'

'Looks like you've got it all worked out,' said Keith.

'No,' said Kathryn. 'I told them I wouldn't commit to anything until I'd spoken to you. I said I'd ring them today. They've been very good about it at work. I told them it was a once-in-a-lifetime opportunity.'

'A bit last minute though.'

'Yes, the girl who's given up her ticket, her mum's just been diagnosed with cancer and not got long to live.'

'Well in that case, what can I say? I was going to talk to you about a weekend away, but I can't compete with Dubai,' said Keith.

'Well we can talk about that when I get back,' she said.

'Yeah ok,' said Keith. 'God, is that the time? I better get going. I told Jack I'd be in by four to lock up.'

'It's only half past three,' said Kathryn.

'Aye,' said Keith. 'But I've got lots to do; you'll never believe the emails I had waiting this morning. Only away for five days, an' all,' he added and smiled.

'Ok,' said Kathryn. 'Oh, you won't forget, I might be out when you get back. Not be late. I'll leave some dinner in the microwave if you're not back.'

'Yeah, ok, I'll see you later then,' he said.

Keith picked up his jacket, kissed Kathryn on the cheek and left. Kathryn was texting before Keith had left the drive.

In Sutherland Close, Victoria had stayed to help the girls settle in. They seemed happy enough and there were no indications of any regrets. At Victoria's suggestion they had decided to get some rest; they were looking forward to the party that was planned for them. By five o'clock they were downstairs helping themselves to the contents of the fridge. Victoria had not yet explained how the cash-book process would work; they were all seriously overdrawn.

Keith was back at the depot and Jack handed over the keys.

'All in, bar Bruce,' said Jack. 'Not due back till late... some rock concert in Newcastle. He'll park up in the street.'

'Oh, he'll be happy. More singing on the way back... rather him than me,' said Keith.

'You're not wrong there,' said Jack. 'I'll get off then. See you Monday.'

'Yeah, thanks for looking after everything,' said Keith.

'No problem,' said Jack, and he walked towards his car.

Keith went inside, switched on his computer and made himself a coffee while it warmed up. He watched the screen doing its thing and was thinking about his journey and wondering what would be happening to the girls. Then his mind turned to the Albanians and his promise to help them; he had been thinking a lot about them during the journey. He felt an obligation and started to work out how he could help them escape without raising any suspicions with Amir. If he was discovered he was in no doubt he would almost certainly kill him. It was that dangerous.

He opened up his Internet browser and searched for train times to London. He checked the details of the refuge house again. He thought about ringing them but decided against it, wanting to avoid answering any questions they were likely to ask. His mission, as that is how he was considering it, was gradually taking over.

By six-thirty Kathryn was getting ready and was hardly able to conceal her excitement. She wanted to giggle like a schoolgirl. She put on some new underwear she had chosen for the occasion which she knew Steve would like, a skirt and a blouse. She took a sip of red wine from the glass on the dressing table and checked herself in the mirror. Not bad, not bad at all, she said to herself. She picked up her new coat from the hanger in the wardrobe and went downstairs. Ellie was out with her friends but Jason was in the lounge watching TV.

'I'm off now, Jason. Your Dad said he wouldn't be late but let him know there's some dinner in the microwave when he comes in.'

'Ok mum,' said Jason, with his eyes fixed to the screen.

Kathryn left the house and drove off to her meeting with Steve. She reached the Royal Oak and Steve's Range Rover was parked up. Kathryn drew up alongside. Steve was smiling and beckoned her over. She opened the passenger door, got in and before she had time to say anything Steve was kissing her. It was the longest kiss she could ever remember and it had aroused every sense in her body. When they did eventually break off she looked at him and just said. 'Missed me then?' and they both laughed.

'You'll never know,' he said.

'Come on, let's get out of here. I have a desperate need,' she said.

Steve drove out to the deserted barn and parked behind it, away from any prying eyes.

'I've got you a present,' he said, and handed her a box.

'What is it?' she said.

'Open it and see,' he said.

Kathryn peeled off the wrapping paper and revealed a bottle of Hermès 24 Faubourg extrait perfume which retails at around $1,500 an ounce.

'Hope you like it.'

'Like it...! It's beautiful,' she said. 'But it costs a fortune.'

'Cos you're worth it,' he said, and smiled.

She opened the bottle and put the tiniest amount on the end of her finger and rubbed it into the pulse area of her left wrist and sniffed. She invited Steve to do the same.

'Hmm good,' he said.

She put the box in her handbag and looked at Steve. 'I've got a surprise for you as well.'

'Yes, you said. Come on tell me.'

'Later, I need something else first,' she said, and she raised her skirt to reveal her nakedness. She had discarded her knickers in the Clio. They too were in her handbag.

To anyone passing there would be no doubt what was happening; the Range Rover was rocking from side to side as Kathryn and Steve satisfied their frustrations.

'God, I had no idea anything could be that good,' said Steve after they had finished. 'I love you so much.'

'Yes, I love you too,' said Kathryn, and they kissed.

'So what's the surprise?' said Steve.

'Is the offer of Dubai still on?' said Kathryn.

'Of course,' said Steve.

'Then you better make it two tickets then.'

'You mean...?'

'Yes,' said Kathryn, and giggled again, before Steve could finish. 'I've cleared everything at home and work are ok about it, so if you still want me, I can come.'

'Want you...? Yes... that's brilliant,' said Steve. He held her hand and started thinking out loud. 'I'll get the tickets on Monday. I have an account with the airline so that won't be a problem. I'll give the hotel a call; they'll be fine, I'm a good customer... It'll be great; I know some terrific restaurants... I hope you won't be bored while I'm working,' he added as an afterthought.

'I wouldn't think so,' she said, and kissed him.

'Well they've got a fabulous spa and swimming pool and shops, so your every need will be catered for.'

'I hope you will be catering for my very special needs,' she said, and kissed him.

'That's for sure,' he said, and his hand moved to her right breast and the kissing started again.

In Sutherland Close the party atmosphere had already started.

Victoria had brought three bottles of red wine and the girls had swapped their cans of Coke for a more stimulating drink. At eight o'clock, Victoria phoned Amir to check everything was ready for the new arrivals. Then she made an announcement to the girls.

'Ok, the party is ready. We will go to another house, very near. They are waiting for us,' she said.

'Will Tyler be there?' said Portia.

'Yes,' said Victoria. 'Everyone is there.'

They put on their jackets and followed Victoria to the end of Sutherland Close. They turned right and first left was Argyle Avenue, just five minutes away.

Amir was waiting by the front door as Victoria approached with the six girls in tow.

'Hello girls,' said Amir. 'Come in, I have some friends to introduce you to.'

The girls went into the lounge and were greeted by Uri and Victor, or Fallon and Tyler as they were known to the girls. There was instant recognition. Victor was Portia's and Vaira's main contact while Brigita and Daina were groomed by Uri. Nicolai was Alise and Velina's contact. There was a moment of nervousness among the girls but the boys soon had them relaxing and took them through to the kitchen to get some more wine.

Marija, Elena and Bijana were on duty in the chat rooms but Nicolai had turned the monitors off for the time being; Victoria wanted to introduce the girls gradually to the other activities. Edita and Delvina were upstairs in their bedroom in the attic. Victoria said she would call them later; she wanted to brief the new arrivals first.

More wine was produced and there was a great deal of raucousness as the wine took effect. Rave disco music played and Alise and Velina got up and started dancing. Nicolai joined them. Uri/Fallon was talking to Brigita and Daina and Victor/Tyler had his arms around Portia and Vaira and appeared to be getting on very well.

After half an hour or so, Victoria sat the girls down and started to tell them about the operation. The boys went back to the computer room to watch the chat room feeds. Victoria told the girls that two would be working in the hotel and four in the factory. They would earn good money, she told them. Then she took out the six cash-books and explained how they would work. Each one had the individual names written on them and started with a balance of minus £500. Victoria explained that this was the cost of the transportation to the UK.

There were some worried looks among the girls.

'Don't worry, you will pay it back very soon,' Victoria assured them, and explained to them in Latvian the various ways they could earn money.

'Come with me and I will show you what else we do,' and Victoria led them into the computer room where the three boys were sat. They could see the three Macedonian girls in various states of undress chatting online with a number of men.

'You can make much money in chat rooms. Girls, they get tips and we also pay very well,' said Victoria.

'If you want to make more money you can make video with Uri or Victor. We pay much money; soon you will earn enough to pay for your education. There are more girls who will be here soon you will meet. They are happy here and earn much money.'

Just then there was a knock on the door and Amir went to investigate. It was the six girls from the other house who normally worked the night shift. Victoria had asked them to call at nine o'clock to meet the new arrivals. The timing was just right and the girls were ushered into the crowded computer room. There were quick introductions. Victoria went up to Portia who she recognised was the unofficial leader of the Latvians. 'Please talk to them. They came five months ago and make much money. They will tell you what it is like.'

With more wine the atmosphere was getting more convivial and Victoria noticed Portia and Victor kissing passionately in the corner. She went over to them.

'Why don't you take her upstairs, Victor? Show her one of the bedrooms.'

Before Victor could answer, the two Czech girls came up to Victoria.

'Can we make video please?' said Irena, a stunning blonde girl who had a string of followers in the chat room. 'Just me and Pavla,' she added. Pavla lived up to her name, meaning 'small', almost doll-like, but was extremely pretty.

'You pay good price?' said Irena.

'Yes,' said Victoria, 'very good price... fifty pounds.'

'That is good,' said Irena, and started kissing Pavla passionately.

Victoria called Nicolai over, who was also getting some serious attention.

'Can you do video for Irena and Pavla?' she said.

Nicolai looked at the couple. 'Yes, of course.'

Victoria turned to Victor and Portia. 'You can watch if you like,' she said. 'Over here,' and Victoria went across the room and turned on the monitors.

The two girls went upstairs while the rest congregated around the screens. After a couple of moments they sprang into life as Nicolai started filming.

As the video progressed the atmosphere downstairs got more and more lively and there were whoops of encouragement. Victoria was delighted, the chat room girls had proved great ambassadors; everything was going to plan.

CHAPTER NINETEEN

Kathryn was suffering a real love hangover as she drove home. Having missed Steve for a week the couple of hours in the back of the Range Rover seemed pretty inadequate. The week in Dubai was going to make up for it. There would be lots to do.

Keith returned home just after eight and managed to revive his dinner that was waiting for him in the microwave. Ellie was in the lounge watching TV, her brother playing computer games in his bedroom. Keith thought he had worked out a way to help the Albanians escape. All being well he would talk to the girls on Monday and outline his plan.

Kathryn walked in around nine-thirty.

'Hmm, you smell nice,' said Keith as she walked in the room, 'new perfume?'

Kathryn thought for a moment. 'Oh... yes, it was just a tester I got on Friday; thought I'd give it a try.'

'Very nice,' said Keith. 'I thought we could...'

'Just going for a shower,' she said, cutting Keith off in mid-sentence.

'Oh, right,' he said.

She returned downstairs about ten o'clock with a towel wrapped around her head. Keith was reading the paper; Ellie was still watching TV. She went over to Keith and pecked him on the cheek.

'I'm going to have an early night,' she said. 'My period's just started,' she whispered.

'Oh, yes, right. See you in the morning,' said Keith. 'I won't be long, I'm shattered.'

Keith <u>was</u> worn out. Despite his sleep earlier he had been busy at the depot till almost eight o'clock. He had taken Sunday off, apart from the meeting with Amir, which he hoped would result in some cash.

Sunday morning, Sutherland Close; the six Latvians were up late and there was a great deal of chatter about the previous evening. It was not what they were expecting, although none of them had really thought through their decision to come to the UK. There had been a promise of glamour, romance even, but Aireford on a cold September morning did not come close to this description.

Portia was worse for wear having consumed plenty of alcohol, and couldn't remember too much. As it happened she was as uninhibited as she had been on her social media posts and had not taken much persuading to make a video with Victor. As it was her first time Victoria had agreed to give her a hundred pounds but it had been worth the investment; having watched the playback the previous evening the results had exceeded expectations.

Victoria arrived around eleven-thirty to check on them.

'Did you have a great time?' she said to Portia.

'I can't remember too much,' she said.

'But the video, surely?' Victoria said.

Then vague recollections; 'Oh, that, yes,' she said, and closed her eyes.

'It is very good... You will get many hits,' Victoria said. 'You will make much money.'

In the cold light of day the realisation that the trip wasn't exactly was what they had envisaged was beginning to dawn on them. Velna was the first to comment about wanting to go home. She was the least outgoing of the group and to some extent didn't fit in. She had had little life experience and only one boyfriend she had confessed; the thought of appearing in a porn movie frightened her to death.

As Portia had said, however, they had little option. They were not going to get their passports returned until the debts had been paid. Nor were they going to get their mobile phones back. Amir had confiscated them; temporarily he had said. Velna was in tears, missing her family and wished she had stayed at home.

Victoria called the girls together and produced their cash-books from her handbag.

'I have your cash-books here,' she said. 'You will see Portia I have deducted one hundred pounds from what you owe. You will soon pay it off, and of course, you have work tomorrow.'

Victoria clarified the working arrangements again, and asked them to choose who did what. 'It is the same pay, three pounds per hour.'

'That is not much,' said Portia.

'It is what we pay,' she said. 'That is twenty-one pounds a day, a hundred pounds a week. That is more than in Latvia, I think... Then of course you can earn much more with chat room and videos, much more,' she said. 'The other girls have nice clothes and money saved for their studies. They are free to go any time they want but they choose to stay... as I do.'

This was true and there was no doubt that the chat room girls did seem to be enjoying life. Victoria told them about her car, her flat and how much money she had earned, just as she had done when the Albanians arrived. She was very convincing and even Velna cheered up.

Uri, however, was worried. Despite the copious alcohol he had consumed he had hardly slept, thinking about his dilemma, but he knew what he had to do.

'I am going to the shop,' he said to Victor, who was in his sleeping bag in the lads' bedroom. The three shared one bedroom; the girls shared the other two. To save space, sleeping bags had been provided instead of beds; not as comfortable, but they did the job.

Once out of sight from the house Uri dialled a London number which was stored on his phone. It was answered straight away in Russian.

'Vasyl...? It is Uri, Uri Popkov, yes, you remember me. I am in Aireford... with Amir. I need to talk with you. I have some information which I think you would want.'

Uri explained that Amir and Victoria had financed the shipment of six girls from Latvia and they were planning on getting more.

Vasyl listened intently. 'When did they do this?'

'The girls arrived yesterday,' said Uri.

Uri could hear the sound of crockery being broken.

'But why do they do this? I have given them best deal, many good girls. Why they double-cross me?'

'I do not know,' said Uri. 'You told me to phone you if I heard anything.'

'No, you did well. I want you to say nothing. Is that clear? Nothing!' Vasyl's voice was raised. 'And when this is over you will join me in London. You can work for me. I need people I can trust.'

'Yes,' said Uri.

'Ok, you go back now. Thank you, I will see you are well looked after. Remember say nothing. I will deal with this.'

Uri rang off, still wondering if he had done the right thing. There would be trouble but sooner or later Vasyl would have found out and there was no telling what would have happened. He would say nothing to Victor for now.

Sunday in Dunfield was spent relaxing. Kathryn was in a bad mood and everyone was keeping out of her way, including Keith. It was nothing to do with any monthly cycle; she was missing

Steve and felt trapped not being able to contact him.

Keith had had enough by four o'clock and decided to return to the depot early to clear some paperwork. He was sat in his office when he heard a car pull up. He got up and looked through the window and saw Amir getting out and walking towards the office. He was alone, holding a carrier bag which at first Keith thought might be a gun. Keith was worried for a moment wondering what to do but before he could do anything Amir walked into the room and just threw the bag on Keith's desk. It made him jump.

'The money, as I said. You did well. We will need you again next month,' he said. 'Be ready, we will call.'

That was about it. Amir turned and left, leaving Keith relieved but also slightly surprised, he was expecting more dialogue. Still, there seemed to be a compliment in there somewhere. Nevertheless, it brought home the potential danger of helping the Albanians.

He had completed the first part of his plan for the girls; it was in a box in his drawer. He took it out and checked again; pay-as-you-go, fairly basic as mobile phones went but it would do the job. He had topped it up with twenty pounds worth of credit. Should be enough, he thought. He put the phone in his pocket and discarded the box in the recycling bin.

Monday morning, and Keith was back on the hotel and factory run outside Argyle Avenue at six forty-five. He watched Edita and Delvina leave but then Nicolai followed and got in the minibus. The girls were stone-faced and said nothing.

'Morning,' said Keith.

'We go, pick up more girls,' said Nicolai, and he told Keith to go around the corner to Sutherland Close.

Keith drove around the block and he could see two girls waiting outside the house. It was Alise and Velna; Keith recognised them from the Latvian trip.

He got out, opened the doors and the girls got in. Nicolai made the introductions.

'This is Edita and Delvina, from Albania. They will show you what to do. You go with them, they are waiting for you at the hotel,' he said.

Keith looked into the rear-view mirror and made eye contact with Edita. He mouthed 'hello' so she could see. She smiled.

There was little conversation en route to the hotel except from Nicolai giving the newcomers some instructions. Keith was wondering what he could do to let the girls know he was working on something for them.

As usual Keith took the minibus to the service entrance of the hotel around the side and got out to open the doors. Nicolai stayed inside. The two Latvians exited first, followed by Delvina, then Edita. In a second Keith had taken the mobile phone from his pocket. He pretended he was helping Edita out of the bus and quickly slipped it into Edita's hand. It startled her for a moment and she wondered what it was. She looked down and quickly put it in her pocket and mouthed 'thank you'. 'Later,' mouthed Keith and Edita nodded in recognition.

The girls went to their work and Keith got back in the minibus; he was sweating. Nicolai was oblivious to the exchange.

After he had completed his morning runs, Keith returned to the depot. He was disappointed he had not been able to speak to the Albanians and wondered if his plan would work now they had company; he needed to speak to them to explain everything. Then he had a brainwave.

Back in his office he took out his phone and sent Edita a text. Keith had made a note of the number. 'Ring me on this number when you can,' it said.

He was in the servicing bay talking to Jack when the call came through about an hour later.

'I've got to take this,' he said to Jack.

Outside, Keith accepted the call and tried to make out the dialogue. Edita was whispering and with her strong accent and the extraneous noise of the yard he couldn't hear understand what she was saying.

'Wait,' said Keith. 'I can't hear you. Stay there.'

He went behind the office wall where it was quieter. The area was strewn with litter.

'Sorry,' he said. 'That's ok,' he added when Edita thanked him for the phone.

'OK, please listen and tell me you understand, ok.'

'I can get you away tomorrow; I have train tickets and some money. What time is your break in the morning...? Eleven o'clock...? Ok, that doesn't give us much time but we'll manage.'

Keith outlined where he would meet the girls; 'at the entrance to the drive.' He made Edita repeat everything. 'Eleven o'clock tomorrow morning,' he repeated.

There were security cameras all around the hotel and he did not want to be spotted in any investigation which would undoubtedly ensue.

Satisfied that Edita understood, he rang off. Hopefully he may have the chance to talk to her on the evening run.

At Hyams, it was a usual busy Monday and Portia and her three friends were being inducted by their supervisor, Sheila Smith. At ten o'clock, the department had an important visitor.

'Hello, Mr Jones,' said Sheila as she saw Steve walk into the packing shed.

'Hello,' said Steve. 'Are these the new recruits? I thought I would pop down and say "hello".'

'Yes,' said Sheila, and Steve introduced himself to the girls.

'Whereabouts in Latvia are you from?' he asked them, and each gave him a brief background. It was like they were addressing royalty.

Although not unusual, Sheila was surprised to see the Managing Director on the shop floor, it was not often he made an appearance in her department and after he had gone she turned to the girls. 'My, you are honoured,' she said.

Steve had a vested interest in the new entrants and was keen to make sure that his investment was being well looked after. He would phone Amir later and express his satisfaction.

Later that afternoon, Keith was again on the hotel run and this time Nicolai was not there. When he arrived at the hotel the four girls were chatting together like good friends.

Keith opened the door of the minibus and they got in. Edita deliberately waited until last and bent down ostensibly to remove something from her shoe. She took it off. 'Just a minute,' she said, and Delvina distracted the two Latvians in conversation in a deliberate move.

'You got the message ok?' said Keith, apparently patiently waiting for Edita.

'Yes, we meet you at the gate at eleven tomorrow,' she said.

'I will bring the tickets and money,' he said.

'Thank you,' she said, and got in the minibus next to her sister.

'Alright girls?' said Keith as he started the engine.

'Yes, today was good,' said Edita.

'What about you girls, I can't remember you names? How was it?' he said.

Alise answered. 'Yes it was ok,' she said. 'The people, they are very nice.'

'Yes,' said Velna.

The four girls continued to chat in English as Keith drove them back.

Tuesday morning, six-twenty a.m., and Edita and Delvina were trying to choose what to take with them. They had acquired some nice clothes during their stay and would have little opportunity to buy the same things when they returned. They were careful not to alert Marija, Elena and Bijana, who were also trying to get ready.

The Albanians both had rucksacks which they had bought on an earlier exploration to the mall and they were pushing tops and trousers into them until they couldn't get anything else in. They did not normally take them to work, however, and were hoping that no-one would notice their additional baggage.

It was Marija who made the comment. 'Why are you taking rucksacks?'

'It's just washing. They have said we can use the hotel machines. It will save our electricity here,' said Edita.

That seemed to satisfy Marija's curiosity and nothing more was said.

As it happened over the last week or so, both Edita and Delvina had appeared less troubled and Victoria had hoped that they were at last adjusting to the new life. No-one suspected they were about to attempt to make a break.

When Keith arrived for them Nicolai was on the computers and did not bother to supervise the departure, failing to see the rucksacks. They got in and Keith drove off, relieved that Nicolai was not accompanying them.

'Everyone ok?' he asked as he joined the morning rush-hour traffic.

'Yes,' said Edita. 'Everything is well.'

That was all Keith needed to hear. He looked at Edita again in his mirror, nodded and then winked. She understood and nodded back. No-one had noticed.

He completed his runs, returned to the depot and having parked up, went to see Jack in the service bay.

'Jack, I need a favour. There was a knocking noise on the Merc this morning as I drove in, it might be nothing, but any chance you could have a look at it for me?'

'Aye sure,' said Jack. 'Give us the keys and I'll check it out.'

'Cheers,' said Keith. 'Oh... just another thing, can I borrow your car for about half an hour this morning. I need to pop out?'

'Yeah, course, no trouble. Give us a shout and I'll give you the keys,' said Jack.

'You're a star, cheers,' said Keith, 'about ten-thirty.'

'Ok,' said Jack, and he continued looking into the bonnet of one of the minibuses.

'Oh, nearly forgot, everything ready for the changeover today?'

'Aye, they're due sometime this afternoon. The double-deckers are all cleaned and ready to go,' said Jack.

Keith walked back towards the office. His plan was in place; next was the tricky bit.

His anxiety increased as the clock ticked inexorably onwards towards the appointed time. At ten twenty-five, he picked up his keys and envelope from his drawer and walked towards the service bay. Jack was on his mobile.

'Shit,' said Keith under his breath. The seconds ticked by and Keith was getting more and more anxious. Jack looked at Keith. 'I'll call you back,' he said into his phone, and rang off.

'Sorry about that boss,' he said.

'Ok, have you got your keys?' he said.

'Oh, aye, forgot. They're in my jacket,' he said, and the two of them walked back to the office where Jack's coat was hung up behind the door.

'There you go,' said Jack, having retrieved the keys from his pocket.

'Do you still want me to have a look at the Merc for you?'

'Aye, if you wouldn't mind,' he said, and handed over his keys.

He shouted to Maggie. 'Just popping out, won't be long.'

'Oh, Steve Jones' just been on the phone. Can you ring him back?' she said.

'Yeah, I'll do it when I get back.'

'He said it was urgent,' she said.

'Ok, I'll get him from my mobile... I have to go,' he said.

Keith looked at his watch, nearly twenty to eleven. 'Shit,' he said again.

He got into Jack's car and left the depot hoping there would be no hold-ups; he was cutting it fine.

It was three minutes to eleven as Keith parked the car just a few yards from the entrance to the drive to the hotel. He hoped that none of the numerous speed cameras had picked him up. His heart was racing. Would they be able to get away? What if they were spotted going down the drive? It was well over a hundred yards from the road to the hotel, nearer two hundred, thought Keith. 'Shit, shit,' he said again, and wondered if he should drive up a way and pick them up. What if they had been stopped? 'Shit, shit,' he said again. He wanted a pee.

Then he saw them hurrying down the drive towards him. The road was lined with horse chestnut trees and did at least offer some cover. He got out and waved to them, and moments later they were in the car and he drove off, breathing a sigh of relief.

'Thank you,' said Edita.

'Yes, thank you,' said Delvina. It was the first time he had heard her say anything.

'Ok, now listen carefully. I have an envelope here. It has the address of the refuge centre in it and their phone number. When you get to London, get a taxi and go straight there. Don't stop for anything; the sooner you are safe the better. Your tickets are there, your train goes at eleven forty-five so you won't have long to wait. I have written down the address you were staying at. You should give it to the people and let them handle it. I hope they will tell the police.'

'We don't want any police. They will put us in jail,' said Edita.

'No they won't, you are the victims here. They may need your statements and then they will get you back to Albania.'

Keith pulled into the station short-stay car park and passed the envelope to Edita. She leaned across and kissed him on the cheek. 'Thank you, thank you,' she said.

'It's ok, you better get going. When you get into the station you will need to look for the platform, remember, the London train... understand?'

'Yes,' said Edita 'We can do that. How long to London?' she asked.

'About three hours,' he said. 'But you have seats booked. You may need to ask someone if you are not sure. You will be fine. Oh and there is fifty pounds in there which will cover the taxi and something to eat for you.'

'Thank you,' said Edita, and they got out of the car clutching the envelope.

Keith watched them walk towards the station concourse and then drove away. He just hoped he had done enough.

While Keith was going back to the office the girls were looking anxiously at the destination board for the London train.

'There... platform two,' said Edita, and they made their way to the platform. Edita stopped and took out the tickets. The money she put in her pockets. A train guard spotted them looking at the tickets, seemingly confused, and went to help them.

'Can I help?' he said.

She saw the uniform, it made Edita jump and for a moment she thought he was the police; then she realised that he posed no threat.

'Thank you,' said Edita, and she showed him the tickets.

'Ah yes, you want coach D,' he said, and walked up to the appropriate coach. 'There you go... seats twenty-three and twenty-four.' He pointed to the seats through the window.

'Safe journey,' he said.

'Thank you,' replied Edita.

The two girls got on the train, found their seats and put their rucksacks on the overhead rack.

They looked out of the window and then minutes later felt the train pull away. Edita looked at Delvina and smiled.

Keith couldn't help wondering how the girls were getting on, and at half twelve he sent a text to the mobile. He hoped they had remembered to switch it on.

'How is it going?'

A few minutes later came the response. 'It is good, on train, thank you,' it said.

Maggie came in with another cup of coffee which distracted him. 'Thanks,' he said as she put it down on the blotter pad in front of him.

'Did you phone Steve Jones back? Only he's been on again,' she said.

'Shit, I forgot. Can you get him for me?'

The call came through. 'Hi Steve,' said Keith. 'Sorry for the delay in getting back to you. It's gone manic here today. New buses due in this afternoon,' he said.

Steve outlined the urgency. 'Keith, I've got an important business associate, his name's Shah Mahmood, due in at Manchester but the flight's been delayed and I've just heard it's been diverted to Birmingham. I was going to pick him up myself but I can't get down there, too much on.'

'What time's he due in?' said Keith.

'About five,' said Steve.

Keith looked at his watch, twelve-thirty. 'Yeah should just be able to make it,' said Keith. 'I can't do it; it'll have to be one of the lads.'

'Yeah, no problem... Don't suppose there's any chance of getting the limo?' said Steve.

'It's a bit short notice, but I'll see what I can do,' said Keith. 'I'll ring you back in about twenty minutes.'

Keith rang off and called Maggie. 'Can you see if Ted Avis has got the limo available? Tell him I need it in half an hour.'

As it happened the limo was available and Keith managed to get one of his contract drivers, Bill Meadows, who was working on one of the minibuses in the yard, to do the run.

'You know the drill, uniform and polite service. You'll need a name board as well; Shah Mahmood is the guy's name, for Hyams. Got that?' Keith said.

'Yeah,' said Bill. He was familiar with airport pick-ups.

With arrangements in place, Keith rang Steve Jones and explained what he had done. 'Thanks Keith, I owe you one. Just let me have the bill,' said Steve.

At two o'clock, the new minibuses arrived and there was a great deal of activity in the depot as the swaps took place. It was all hands to the pump as the double-deckers were driven away. Keith felt a touch of sadness as he watched them go out of the depot for the last time.

At three o'clock, Keith received a text. 'We are in London,' it said.

'Let me know when you get to the refuge,' he replied.

Jack came into the office at four to let Keith know that he couldn't find anything wrong with his car but he had tightened the fan belt as he noticed it was a bit slack.

'Thanks Jack,' said Keith.

At the hotel, all hell was breaking loose. Anna, the supervisor, had reported the girls missing when they hadn't returned from their eleven o'clock break. Eventually, Shalik was informed and a search of the hotel was ordered. Their cleaning trolleys were found locked away in one of the rooms. Concern was growing.

Shalik called Amir at the recruitment agency at just gone midday.

'Gone, what do you mean, gone?' said Amir.

Shalik explained the course of events as they saw it.

'What about CCTV?' said Amir.

'We are just checking,' said Shalik.

Grianne thought it was all a bit over the top. 'Maybe they just went to the shops,' she said, having no idea of the real situation. She was running the CCTV while Shalik watched.

'There,' he said after a few minutes. 'There they are,' and he watched them heading down the drive before disappearing off camera.

Shalik phoned Amir and told him what they had found. Amir was beside himself with rage.

'You let them escape,' he shouted at his brother.

At five o'clock, as Keith was nonchalantly waiting for the girls outside the hotel as usual, he received the text he had been waiting for. 'We are safe, God bless you.'

Keith had tears in his eyes.

By ten past five nobody had appeared and so to keep up appearances Keith walked to the hotel reception and rang the bell.

It was Grianne who answered. She had seen Keith before.

'Here for the girls, no-one's about,' he said.

'Wait here,' she said, and a moment later Shalik appeared. Keith was bluffing this.

'There has been a problem,' said Shalik. 'Two of my girls are missing.'

'Well, what do you want me to do? I've got to pick up at Hyams. Do I wait or what?' he said, trying to maintain his composure and a modicum of control.

'Wait, one moment,' said Shalik, and he went back into the office.

Five minutes later he reappeared with the two Latvian girls following him. 'They go back to the house,' said Shalik.

As he got them in the bus he noticed one of them was crying.

'What's up, love?' said Keith.

'That man is evil,' said Alise. 'He said we helped other girls escape.'

'What did you say?' asked Keith.

'I say we know nothing. We here only short time, but he did not believe us,' she said as Keith headed back to the house. He had stirred up a hornets' nest.

'I wouldn't worry love,' said Keith. 'They must have believed you.'

That was just the start of the repercussions. Victoria returned to Argyle Street as soon as she heard the news. With everyone at work only Nicolai and Victor were about. Uri was on the building site.

She went up to the attic to check their stuff. There were some things still there but Victoria noticed that their better clothes and personal possessions, including toiletries, had gone. They were definitely not intending to return. She considered the repercussions.

Amir turned up mid-afternoon and they discussed the situation at some length. There were two main questions; where would they go and who, if anyone, had helped them?

'But if they have left, will they go to the police?' said Victoria.

'They might,' said Amir.

The Macedonian girls returned from work around five-thirty and there was an immediate inquisition. They were asked if Edita and Delvina had said anything or indicated in any way their intentions to leave.

'I noticed they were carrying their rucksacks today,' said Marija.

'What did you do? Why didn't you say anything?' said Amir, snarling at her in anger.

'Edita say she was taking clothes to the hotel to clean, use their wash machines... I did not know they were going to leave,' she said, and started to cry.

It was clear to Amir that this was going to be a fruitless line of enquiry. The key questions remained, where had they gone and who had helped them? The other question of what might be the ramifications had not been considered in detail at this stage, but Amir and Victoria were concerned.

Earlier, Edita and Delvina had arrived in London on time and were amazed when they reached King's Cross. They had never seen anything like it before. They immediately set about trying to find a taxi. Edita checked the address again on her piece of paper. They followed the signs and waited in a small line but in a few minutes they were on their way to the refuge. It was in a leafy suburb of West London and as the taxi pulled up they could see it was a large private house. They paid the taxi driver, got out and went to the front door. Edita looked at Delvina and rang the bell.

A smart dark-haired lady in her fifties answered the door.

'Can you help us please?' said Edita in English. 'We have been kidnapped.'

The woman spoke in Albanian. 'Of course, come in,' and Edita looked at Delvina, then hugged her.

The house was large with extensive grounds at the back; the girls were led into a small room.

'Please wait here. Can I get you some tea or a cold drink?' she said. Edita declined.

A few minutes later the woman returned with a pocket recorder and a piece of paper.

'You are sisters, I think; so alike,' said the woman trying to relax the girls.

'Yes,' said Edita.

'Do not be concerned,' she said. 'I just need to ask a few questions and then I will explain what will happen.'

The woman introduced herself as Mimoza Latifi. 'But everyone calls me Mimi,' she said and smiled.

CHAPTER TWENTY

The girls gave a detailed account of what had happened to them, their kidnapping, transportation, the rape, their journey in the bowels of the lorry on the ferry and their subsequent delivery to Aireford.

Edita produced the piece of paper with the address on it which Keith had given them. 'We had help from the taxi man called Keith,' and she explained what Keith had done for them.

'He is a very brave man,' said Mimi. 'These people are *pamëshirshme...* ruthless.'

Edita understood the word in both languages and was suddenly concerned for his safety.

'What will happen?' said Edita.

'We will get you settled in here and as soon as we can, we will get you away. I will contact the embassy and arrange for new passports and once we have them you will be flown home,' said Mimi.

'What about the police?' said Edita. 'These people should be stopped.'

'Yes, of course. We do have a contact at Scotland Yard... the police in London,' she clarified, 'and we send him all the information. You won't need to make a statement. They will have a tape of your conversation. The address you have given me will be very useful. Most girls have no idea where they have been. Some are still on drugs.'

Edita looked at Delvina. On hearing this it would seem they appeared to have got off relatively lightly.

It was almost eight o'clock by the time Keith had got home. Kathryn was in the lounge watching TV, Jason and Ellie upstairs in their rooms.

'Anyone at home?' said Keith as he came into the lounge.

'Hello,' said Kathryn. 'Dinner's in the oven. How was your day?'

'Busy,' said Keith. 'Got the new buses today,' he said, and started to explain the makes of the new vehicles, how fast they would go and how many passengers they could carry. Kathryn had switched off after about ten seconds and was concentrating on her TV programme.

'How was your day?' said Keith as he put his jacket in the hall and went to retrieve his dinner from the oven.

'Ok, thanks,' she said.

Inside, Kathryn couldn't wait for the week to pass. Next Monday she would be with Steve; she was counting the hours. The text messages between them had continued to flow and they had agreed not to meet up during the week but, as Steve put it, 'save themselves for Dubai'.

Kathryn reluctantly agreed, recognising it made sense; no point in jeopardising things.

In Argyle Street, the investigation and recriminations continued. Amir started to blame Victoria for not keeping a tighter rein on the girls, which she defended vehemently. Then there was the question of the Latvians. How should they treat them? Victoria suggested they play it low-key, no big deal. 'It makes a lot of sense,' she said. 'We do not want the Latvians to think they are prisoners. It will cause even more problems.'

Amir concurred and Victoria agreed to call round to Sutherland Close and explain what had happened.

She eventually called round at eight o'clock with two bottles of wine; the six girls were eating and watching TV.

They seemed pleased to see her when she walked in.

'How was your day?' she asked, and the Hyams girls responded positively. The hotel girls, not so, and Alise explained her interrogation by Shalik.

'I am so sorry you had to put up with that. It has been a misunderstanding. I will speak to Shalik... Edita and Delvina have decided to return home, that is all. They have made much money. They will continue their university studies. I have asked them to write to us and tell us how they are getting on,' she said.

This seemed to placate the girls and they brightened up. Victoria opened the two bottles and poured them all a drink. She recognised that for the time being they would keep the Latvian girls away from the Macedonians until things had calmed down.

'I came to see if anyone would like to make some extra money tonight. We will be doing another video with Uri. Does anyone want to go with him? We pay one hundred pounds.'

'Uri is Fallon, yes?' said Brigita.

'Yes,' said Victoria.

'I would like to go with him,' she said. 'But you will have to tell me what to do.'

'Of course,' said Victoria.

The rest of the girls started to giggle.

'Can we watch?' said Portia.

'Of course,' said Victoria, 'if Brigita doesn't mind.'

'No, it is ok,' said Brigita.

'I will call for you in one hour,' said Victoria, and she left the girls chatting animatedly; the first bright spot of the day.

Back in Argyle Street, Victoria explained what she had said and her plan for maintaining control. Amir was not totally convinced but went along with it. He was desperate to find out if there had been some sort of conspiracy.

'What do we do if we get a visit from the police?' said Victoria.

'I have been talking to Nicolai and I think we should move the computers to one of the other houses,' he said.

Victoria thought for a moment. 'Yes, that is good.'

'There is room with us,' said Uri, who was monitoring the chat room feeds with Nicolai.

It had cost a lot of money to set up all the equipment and rooms in Argyle Street and the transfer would not be straightforward.

'Yes, we will do that... tonight,' said Amir.

'What about the chat rooms?' said Victoria. 'We must not stop those. Too much money we will lose.'

'We can take everything except the chat room. Then tomorrow when we close we can move the chat room,' said Amir.

'Yes,' said Victoria. 'That would be ok.'

'What about the video? I have one of the Latvians with Uri later... I want to do that one. It will encourage the others,' she said.

'Yes, ok, after video we will start work,' said Amir.

Amir and Victoria worked out a plan. The entire operation would move to Bute Close. Four of the girls would relocate into the vacant rooms in Argyle Street and the boys would see to the trunking of the wiring and redecoration.

At nine o'clock, Victoria went to Sutherland Close to collect Brigita. She had drunk three glasses of red wine and was ready for anything. The other girls were giving her plenty of encouragement; it had become a game, like a wild hen night. All six had decided to go to Argyle Street; no-one wanted to be left out, even Velna was starting to become more adventurous.

Inside, there was a great deal of activity. Nicolai had already started to disconnect any wiring that was not needed; just the chat rooms and the empty room they would use for the video were left.

The girls came in and Victoria produced more wine. Brigita was nervous but then Uri explained how it would work and after a few minutes she said she was ready.

Twenty minutes later the video had been shot and the girls applauded her as she came into the lounge. Victoria went up to her and kissed her. 'How was it?'

'Good,' said Brigita, 'very good,' and she held onto Uri, who was standing next to her.

'I don't want to spoil the party,' said Victoria, 'but we have much to do and you girls have work tomorrow. Nicolai will take you back.'

'But I want to be with Uri,' said Brigita.

'You will see him tomorrow, promise,' said Victoria.

'It's alright, I will take them back,' said Uri. 'Nicolai should be here.'

Victoria looked at Amir, who shrugged his shoulders.

'Go on then,' she said. 'But don't be long. There is much to do.'

Uri and the girls left and went back to Sutherland Close, with Brigita hanging onto his arm.

After he had walked them back, Uri took out his phone and made a call. This was the first opportunity he had had.

'Hello, Vasyl? It is Uri... Yes, I am fine... I have more information. Two girls ran away today. The Albanian girls you sent us.'

Uri could hear Vasyl ranting at someone. 'They have run away you say? Where have they gone?'

'No-one knows,' said Uri.

'But they will tell the police, they will come for Amir and he will tell them everything,' said Vasyl.

'No, he would not say anything,' said Uri.

'Of course he will. He is weak. He will betray us to save his own skin. I know this,' said Vasyl.

'What are you going to do?' said Uri.

'I do not know yet. But say nothing, to anyone. Do you hear?'

said Vasyl.

'Yes,' said Uri, and rang off.

It was gone midnight by the time they had packed most of the stuff in three large cardboard boxes. It was just the routers and chat room wiring left. The video room had been cleared and the bed dismantled. The girls would be in their sleeping bags. The Macedonians would be moved to one of the free bedrooms and the attic cleared. By tomorrow it would look just like any normal house with a group of students in residence.

While they were working, Amir looked at Nicolai.

'Do you trust the taxi driver?' he said out of the blue.

'What do you mean?' said Nicolai.

'Do you trust him?' he repeated.

'I don't know him. You were with him to Latvia,' said Nicolai.

'Yes,' said Amir, 'and I don't trust him.'

Victoria heard the conversation. 'You think the taximan helped them escape?'

'I don't know but I have been thinking about it. It is not any of us, or the other girls, I am certain,' he said.

'But they could have just run away,' said Victoria.

'But they had no money, no papers. Where would they go?' said Amir.

'They could be begging somewhere,' said Amir.

'Or have gone to the police,' said Nicolai.

'No, I don't think so. They were scared of the police,' said Victoria. 'I explained what would happen if they were caught. I told them they would be thrown in jail and I think they believed me.'

'I think we should speak to the taximan... just to make sure,' said Amir.

Wednesday morning at the depot, the area looked bare without the double-deckers but today was the start of a new era, thought Keith. He was overseeing the branding of the new minibuses like a kid at Christmas. It had been several years since they had had any additions to the fleet and the sign writer was carefully completing the "Woodley's Of Aireford" logo with all the care of the master craftsman he undoubtedly was. Keith couldn't be any prouder. As the first one was finished, Jack and the other drivers who were about broke into a round of applause. 'Can't wait to drive 'em,' said one of the lads. One or two took pictures with their mobile phones.

The celebrations were interrupted by Maggie screaming at the top of her voice. 'Keith! Telephone.'

He left the lads watching the second minibus being emblazoned and went to the office. Maggie saw him come in. 'It's a Mr Aziz. Wouldn't say what it was about.'

Suddenly any joy that Keith was feeling disappeared. Maggie left him to the call.

'Hello,' he said anxiously.

'It is Amir. I will come to see you tonight at six o'clock. I have some business we will discuss.'

'Ok,' said Keith. 'I'll be here.'

'Good,' said Amir, and hung up.

Keith stared at the phone; the anxiety had returned. He wondered if it was about the girls.

Back at Argyle Street, with the occupants at work, it was all hands on deck to transfer the operations to Bute Close, about a quarter of a mile away. It was a similar-size building as the house in Argyle Street, a three-bed terraced house.

With the chat rooms closed, Nicolai soon had the wiring out and packed away together with all the computer paraphernalia needed to mount the operation. It would take him all day to configure the set-up in the new home. Both Uri and Victoria had taken the day off work to convert the house into a similar fashion to Argyle Street. Victor was ferrying equipment and stuff between the two properties in a borrowed van.

By the time Keith had dropped off the girls at five o'clock the new arrangements were virtually in place. The three boys would stay in the Bute Close house while the former residents would move into Argyle Street. There was nothing left that could link it to any business operation.

At ten to six, Amir called to check progress and pick up Uri. 'We go to see taxi driver and have discussion,' he said.

Uri was using a claw hammer to secure the trunking for the computers.

'Bring that with you,' said Amir.

'Ok,' said Uri, and he put the hammer in his jacket pocket.

At the depot, Keith did not have a good feeling about the forthcoming meeting and he paced up and down his office. He wished he had asked Jack or one of the other lads to hang around but this was his mess and he needed to deal with it.

He heard the car pull up and Amir and Uri walked in.

Amir pulled up a chair and sat opposite Keith. Uri stood just behind the Iranian looking menacing.

'You know about our little problem,' said Amir.

'What do you mean?' asked Keith, trying desperately to look calm. He leaned back in his chair to put some distance between him and the halitosis.

'We have lost two girls,' he said.

'Yes,' said Keith, 'I heard.'

'What do you know about it?' said Amir.

'I turned up at the hotel to pick them up last night and they weren't there; that's all I know.'

Amir looked at him, carefully scrutinising his body language for any tell-tale signs.

Amir looked up at Uri. 'Do you believe him?'

Keith's hands were on the desk, stretched out in front of him like an executive giving an annual appraisal to one of his staff; formal and giving nothing away.

In an instant, Uri had taken out the hammer and brought it down with a crash on Keith's right hand.

For a nanosecond Keith saw the hammer land and then his brain registered with an explosion of excruciating pain. Instinctively he cradled his damaged hand, tears were in his eyes. It felt like a million fires had been lit under his flesh.

'Well I don't think I believe you,' said Amir,' and if you don't tell us we will do the other one, then other parts of your body that are extremely sensitive to pain.'

'I can't tell you what I don't know,' Keith screamed. He put his other hand back down on the table.

'Go on, hit that if you want, I don't know anything, if I did I would tell you. Come on, I have done everything you have asked of me; more even.'

It was a bluff, but a brave one.

'Go on, hit it if it makes you feel better but it will not change anything; I don't know what happened to your fucking girls.'

Amir looked at Keith. 'If I find you are lying I will kill you,' he said, and got up and walked out. Uri stared back at him as he left the room.

Keith was in a bad way, his hand definitely broken. He looked at the clock, it was six-thirty; he picked up the phone and dialled home.

'Hi it's me,' he said falteringly. 'I'm at the depot, can you pick me up? I've had an accident. I need to go to hospital... No, ok, I'm not going anywhere.'

It would be at least twenty minutes before Kathryn would get there. He went to the toilet and ran some cold water. He screamed again as the cold flow hit the spot. He looked at the back of his hand. There was a red circle, the imprint of the hammer butt starting to form. He sat and waited. Then had a horrible thought; his mobile phone still had the text messages from the girls. 'Shit,' he said to himself; now that would have been a giveaway. He took it out of his pocket and managed to delete the messages with his left hand.

Kathryn drove into the depot and Keith was waiting outside. He had wrapped a towel around his hand but he was shivering from shock.

'What happened?' she asked as he got in.

'I had a filing cabinet drawer drop on my hand. I think it's broken. Can you drop me off at A & E? I'll get a taxi back. God knows how long I'll be.'

'I'll stay if you like,' she said.

'No, it's ok. You get back to the kids. I'll ring you when I finish.'

'Ok, just as you like,' she said.

Kathryn pulled up outside the admissions entrance and Keith got out. 'See you later, love,' he said, and she drove away. Keith needed to make a call. He managed to extract his phone from his pocket and dial.

'Jack? It's Keith. Look, I've had a bit of an accident, think I've bust my hand. Can you drop by the depot for me and lock up. No, nothing serious... just had one of the filing cabinets fall out on it, that's all... What time will you be in tomorrow? I may need you to do the hotel and factory run for me. I don't think I'm gonna be able to drive for a bit.'

'Yeah ok, see you in the morning,' he said, and rang off.

It was, as predicted, a long wait, and at half past ten Keith emerged from the emergency room with his hand in plaster and elevated in a sling. He would need this for four to six weeks, the doctor had said. The hand was also badly bruised and it would not be possible to see if there was any damage to the tendons until the swelling had subsided. He had been prescribed some painkillers and a revisit appointment to outpatients in a fortnight. As he waited in the cool air outside the hospital for the taxi he was thinking, it wasn't like this in the Western movies. John Wayne was never in a sling and out of action for two months after a day of fisticuffs.

'Bollocks,' he said as the taxi drove off. He was trying to think about what arrangements he would need to make. He wouldn't be able to drive for a while, that was certain.

Kathryn opened the door for him as she heard a car pull up on the drive. She looked at him with his jacket wrapped around his shoulders and his right arm in the sling and suddenly felt sorry for him, and for the first time a touch of guilt had crept in.

'I might need a hand to dress for a day or so,' he said.

Suddenly, a thought went through her mind. 'You will be all right for next week?' she said. 'You know, Dubai?

'Yeah, be right as rain. I'll have this lot off by the weekend. Can't be bothering with all this palaver, too much to do.'

Inside, she breathed a sigh of relief.

Keith had a dreadful night, the painkillers only providing marginal relief. In his darkest hour, he was wondering if he had really convinced Amir but he guessed he must have done. He wouldn't have been standing otherwise.

Thursday morning, and the alarm rang as usual at five-thirty. Keith was in agony and had hardly slept. Kathryn was not there, she had made up a bed on the sofa in the lounge to try to get some sleep; Keith had been so restless. He had dispensed with his sling and was able to lift his arm, but there was no movement in his fingers. Driving would be impossible. He went to the kitchen and made some tea. Kathryn was dead to the world. The spare alarm clock was on the floor; it was set for seven-thirty.

He took his tea back upstairs and swallowed another painkiller. He called Jack, who would be on his way to the depot to open up. He was driving but on a hands-free.

'Jack? It's Keith... not good... I won't be coming in today... No, it looks like I'm gonna be out of action for a while,' he said. 'I've been thinking, forget about the hotel and Hyams run today. I'll ring 'em and ask them to make their own arrangements for today. Yes, it'll be fine... you have enough on your plate. I'll call Maggie later and get her to forward me any emails. I can do some work from here.'

Keith made another call. 'Amir, it's Keith Woodley,' he said when the call was answered. 'You're gonna have to make your own arrangements for the runs today. I won't be driving for a while thanks to your fucking henchman. No, I can't; there isn't anybody. No, you should have thought about that before you got heavy-handed. It wasn't necessary.'

Keith hung up and crawled back into bed; there was nothing else he could do and the latest painkiller was starting to take effect.

He woke as Kathryn was getting ready for work. She was in her underwear and about to put on her work clothes. 'You sleep ok?' she said.

'No, had a dreadful night.' He winced as his brain reminded him of his broken hand. 'Shit,' he said.

'Are you going into the depot today?' she said.

'No, I'll stay here today. I'll get Maggie to send over any emails and she can phone me with any messages.'

'Right,' she said. 'Kids are having breakfast. I'm off to work, I'll see you tonight.'

'Aye, ok,' he said as she walked out of the bedroom.

Amir was in Bute Close and went upstairs to wake up Nicolai to take the girls to the hotel and factory. 'Where's the taxi?' said Nicolai as he put on his jeans.

'Had an accident,' said Amir.

Uri and Victor were still asleep.

'Uri, Victor, get up, we have work to do,' he shouted, and there was movement in the two adjacent sleeping bags.

Last night had been the first chat room session in the new house. The computer systems seemed to be working fine and the hits on the website indicated they were getting plenty of customers logging in.

One or two observant punters noticed the new surroundings but the girls just said they had had a change round. It wasn't the decor they were interested in. Marija, Elena and Bijana had done the evening shift as usual, and the former Bute Close girls from eleven till four. They had to walk from Argyle Street to the new chat room sets but there were no complaints. Victoria had agreed to pay them a bonus as it was their first night and had paid out for some new clothes for them. The girls' cash-books were looking very healthy.

The Latvians in Sutherland Street were also content. Victoria called in around seven to see if they were alright and was bombarded with requests to do videos, them having watched Brigita the previous evening.

'Tomorrow,' said Victoria, and she explained they were still sorting out the rooms.

Mid-morning at Hayfield Manor, the inquest into the disappearance of the two Albanian girls continued. Shalik was interviewing the last of the waitresses who were on duty on Tuesday morning, but was beginning to think that Edita and

Delvina had just decided to walk out.

A nervous, mousy-looking girl called Eliza walked into Shalik's office, responding to the summons. She had been warned what it was about by her colleagues who had also been interrogated.

'Hello Eliza, come in and sit down... you have nothing to worry about,' said Shalik, which did nothing to ease the poor girl's anxiety.

'You were on duty in the breakfast room on Tuesday, in the morning. Is that right?' he asked.

She looked down at her fingers, which were wrapping themselves around each other nervously.

'Yes,' she said.

'Do you know the two girls who have gone missing?' he asked.

'I have seen them around,' she said.

'Now think carefully, did you see them at all on Tuesday morning walking to the hotel gates at all?' he said.

'Yes, I think so,' she said.

Shalik jumped. 'You think so?' he shouted, which frightened the girl even more.

'Did you or didn't you?' he repeated.

'Yes,' she said. 'I saw them go to the gate and get in a car.'

'What sort of car? Did you see the driver?' he leaned forward and looked her straight in the eyes.

'Yes, it was the man who drives the taxis. I see him bring the girls in the morning. Sometimes he waves,' she said.

'You are sure?' said Shalik, 'the man who brings the girls here in the morning.'

'Yes, it was him,' she said. 'I thought he was taking them home, perhaps they were ill.'

'Thank you, Eliza. There will be a small bonus for you this week,' he said. 'You can go.'

'Thank you,' she replied, and walked out.

It was Shalik's turn to rage. He picked up his desk phone and called Amir.

'Amir...? Shalik, I have just spoken to one of my waitresses and she saw the two girls get into a car on Tuesday morning. Yes, they saw the driver. It was the taximan, she said. She was certain. I asked her many times... What will you do?' he said. 'Yes, that will be best.'

Amir was in Azure's offices and was almost red with anger. He called Victoria in. Straightaway she could see his distress.

'Are you ok?' she said.

'It was him, the taxi driver. I knew it,' he said. 'He is a dead man.'

'What are you going to do?' said Victoria.

'I will speak to Uri and Victor. We will pay him a visit I think.'

Meanwhile, in London, two separate and very different incidents were unfolding.

In the leafy suburb of Fulham, Edita and Delvina were in one of the lounges reading when Mimi came into the room. There were three other girls in the house at this time, also waiting for their documents. They were watching TV. Edita and Delvina had talked to them the previous evening and their stories were equally as harrowing. Like them, they were kidnapped in Tirana but sent to London where they were tortured with cigarette ends and raped, then forced into prostitution. One of them had had an abortion. Then they heard about the refuge and planned their escape. They would be killed if they were discovered, they were certain.

'Edita, Delvina,' said Mimi, and they got up and followed her into another room which served as an office. There was a desk with a computer monitor to one side.

'Sit down, I have some news for you,' she said, and they pulled up two chairs.

Mimi opened the desk drawer and handed them two passports.

'These are your replacement documents. The embassy always prioritises the "taken" so we can get you home to your families as quickly as possible,' she explained.

Edita and Delvina took them from her. 'Thank you,' they said together.

'I also have your plane tickets. You will leave this afternoon and fly at five o'clock. You can ring your parents and let them know. Maybe they can pick you up from the airport in Tirana. I will give you the times.'

Edita and Delvina looked at each other; Delvina started to cry. Their ordeal was almost over.

'We have a car which will take you to the airport here. It is too dangerous on the Tube. We will not risk you being captured again.'

'Thank you, thank you,' said Edita.

'I think you should thank your taxi driver. He is the one who saved you,' said Mimi. 'We just try and put the pieces back together.'

Earlier in Holloway, North London, just off what was once The Great North Road, in the dingy flat above the kebab shop which served as their headquarters, there was a different atmosphere entirely.

Vasyl Hudzik, former Russian Mafia member, Oleksi Bolyk, who had acted as courier and Kasper Paviosky, occasional enforcer, were in discussion deciding on the course of action they would take against their erstwhile customers in Aireford.

There was a general consensus they needed to be dealt with.

CHAPTER TWENTY-ONE

Late afternoon at Bute Close, Amir had arrived and was in discussion with Uri and Victor.

'Tonight we will visit taximan and deal with him,' said Amir; his fury was unabated and he had been working on what they would do.

'We know where he lives, we will go to his house tonight and kill him, but first we will kill his family. Uri and Victor, you can decide if you want to have the mother or daughter. The taximan will watch as you love them. Then they will die, then the boy, then taximan. He will feel more pain than before, I will see to it,' he said.

Uri and Victor smiled. 'You can have the girl, Victor, I need a real woman,' Uri said, and laughed.

Uri was in the back room when he received a text message. 'Ring me,' was all it said.

'Just going to mini-market,' he said on returning to the lounge where Amir and Victor were sat discussing the finer points of Amir's plan to dispatch the Woodley family.

They took little notice as Uri left the house and went around the corner out of sight.

He dialled the number. 'Vasyl?'

'Uri, we are in the car, we are coming to see Amir. You must not alert him... ok?' said Vasyl.

'Of course,' said Uri.

'We need to talk to him. Is there anywhere we can take him? Not at his house,' said Vasyl.

Uri thought for a moment. 'Yes, we are working at a place. There will be no-one around after six o'clock. It will be easy there.'

'Good,' said Vasyl. 'We will be there at eight o'clock. Make sure Amir is with you.'

'Do you know the address?' said Uri.

There was a pause and some discussion. 'It is Argyle Street, I think.'

'No,' said Uri. 'We have moved,' and he provided them with details of the Bute Close house.

'Eight o'clock... make sure Amir is there,' said Vasyl again, and rang off.

Uri went back to the house. Suddenly, he was worried; if Amir were to find out he had betrayed him, he would be killed.

Back at the Woodley residence, Keith had not had an easy day. He was in excruciating pain from his hand and was running out of tablets. He had managed to answer his emails; he could just about manoeuvre the mouse with his damaged hand, and had taken a call from Steve Jones who wanted to arrange the limo for Friday to return his VIP visitor to Manchester; again Ted Avis's vehicle was available. Keith wondered if he should make Ted an offer for it if this was going to be a regular occurrence. He would give it some thought. By mid-afternoon he was asleep in the chair in the lounge, oblivious to matters that were unfolding elsewhere.

In the benefits office, Kathryn was having difficulty concentrating. She continued to receive texts from Steve and the excitement for Monday was growing; just four days to go. Everything was set for the journey to the airport. Steve would meet her at the station in town and take her to the airport in the Range Rover.

By seven o'clock, the atmosphere at Bute Close was getting very tense. It was eerily quiet; usually it was a hive of activity but Amir had cancelled the early chat room; he and the boys had a prior meeting. Given she would not be required to supervise, Victoria had decided to stay at the office in town to catch up on some work.

Amir, Uri, Victor and Nicolai were sat discussing the arrangements for the hit on the Woodleys' house. The question of disposal was giving them some issues; how would they get rid of the bodies? Although it was a detached house with its own drive, there were neighbouring houses and they would need to make their escape without being seen. Carrying bodies out would be very risky.

'If we go after nine o'clock,' Uri argued, 'everyone would have their curtains drawn.' He was desperate to make sure Amir was around when Vasyl turned up. 'We can just leave them there and set fire to the house,' he added. 'There will be nothing to link them with us.'

'Yes,' said Amir, 'you may be right.'

He was sat in a chair fiddling with a gun, making Uri even more nervous. It was only an hour before Vasyl and his people were due at Bute Close, but if they were late for any reason Amir would be on his way to Dunfield with no idea when they would get back and there would be nothing Uri could do.

He was looking at his watch almost every couple of minutes it seemed, which hadn't gone unnoticed by Amir. Victor and Nicolai were in the computer room doing some editing to Brigita's video before posting it online.

'Do not look so nervous, Uri, very soon you will be loving Mrs Taxi man,' he said, and laughed.

Suddenly Uri felt a vibration from his mobile phone in his pocket. It was a text. He retrieved his phone and switched it on. 'Five minutes' was all it said.

Amir was also feeling restless and got up from his chair. 'I think we should go now,' he said. 'It is dark enough. I will get

Victor and Nicolai.'

Uri quickly countered. 'No, no it is not time,' he said. 'We need to wait.'

Amir looked perplexed. 'But why, the sooner we get it done, the sooner we will be back. Victoria said another of the Latvians wants to make a video and we should not disappoint her.'

'I think we should wait... it is what we said,' said Uri.

Amir looked at him and accepted his council. 'Yes, you are right. It will not be so long.' He sat back down.

Uri was watching Amir's gun like a hawk. If Amir spotted Vasyl there would almost certainly be a fire-fight. Amir got up again and started walking around. The nerves were getting to him. 'I think I will go to the shops and get some things,' he said.

'Sit down, Amir, you are making everyone nervous,' said Uri. Amir sat down and put his gun on the table next to him.

Then there was an urgent knock on the door. Amir looked at Uri, but before he could move Uri had snatched the gun. 'What the...?' said Amir.

'Wait there,' said Uri, and he went and opened the door.

It was Vasyl and his three companions. Uri put the gun in the back of his jeans and let them in.

Vasyl barged in and saw Amir sat in the chair. Oleksi pulled out a gun. 'You come with us,' said Vasyl. Amir looked at Uri and snarled. 'You are a dead man,' he said as he got up.

'Uri, you come. Kasper, you stay here. Victor and Nicolai heard the kerfuffle and came to investigate.

'Victor, it is good to see you. Do not worry, everything is ok. We want to talk to Amir; we will be back soon,' he said. Kasper moved his jacket to one side so the lads could see the revolver in his waistband.

The men got into Vasyl's large Volvo and followed Uri's instructions to the building site.

Someone was watching what was going on from the street corner. It was just good fortune; there was no room to park outside the house. All the neighbouring residents were at home watching TV and their cars had taken up every inch of space. She cursed when she saw someone had parked in her normal place outside the house. Victoria had no option but to park in an adjoining street; it had probably saved her life.

She got out of her car, locked up and made the two blocks to Bute Close. She was just about to cross the road when she spotted three men loitering outside the house; she recognised Oleksi straight-away. She waited to see what was happening and watched the men go inside. After a few minutes a car drew up and the men came out dragging Amir and bundling him into the waiting vehicle. She knew straight-away what was happening. She was in no doubt that she was in danger, and so were the other girls. She made a quick decision.

She went back to the car, an old Fiat she used for driving around town, and headed off to Argyle Street. She let herself in and went to a cupboard in the kitchen. A couple of the girls were milling about. She shouted to them, 'Get everyone together... you are in great danger. Get your things, quickly.'

While they were gone, she lifted the front off one of the cupboards and revealed a safe at the back. She flicked the dials left and right and pulled sharply. The heavy door opened towards her. Victoria quickly scooped up the packets of bank notes and put them into a supermarket carrier bag, Euros, dollars, pounds sterling, all hidden in case of emergencies. This was an emergency. There were also the passports of all the girls.

When she returned to the lounge, the six late-shift girls and Marija, Elena and Bijana were waiting. Victoria spoke to them. 'Listen carefully, you are in grave danger, you need to get away.'

She put the passports down on the table. 'Your passports are here. Find them quickly,' she said, and the girls rummaged through.

She took out one of the bundles of English money and put it on the table.

'Here, there should be five thousand pounds there, spilt it between you. There is a bus stop on the main road. You know where that is. Take a bus to the station and get a train to Leeds. It is not far. Do not go to London, they will be waiting for you. They will find you.'

'Who will find us? What is happening?' said Marija.

'There is no time to explain... you must go... now. Remember, go to the station, then go to Leeds. Get a place for tonight somewhere, then go to the airport there in the morning. There are flights to many places. You may even get a flight home but you can fly to Amsterdam and you can get anywhere from there. Try and make your way home. Do you understand?'

'Yes,' said Marija.

There was another scrum for the money and Marija took charge. 'Come, we will do this at the bus stop,' she said.

'Go quickly,' said Victoria.

She led the girls out. They were each carrying small backpacks containing as many belongings as they could cram in. There were some brief farewells and then they walked away down the drab streets towards the main road, which shone like a beacon in the distance.

Victoria got in the car and headed for Sutherland Close and the Latvians. She walked in and again called them together. She spoke quickly in Latvian, outlining the same message she had given to the other girls. She produced their passports. 'You must go, if they catch you they will take you away.'

They gathered up their rucksacks and belongings. Victoria

gave them some money, including a wad of Euros. 'There should be enough there to get you home, and she gave them the same instructions. Remember Leeds, there is an airport there. Do not go to London, they will find you.'

The girls were trying to make sense of everything. 'Thank you,' said Portia, and they left the house with their belongings and headed towards the bus stop.

There were other things that Victoria needed to do, but they would have to wait until the banks opened tomorrow. She thought about her next move; should she return to her flat? Given her connection with Amir, Vasyl and his associates would almost certainly be looking for her. She made a decision and took a gamble, thinking that they would be spending some time with Amir. Ten minutes later, she approached the apartment block and made a drive-by to check there was no-one waiting. She couldn't see anyone about in the immediate vicinity; a few passers-by going about their business. She took a chance and parked the Fiat in a side street and quickly walked the couple of blocks with the carrier bag containing the remainder of the money and her handbag.

Her flat was in one of the few desirable areas of the city and on the top floor with views across the neighbouring park. There was a security door to the complex which she accessed by code and on the ground floor, the lift. She pressed the call button and waited anxiously for it to arrive. 'Come on, come on,' she said to herself. Thirty seconds seemed to take a lifetime but the lift arrived and opened. She got in and pressed the button for the third floor. It juddered upwards. 'Come on, come on.'

It arrived on the top floor and the keys were already in her hand to save time. Her front door was directly opposite the lift. She was shaking and had difficulty negotiating the key into the lock, and then the door opened. She went straight to the bedroom and collected all her jewellery. She put all her make-up and toiletries in another carrier bag, and then packed her most expensive dresses and the rest of her stuff in two suitcases. She had a final check – it was almost ten o'clock; there was nothing left of any real value. She would replace her CD collection.

She made her way down in the lift to the basement and the underground car park, lugging the two suitcases, two carrier bags and her handbag. She opened the boot of the Porsche which was parked in its allocated bay, stowed the gear, and then drove away. She headed out of town towards the motorway, found a budget hotel close by and booked in for the night, just as a base. There were things she needed to do tomorrow.

Earlier, Amir hadn't fared quite as well.

Oleksi had brought the Volvo to the front door and was waiting in the middle of the road with the engine running. The door opened and Vasyl hauled Amir out of the house and bundled him into the back. Oleksi pulled away with Uri directing them to the disused factory where he had been working. The complex was about two miles away from the house and was being converted into "desirable" flats in a phased project; part of the site was still derelict. The car pulled up in an alleyway beside a crumbling wall. Weeds and litter reflected the disuse and neglect. Uri got out and opened the door for Vasyl to exit.

'Out,' Vasyl shouted, and thrust a gun into Amir's ribs. Uri and Oleksi followed.

'This way,' said Uri.

They went through a door and down a long corridor; broken glass crunched beneath their feet as they walked. It was not yet completely dark yet but getting close. As this part of the site was in the process of being cleared the electricity supply was still connected, and Uri threw a switch to illuminate a single bulb.

'In here,' said Uri, and he opened a door which led to a large room, probably an old storage or office facility.

'Get the rope,' said Vasyl, and Oleksi ran back to the car and returned with a length of rope used for towing cars.

There was a large exposed RSJ beam running across the ceiling and Vasyl threw the rope over the steel joist.

'Oleksi, tie him,' he shouted, and Oleksi wrapped the rope around Amir's waist and knotted it.

'Here, help,' said Vasyl, and the three of them pulled Amir off the ground. The rope slipped up Amir's torso and held firm under his arms. The room had bars on the window to keep intruders out just a few feet away, and Vasyl threaded the rope and tied it off, leaving Amir's legs dangling three feet from the floor.

'What do you want Vasyl? What do you want?' shouted Amir, who was towering over them, his legs kicking.

'Some answers, my friend,' said Vasyl.

He took out a sheath knife from a holster around his right leg, leaned up and slit the belt of Amir's trousers. He gave them a tug and then slowly pulled them down with his underpants. He watched Amir dangling there, totally naked from the waist down.

'Why did you bring in new girls?' Vasyl shouted.

'I had to... I had an urgent order... from... from our customer,' stammered Amir. 'There was no time to get them from you.'

'But we said we were getting in a shipment. We told you that... You were trying to cheat us.'

'No, no I wouldn't do that,' said Amir.

Vasyl plunged the knife into Amir's pelvis around the hipbone and he shrieked in pain. Blood spurted down his leg.

'That was the wrong answer,' said Vasyl. He paused for a moment, considering his next move. 'Who is this customer?' he said.

'It is Jones,' he said. 'He has a factory... where the girls work.'

'Where is this factory?' asked Vasyl.

'It is Hyams, the factory. Jones... he give us the money to get them. It is he who should be here, not me. We were only doing what we had to do. He... he said he would not use us if we did not get them for him.'

Amir was trying desperately to deflect the blame in some way. He continued pleading.

'What could I do...? There was no time... I did not want us to lose business. It was only one deal... that is all... We can share the money,' said Amir, who was now having difficulty speaking.

Vasyl was not for placating, his anger was overwhelming and he repeated the stabbing on the other side. Amir again shrieked in pain and blood flowed freely down his leg from the wound. 'So this man Jones was providing the money?'

'Yes, yes,' said Amir, crying pitifully. 'It is him who has the girls. He pays them small wages.'

There were two separate pools of blood below his feet.

'Why did you not tell me?' asked Vasyl.

'It was as I said, there was no time. This man said he would cause much problem for me,' said Amir.

'What do you mean, cause problem?' said Vasyl.

'He has many connections in the Middle East, Iraq, Saudi, my country... He said he would have my family shot if I did not give him cheap girls,' said Amir.

This was not really plausible, but Amir was desperately trying to save himself. It was all he could think of.

'Should we believe him?' said Vasyl to Oleksi.

'I don't think so,' said Oleksi.

'What about you, Uri?' said Vasyl.

'I know this man Jones, Amir does much business with him. I don't know about his connections,' said Uri.

'You are right, Amir. Maybe we should speak to this Mr Jones, but do you know what I think...? You were... what is the word in English...? I cannot think. Going on your own... That is what I mean. You don't pay me money. Maybe you sell girls to other peoples, get all the money for yourself and you say "fuck Vasyl", that is what I think.'

'Well fuck you Amir,' he said, and plunged the knife into Amir's lower abdomen. He slit sideways until parts of Amir's intestines were visible. Amir dropped into unconsciousness.

'Leave him,' said Vasyl. 'We go back to the house, there are matters to discuss.'

Amir's legs were twitching; blood was running down his body and dripping off his genitals; the pool on the floor expanding outwards.

The three left the building and drove back to Bute Close. Nicolai, Kasper and Victor were waiting anxiously.

They parked outside and Uri let them in.

'Do you have vodka?' said Vasyl.

'I don't think so,' said Nicolai.

'Then get me some,' barked Vasyl, and Nicolai was duly dispatched to the nearby off-licence.

'So what do we do with the girls?' said Uri.

'How many do you have working for you?' asked Vasyl.

'Fifteen it is now,' said Uri.

'Do you know how to run this operation?' said Vasyl.

'Not all of it. Victoria looks after the girls and the money,' said Uri.

'Victoria, ah yes, the lovely Victoria, a particular friend of yours Oleksi. Am I right?' said Vasyl.

'Oh yes,' said Oleksi. 'Very beautiful, very energetic, make love all night.'

'Where is she?' asked Vasyl.

'At one of the other houses, I expect,' said Uri.

'Uri, you and Victor find her, bring her here. We need to have a conversation; Kasper, you stay here,' he said.

While Nicolai was getting Vasyl's vodka, Uri and Victor went to Argyle Avenue and found it deserted. The girls had gone, along with most of their belongings. Uri searched the house and found the empty safe in the kitchen.

'Come on, we must check the other house,' said Uri, but of course they found the same thing.

As it happened, by this time, the girls were on the train to Leeds. The two groups had met up at the station in Aireford and decided to stick together. They eventually found a budget hotel in the city centre in Leeds, not far from the station, and would catch a bus to the airport the following morning to book flights home.

Uri returned to Bute Close with the bad news. Vasyl had already started his vodka and went into another rage, throwing his glass across the room. Without any girls there could be no operation.

'Where is Victoria?' said Vasyl.

'She was not at the houses,' said Uri.

'Then we must find her... we need to ask her some questions,' said Vasyl. 'Where does she live?'

'She has a flat in town,' said Uri.

'Right, we better pay her a visit... You, Uri, come, take us there. You two wait here,' he said to Nicolai and Victor, who were also looking anxious.

It was almost ten o'clock by the time Oleksi pulled up outside the flats.

'It is the top floor,' said Uri from the back of the car.

Vasyl looked up at the building, just four floors and an underground car park.

'Uri, you come... Oleksi, Kasper, you stay, wait for us,' said

Vasyl.

Uri and Vasyl reached the front door.

'It is locked,' said Uri. Vasyl cursed.

Just then, two residents came out of the lift and pressed the access button and there was a click as the door unlocked. Vasyl barged in, almost knocking the couple to the ground. Uri followed. They ignored the lifts, deciding to take the stairs. They reached the penthouse flat which took the top floor and Uri knocked on the door. There was a glass spyhole, and Uri stood in front of it; Vasyl was out of sight. There was no reply.

Vasyl looked at the door, which seemed fairly substantial. 'We need to get in,' he said.

Uri took a run at it with his shoulder. There was a crunching sound as he made contact. The door moved reluctantly on its hinges. Uri made another run. This time the door latch was unable to resist the force and the door flew open. The men rushed in.

'Check in there,' said Vasyl, pointing to the bedroom.

Uri went in and looked around. 'She is gone,' he said as he walked back into the lounge, 'her clothes, everything,'

Vasyl cursed in Russian. 'We must find her.'

'There is nothing we can do tonight. She could be anywhere,' said Uri.

Vasyl continued to curse. 'Ok, we go back,' he said, and the two of them left the apartment.

A few minutes earlier Kasper had watched an orange Porsche Boxter glide by, admiring the car but making no connection with the attractive owner.

Friday morning, the girls in Leeds, with directions from the helpful hotel receptionist, had made it safely to the airport via the regular shuttle bus from the station. All of them had managed to get fights to their respective homes, some direct, some via Amsterdam.

Portia and her Latvian friends were only just coming to terms with their situation. They had unwittingly become prisoners and, but for Victoria's intervention, there was no telling what would have become of them. There was a subdued atmosphere in the departure lounge as they waited for their flight to Riga.

Victoria knew she too would have to get away, but there were things she needed to do first. She was always immaculately dressed and looked like a glamour model, but today would be different. She was wearing her baggy sweatshirt with her hair tied back. She was also wearing no make-up. Even her own mother would have had difficulty in recognising her. She left her baggage in the hotel room and ordered a taxi. The Porsche was parked behind the hotel, out of sight of any passing traffic.

Her first port of call was to the financial district of the city and the bank where they kept a safety deposit box; she and Amir had lodged it there a few months earlier. There was a delay as her identity was checked and she started to feel nervous. She kept looking around making sure that no-one was watching. After a few minutes she was escorted to the vaults by one of the staff. The young man waited outside as she entered the secure room. There were rows of small boxes and she produced her key and accessed number 1073. She took out the small cloth bag and put it in her handbag and then relocked the box. At the last count the diamonds would be worth at least 250,000 Euros. She then went to the cashier and drew out the balance of her personal account.

She left that bank and went across the road to another, The National Bahamian Trust. This was the big one. The manager had been regularly entertained by Amir and although Victoria had met him when they first set up the account, she was not sure if he would recognise her. Given the balance on the account, the manager would almost certainly need to authorise any significant withdrawals. Sure enough he was summoned.

'Hello Charles,' said Victoria as he approached. She was led into a small interview room and offered a seat; the manager sat down opposite her.

'Victoria, my dear, how lovely to see you again, I understand you want to close the account?' he said.

She used all her charm on him and explained that Amir had gone abroad to set up a new business and needed the money urgently. She breathed a sigh of relief as there was little more interrogation. The manager had done what was required. 'Give Amir my best wishes when you speak to him. Tell him we will meet up when he returns and it will be my turn to pay,' he said, and let out a raucous laugh as he got up and left.

Another member of staff came in and Victoria completed the paperwork and transferred the balance of the high-interest account which had been receiving the website money to her private account in the Bahamas by telegraphic transfer; nearly £750,000.

She left the bank and breathed a sigh of relief, then got a taxi. She returned to the hotel and packed her bags and loaded up the Porsche. It was only ten o'clock but within a few minutes she was on the motorway and heading towards Hull. She would be in time to catch the afternoon ferry to Zebrugge. Then she would head home to Riga, a very rich, but also a very wanted, woman.

In Bute Close, there was significant frustration in the inability to track down Victoria. Vasyl was stomping up and down in the living room like a bear with a sore head.

He turned to Uri, who was playing a game on his mobile phone.

'What do you know about this man Jones?' he said.

'He is very important, I think. Amir always said so,' replied Uri, who was giving Vasyl his full attention.

'Do you know where he lives?' said Vasyl.

'No, but I know where he works,' said Uri.

Vasyl thought for a moment. 'We need to return home,' he said. 'But you and your two friends here, you stay and find out about this man for me. Call me next week and I will decide what to do.'

'Yes,' said Uri. 'We can do that.'

'And if you can find the bitch Victoria, tell me straight away. I will pay you, or anyone else, ten thousand Euros if you find her.'

On the building site, there was a nasty surprise waiting for a couple of workers who were opening up for the day. They were walking to the work area down the alleyway where Oleksi had parked the previous evening.

'Hang on Stan, what's that?' said Brian Long, a doyen of the bricklaying trade. Something had caught his eye to his left through the broken glass in the former office space.

'Looks like someone's topped themselves,' said Stan Willis, his buddy for many years, following the gaze.

Stan pushed open the door and could see the figure of a man dangling from a rope attached to the ceiling.

'Jesus,' said Brian, 'you better call the police.'

Nine-thirty a.m., Hyams Fabrics, a call came through to Steve Jones' extension.

'Steve, it's Patsy... just had a call from Packing and none of the Azure girls have turned up today. Thought you would want to know.'

'Thanks Patsy, can you give them a call and see what's going on?' he said.

'Bugger,' he said under his breath, 'today of all days.'

He had just returned from Hayfield Manor and breakfast with Shah Mahmood, his VIP visitor; he wanted to see him off, an important courtesy gesture which the Arab appreciated. Bruce

Merryweather had got the run and arrived at the hotel in Ted Avis' limo to pick him up and take him to the airport. Bruce was dressed in Keith's chauffeur uniform which was kept at the office and available to anyone on "posh" job duty. The fitting was not always comfortable and Bruce's jacket was definitely looking tight on his portly frame. There was no way he could do up the buttons.

It was Steve's last day before his trip to Dubai, and he had blocked out his diary to enable him to ensure his work was left straight.

A few minutes later, Patsy came into his office with a coffee.

'Just spoken to Azure and they don't know what's happening. There's no sign of Mr Aziz or his assistant. I've asked them to let us know.'

'Thanks Patsy,' said Steve. 'Have a word with H.R. and tell them to get onto another agency and get cover.'

'Will do,' said Patsy.

Following the discovery of the body of Amir Aziz, a police investigation had been launched. It had been a particularly gruesome murder and was being considered a major incident. There was nothing to identify the body and that was going to be the first priority.

At Hayfield Manor Hotel, Anna Dyszatow, the House Manageress, was in urgent discussion with Grianne Jamieson, who was today's duty manager. The Azure girls had not turned up. Shalik was in the dining room arranging lunch menus with the chef when Grianne interrupted and gave him the news. Shalik finished his discussion, and then called his brother. His phone was in his jacket pocket, which was still at Bute Close, and Uri heard it ring. As soon as it had stopped Uri removed it from the pocket and took out the SIM card.

He handed the phone to Nicolai. 'Can you get rid of this... and Amir's jacket?' he said.

Shalik tried again a few minutes later but this time there was no ringtone, just a discordant noise. He looked concerned. He phoned Victoria's number. She was on her way to the ferry and heard it but made no attempt to answer. She would get a new phone, she reminded herself.

Shalik tried the Azure office and was given the same news as Steve received. He was starting to worry about his brother.

CHAPTER TWENTY-TWO

Friday, back in Dunfield, and Keith was enduring his second day stuck at home and was crawling up the wall in frustration, but there was nothing he could do. His hand had been less painful but he was still not well enough to do a full day's work. Maggie had been phoning him regularly with updates and sending emails but the lack of control he was feeling was exasperating. Jack had brought him up to date with the Hyams delivery business transfer, which was going well, he was assured.

His day dragged and he was laid on the sofa resting when the kids came in from school; they were not used to him being at home during the day. Kathryn turned up at five-thirty. She had been shopping at lunchtime and had bought some nice surprises for Steve which she would wear for him in Dubai. She had never been in the Fantasy Store before; a shop specialising in erotica and particularly risqué lingerie. In fact she would tend to avoid walking past, just the occasional glance out of curiosity, but here she was with her purchases hidden at the bottom of her carrier bag. She had discarded the store wrapping in a Jiffy bag at work. Actually, the experience was different to what she was expecting. The staff were friendly and the atmosphere not intimidating at all. She viewed the other customers suspiciously but they seemed normal, like her. She laughed when she saw one or two of the items on sale; Rampant Rabbit, now that was an eye opener! She felt extremely brave as she left the store, but hoped she hadn't been spotted.

She handed the evening paper to Keith, who was now sitting up, having heard her arrival.

'How was your day?' he said.

'Fine, how was yours?' she said as she took off her jacket and hung it in the hall.

'Don't ask,' he said.

'How is your hand?'

He looked at the strapping. 'Sore, but not as bad as yesterday,' he said. 'Kids are upstairs doing their homework,' he added, anticipating her next question.

'Right... just going to change,' she said, and went upstairs with her bag of purchases.

Keith sat at the dining table and started to read the headlines in the newspaper.

'Police investigate gruesome murder,' it said.

It caught his attention and he started to read the narrative.

'From our crime correspondent: The body of a man was found hanging from the ceiling of a derelict property in the Deeppool area of the city by two workmen early this morning, a police spokesman has told the Evening Argos. Police would not go into detail but said it is being treated as a murder investigation and that early indications were that the man had been tortured before he had been killed. His identity is not known but he is said to be in his late thirties, early forties, about five feet ten inches and of Middle Eastern origin. Forensic tests are continuing. Police are requesting that if anyone might know the man's identity to come forward. An incident room has been set up and anyone with information is asked to call 0800 600 5488.'

Keith made no connection and turned to the sports pages.

Five o'clock at Hayfield Manor Hotel, a supply of the evening paper had been delivered. They were offered free to guests and were popular as they enabled them to check details of the entertainment that was on in the locality.

Shalik was in his office and was really concerned. He had been trying to contact his brother all day; something was not right. If he hadn't heard from him by morning he would call the police.

One of the porters brought in a copy of the paper and handed it to Shalik, who also liked to keep up to date with local events and any articles featuring the hotel. He started reading the front page and let out a shriek, then cursed in Farsi.

'Whatever's the matter?' asked Grianne, who was just coming to the end of her shift.

'No, no, no,' said Shalik, and held his head in his hands; the newspaper fell to the floor.

Grianne picked it up and looked at the front page; she read the words.

'You don't think this is your brother, do you?' she said.

'Yes,' he said. 'It is Amir... I am certain.'

'You must call the police,' said Grianne, and started dialling the contact number. 'Here,' she said, and passed the phone to Shalik.

Shalik had difficulty in speaking, but managed to tell the police officer on the other end that he thought the man in the newspaper might be his brother.

Within twenty minutes a police car had pulled up outside the front entrance to the hotel and two plain-clothed detectives got out and went inside. The officers introduced themselves at reception and they were quickly ushered into the office where Shalik and Grianne were waiting.

'I am D.I. Spencer; this is D.C. Cummings,' said the senior man.

'Shalik Aziz,' he said, and looked down. Grianne left the room to give them some privacy.

'I believe you have some information for us?' said Spencer.

'Yes,' said Shalik. 'I think it might be my brother, the man in the paper. I have not been able to speak to him today and he has not been at work.'

'I see,' said the D.I. 'Do you have a photograph of your

brother?'

There was a colour picture of himself and Amir taken about twelve months earlier in a frame on his desk; Shalik turned it around.

'This is him,' said Shalik.

The D.I. picked up the picture and examined it.

'It is him, yes?' said Shalik.

'We'll need you to come down to the station, Mr Aziz, to ask you some more questions and make a formal identification,' said the officer.

After Vasyl and his cronies had left Bute Close, Uri, Victor and Nicolai were in deep conversation.

'What do we do about Mr Jones?' said Victor.

'We need to find him and tell Vasyl,' said Uri. 'I know where he works.'

'We can't just go there. They will have security,' said Victor.

'We will wait outside the factory and follow him,' said Uri.

'But how will we know him? He might not be there... at the factory,' said Victor.

'There is only one way to find out,' said Uri.

'Nicolai, fetch the laptop,' said Uri, and Nicolai went to the computer room and grabbed one of the laptops.

Uri found the website and took a note of the phone number from the "contact us" page. He dialled.

'I want to speak to Mr Jones please,' said Uri. 'A friend of Mr Aziz,' he added when asked of his identity.

There was a pause. 'Who is this? What's happened to the girls?' said Steve. Uri hung up.

'Well he's there alright,' he said, looking at Victor.

Steve looked at the phone and shrugged his shoulders.

Later, Uri, Victor and Nicolai were in Amir's BMW, of which

they had now assumed ownership, and were waiting outside Hyams factory.

'How will we know him?' asked Victor.

'He is the boss, right?' said Uri.

'Yes,' said Victor.

'He will have the best car,' said Uri.

There was considerable traffic going in and out, and at the gate a security guard was checking all arrivals and departures. At five o'clock, the gate barrier was opened and there appeared to be a mass exodus of people; the queue snaked right the way back to the staff car park as they waited to move into the evening rush-hour traffic. By ten past five, the barrier was closed again and the comings and goings resumed to earlier proportions. At five-thirty, the distinctive Range Rover with its personal number plate SBJ 10 appeared at the barrier. It was raised immediately and the security guard seemed to stand to attention as it moved out into the main road.

'There,' shouted Uri. 'That will be him.'

Nicolai was driving. He turned on the ignition and started following as discretely as possible.

After about twenty minutes they were in open countryside. The lanes were narrow and Nicolai had difficulty in maintaining visibility without being conspicuous. Eventually, there was a large mansion on the left surrounded by ten-foot tall iron railings. The Range Rover stopped outside the entrance and waited while the electronic gates opened.

'Wow,' said Victor. 'Look at that place.'

'Ok,' said Uri. 'Let's get back and I will call Vasyl.' He looked at his phone; no signal.

Once they had reached the suburbs of Aireford the mobile reception had been restored and Uri reported in to Vasyl.

'We know where the Mr Jones lives,' he said. 'What do you

want us to do?'

Vasyl gave Uri instructions and rang off.

'What does he want us to do?' said Victor.

'Nothing,' said Uri. 'They have problems there they have to take care of. He will let us know.'

They headed back to Bute Close.

Later, they were in discussion, wondering what to do about the operation.

It was Nicolai who made a suggestion. 'I have been thinking about this,' he said. 'We still have the website and many videos and we are still getting many hits.'

'But we have no chat room,' said Victor.

'No but I can open another feed so that any payments will be diverted to a new account. We can still make much money,' said Nicolai.

'You can do that?' said Uri

'Yes, it is not difficult, one hour maybe,' said Nicolai.

'But how do we get the money?' said Uri.

'We will need a bank account,' said Nicolai.

'I have one in Kiev,' said Victor.

'We could use that,' said Nicolai.

There was some debate but eventually they decided to use Victor's account in the Ukraine to be the destination of the funds generated by the video sales. It was the only way; without valid visas they would not be able to open an account in the UK. Other events unfolding elsewhere, meanwhile, were set to disrupt their plans.

Saturday morning, six a.m., officers from Scotland Yard's serious crime division were outside 29 Argyle Street, Aireford. They made a forced entry and searched the property; it was empty.

Later that morning they raided the premises of Azure Recruitment and took away their computer equipment as part of an ongoing investigation.

Late that afternoon, Keith was reading the headlines in the evening paper, this time with more than a passing interest. 'Deeppool murder case, police identify body', blazed across the front page.

'From our crime correspondent: Police say that the body of a man found tortured and murdered in a derelict factory in Deeppool has been identified as local businessman Amir Aziz (41). Mr Aziz was a partner in the Azure Recruitment Agency which employs ten people in the city centre. Mrs Dawn Wyatt, one of the employees, told our reporter that they were stunned by his death. He was described as a good boss and generous with his staff. In a separate development, police from Scotland Yard's serious crime division raided a property in Argyle Avenue, Aireford, believed to be owned by Mr Aziz. Police would not confirm any possible link, describing their investigation as ongoing.'

Keith read the piece again and contemplated the news. He would be safe now, surely, but he then started worrying if he would be implemented in any way. Should he go to the police? He was not sure.

News of the raid on Argyle Street quickly reached the Bute Close lads. They made a quick decision.

'We must dismantle everything,' said Uri. 'We can hide it in the car.'

So while Nicolai started taking out all the wiring that he had so diligently set up only a few days earlier, Uri brought the BMW to the front door. Within an hour all the monitors and computer towers were neatly packed in the boot of the car. Then Uri and Victor started moving their personal possessions into the bedrooms that were reserved for the chat rooms.

By mid-afternoon the transformation was complete and there would be nothing to link them to Aziz's operation; he was just their landlord.

At six o'clock, Uri received a phone call; it was Vasyl.

Uri listened to him, and then spoke to Victor and Nicolai.

'That was Vasyl, he has heard about the raid. He is moving his operation in London but wants to deal with Mr Jones. He is coming here tomorrow and wants us to check on him, and Vasyl will decide what he will do.'

Back in Dunfield, Kathryn was trying to hide her excitement and nervousness about Monday from the rest of the family. Text messages were still criss-crossing between her and Steve, which only heightened the anticipation. Keith had noticed the change of mood but ignored it once his enquiry of 'are you ok, dear?' had been rebuffed quite sternly. 'Of course, why do you ask?' was Kathryn's response.

Keith was starting to get more movement in his hand and at least was able to dress himself on his own, albeit slowly.

Around six o'clock, there was another text from Steve. 'Please ring me as soon as you can.'

She replied. 'Ok, five minutes.'

'Just popping to the supermarket, we're running low on milk,' she said, and before Keith could say anything she was putting on her jacket and heading out of the house.

She pulled into a lay-by just up the road and dialled Steve's number.

'Hi,' she said on hearing his voice.

'Hi...' There was a pause. 'Look, I'm sorry to spring this on you but I have some news.'

Kathryn was suddenly preparing herself for a disappointment.

'I can't do this anymore?' he said.

Her heart sank. 'What do you mean?'

'Go on like this. It's driving me crazy... I told Sophie about us. Well not you exactly but I told her I'd found someone else.'

There was a long pause. 'What did she say?' said Kathryn.

'See you in court... that's all she said. Then she took the kids to her mother's. She's gone.'

There was another long pause. Kathryn was trying to take it all in. Steve continued. 'As I said I'm sorry to spring this on you, but I didn't know what else to do,' he said. 'I love you and I want us to be together.'

'I love you too,' she said. She thought about Keith with his broken hand, and the kids. She was torn.

'We only get one shot at this,' he said.

'Ok,' she said, 'but what about Monday?'

'That can be our honeymoon... Don't worry I have plenty of money Sophie doesn't know about. We'll be fine.'

Kathryn was still trying to absorb the enormity of the decision she was about to make.

'I can't do it today, I need to plan things,' she said. There was another long pause.

'Ok, I'll tell Keith Monday morning before I leave,' she said.

'Are you sure? It's a big decision.'

'Yes, I'm certain,' she said.

She rang off and returned home having completely forgotten about the milk.

That evening, Kathryn was at home coming to terms with what was going to happen. She watched Keith looking quite pathetic with his broken hand, and felt sorry for him; but that wasn't love she convinced herself.

The kids were another matter, but with Keith's work they

could move in with her and Steve. It would mean some disruption initially but they would soon get used to it; they would be fine.

She hardly slept that night and Sunday was even worse. She had continued to receive texts from Steve. He was worried that she would change her mind but she reassured Steve she wanted to be with him.

Sunday night, when Keith had gone to bed, she decided to compose a letter; she couldn't bear the thought of confronting him with the news. He might persuade her to stay and she knew that was not what she wanted.

'Dear Keith, I am so sorry to have to write this letter. I wanted to tell you to your face but I guess I am a coward. The truth is I have found someone else and I want to be with him. I will always love you but it is a decision I must make for my future. I hope one day you will forgive me.

Kathryn'

She put the letter in an envelope and sealed it.

Monday morning, almost six a.m., Kathryn had packed her bags, a suitcase and a carry-on. Travelling business class, there was some leeway with the weight, but twenty kilos would cover her needs. She had hardly slept, a mixture of excitement and anxiety, and by five a.m. was already showered and made up. Keith was not yet awake. Kathryn insisted she would sleep on the sofa so as not to disturb him. She had said her farewells the previous night.

He had of course offered to drive her to the train station where she and Steve had agreed to meet; his hand was feeling better, he had said, but she declined. She also refused a lift from one of the lads from the depot. 'Don't be silly you'll have to pay them overtime... It'll be cheaper for me to get a taxi,' she said. Keith could see the logic and didn't press; given recent events an early morning call was not a welcome proposition.

She paced the living room waiting for her lift, counting down the minutes, looking anxiously through the window. The taxi turned up on time and the driver carried the bags to the car. Kathryn felt a pang of guilt as she had one last look around the lounge before picking her coat up and folding it over her arm. The taxi driver held open the door for her and she got in. As it pulled away she looked back at the house as it disappeared from view and was overwhelmed by sadness. The envelope was on the kitchen table.

The taxi pulled up outside the station around six-thirty. Steve would drive them to the airport in good time for the lunchtime flight to a new world. He was waiting in the short-stay car park and saw Kathryn get out of the taxi. She paid the driver, looked around and saw the Range Rover. She did not notice the old Volvo parked in the approach road and its three occupants staring at the comings and goings in the car park.

It was a cool morning; she had put on her new coat in the taxi and she stopped momentarily, put down the bags and pulled up the fur collar to protect her from the breeze, a move that would probably save her life. Kathryn could see Steve looking at her; he was smiling broadly. She returned the smile and walked slightly unsteadily towards the car, pulling her two suitcases, her handbag in the crook of her right arm.

He started the engine; Kathryn was only a few yards away.

Then there was a blinding flash. The car just seem to disintegrate in front of her eyes; metal, glass... fragments of all kinds propelled through the air at lightning speed. For a split second it was as though time had frozen everything into a snapshot. Then the blast wave hit her and she flew backwards through the air, landing on the pavement. Bits of shrapnel descended from the sky. The fireball reached sixty feet, bystanders would say later – a car bomb, detonated remotely. Kathryn looked down at her coat; it was torn to shreds, blood starting to ooze from some of the tears. Then she lost consciousness. The Volvo pulled away, mission accomplished.

EPILOGUE

After the hit on Steve Jones, Vasyl, Oleksi and their weapons expert Kasper Paviosky, who had constructed the car bomb, returned to London with Uri in the Volvo, Victor and Nicolai following in Amir's BMW. They could not remain in Aireford; it would only be a matter of time before the police discovered them. Both cars would be quickly destroyed.

On hearing from Uri about the success of the chat room and video enterprise, Vasyl decided to set up a similar operation in London. It made a lot of sense and there would be no shortage of girls only too glad to provide the glamour; kidnapping would not be needed. Nicolai had all the equipment and access to the website and would be in charge of the logistics and computers; Uri and Victor would continue in their roles as studs.

Nine a.m., back in Dunfield; Keith had found Kathryn's letter and was sat on the sofa stunned. He had managed to get the kids off to school but decided not to say anything; he didn't know what he was going to tell them. He was shaken out of his retrospection by an urgent knock on the door. He looked through the window and could see a police car in the drive.

'Mr Woodley?' said the officer. 'Can we come in?'

Straight-away Keith's worse fears had been realised. They must have come to interview him about Amir Aziz. He tried to get his thoughts into order; he had worked out a plausible story just in case.

He let them in.

'What's the problem officer?'

'I'm afraid I have some bad news for you. Your wife has been injured... she's in Aireford General.'

'What do you mean injured? How...? What happened?' said Keith.

'We're not sure what happened. We're still investigating, but I think you should get to the hospital as soon as you can,' he replied.

'But I can't drive,' said Keith, holding up his damaged hand.

'Ok,' said the officer. 'We can drop you down there.'

Within five minutes Keith was sat in the back of the police car with the sirens blaring as they made the journey in ten minutes. Outside the access road to the hospital there were vans of all shapes and sizes, many with satellite dishes on top, parked in every available place and making progress difficult. The police car manoeuvred through and pulled up outside the main entrance door. Keith thanked the officers and ran into the hospital building. He was directed to the Accident and Emergency department. He knew where it was, having visited only a few days earlier; his heart sank as he retraced his steps. The pain in his hand returned as he re-lived the memory. He reached the enquiries desk and the receptionist took the details. 'Just wait over there. Someone will be with you shortly,' she said. Keith was in a daze and just complied.

He managed to find a seat and was looking at the other people in the waiting area. The department was heaving with people, nursing staff were dealing with minor injuries resulting from the earlier explosion, mostly cuts from flying glass, it seemed. Several people had blood on their clothing; others were stemming wounds with handkerchiefs or other material. It was a hive of activity. Porters and doctors were coming and going, police officers with notebooks talking to people, and, of course, journalists. Looking through the window, Keith could see a film crew reporting for the lunchtime schedule; a bomb was certainly big news.

Keith couldn't settle. Several times he got up and asked for news at the reception desk, but each time he was told to wait.

'It shouldn't be much longer,' the girl said after twenty minutes. Eventually, after what seemed to be a lifetime, a doctor entered the department and Keith noticed him scanning the twenty or so people left sat in the waiting area for their turn to be seen. He made eye contact with Keith and approached him.

'Mr Woodley?' he said.

'Yes,' said Keith.

'Your wife has just gone up to theatre,' said the medic.

'Theatre...? Theatre...? What's happening...? How is she?' said Keith.

'Well, she's out of danger but it was touch and go. We've managed to save her right eye. It was badly damaged,' he said.

'But how...? What happened? No-one's told me anything,' said Keith.

'The explosion... at the station this morning. It was on the news.... They think it might be terrorists,' he explained.

'But... my wife... how is my wife?' said Keith anxiously.

'As I said, she's out of danger. Her left leg is badly broken which is why she has gone to theatre... and she has many cuts and bruises to her face and head. She was very lucky... there were a couple of fatalities,' said the consultant.

Keith just sat there staring into space.

'Look, stay here. I'll find out how she is and I'll come back in a few minutes,' he said. 'I will say this though.'

Keith looked up at him.

'That coat.'

'What about it?' said Keith.

'Almost certainly saved her life,' said the consultant. 'It protected her... you know, like a motorcyclist's leathers. If she hadn't have been wearing it, there's no doubt she would have died.'

THE END

ALAN REYNOLDS

Following a successful career in Banking, Alan established his own training company in 2002 and has successfully managed projects across a wide range of businesses. This experience has led to an interest in psychology and human

behaviour through watching interactions, studying responses and extensive research. Leadership has also featured strongly in his training portfolio and knowledge gained has helped build the strong characters in his books.

His interest in writing started as a hobby but after completing his first novel in just three weeks, the favourable reviews he received encouraged him to take up a new career. The inspiration for his stories comes from real life events with which many people can easily identify.

Alan now has a world-wide following with his books selling in the US, Canada, Australia, across Europe and throughout Asia. In 2015 Flying with Kites won a prestigious Wishing Shelf Award for Adult Fiction and in 2015 The Sixth Pillar was a shortlisted finalist.

Milton Keynes UK
Ingram Content Group UK Ltd.
UKHW020855250124
436675UK00001B/7

9 781910 406311